Cassie Miles, a *USA Today* bestselling author, lived in Colorado for many years and has now moved to Oregon. Her home is an hour from the rugged Pacific Ocean and an hour from the Cascade Mountains—the best of both worlds—not to mention the incredible restaurants in Portland and award-winning wineries in the Willamette Valley. She's looking forward to exploring the Pacific Northwest and finding mysterious new settings for Mills & Boon Heroes romances.

A *USA Today* bestselling author of over one hundred novels in twenty languages, **Tara Taylor Quinn** has sold more than seven million copies. Known for her intense emotional fiction, Ms Quinn's novels have received critical acclaim in the UK and most recently from Harvard. She is the recipient of the Readers' Choice Award and has appeared often on local and national TV, including *CBS Sunday Morning*. For TTQ offers, news and competitions, visit tarataylorquinn.com

FUGITIVE HARBOR

CASSIE MILES

MISTAKEN IDENTITIES

TARA TAYLOR QUINN

MILLS & BOON

First Published in Great Britain 2024
by Mills & Boon, an imprint of HarperCollins*Publishers* Ltd
1 London Bridge Street, London, SE1 9GF

www.harpercollins.co.uk

HarperCollins*Publishers*
Macken House, 39/40 Mayor Street Upper,
Dublin 1, D01 C9W8, Ireland

Fugitive Harbor © 2025 Kay Bergstrom
Mistaken Identities © 2025 TTQ Books LLC

ISBN: 978-0-263-39697-3

0125

FUGITIVE HARBOR

CASSIE MILES

To all those dedicated to repairing and maintaining
the Oregon lighthouses. Shine on.

Chapter One

A jagged shard of lightning pierced the low-hanging clouds and streaked across the night sky above the Cape Absolute lighthouse on the Oregon coast. The bolt might have struck a tall Sitka spruce, or torn a chunk off the basalt cliffs, or spent its force plunging to the depths of the roiling Pacific. Standing at the mullioned window in the dining room of the lightkeeper's cottage, Ava Donovan touched her fingertip to the cold glass and traced the path of a raindrop down the pane. She braced for the thunder. In seconds, an explosive boom rattled her eardrums.

A lightning storm was unusual for the coast. They got plenty of rain, but only a few of the storms erupted into lightning. The celestial light show mesmerized her and sent shivers marching down her spine. Not that she was cold. Her plaid, flannel pajamas and wool socks kept her plenty warm.

She turned away from the window and padded down a short hallway to the study where a desk lamp shone on a document she'd been studying—a copy of a lightkeeper's log from the 1920s, one of the few written by a woman, Elizabeth Mayes, known as the Widow of Cape Absolute.

Ava took a seat at the rolltop desk, straightened her shoulders and shook off her tension. *Nothing to be scared of.* The lightning was odd, but rain was typical for late April when the daffodils were up and rhododendrons started to bud. Night temperatures hovered in the forties. Gusting winds kicked up to thirty miles per hour. If she'd been an official lightkeeper, like Elizabeth, she would have paid attention to the tide charts and barometric readings, but she wasn't here to maintain a daily record. Her job for the next six to eight months was to renovate the buildings on this property in an accurate manner to satisfy the National Historic Landmark requirements.

Uniquely qualified, she had an MA in archeology and another in American history with a published thesis highlighting landmarks of the Pacific Northwest. In addition, she'd put herself through college working on home remodels. Happily, Ava had accepted the lighthouse project, which marked a step forward in her career, and moved into the cottage on a cliff jutting into the Pacific. The only access was an unmarked dirt road that veered off the paved route through the Siuslaw National Forest and wove through the old growth forest for 2.7 miles.

No traffic. No neighbors. No problem.

Though her family—three brothers and a sister—told her she'd be lonely, solitude didn't bother her. Still, she'd felt restless tonight, apprehensive for no particular reason. At eleven o'clock, she should have been tucked into bed. Instead, she wandered. After living here for two-and-a-half weeks, she knew her way around and left most of the lights off.

In spite of being referred to as a "cottage," the lightkeeper's residence was substantial—a two-story house that was separate from the lighthouse tower. The cottage had five bedrooms, an extra-large primary suite and three other rooms that could be converted to more bedrooms for the proposed B and B. Built in the late 1800s and refurbished several times since then, the cottage had a lot of square footage, lots of windows, lots of hallways and even a couple of secret passages, rumored to be used by ghosts of former lightkeepers.

From outside, she heard a crash.

Ava bolted to her feet and dashed back to the dining room window. Another flare of lightning illuminated the forty-eight-foot-tall tower at the edge of the headland cliff. The lighthouse stood about fifty yards away from the lightkeeper's cottage. The once proud beacon warning approaching vessels of dangerous rocks and shoals had been dark for over fifty years.

Peering into the night, she couldn't see well enough to know what caused the noise. The battery-powered light she'd installed over the lighthouse entrance wasn't very bright—just a glimmer. On a cloudy, rain-soaked night like this, moonlight provided scant illumination.

She waited for another lightning flash to give her a clearer view. An aluminum ladder had fallen outside the tower and smashed into a couple of sawhorses. Though she recalled using the ladder earlier, she couldn't imagine herself being so careless as to leave it standing unattended. A chilling thought occurred: someone else might have tampered with the ladder.

Though she didn't see a shadowy figure creeping through the night, Ava had legitimate reason for concern. Over the years, graffiti artists had literally made their mark on the whitewashed exterior of the tower. Of course, they wouldn't attempt to paint in the rain. But what about the interior? She'd purchased a lock for the door to discourage them from entering, but someone might use the cover of the storm to break inside and scrawl their mark on the walls. *Not on my watch.*

In the kitchen, she flicked on the overhead light before going out to the enclosed back porch to don a heavy-duty rain poncho over her pajamas. Rubber galoshes covered her socks. Armed with a Maglite from a shelf by the door, she turned on the back porch light and paused. Though she didn't see a vehicle parked beside her truck in the rear parking lot and hadn't heard a car approaching, intruders could have hiked through the forest.

She might be facing a vandal. An intruder. A dangerous person.

When her oldest brother—the notorious Barry Donovan—helped her move in, he warned about the dangers of a twenty-seven-year-old woman living alone in a secluded place like this. He disregarded her comment that she had practiced tai chi—which was, in fact, a martial art—for years. Moves like Cloud Hands and Grasping Bird Tail probably wouldn't stop an assailant.

Barry had taken her shopping for a gun.

Now might be the time to use it. Clumsy in galoshes, she ran through the dining room and down the hall to the desk in the study. In the lower right drawer of the old rolltop, a locked box held her brand-new Glock 48. Both Barry and the saleswoman told her it was lightweight, easy to handle and held ten rounds. To operate the weapon, she only had to aim and squeeze the trigger, unleashing the automatic safety. Just pull the trigger. *Easy enough.* Plus, the neon pink Glock gleamed with bravado.

Ava punched in the combination code to unlock the small gun safe, retrieved her weapon and checked the clip the way Barry showed her. *My phone!* She definitely needed her phone in case she had to call for backup. Taking it off the charger on the desk, she stuck the phone into the flappy pocket in her poncho and returned to the kitchen. Holding the flashlight and Glock in her left hand, she used her right to unlock the back door and pull up her hood. Glock in hand, she went down three rickety stairsteps. The wind from the northeast blew rain onto her back and shoulders, pushing her toward the lighthouse and the edge of the cliff. The crashing of waves against rock accompanied her footsteps with a primeval rhythm. The beam from her Maglite barely kept the darkness at bay.

She trudged onward. Though she'd pulled the hood over her head, rain spattered her nose and cheeks. With the hand holding the gun, she pushed her bangs off her forehead. Lightning burst across the night sky, and the trees became grasping shadows, threatening to drag her into the foreboding forest. She stumbled and fell to her knee in a puddle. Accidentally, her finger squeezed. The gun went off. An explosion rocked the air. She had fired into the dirt.

"Damn, damn, damn." She bounded to her feet and ran the last several yards, trying to ignore the twinge in her wrist from the pistol's recoil. A twenty-eight-foot aluminum extension ladder lay on its side blocking the lower portion of the closed door, but the lock remained firmly in place. Even if someone had gotten inside, they couldn't have reached out to refasten the hasp. Unless they had an accomplice. *There might be more than one of them.*

Peering through the rain at the back porch, she saw the cottage door hanging wide-open. *How could that be?* She thought she'd shut the door but had been busy juggling the gun, her phone and the flashlight. Apparently, she hadn't fastened the latch tightly enough.

Splashing through puddles, she hurried back to the cottage, climbed the three steps, entered, pulled the door closed and turned the key in the dead bolt. Off with the poncho. She hung it on a hook, kicked off her boots and returned the Maglite to its place on the shelf by the door. Still carrying her Glock, she padded into the kitchen in her damp socks. The overhead light shone on the worn green-and-yellow-patterned linoleum floor where a trail of watery footprints led into the adjoining dining room. *Trouble!* Her heart thumped heavily. While she'd been outside, an intruder must have crept into the cottage. Gaining entry might have been their plan all along.

She needed backup: 9-1-1. Her phone ought to still be in her poncho, but when she went back to the porch to look, the phone was gone. She must have dropped it when she fell or when she was running. Going outside and searching in the dark seemed futile. But calling for help seemed like the best option, even though emergency responders would take at least a half hour to get here. In the study, there was a land-line and her car keys. All she needed to do was go through the kitchen to the dining room. From there, the study was down a short hallway. Place the call. Take the keys. And make a mad dash for her truck.

Cautiously, she inched toward the doorway leading to the dining room, which was dark except for faint moonlight through the windows. She reached around the corner and groped for the switch. A rustling noise crackled in her ears. She heard a shuffle, sensed his presence before he grasped her wrist and yanked hard.

Off-balance, she stumbled into the dining room. He clamped an arm around her belly and pulled her back against his chest. He easily overpowered her. Releasing her wrist, he twisted her arm and took the gun from her hand.

She inhaled and prepared to scream. Not that anyone could hear her. There were no neighbors. Just forest.

"I'm sorry, Ava."

"Who? What?"

"Let me explain."

She craned her neck and tried to see his face, but she couldn't turn her head far enough. "Who are you? How do you know me?"

"It's been a long time. Six years."

"Let me go." Her muscles tensed, but she couldn't move.

He held her too tightly. His wet clothing soaked her flannel pajamas."Just relax."

"Tell me who you are?"

"You came after me with a gun. Let's make sure we're on the same page. Okay?" His tone softened, but his grasp stayed firm. "Six years ago, how old were you?"

"Twenty-one."

"Where were you?"

"Eugene." She'd been in grad school at the University of Oregon, working on her MA in archeology. She couldn't imagine why he was asking these mundane questions but figured the conversation might work in her favor. If she kept him talking, he might relax his grip, and she could escape. She asked, "Were you at U of O? Are you a Duck? Did we have a class together?"

"You wore your long, dark hair in a ponytail. You've cut it."

He knew her name, knew what she looked like. "Have you been stalking me?"

"Hell, no." He sounded offended as though he wasn't the sort of man who stooped to stalking. "I saw an article in the *Register* when you signed on for this project. And a recent photo."

She glanced toward the hallway that led to the study. If she could get there, she'd lock the door and make her call. There had to be something in that rolltop she could use as a weapon.

"I remember," he said, "you were an excellent swimmer. And diver."

His mention of her water skills was a clue. "We both must have been in the nautical archeology course that studied shipwrecks near Coos Bay."

"You were the only woman in the class."

"Yeah, I was popular."

A chuckle rumbled in his chest, and she felt his grip loosen. *This is my chance.* She jabbed her left elbow into his gut and dodged to the right, slipping out of his clutches and falling to the floor. Though she wanted to go left, she was facing the opposite direction. On hands and knees, she crawled frantically toward the light in the kitchen.

He followed. Before she got very far, he grabbed her arms and pulled her up. Though caught, Ava didn't quit. She kept wriggling, fighting to free her arms and wildly kicking back at him. *To no avail.* He lifted her as though she weighed no more than a rag doll and carried her to a straight-back chair at the kitchen table. After he sat her in the chair, he stepped back a pace.

In the overhead light, she stared up at him. Her jaw dropped. "Professor Brody?"

"Are you okay? I didn't mean to hurt you."

"Why did you hide? You grabbed me. Why?"

"The gun." He reached behind his back and took her pink Glock from where he'd stashed it in the waistband of his jeans. Her lethal weapon looked tiny in his large hand. "When I heard gunfire, I didn't want to take the chance that you'd shoot first and ask questions later."

His response almost made sense. *Almost.* "Is there some logical reason why you couldn't come to the door—like a normal person—and ring the buzzer?"

"Would you have let me in?"

She pinched her lips in a tight, angry line and looked away from him, unwilling to be influenced by the glow emanating from his stormy gray eyes—eyes she remembered much too well. She'd spoken to him on the phone less than two weeks ago and couldn't believe she hadn't instantly recognized his voice. "I'd have slammed the door in your face."

"Haven't changed your mind."

"No."

Dr. Liam Brody placed her gun on the stained, cracked, beige tile countertop. "I need your help, Ava. But I'll understand if you refuse. You don't owe me anything."

As she stared at him, her firm resolve weakened. He had a mesmerizing effect on people, particularly on her. "If you understand that I don't want to get involved, why are you here?"

"I hope you'll give me a chance. Will you, at least, listen to me?"

Six years ago, she'd imagined herself in love with this tall, darkly handsome professor. They'd flirted and teased but kept a distance, except for one night when they were out on the dive boat, drinking beer on the deck and watching starlight dance across the waves. He embraced her. The warmth from his body raised her temperature several degrees, and she melted like chocolate in a double boiler. His kiss took her breath away.

Too quickly, he had turned away and apologized. An intimate relationship between professor and student was inappropriate. He never touched her again, much to her disappointment.

For years, his likeness had haunted her dreams. Liam Brody was educated, accomplished and looked great in his black wet suit with orange markings. Back then he was only thirty—young for a PhD—and had garnered international renown for the archeological reclamation of shipwrecks in the Strait of Juan de Fuca between Washington state and Canada. On the U of O campus, he'd been kind of a celebrity. A documentary crew had covered his accomplishments and praised him to the skies.

Recent news reports about him weren't so complimentary. He was charged with murder.

"Is it true, Liam? Did you kill Stuart Whitcomb?"

"I don't think so. But I don't know for sure."

She'd followed the reports on his arrest and had heard

that his defense centered on not remembering what happened. Certainly, that was a possible explanation. Amnesia often occurred in cases of trauma, especially when accompanied by a bout of unconsciousness. Still, selective forgetting seemed like an awfully convenient alibi for an accused murderer. "My sister is good friends with Stuart's ex-wife."

"I know. Stuart grew up in your hometown."

That coincidence was, of course, the reason he'd come to her for help. As a lifelong resident of Narcissus, she knew the ins and outs, the disasters and the triumphs of that small town on the Yaquina River. The Donovan family was an intrinsic part of the community. Her oldest brother had frequent confrontations with the local police, usually while drunk. Jerome, her youngest brother was a contractor who she'd hired to work on the lighthouse. Unlike Barry, he had a reputation as a hardworking, well-behaved pillar of the community with a wife and kids. Memories of the brother between those two, Michael, filled her mind and clenched her heart. Michael was eight years older than Ava who was the youngest. Shortly after he turned eighteen, he had been accused of murdering his girlfriend and wrongly convicted, sentenced to life in prison.

Ava had only been ten years old, too young to help her brother. All she could do was cry herself to sleep every night. It took twelve years to discover fresh DNA evidence proving his innocence. When he finally came home, she made it her mission to support him in spite of the townspeople and former friends who sneered at an ex-con even though he'd been proven innocent. When Michael decided to leave Narcissus and start over someplace new, she begged him to stay, offered to come with him and help out. She'd been twenty-four, old enough to make a difference in his life.

He refused to take her along. She'd just completed her university studies and had several relevant jobs and research studies lined up. Her life was going well, and Michael didn't want to disrupt her progress. He was proud of her. Told her how much her acceptance meant to him while he was incarcerated.

She'd always known he wasn't a murderer. Never ever stopped believing in him.

And now, there was Dr. Brody—a man in a similar predicament. If he wasn't guilty, she needed to take the risk and try to help him. If someone had stepped up and supported her brother, his life would have been different.

"I'll listen," she said, "but you'd better talk fast."

Chapter Two

With his thumbs hitched in the pockets of his wet jeans, Liam Brody leaned against the kitchen cabinets and studied Ava, remembering the way she'd looked six years ago with her long, curly, chestnut brown ponytail and striking blue eyes. He liked the new chin-length haircut with bangs that framed her triangular face and dimpled chin. Even though her mad dash through the storm left her disheveled, she kept her poise.

He needed to convince this cool, levelheaded woman to take his side. Grabbing her in the dark hadn't been a real smooth way to reintroduce himself, and he was lucky that she hadn't snatched her pink Glock off the kitchen counter-top and shot him in the ass.

She went out the back door to the porch and came back wearing a faded red hoodie over her pajamas. "It feels like I'm missing something important. Aren't you in the middle of a trial?"

"Correct."

"Are you out on bail?"

"Correct, again."

"Do your terms of bail allow you to come out here to the coast? Shouldn't you be wearing one of those ankle brace-lets to monitor your location?"

"I'm not allowed to go more than ten miles away from

Eugene. And I should be wearing a GPS tracking anklet. I took it off. Before you ask, that's illegal." He might as well give her all the bad news at once. "There are probably police, deputies and US marshals looking for me right now. I abandoned my car twelve miles up the coast and cut through the forest."

"You're a fugitive," she clarified.

"If it turns out that I killed Stuart, I'll do my time. But if not…"

"Wait a minute!" Her blue eyes narrowed to slits. "By allowing you to stay here at the lighthouse, I'm harboring a fugitive. Also illegal?"

"Correct."

"And you can't even tell me that you didn't kill the guy."

"Here's what I remember."

"This had better be good," she said, "or our conversation is over right now."

He'd recited this account dozens of times for the police and attorneys. The words rolled out like a well-worn mantra. "Stuart and I were out on a thirty-nine-foot-long cabin cruiser with all the bells and whistles. A classy little rig."

"Alone?" she asked.

"Yes."

"Were other boats nearby?"

"We'd gone five or six miles from the marina. I didn't notice anybody else. We were considering buying this midsize craft for our fleet. We shared ownership of the salvage company: BW Deep Dive. I'm majority shareholder with 51 percent."

"I knew you worked together on some projects. Didn't know you were partners." She nodded. "So you were on the boat. Then what happened?"

"I felt woozy, sat down. My head was spinning, then I

blacked out. Maybe I was drugged. Earlier, I drank a beer from a bottle and had a sandwich."

She held up her hand to stop his narrative. "Did the police test the food for drugs?"

"Yeah, and they didn't find anything." To his mind, the lack of drugs didn't mean much. The killer could have tossed the beer bottle overboard.

"What about you? Did they run a tox screen to see if there were drugs in your system?"

"By the time they got around to taking those tests, it was several hours later. Too long to come up with definitive results."

Her gaze leveled as she studied him. "Tell me the truth, Liam. Are you on any sort of medication? Do you take recreational drugs?"

"Not since I was eighteen." He'd lost both his mom and his best friend to drug overdoses. Not at the same time but close enough to make him a lifetime member of twelve-step programs for people who have had their lives overturned by drugs or alcohol. "Anyway, when I woke up, the motors were off, and we were drifting. Stuart had collapsed near the helm and was bleeding from a head wound."

"From what I recall reading about the case, he wasn't shot. Correct?"

"The autopsy said his injury was the result of blunt force trauma, but I didn't see a club or anything else that could have been used to whack him."

"Wouldn't be difficult to dispose of the murder weapon," she said.

He continued, "I tried CPR and called the Coast Guard. Too late. Stuart was dead by the time they arrived."

"From what I've read on the internet, you two guys weren't all that friendly. Witnesses reported that you fought about the direction of your work together."

"We're explorers," he said, unable to keep a note of pride from his voice. Liam appreciated his ability to make a living from the sea. "I was interested in research. Stuart wanted to do more salvage. And, yeah, we argued."

She stepped past the mid-century modern kitchen table that would have been worth something if it had been in better condition and walked to the avocado-colored stove that matched the fridge—a vintage 1950s look but not historical. This place would require careful refurbishing to be designated a national landmark.

Her movements were deliberate as she filled a teapot with tap water, flicked on the front burner and moved the pot onto the flame. "It's your contention that you were drugged, but you don't know how or who did it. And then, while you were unconscious, another person boarded the cruiser and killed Stuart. Again, you don't know who or how."

"That's an accurate summary." Six years ago, she'd been in his class, and he'd been aware of her talent for logical thinking. Also, he'd been impressed by her smile, her athletic body and those beautiful blue eyes. She was the only student who tempted him to break the rules. He cleared his throat. "That's the starting point for our investigation. Are you game?"

"So far. But I want to know more."

"I'm glad we'll be working together." A few years after she graduated, he'd tried to contact her and discovered she was living with a guy. "Is that going to be a problem? I heard you had an arrangement with a lawyer in Portland."

"Portland Jimmy the urban jerk." She gave a dismissive snort. "We've been off and on for a long time, and we broke up for good a couple of months ago. He wanted a woman who liked to throw dinner parties and keep his condo clean. I preferred excavating at the Chinookan village or studying basketry from the Klamath Tribes or upgrading markers on the Lewis and Clark Trail."

Liam knew from experience that no mere human male could compete with the passion for archeological field study. "Then you got this project."

"I campaigned for the job, spent a lot of time with Georgina Solomon, the great-granddaughter of George Solomon, the lumber baron who bought the lighthouse in 1956. I think one of the main reasons she hired me was my connection to Narcissus. Georgina liked using a local. I think her husband, Peter Quincy, also runs a salvage business from Newport."

"I'm aware." Liam considered Quincy, a competitor, to be one of his primary suspects. "He and Stuart worked some deals together. I think Quincy was smuggling."

The teakettle screeched on the stove. She lifted it off the flame. Given the fact that he'd just admitted to being a fugitive, described a suspicious scenario for Stuart's murder and cast aspersions on the husband of her employer, her composure was admirable. In a calm voice, she asked if he'd prefer herbal tea or coffee. Sugar? Milk? While she prepared their beverages—chamomile tea for her and coffee through a French press for him—she said nothing. She placed their mugs on the kitchen table, produced a package of chocolate chip cookies and sat in the straight-back chair across from him.

"Here's the deal, Liam. You could be taken back into custody at any moment."

"True." And his cushy time under house arrest would be over. If the US Marshals caught up with him, Liam would likely be incarcerated, having proven himself a flight risk. He kept those fears to himself and sipped his coffee. Caffeinated heaven.

"Level with me," she said. "Tell me about the investigating you've done so far."

"I started by hiring a PI, Wyatt Willis. He wasn't much help but still better at gathering evidence than the police. They came up empty-handed." Since he'd been confined to his house, he couldn't track down witnesses and set up interviews. "And I went to a psychologist who specializes in hypnotism to test me and find out if my subconscious mind picked up any clues."

"Psychic investigating. Awesome." She tasted her chamomile and licked her lips. "I'm guessing the hypnotist didn't figure anything out."

"Bits and pieces that don't make sense. What I need is more research, more investigation. And you're good at that."

"I appreciate the compliment, but I'm not Sherlock Holmes." She shook her head. "Let's get real. I'm not even Nancy Drew."

"But you know people in Narcissus, Stuart's hometown. His mom is still there, but his dad took off with a trophy wife and lives in Hawaii. Stuart has a sister, also in Narcissus." He knew Ava would be an asset. "Because you're a local, these people will talk to you."

"Not necessarily. His mother and sister consider themselves to be more elite than the Donovan family. For the most part, the Whitcombs aren't nice folks. Wouldn't surprise me if mom or sis popped old Stuart." When a sly grin spread across her face, he remembered why he'd found her so attractive. "His sister dated my oldest brother, Barry. Didn't end well. He wrecked her BMW."

"Is Barry the brother you used to work for?"

"No, that's Jerome. He's settled down with a wife and two kids. He still does contract construction work, specializing in renovations. Matter of fact, he and his crew are working here. Also, I have a sister, Rachel, with two more kids. And another brother who is single."

A shadow darkened her expression. He suspected something in her family history had hurt her deeply. "What is it, Ava? What's wrong?"

"Don't want to talk about it." She took another sip of tea. "Rachel and her family still live in Narcissus."

"You mentioned her before. She's friends with Stuart's ex-wife."

"Do you know the ex?"

"I've met Holly. Been to a couple of parties where she was a guest." She hadn't made much of an impression on him until recently when she showed her blatant greed. "She expects to inherit Stuart's shares in Deep Dive. Actually, the estate and business go to his son, and she'll be the executrix which gives her a lot of control of the funds. He never got around to changing his will after their divorce."

"Sounds like a good motive for bumping him off."

"She has an airtight alibi. At the time of Stuart's murder, Holly was on an Alaskan cruise."

"Hush." Ava went silent. For a tense moment, she listened, then she pushed away from the table and ran across the linoleum to the windows in the dining room. "I see headlights in the front parking area."

"How could you hear cars approaching over the rain and wind?"

"I'm accustomed to the silence. I don't get many visitors." Her voice quavered. "Two vehicles. A cop car and an official-looking van."

He couldn't believe the police were able to track him so fast. He'd ditched his phone and ankle bracelet. While he was driving from Eugene, he'd taken a circuitous route and abandoned his car before hiking twelve miles through the forest.

"How did they know?" He shook his head. "I didn't tell anybody I was coming here."

"Two weeks ago, you called me," she said. "No doubt your phone was monitored."

"I used a burner."

"For somebody who isn't a criminal, you're kind of clever."

"Thank you," he said.

"Not a compliment." She stepped up to confront him. "You convinced me. I want to know more about your investigation. What can I do to help?"

"Don't turn me over to the police."

Chapter Three

Moments after she'd seen the headlights, Ava scurried through the first floor of the lightkeeper's cottage to the entryway. The doorbell buzzed insistently and a heavy fist pounded on the solid oak door, which was one of the few architectural features she didn't need to replace. Details on the intricate carving of a double-masted schooner at full sail were still clearly defined. Clutching her red sweatshirt closed to hide her pajamas, she opened the door. The porchlight illuminated two men, sheltering from the rain under the triangular portico.

She recognized Deputy Don Jessop, a Lincoln County officer, from the many times he'd visited her family's home while she was growing up, usually to harass or arrest Barry. Standing in the storm with his buck teeth bared and rain dripping from the tip of his long nose, he looked as angry as a carnivorous weasel. From Barry's first run-in with the law in ninth grade, Jessop had picked on her linebacker brother who had a big mouth to match his broad chest and bad attitude.

The other man was tall and lean with a thick gray mustache that reminded her of her dad, a quiet, decent man who did his best to support his large family but died before she really got to know him. The guy on the porch wore a five-pointed badge on his dark gray rain jacket. The brim of his black cowboy hat shaded his deep-set eyes. "Are you Ava Donovan?"

"I am. And you are?"

"Deputy US Marshal Todd Woodburn."

Though Barry taught her to stand up to law enforcement and never show fear, Ava knew better than to be rude. She wanted this encounter to be over quickly, preferably before they sniffed out the entrance to the secret passage where Liam was hiding. Infusing her tone with righteous indignation to mask her nervousness, she asked, "Why are you here?"

"This conversation would be easier if we were inside," the marshal said.

Should she ask for a search warrant or would that make her look guilty? She blurted, "What do you want?"

"There's an escaped fugitive in the area, and we need to make sure you're safe."

Concern for her safety sounded rational. She couldn't think of a reason to refuse.

After they'd tromped inside and wiped their boots on the mat by the door, she indicated a series of hooks where they could hang their coats. Both men declined her offer, which she considered good news, an indication that they didn't intend to stay long. She might get out of this situation without being arrested. Her fingers wrapped around the neon pink Glock tucked into her sweatshirt pocket.

Jessop looked down his pointy nose and sneered. "I should have known that a Donovan would be involved in this."

"Involved in what?" She glared at the deputy. "Has something happened to my family? Is something wrong?"

"There's so much wrong with you people that I can't list it all." He turned toward Marshal Woodburn and continued,

"Her oldest brother has been arrested a dozen times. Another brother spent twelve years in prison for murder."

A burst of anger eclipsed her anxiety. "Michael was released. Wrongly accused and convicted due to incompetence from the officers in your jurisdiction. You made mistakes, and my brother paid the price. He's received some compensation from the state of Oregon, and the Exoneration Network, that's ExNet, is working to get more. A lot more."

"A waste of taxpayers' money."

Her fingers twitched near the trigger of the Glock. Might be worth jail time to shoot this guy. Barry had always referred to Deputy Don Jessop as Jess-hole, and she had to pinch her lips together to keep from shouting the insult. Stiffly, she said, "Get out of my house."

"Not your house. Don't belong to you."

"Get out."

"First, I got a couple of questions," Jess-hole said. "We saw your lights when we parked. You're out of bed in the middle of the night. How come?"

"I wasn't aware that being awake was against the law."

Woodburn took off his cowboy hat and smoothed his thinning gray hair off his forehead. "We got off on the wrong foot, Ms. Donovan. Let's start over. I don't want to leave you here alone when you might be in danger."

"I won't tolerate insults to my family."

"I'm sure Deputy Jessop is sorry." Woodburn held up his hand, blocking any comment from Jess-hole. Though the federal marshal didn't have command in Lincoln County, he was clearly in control. "This is an unusual house."

"The lightkeeper's cottage," she said.

"But the lighthouse has been decommissioned."

"Hasn't been lit since 1976. The owner, Georgina Solomon Quincy intends to apply for status as a National Historic Landmark."

"Yeah, yeah, yeah." Jess-hole cleared his throat. "Still doesn't explain why you're up and pacing around. Maybe you're hiding somebody in here."

"Not that I owe you an explanation," she said, "but I was in the study doing research, reading the lightkeeper's log of Elizabeth Mayes, the Widow of Cape Absolute, written in the 1920s. Her husband was lost at sea, and she took over his job. According to legend, she stood on the platform of the widow's walk at the upper level of the lighthouse and kept watch every night. The double-masted schooner carved on the front door is meant to represent the missing vessel."

Woodburn nodded. "I can tell that you love your work."

"I do," she said. "The history of a place informs and explains the present."

Unlike Jess-hole, the federal marshal seemed intelligent. His dark eyes scanned the entryway and the staircase leading to the second-floor bedrooms. He peered into the large living room with the old, worn furniture, threadbare rugs and carved rocking chairs set in front of a rugged, stone fireplace. After taking his time to carefully examine his surroundings, he turned his attention back to her. "Your socks are damp. Have you been out in the rain?"

Though Ava wasn't good at lying, Barry had coached her. He'd told her the most effective deception was based on telling as much of the truth as possible. *Honesty is the best policy, right?* Besides, she couldn't very well deny that she'd gone outside to look around when water splotched all over the floor. "I heard a crash near the lighthouse and went to investigate."

"What caused the noise?"

"Earlier today, I was doing work with a ladder and left it leaning against the tower. The wind must have blown it down, but I couldn't see from here." She'd spoken the truth but felt like she had a flashing red light on her forehead proclaiming her a liar. "I'm nervous about intruders."

"Why?"

"Graffiti," she said. "Vandals scrawled all over the outside of the lighthouse, but the interior is unmarked. I worried that they might use the cover of the storm to break in."

The federal marshal held her in a suspicious state of scrutiny. "If you had encountered an intruder, how did you intend to protect yourself?"

Outsmarted. He'd set a trap for her, and she'd jumped in with both feet. Holding her Glock 48 with two fingers, she lifted the weapon from her sweatshirt pocket. "I'm armed."

Jessop whipped his gun from the holster and aimed it, two-handed, at her. "Gun on the floor. Hands on your head. Do it. Now."

Staring down the bore of his over-size sidearm, she didn't think of the deputy as a joke. As dangerous as the furry but deadly wolverines that had begun to establish colonies in Deschutes County, Jessop scared her. She looked from him to the marshal. Slowly, she held the gun toward Woodburn. "Take it."

Woodburn gently removed the Glock from her two-finger hold and lifted it to his nose. "This weapon has been recently fired."

While she bobbed her head, Jessop holstered his gun and roughly spun her around. He yanked her right wrist behind her back and twisted until she yelped. Then he snapped on a handcuff. "You have the right to remain silent."

"That's enough," Woodburn said. "Release her."

"She pulled a gun on us," Jessop whined. "She can't do that."

From the corner of her eye, she saw Woodburn dangling her pink weapon. "Did this nasty, little Barbie Glock scare you?"

"You said she fired it."

"It was an accident," she said.

He kept hold of her arm and shook her. "Explain yourself, Ava Donovan."

"Let go of me."

"Not until you promise to be a good girl." He sounded like he was enjoying himself. Causing her pain gave him pleasure, and there wasn't anything she could do to stop him.

Without raising his voice, Woodburn gave the orders. "Deputy, remove the handcuff. Then I want you to go upstairs and search. Look in every closet and under every bed."

Jessop hadn't been terribly rough, but she still felt violated. She rubbed her wrist where the handcuff had been. "I never gave you permission to search."

"I told you so," the deputy said. "She's hiding something."

"I just don't want you pawing through my things with your grubby hands," Ava said. "Marshal, please do the right thing."

"You're within your rights to demand a warrant," Woodburn said. "It'll take a couple of hours for us to locate a judge in the middle of the night. Could be damn inconvenient. We could be here all night."

She hated that idea. "Maybe you can go upstairs with the deputy and supervise."

Jessop glared at her. "I promise not to touch your precious things. I'm on the hunt, looking for a fugitive."

The thought of him in proximity to her clothes, perfume and mementos sickened her, but she supposed it would be worth it to get rid of these two. "Don't touch anything."

While he clomped up the stairs, she turned to Woodburn. "I suppose you want to look around down here. I can give you a tour."

"I appreciate your courtesy." He fell into step beside her as she led the way through the lower level. A large living room stood opposite the dining room. Down the hallway was a sitting room, a nursery and a game room—one or more of which would be converted into bedrooms for the B and B. In the kitchen, there was a breakfast nook and a huge pantry, well stocked to provide meals for the crew working on the renovations.

She looked up toward the ceiling. "Shouldn't Deputy Jessop be done by now?"

"Soon enough," Woodburn said. "You told us that history shapes and predicts present events."

Not exactly what she'd said, but close. "Go on."

"I'm curious, Ms. Donovan. What does past experience tell you about the murder of Stuart Whitcomb?"

"I don't have enough information," she said, quickly and honestly. "I know he grew up in my hometown of Narcissus and wasn't well-liked. Other than that, I've followed media reports on the trial. Just like everybody else."

"The accused murderer is someone you know," Woodburn said. "A former professor of yours. Liam Brody. Do you recognize the name?"

"Of course. Professor Brody was an excellent teacher and a decent human being. When I heard he was arrested, I couldn't believe it."

"His car was abandoned near here."

Liam had told her it was hidden behind a storefront. How did they locate it so quickly? "Did somebody follow him?"

"The vehicle has a GPS tracker."

That explained it. "I haven't seen a car."

"According to my information, you talked to him on the phone a few weeks ago."

Apparently Liam's strategy of using a burner had been unsuccessful. Law enforcement probably had his house bugged. "He called," she admitted. "And he wanted to chat about people in my hometown. I wished him luck on the trial but didn't know anything that would be useful in his defense. Stuart's family and mine ran in different circles."

"Ms. Donovan, I'll need to see the paperwork for your gun."

While she led him down the hallway, her heart pumped faster with every step. In the study, the secret passageway was accessed by unfastening hidden hinges on a floor-to-ceiling bookcase that turned outward to allow access. Inside the closet-sized space with a ladder leading to the second floor, Liam was hiding. If he sneezed or dropped his coffee mug, Marshal Woodburn would tear out the books and claw through the fake wall.

Purposely, she looked away from the entrance to the passageway and concentrated on the rolltop desk. "Here's the lightkeeper's daily log written by Elizabeth Mayes. This is actually a copy. The original pages are too fragile to leave the research library at the Oregon Historical Society Museum."

He perused the handwritten notations that included time, temperature, barometric pressure, wind velocity and so forth. In addition, Elizabeth added personal notes, ranging from a sighting of a family of river otters in the Yaquina to a lover's dream of her missing husband. Ava had considered starting a daily log of her own. Lots of people followed that procedure to keep track of events. She'd have to ask Liam if he had a captain's log.

"Where do you keep your gun?" the marshal asked. "And why pink?"

As she opened the locked lower drawer and showed him her gun safe that also held her registration and paperwork, she explained, "I don't know anything about weapons, but my brother talked me into getting one so I'd be safe. The neon pink made me feel less frightened. I haven't been to a firing range yet, but I'd better get some practice."

"You don't want any other accidents." He ejected the clip

from the weapon. "Here are a couple of tips. Don't keep your gun loaded. Also, you need to store the ammunition separately."

"Yes, sir." The marshal seemed so calm and natural. She wanted to believe that he'd help her and Liam. "Earlier you agreed with me when I said the past provides a foundation for the present and the future."

"I believe that."

"Do you think the motive for Stuart's murder could be something that occurred a long time ago and has nothing to do with Professor Brody?"

"Do you?"

"I don't know." If she'd learned anything from Michael's wrongful conviction, it was that the initial investigation needed to be completely, utterly, totally comprehensive. The truth might hinge on a seemingly inconsequential detail. "The police need to do more digging into Stuart's background. And his family's history."

"My job doesn't include investigation," Woodburn said. "In this case, the US Marshal Service was contacted by the Oregon State Police for assistance in guarding and transporting Liam Brody while he's on trial."

She'd never really understood the layers of legal and judicial bureaucracy, but since Woodburn was an officer, it seemed like he ought to be a crime-solver. "What if you uncovered evidence that proved his innocence?"

"My task is to locate and arrest the fugitive." He placed her gun in the small safe, closed the drawer and locked it.

"But what if—"

"I'm good at my job, Ms. Donovan. Like they say in the Mounties, I always get my man."

Not this time, Marshal.

Chapter Four

Thus far, the unwarranted search in the lightkeeper's cottage had taken thirty-three minutes according to Liam's glow-in-the-dark dive watch. He'd spent the whole time tucked inside the secret passage behind the floor-to-ceiling bookcase in the study, breathing the thick, damp air until his lungs felt clogged. The enclosed space reminded him of an elevator shaft, six feet deep and five feet wide. The height stretched two stories high, all the way from the ground floor to the attic above the upstairs level. Using his pocket Maglite, he studied the unfinished wood and two-by-four wall studs.

He closed his eyes and tried to imagine how the secret passage fit into the overall floorplan for the cottage. On one side, there was a linen closet that opened into the hallway. A small bathroom next to the kitchen bordered the other side.

With his ear pressed against the thick wall of books, he concentrated hard, straining to hear what was being said in the study and entryway. From what he could tell, Deputy Jessop—a Lincoln County officer he'd never met—held a grudge against the Donovan family, especially Ava's ne'er-do-well brother. Jessop's rude attitude toward Ava irritated Liam.

On the other hand, Woodburn showed himself to be a fairly decent guy. No surprise. Liam had already drawn that conclusion. The marshal had been escorting Liam back and forth to hearings, depositions and court dates since his arraignment. These trips started with Liam being shackled and cuffed behind the wire-mesh barrier between the front seat and the prisoner transport section in Woodburn's official US Marshals van. Now Liam was allowed to ride in the passenger seat with only a pair of standard-issue handcuffs. Though definitely not friends, they'd developed a cordial relationship. When the marshal told Ava that he wasn't an investigator, Liam understood. Woodburn didn't care about guilt or innocence. His duties revolved around transport, and he made sure Liam arrived at all required appointments in a timely manner.

The marshal's single-minded focus made him a far greater threat than Jessop, who didn't seem capable of locating his toes at the ends of his feet. When Jessop was sent to search in the upstairs, Liam worried. The second-floor exit from the secret passage emerged inside Ava's bedroom closet. The hinges for the escape hatch were more noticeable than those for the bookcase in the study. Liam climbed a crude ladder—two-by-fours nailed to wall studs—to the second-floor ledge and peeked through a narrow crack between the boards while Jessop bumbled through Ava's bedroom, muttering to himself. Liam held his breath while the deputy yanked the closet door wide and poked his head inside. He flipped through the clothes on hangers and smirked at the row of shoes lined up on the closet floor, purposely mixing two matching shoes. Then he clomped out the closet door, leaving it open.

For the time being, Liam was safe. He climbed down to the main floor.

When the two officers and Ava went to the kitchen for a cup of tea, he couldn't hear their conversation and had a moment to consider where he'd spend the night. The secret passage would work, but the tiny space was uncomfortable. He could barely stretch out on the floor. After Jessop and Woodburn left, he might risk sleeping in one of the many bedrooms. Not really a good option. Ava hadn't welcomed him with open arms and just might tell him to get lost. In a bedroom, he'd be vulnerable if they returned. And he couldn't help leaving traces of himself in fingerprints and fibers that might implicate Ava.

That left the lighthouse.

Earlier tonight in the midst of the storm, he'd tried to access the interior of the tower. He climbed the aluminum ladder to reach one of the narrow windows halfway up, about twenty feet off the ground. The glass had been broken from the window frame, and he peered inside using his flashlight. Darkness obscured most of the architectural details, but he saw damage to the winding staircase that hugged the outer wall. Several stairsteps were broken or missing, especially near the bottom. Just below the window, a four-foot section had been torn from the wall, making it impossible to climb to the highest point where the beacon had been housed when the lighthouse was functional. If he could reach that upper level, which was surrounded by a metal widow's walk outside the windows, it would be a decent hideout.

Fearing he might be caught, he'd taken off his backpack and reached through the window to stash it on the busted stairs where it couldn't be seen from the floor below. If Ava told him to hit the road, he could retrieve his pack without too much trouble. And if she allowed him to stay—*please, please let that happen*—he'd come back to the lighthouse to access his laptop, his notes on the investigation and other personal items.

Huddled against the wall in the passage, he heard a door slam. A moment later, Ava spoke quietly outside the bookshelf. "Liam, are you okay?"

"A little cramped. Are they gone?"

"No, they just went out to look at the lighthouse. I told them there was nothing to see and gave them the key to unlock the door. They'll be back in a few minutes."

A knife-edge of fear sliced through his already shredded composure. If Woodburn somehow managed to locate Liam's backpack, they were in big trouble. "Are they suspicious?"

"Oh, yeah. Woodburn noticed the grounds in the French press I used to make your coffee."

A good thing he'd taken his mug into the passageway. "What did you tell him?"

"Told him that I'd prepared coffee for myself, then changed my mind about drinking the caffeine and dumped it in the sink. I'm not sure he believed me."

He heard her suck down an anxious breath and regretted putting her in this difficult situation. "Anything else?"

"They tracked your car with a GPS bug and listened to our conversation on the burner phone. Marshal Woodburn is smart, really smart."

He noticed a note of confusion in her tone. "And?"

"On some level, it feels like he's on your side. He made a comment about understanding how the past might lead to a solution in the present. As if researching Stuart's background could result in useful evidence."

"I overheard a piece of that conversation when you were here in the study." During the time he'd spent in Woodburn's van, Liam had gotten the impression that the marshal wasn't impressed with the evidence, or lack thereof, compiled by the local police.

"He also asked if you or Stuart were friends with Peter Quincy or Charles Tancredo."

"I wouldn't say we were friends, but we know each other." Quincy was Georgina's husband and Tancredo was the harbormaster at the Port of Newport. He managed both the commercial docks and the recreational marina. "Why?"

"Something about trafficking illegal cargo."

"Drugs." Cartels operating from Mexico to the south distracted from the northern border with Canada where gangs and organized criminals took advantage of less stringent surveillance. "Stuart wasn't a law-abiding person, but he wasn't a fool. I can't imagine how or why he'd get involved with drug dealers."

"Still, his murder sounds kinda like a hit. Don't you think?" Before he could comment about her unexpected familiarity with cartel violence, she gave a squeak and said, "Gotta go. Woodburn and Jess-hole are back."

Jess-hole? He liked the nickname.

From the kitchen, he heard murmurs of their conversation. As he listened, the three of them made their way through the hallways to the front door. Ava chirped a thank-you to Woodburn for finding her cell phone outside near the path to the lighthouse and told them they were welcome to come again, but she'd appreciate advance notice next time. Jessop lashed out with a snide comment. Woodburn said nothing until they reached the front door.

"If you see Liam Brody," he said to Ava, "call me immediately. Here's my card."

"Thank you," Ava said.

Liam pictured the tall, gray-haired marshal with his darting gaze and thick mustache. Woodburn offered kind advice. "Running away makes him seem guilty. If he contacts me, I can get him back on track for his trial."

"I'm not sure I understand," Ava said. "Would you cover up the fact that he ran?"

"I didn't say that."

"What exactly could you do for him?" she asked. "What can I tell him you'd do?"

"I'd be willing to testify about his cooperation. That way, his attorney can put a positive spin on the situation."

"Would he be able to remain out on bail?"

"Not a chance." His voice sounded definite. "Good night, Ms. Donovan."

The heavy front door slammed loudly. Woodburn had made Liam an offer, which he appreciated. Instead of tearing the lightkeeper's cottage apart in an intrusive search, Woodburn held out an olive branch. Liam had to wonder why. Did Woodburn know something he didn't?

Why didn't the marshal pursue a more diligent search? Had Ava threatened him with a lawsuit if he didn't provide her with a search warrant? Maybe Woodburn had come to the conclusion that he ought to return with a more effective investigative team than Deputy Jessop. Possibly, after a quick study of the cottage, the marshal decided they should concentrate on more promising leads. Liam had set a couple of false trails before he left Eugene. One pointed to a local airfield. Another went to the docks at Newport where he had a fleet of four boats, including a high-performance motorboat that could outrun most of the Coast Guard vessels and take him to Canada before a search got underway.

If fleeing from the area had been his goal, he had many options. But that wasn't the reason he came here. He wanted to stay and investigate, using the specialized knowledge that Ava knew from growing up in Narcissus. He heard her outside the passageway.

"They're gone," she said. "But there's no guarantee they won't be back. Meet me upstairs in my bedroom."

He'd been waiting for that invitation ever since they first met, six years ago on his dive boat. But the context was all wrong. They wouldn't be sharing a bed. Not tonight.

AFTER SHE LEFT the den, Ava circled through the first floor, turning off the lights as she went from the study to the dining room to the kitchen and back to the entryway. Her path progressed slowly and deliberately, giving her time to calm down and gather her thoughts. Though she didn't want to give in to fear, the visit from the police had left her shaken.

And the approaching confrontation with Liam would be difficult. Though she cared about him and about seeing justice done, Woodburn's advice made her stop and reconsider. Harboring Liam was breaking the law. No two ways about it. And she didn't want to go to jail.

Though she'd thought of him many, many times during the past six years and he played a major role in her fantasy life, Ava didn't owe him anything. It was presumptuous of him to ask for her help, very demanding, very alpha male. Without warning, he'd strolled back into her life and upset her plans. The lighthouse project could be the taking off point for an interesting, lucrative career in historic renovations. Exactly the sort of thing she'd been hoping for. The smart thing would be to tell Liam to contact Woodburn and wish him luck at his trial.

But she didn't trust the justice system. Innocent people were convicted all the time. She remembered her brother, incarcerated for twelve years because the police failed to investigate thoroughly. How could she refuse to help Liam in the same situation? He needed her. And she was a sucker for reclamation projects, whether it meant feeding the runt in a litter of kittens with an eyedropper or performing a makeover on a friend for a special date.

She made her way to the carved staircase that ascended from the entryway through the center of the house. Unlike the carvings on the front door, the oak balustrades and newel posts had been painted several different colors over the years.

She'd have to research the history of the house before she stripped the paint and restained the original wood.

At the top of the staircase, she turned left on the landing. The primary bedroom—her room—boasted a worn armchair and table by the window along with other heavy oak furniture. Also, there was an attached bathroom with a claw-foot tub and, of course, the large walk-in closet where the secret passageway connected from the den downstairs. The glow from a small bedside lamp shed just enough light for her to notice Liam, standing by the window and holding the curtain aside so he could see out. The rain had begun to let up, and moonlight filtered past the edge of the curtain to outline his profile.

To help him or not to help him? That was one of many questions. Could she turn her back on someone who might be wrongly accused? Was she being a fool to accept Liam's amnesia alibi? Was her former professor, in truth, a killer?

He turned his head toward her and grinned. His dark eyebrows gave his face character while his sharp cheekbones and square chin provided structure. He'd taken off his rain jacket and rolled up the sleeves on the plaid shirt he wore over a long-sleeved thermal T-shirt. Tall and lean and sexy, he was the whole package. Not that she had any intention of unwrapping him.

"We need to talk," he said.

"Sounds like you're breaking up with me."

If so, she had the perfect breakup speech, starting with the classic: *It's not you. It's me.* She'd explain how she didn't want to get involved, didn't want to take a chance on blowing her reputation and losing this renovation project. As these arguments circulated in her head, she hated the cold, callous direction of her thinking. How had she turned into a person who valued her profession more than his freedom?

She climbed onto the queen bed with the four-poster frame

and curled her legs up under her bottom. He took the armchair. "Okay, Liam. Talk."

"I put you in a lousy position. When I heard Jess-hole berating you and Woodburn posing his questions, I realized that it wasn't right for me to ask you to take this kind of risk. You hardly know me."

All true. "Actually, it'd be worse if you knew me better and took advantage."

"If I knew you well…" He flashed a rakish grin and arched his left eyebrow like a caricature of a rogue. "If I knew you in the biblical sense, we'd have some awesome memories."

"Awesome, huh?" She scoffed. "You might be overestimating your allure."

"Only telling the truth."

She glided her hand down a bedpost, ornately carved with delicate flowers. Though she hadn't meant for the gesture to be sexy, she felt the smooth, sanded texture of the wood beneath her fingers. His steady gaze lit a flame inside her. "What else did you want to say?"

"I'm proud of you, Ava." He cleared his throat and keyed his tone to sound more like a proper professor. "You're a top student, even if you didn't go into maritime archeology. You've built your research skills, worked tirelessly in the field and gained the respect of academics and others involved in the preservation of history. This restoration at Cape Absolute should place you at the forefront in your profession."

His compliments made her blush. "Have you been following my exploits in the alumni bulletins and on local news?"

"Damn right," he said. "I would have sent a congratulations bouquet when I heard about this lighthouse job, but the timing wasn't right. I was tied up with these pesky murder charges."

When she read about his arraignment, she'd wanted to offer her support and had been tempted to reach out. At the time, she'd had her own life to consider. Preparing to move here, finally abdicating her relationship with Portland Jimmy and gathering research materials took time and energy. *An excuse, and not a very good one.* While she'd been occupied with her hotshot career, Liam was drowning offshore. The least she could have done was throw him a life preserver.

"Anyway," he said, "I'll be moving on. No one needs to know I was here."

But I'll know. And she'd feel forever guilty. "At the very least, you need to stay for a couple of hours in case Jess-hole and Woodburn are watching the house."

He shook his head. "It won't take much for me to sneak into the forest and disappear."

Half of her brain screamed for her to let him go. But the other half was louder and would not be ignored. This time her decision was final.

"Stay," she whispered.

"Do you believe I'm innocent?"

"This isn't about you, Liam. It's about the truth." A shadow darkened her thoughts. If someone had helped her brother and investigated more thoroughly, the jury would never have sent him to jail.

Liam's voice was gentle. "What is it, Ava? What's wrong?"

"My middle brother, Michael was wrongly convicted of murder. If someone had listened to him earlier, he'd have twelve years of his life back. I'm doing this for him."

The stakes couldn't be higher. If she'd misjudged him and his claim of amnesia was a sham, Ava had just invited a cold-blooded killer into her life.

Chapter Five

"In the meantime…" Ava hopped off the bed and headed toward the closet "…we should get you settled in a safe place to spend the night."

"The lighthouse," he suggested.

"I've got a better idea." Elizabeth Mayes, the long-ago lightkeeper, would have approved. She loved the passageway, and Ava had improved it. "A secret within a secret."

Inside the bedroom closet, she rearranged her shoes in front of the secret passage entrance, noticing that two pairs had been shuffled. Had to be the work of Jess-hole, what a jerk. She opened the hatch, sliding the door aside and stepped over the neat row of shoes onto the ledge. Climbing down the crude ladder—thick boards nailed to vertical studs—required very little concentration though she was descending into darkness.

If she and Liam were going to bring this investigation to a successful close, they needed to get started right away. She considered how to proceed and decided the first order of business would be to get the lay of the land by talking to someone she trusted. Her sister, Rachel, worked part-time at the pharmacy adjoining the market and heard enough gossip to provide an accurate picture of how the folks in Narcissus viewed the murder of Stuart Whitcomb.

Rachel, only two years older than Ava, had followed in their mother's footsteps by getting married when she was eighteen and popping out two wonderful, smart, healthy children before she was thirty. Rachel's greatest talent was baking. When upset or troubled, she retreated to the kitchen and got busy, whipping out breads, muffins, cakes and cookies. She claimed the activity settled her mind and gave her focus. Nobody in the family contradicted, mainly because they couldn't talk with their mouths full of the delectable sweetness she created.

Ava had a similar habit. Instead of cooking, she built stuff. At age four, she constructed an elaborate, three-story dollhouse. During the summer after first grade, she built a clubhouse from scrap wood. With a sheet of plastic over the window and a door that opened and closed, she sanded, swept and decorated using a leftover paint from projects around the house. The end result was too cool. Her three obnoxious brothers begged to be let in, and she complied. *Big mistake!* They took over.

While she climbed down the crude ladder in the secret passageway, she told Liam about her construction efforts. "The best," she said, "was in third grade. I built a tree house in the giant hemlock at the edge of our property. Heavy work and complicated, but I didn't ask my dork-face brothers for help. This new, improved clubhouse would be No Boys Allowed."

"Sounds fair to me." His deep voice echoed in the passageway. "You did the work, so you deserved the privacy."

"A tree house is easier to defend. I gathered a bunch of pinecones and pelted the dorks whenever they tried to climb inside."

"You were a tough little third grader."

"Better believe it."

On the first floor, she waited for him to step down beside

her with his pocket-size flashlight showing the way. In the five-by-six-foot rectangle, they were forced to stand within inches of each other. The natural heat from his body radiated toward her, and his jeans—still damp from the rain—moistened her flannel pajamas. Too easily, she imagined their legs entwined as the distance between them vanished. She could almost feel the hard planes of his chest and the sheltering strength in his arms.

Without meeting his gaze, she took the flashlight from his hand, ignoring the sizzle when their skin touched. She inched toward her left until she reached a wall of unvarnished siding, made up of eighteen-inch-wide boards. At the farthest edge, hidden by shadows, she found a small handhold and pulled. The wall folded on invisible hinges like an accordion. "Ta-da," she said. "It's a secret room within a secret passageway."

He murmured, "No boys allowed."

"Well, you're welcome to come in." She tugged on a dangling cord, and a bare 75-watt bulb came to life.

"Did you build this secret hideout?"

"Actually, no. Someone else put it together, but I found it and made a few repairs, mostly just oiling the hardware. It only took a couple of hours."

The ceiling in the secret room was as tall as the study. Liam could stand without bumping his head. In other ways, the dimensions matched the typical size of a prison cell: six-by-eight feet. She used the space to store her camping equipment, including sleeping bags, a couple of tents, a lantern, a Coleman stove and tarps that smelled faintly of old campfires. Never had she considered using this stuffy, little area as a guest room. But she enjoyed the idea of having a secret place inside the lightkeeper's historic cottage.

"Electricity," he said, looking up at the bulb. "That could come in handy."

"Is there something you want to plug in?"

"My laptop."

She raised her eyebrows. "I don't see a computer."

"I left it in the lighthouse," he said, "before I tipped over the ladder."

This was a story she wanted to hear. What was he doing with the ladder? She spread one of the sleeping bags on the dusty wood floor and sat. "I'm going to need more explanation."

"When I got here, I had second thoughts about coming inside and putting you in jeopardy. Especially in the middle of the night." He folded his long legs and sat beside her. "I had a plan. I figured I could stay in the lighthouse until dawn."

Not a clever move. "What made you think nobody would look for a runaway fugitive in a forty-eight-foot-tall tower? The lighthouse doesn't exactly fade into the background."

"I said that I had a plan. Not necessarily a *good* plan."

"Then what?"

"I set the ladder so I could climb up and look in one of the windows."

"Let me get this straight," she said. "You decided to use an aluminum ladder during a lightning storm."

"I took my chances. When I looked inside I saw how badly the stairs were damaged. There's a large section—probably four feet—torn away from the wall. There's no way to reach the top floor of the lighthouse until repairs are made." He gave a self-deprecating shrug. "That was when I came up with another idea. I tucked my backpack—holding my computer, clothes, a couple of burner phones and other supplies—into a dark corner of the busted stairs."

"When you were climbing down," she concluded for him, "you tipped the ladder over."

"I should go out and get my backpack."

For a long moment, they sat quietly. Outdoors, the thunder continued to roar and the heavy rain thrummed against the windows. Farther away on the road or in the forest, there might be officers watching for a sign that Liam was here. "I don't think you should risk going out there tonight. Apart from the danger of a lightning strike, it's too easy for Woodburn to set up surveillance. What do you need your computer for?"

"I've made notes on my investigation into Stuart's murder."

"That would be helpful in planning our next step. I'm scheduled to see Georgina tomorrow and might get a chance to talk to her creepy husband."

"Tomorrow? But it's Sunday."

"The one day of the week when I don't have workers scheduled. Sunday afternoon is a great time to see Georgina. Plus I want to talk to my sister who happens to be friends with Holly Louise, Stuart's ex-wife."

"Holly is on my suspect list. She and her son, Oliver, will both inherit access to what's left of his fortune."

Ava stood and turned toward the door. "I'll get my laptop. You can access your files on the cloud. Is that possible? If so, can other investigators trace your progress?"

"Yes, you can access. No, others can't. I'm not a computer genius, but I'm pretty good. My data is secure."

"Good."

Before she left the secret room, he caught her hand. She looked down into his silver-gray eyes. He whispered, "Thank you."

"You're going to owe me big-time for helping you get acquitted."

"I won't forget."

And if he wasn't innocent, she hoped he wouldn't blame her for failing him.

GRATEFUL THAT HE didn't suffer from claustrophobia, Liam spread out a second sleeping bag opposite hers and created a sort of table from a couple of cardboard boxes with "Camp" scrawled on the side with marker. His gaze bounced off the rough wood walls. The secret room was too small, grungy and stuffy to be comfortable; however, for the first time since he discovered Stuart's body and started CPR, he felt safe. Finally, he had someone on his side. His breathing settled into an easy rhythm, and his tension relaxed enough for him to turn his head without hearing the pops and crackles of knotted muscles across his neck and shoulders. Thanks to Ava, he might get through this trial.

When she returned, her arms were full. In addition to the laptop, she brought a thermos—which he hoped was filled with coffee—a six-pack of water, her phone and a reusable grocery bag holding paper plates and snacks. She set him up with pita chips, an apple and a container of roasted red pepper hummus, all of which he scarfed down.

"Hungry?" she asked wryly.

"A twelve-mile dash through the forest burns a lot of calories." He was usually in better physical condition. Not only did he scuba dive a couple of times a week but he jogged nearly every morning. The GPS ankle bracelet had curtailed his outdoor workouts, limiting him to running on a treadmill and a couple of daily sessions on his ergometer rowing machine that he called "the erg."

She handed over her computer. "You can get started. I'll make you something more substantial to eat."

He would have told her not to go to any special trouble, but that ship had left the marina. He'd already thrown her life into chaos, and he didn't expect the situation to get less complicated. In minutes, he accessed his data on her laptop and opened a file named "Holly Louise and Oliver."

When it came to renovation and home construction, Liam

doubted he was as talented as Ava, but he sure as hell knew his way around electronics. Among the devices he carried in his backpack were bugs for listening and for tracking. He'd also rewired earbuds to make a portable, invisible walkie-talkie, something that would come in handy when they were working together and he couldn't show himself.

She slipped back into the secret room and passed him a plate containing a ham, tomato and cheese sandwich on a ciabatta roll. In her other hand, she held a steaming bowl of chili.

"Microwaved," she informed him. "I have plenty of food in the pantry and the freezer. My brother Jerome and a two-man crew have been working here all week, and they've got to eat."

"Does Jerome know about the secret passage?"

"No boys allowed," she reminded him of her motto. "This is *my* secret. No doubt, he'll eventually find out. But I like having a place where I can disappear."

"The guys in his crew, are they from Narcissus?"

She nodded. "Josh Ableman and Fish Finley. I think his real name is Edward, but everybody calls him Fish because of the 'fin' in 'Finley.'"

"I know him." Fish Finley worked part-time for him at Deep Dive. Until recently, Liam thought he and Fish were friends. "He's scheduled to testify at trial. Supposedly, Fish overheard an argument I had with Stuart."

"Yikes! Is there anybody in Narcissus who isn't involved in this murder?"

"Small town." He took a bite of the sandwich and chewed. *Delicious.* During these weeks at home with his anklet and little human contact, food had tasted like sawdust, and the aroma made him sick. Depressed? Maybe. He'd lost weight. One taste of Ava's sandwich and chili energized his will to live.

"Tomorrow," she said, "my first stop will be at Rachel's house. She always has a potluck starting at one. My regular meeting time with Georgina is at four."

"I want to be able to listen in. Also to communicate with you while you're talking."

"Not sure how you can pull that off. You're too big to be a fly on the wall."

"I have a few ideas."

"Maybe I can record the conversations on my phone. I've done that before when a client like Georgina comes up with detailed instructions I need to get exactly right."

"I have a walkie-talkie device. It's just an earbud and a tiny microphone. The problem is that we need to be within a hundred yards of each other for it to work."

"Which means you'd have to ride along with me." She thought for a moment, then said, "I can manage that. There's a huge toolbox in the back of my truck. Maybe a bit too short for your legs, you'll be cramped. And you'll feel every bump in the road."

"That's fine." Grateful for every bit of help, he had no room to complain. He dug into the homemade chili, savored the beef and beans and exhaled a sigh of sheer contentment. "All I need now is my backpack."

She took her phone from her pocket. "I'll check the weather app to find out when the rain is going to stop."

He smiled to himself. Following the weather was second nature to most Oregonians, ranging from farmers to skiers, to those who made their living from the sea like him. His salvage business took rain and wind into account before and during most of their dives. Though not totally accurate, especially when trying to guess a few days in advance, the predictions were mostly right on target. "I don't mind the storm. I can go out right now if you give me a key to the lighthouse door."

"What if somebody's watching?"

"I'll run."

She exhaled in a huff. "You really aren't good at planning, are you? According to my app, the storm is going to let up in forty-four minutes. We'll wait. Then I'll go to the lighthouse. Alone."

"How will you know where my backpack is hidden?"

"I'll figure it out."

No way would he let her take all the risk. If he got caught on the way to the lighthouse, she still had plausible deniability and could say she hadn't seen him. He finished off the sandwich and turned the laptop so she could see the screen. "This is what I've got so far about Holly Louise and Oliver."

She scrolled through the document. "Neatly organized. You start with factual data about the individual, the next section details their connection to the crime and finally you have your theories about possible motivations."

"I'm not a detective, but this investigation seems like another research project. I've added details that won't prove relevant. Better to have too much than not enough."

"Are you kidding with this motivational theory for Holly Louise?" She pointed at the screen. "Alien or ghost intervention."

"You've lived in Oregon long enough to recognize the indigenous wackiness. Consider the motto for our largest city, Keep Portland Weird. Holly Louise might believe she was directed to kill her ex-husband by otherworldly sources. I've heard that she's a big fan of horoscopes, psychics and crystals."

"True. She has a bracelet made entirely from blue and gray agates she gathered herself. It's supposed to ground her and bring good fortune."

"Yet, she still married Stuart."

"My sister chalks that up to teenage hormones. Holly was only eighteen and pregnant when they tied the knot."

"I never knew."

"Not surprised," she said. "Guys don't tend to talk much about their relationships, not even to their business partners."

"Definitely the case with me and Stuart. We hardly ever talked about personal stuff." He finished the chili and considered licking the bowl before he politely set it down beside his makeshift table. "His son, Oliver, is seventeen. Old enough to have formed his own opinions about his father."

"Old enough to commit murder," she said.

"That theory had occurred to me. Oliver is an experienced diver."

She cocked her head to one side. "Are you thinking the murderer is a scuba diver who came aboard after you were unconscious?"

"Only a theory." If Oliver came onto the boat, it meant he'd already made a plan with his father. Stuart would have administered the knockout drug to Liam. Father and son were working together. But why? Why would the young man have drugged Liam and tried to pin the murder on him? And why would Stuart plan his own murder? "I don't even know the kid."

"Neither do I," Ava admitted. "But my sister can fill in some of the blanks. Can you show me some of your other profiles?"

He shuffled through the computer screens. In addition to Holly Louise and Oliver Whitcomb, he'd listed Georgina Solomon Quincy along with her husband. He had files for Serena Whitcomb, Stuart's sister, and Charles Tancredo, the harbormaster at the Port of Newport. He managed both the commercial docks and the recreational marina. Tancredo claimed that Stuart owed him a quarter million dollars.

Ava pointed out a wide omission. "What about his parents?"

"His dad lives in Hawaii with his second wife. A neat alibi, plus he's filthy rich. Same for his mother, a Realtor who invested brilliantly. Serena, on the other hand, has blown through a lot of her inheritance."

"I'll talk to Rachel about her." Ava checked the time on her phone and gracefully rose to her feet. "It's just after two in the morning. I'm going to change clothes and dash out to the lighthouse. Might be good if you came out of hiding and kept an eye on things in the cottage. Stay away from windows so nobody can see you."

He followed her out of the secret passage to the foot of the staircase and watched the athletic sway of her hips as she jogged up the stairs. He went from room to room downstairs, avoiding windows, but when he cautiously peeked out, he saw that the weather forecast had been correct. The rain had ended, and the half-moon peeked out from behind a cloud.

Moonlight shone against the white lighthouse tower making the wear and tear of many years seem irrelevant. Though the beacon hadn't been activated for over fifty years, the tower stood as a symbol of safe passage. He hoped his journey would lead to a verdict of not guilty. Then he'd be free to tell Ava the truth about his feelings for her.

Chapter Six

"Don't follow me." In the enclosed back porch behind the kitchen, Ava stuck her arms into a hooded, lavender rain jacket that draped long enough to cover her bottom. She slipped her phone in the pocket. "If you see anyone approach me on my way to the lighthouse, go back to the secret passage, lock yourself in and wait for me to come back."

"You're the boss," he drawled.

"That's right. I am."

She figured Liam to be one of those guys who saw himself as the skipper rather than the deckhand who saluted, followed orders and said, Aye, captain. *Too bad for him.* She had to be in charge, couldn't take the risk of having Jess-hole or the marshal come back and arrest her. She had to summon all her confidence and give orders like she meant them. From her years working construction with her brother, she knew how to act like a boss.

The overhead kitchen light outlined his shoulders and streaked through his thick, dark hair while he drank another cup of coffee. She resisted the urge to order him to lay off the caffeine or he'd never get to sleep. Maybe he was one of those odd people who could have coffee right before bed. In any case, she was a boss. Not his mommy.

She cleared her throat. "Does it bother you to have a woman tell you what to do?"

"I expect nothing less from you." Though respectful enough, she heard a touch of irony as he continued, "When I came to you, I didn't expect to find a nervous, little dormouse. I like a woman who takes charge."

"Word of advice," she said, "that's enough coffee."

Wearing her rain-resistant jacket, a thermal shirt, jeans and waterproof boots, she felt a hundred times more prepared than during her last mad dash to the lighthouse tower. The rain had slowed to a drizzle, and the cloudy skies—unmarred by lightning—painted the rocks and forests with a pale blue serenity. After she descended the back stairs to the yard carrying the Maglite, she glanced over her shoulder toward the kitchen door. She couldn't see Liam, which was a good thing. He knew better than to stand at a window where someone could see him.

The misty air outside the house brushed her cheeks. Chilly but not cold, the night refreshed her almost as much as reviewing the information Liam had put together. He'd compared his investigation to a research project, and she agreed. They'd work well together.

She moved quickly across the fifty yards separating the cottage from the lighthouse. The half-moon and stars lit her path, making the flashlight unnecessary. She turned it off. Though she doubted any law enforcement officers had been assigned to watch the cottage and surrounding properties all night, she'd rather not call attention to herself by waving a Maglite through the darkness.

At the outer entrance, she unlocked the lighthouse door and pushed it open. Moonlight spilled through the two high windows, creating shadows against the dirty white walls and splotches of naked brick where the plaster had peeled away. A six-foot mound of scrap wood piled up beside the door. Ava had tried to clear away the broken furniture and the damaged stairs that formerly clung to the circular wall and climbed to the room at the top where the beacon had been housed a long time ago.

Using the flashlight beam, she studied the damaged staircase. The first four steps on the bottom were intact but the railing was gone. Theoretically, the risers were usable, but so shaky she hardly dared put her weight on them. After more broken stairs came the long break where the staircase had been completely torn away, which was about four feet long. She estimated that the semi-intact lower stairs rose twenty-seven inches, followed by damaged stairs leading to four feet of empty space. The first solidly anchored stair was almost ten feet from the floor. That riser was bolted to the wall. When she was ready to start work on the staircase, she'd reach the upper stairs with a ladder. For now, climbing was unsafe.

She aimed the flashlight beam higher and spotted Liam's black backpack tucked into a corner of a higher stair directly below the window, approximately fifteen feet off the floor. Reaching it wouldn't be easy. She needed something long to extend her grasp. Since she'd been using the lighthouse to store carpentry equipment and yard implements, she had options. Poking through the tools, she discovered a bow rake with tines she could use to hook the straps on the backpack...if she could reach it.

Getting into position below the stairs, she extended the rake as far as she could, still coming up short. She wished for an additional six inches in height. There had to be something in here that she could stand on.

She heard the door open. Liam whispered, "Deputy Jessop is hammering at the front door of the cottage."

She'd been so focused on the immediate problem of snagging the backpack straps that it took a moment to comprehend what he was saying. "Why is he here?"

"Didn't think I ought to ask." He took the rake from her. "Go out there and talk to him."

"What about you?"

"I'll figure something out."

"We should have done this your way. If I'd stayed in the cottage, I could have answered the door and gotten rid of—"

"Just go."

She dodged around the junk inside the lighthouse and went out the door. In the moonlight, she saw Jessop charging around the side of the house with a flashlight in one hand and a gun in the other. She and her brothers made fun of the mean-spirited deputy, but she knew he had a vicious temper. *Jessop was no laughing matter.* Once, he'd beaten Barry into unconsciousness. Only a few hours ago, he'd slapped a handcuff on her wrist, twisted her arm and aimed his weapon at her. If Woodburn hadn't been there to rein Jessop in, that situation could have gotten real messy real fast.

Now Jessop was back. Alone.

Her confidence evaporated, leaving her vulnerable. Somehow she had to convince him that she had nothing to hide and he shouldn't enter the lighthouse. If he found Liam, he'd probably shoot both of them. She raised her trembling hand and waved to him. "Over here, Deputy."

He halted and braced the pistol in a straight-armed, one-handed stance while still holding his flashlight with the other. "Stand still. Show me your hands, girl. Don't move."

She did as he ordered, being careful not to provoke him. Keeping her voice gentle and nonthreatening, she said, "Let's go inside. I'll make herbal tea, and I think I have some leftover marionberry pie that I can heat up."

"I'm not here for a damn snack. I'm here to apprehend your damn boyfriend."

"Who?"

"The fugitive, Liam Brody."

Her mouth went dry. It took all her restraint to keep from looking over her shoulder at the lighthouse. "I don't know what to tell you, Deputy. You and Marshal Woodburn already searched everywhere."

"You're up to something. Don't tell me you're not."

Jessop came closer, stopping when only three feet away from her. Still holding his gun, he swept the flashlight beam from the top of her head to the tips of her toes. The light lingered on her breasts, and he stared hard. But she didn't move, didn't flinch. *Don't do anything to make him angrier.* "Please, let's go inside the cottage."

"You're in a heap of trouble," he said as he turned off the flashlight and slipped it into a holder on his utility belt. "What the hell are you doing out here?"

"I had to check on something in the lighthouse." She kept herself from saying too much. The more she elaborated on an excuse, the more ways he could trip her up.

"How come?"

"I need to make sure the report on my progress is accurate. Tomorrow, I meet with my employer, Georgina Solomon Quincy." She emphasized the name, hoping to impress Jessop. Everybody in Lincoln County knew of the wealthy Solomon family.

"Miss Georgina is friends with Stuart's family. You know how those rich people stick together. And I'm damn sure she'll be angry when she finds out that you're harboring his killer."

"I'm sure you're right, Deputy." She knew for a fact that he was dead wrong. Georgina despised Stuart, his ex-wife, his mother and his sister. But Ava knew better than to contradict Jessop. Her brothers had taught her to never poke a skunk. Cowards were most dangerous when proven wrong. "Is it all right for me to put my hands down?"

"Not yet." He thrust the pistol toward her. "I'm stiff and tired, and it's all your fault."

"Sorry," she murmured. *Don't contradict him.*

"I've been parked in the forest, watching and waiting after Woodburn took off to search in other places. I saw lights come on in your bedroom and your kitchen. Don't you ever sleep?"

"My nerves are on edge. I don't usually get visits from the police in the middle of the night."

"Don't lie to me." He barked a harsh laugh. "Plenty of times I showed up on the Donovan doorstep to arrest Barry in the middle of the night after the bars closed. And don't get me started on Michael. I'll never believe that punk is innocent."

Her jaw clenched. Anger sliced through her fear as she instinctively reacted to his cruel comment about her unjustly accused brother. She took back a sliver of her self-control. "How can I help you?"

"I want to see inside the damn lighthouse. Use your key to open the door." He gestured with the gun. "Come on, let's go."

"You were already in there."

"Do what I say. I'm not going to ask politely again." He took another step closer and shoved her shoulder, throwing her off balance. She caught herself before falling. He shoved again. "Do I need the cuffs? Maybe you like being restrained. Do you like it when your boyfriend ties you up?"

Disgusted and outraged, she pulled her phone from her pocket. "I'm recording this conversation. Starting now."

"What the hell?"

"I need a record of what you're saying to use in court. I

might sue the sheriff's office for police harassment. Touch me again, and the charge goes up to police brutality."

His thin lips curled in a sneer. "Bitch."

"Speak up, Deputy Jessop. I didn't catch that word."

"No more games, little girl. I want to look inside the lighthouse. A reasonable request." Still holding his gun at the ready, he strode past her toward the door. "I'm an officer of the law, just doing my damn duty."

She wanted to shout at him, but panic choked her words. If the deputy walked inside, he'd find Liam. "Wait! You don't have a warrant."

"Well, look here." His long nose twitched as if catching the scent of his prey. "The door isn't locked, and I hear sounds of a fight going on inside."

"That's a lie. Nobody is in there."

"Not the way I see it. I need to investigate."

When he grasped the doorknob, she felt her life crumbling. All her years of study and hard work would be wiped away. She'd have a criminal record. No one would ever hire her to do another historic renovation.

Jessop shoved the door open and burst inside, holding his pistol with both hands. Triumphantly, he shouted, "I've got you now."

Frozen in place, she looked to the skies, seeking solace in the stars and the moon. *No regrets.* Even if she went to jail, she knew that helping Liam had been the right decision. She believed him innocent, unjustly prosecuted for a murder he didn't commit, and he had no one else on his side. *Sometimes, you just have to do what you think is right and accept the consequences.*

Her gaze was caught by a flash from the beacon room at the top of the lighthouse. Concentrating hard, she saw a glimmer of light from one of the windows. It drew a circle on the glass, then paused, then drew a circle again. Sometimes on scuba expeditions at night in dark seas, they used flashlight signals to communicate. Drawing a circle with a light was code for "everything is okay." Somehow, Liam had made it to the top of the tower, and he was letting her know he was all right, using his powerful pocket Maglite.

From inside the lighthouse, she heard Jessop yelling. "Son of a bitch! Where the hell are you?"

She exhaled in a gush, unaware of holding her breath. Her pulse rate steadied as energy flowed back into her body. She had no idea how Liam had managed to reach the upper floor of the lighthouse tower. *Sprouted wings and flew to the rafters?* It felt like a miracle—a sign that she was supposed to be working with him.

With her feet braced in a solid stance, she raised her phone to record Jess-hole when he emerged from the lighthouse. "Well, Deputy, what do you have to say for yourself?"

His eyebrows lowered, and his chin stuck out. In spite of the chilly night air, his forehead dripped with sweat. She'd won this round, and her victory felt good.

He rushed toward her. When close enough, he slapped the phone from her hand into the mud. "You're not going to get away with this."

She squatted down, picked up her phone and brushed off the mud, impressed that the screen was still lit. "Second time today," she muttered. "I just finished cleaning this thing off."

"I'm not giving up. I'm going to watch you and follow you until that fugitive is caught and you both go to jail."

When she looked up and saw the hatred in his eyes, Ava couldn't help being scared. Bravely, she stood up to him. "Is that supposed to be a threat?"

"A promise, Ms. Donovan."

When he pivoted and stalked away from her, she saw cruel determination in the rigid set of his shoulders. Deputy Jessop meant what he'd said.

Chapter Seven

Looking down from the windows in the circular room at the top of the lighthouse, Liam watched Jessop stomp around the cottage to where he'd parked his black SUV with the Lincoln County Sheriff's Department logo. Walking at a fast and furious pace, the deputy looked like the definition of a frustrated, angry man—a guy who wanted to kick butt and take names but didn't have a pencil.

Liam shifted his focus to Ava, who stood frozen between the cottage and the lighthouse in the exact same place she'd faced Jessop. The light purple hood on her jacket had fallen back, and the wind ruffled her dark, curly, chin-length hair. Her arms wrapped around her middle as if holding herself together. She was too far away for him to see if she was shaking with fear or to hear a tremble in her voice, but he'd seen Jessop knock her phone from her hand and snarl. She didn't deserve this kind of bullying from the law. Nobody did.

Using one of the burner phones he had stored in his backpack, he sent her a text. Come to the tower. Pretend you're locking up but come inside.

He saw her wipe the screen on her cell phone, nod once and take a shaky step toward the lighthouse. Meanwhile, Jessop had slammed the door of his SUV and driven away. Liam watched the red taillights disappear into the forest.

This time, the departure was real. The deputy wasn't hanging around. Once again, Liam had escaped discovery.

Earlier tonight, he wasn't sure he'd make it, but he'd found a way. When he reached the room at the top, he'd discovered that other people had been here before him. They'd left a couple of sleeping bags and a long, double-strand rope with thick knots every eighteen inches to use for climbing. Anchored to the pedestal for the beacon, the rope felt like a solid support. He opened the hatch and tossed it through, pleased to see that it almost touched the floor, nearly forty-two feet below.

He lowered himself onto the rope and descended, grateful for the upper body strength he'd developed during the weeks he'd spent confined to his house. Twice-daily workouts on the erg had paid off big-time as he gripped the rope and used his legs and feet to balance on the knots. About five feet from the floor, he let go and dropped. Ava awaited.

Before he could explain and apologize, she set her flashlight down on the floor. With her hands free, she joined her body with his. Her arms wrapped around his neck, and she buried her face against his chest. Not weeping but breathing heavily, she clung to him with fierce strength as though he were her lifeline—the only thing keeping her from floating into the night sky like a lost balloon.

Her words trickled out between gasps. "I thought we were caught. Going to jail. No way out. Can't believe it. Jessop outsmarted me."

He caressed her shoulders and slid his hands lower to her slender waist. "He's not clever enough to beat us. Luckier than he has any right to be. And as stubborn as a hungry honey badger. That makes him dangerous."

"Yes," she whispered, "he won't give up."

"Neither will we." The fragrance of her shampoo reminded him of lilacs in the spring. "There are two of us. We're tough, and we smell good."

"What?"

"You and me. Champions of the world."

She tilted her head and gazed up at him. Moonlight from the high windows glistened on her cheeks and sparkled in her blue eyes. She cleared her throat. When she spoke, her voice was calm. "You changed clothes."

"I had other stuff in my backpack. I needed to get out of the wet jeans."

"Where did you find the fancy rope?"

"Ava, we don't have time to talk. I watched Jessop drive away, but he might come back or send someone else for a stakeout."

She bobbed her head. "The rope?"

"I found it in the room at the top. Somebody else must have been here."

"That room is called the lantern room. Above is a metal dome or cupola with an air vent and lightning rod on top. And the stairs…" She paused her lecture to gaze at the snaggletoothed spiral staircase with impossibly large gaps. "How did you get up there?"

"Free climbing," he said, again pleased about his rowing muscles. "I jumped up to grab the lowest stair that was still attached to the brick wall. Twisting and turning, I maneuvered from stair to stair. When the boards creaked and buckled under my weight, I supported myself with my arms. And vice versa. Not a trip I want to make again."

"When I saw you make the sign for okay in the window, I almost fainted from relief." The tiniest hint of a smile touched her lips. "Before that, I was almost too scared to breathe. I thought Jessop was going to shoot both of us."

"If you've changed your mind about helping me and want to end this collaboration, I can live with that. When I saw Jessop pushing you around, I regretted being here and wanted to kill the son of a bitch."

"Don't say things like that. When you talk about murder, it makes me doubt the wisdom of playing on Team Liam."

In spite of his need to get moving and seek a safe haven, her nearness calmed him. He whispered, "I'm sorry."

She reached up and held his face in her hands. "Earlier, I agreed to help you. But now… I'm committed. I believe in you, maybe more than you believe in yourself."

Rising up on her tiptoes, she confirmed her words with a light kiss. The softness of her lips wakened his strength and his determination. He pulled her close, savoring the delicate pressure of her pliant body against his chest. He kissed her back, tender at first and then with rising passion. The taste of her sweet, warm mouth drew him deeper. His tongue probed between her lips, gliding across the slick surface of her teeth and then went deeper. A growl vibrated in his throat. He wanted more of her, wanted everything from her.

But he wouldn't take advantage. Yes, she'd kissed him. But would she agree to more? "The view from the lantern room is magic. The topmost branches of Sitka spruce waving in the wind. Moonlight shimmering. Breakers churning."

She inhaled a ragged gasp. "Captains on passing ships reported they could see the lantern's beam from twenty-three miles out, and I expect the same is true in reverse."

"Ava, will you stay here with me tonight? In the lighthouse."

Though he expected a no, she didn't immediately turn him down. Instead, she stepped away from his embrace and eyed the knotted rope. "I'm not quite ready to make that climb."

"I'll help."

"I bet you will." She gave a light chuckle. "Might be easier if you came back to the cottage with me."

Every bone, muscle and nerve in his body urged him to

say yes. His arms felt empty when he wasn't holding her. She was perfect. He wanted to make love to her. But he couldn't risk it. "Tonight I stay here."

"You're sure?"

"Being here is strategic."

"How so?"

"If Jessop or anybody else finds me, you can claim that you didn't know I was there."

She tensed. "You want me to lie?"

"In the service of a greater truth," he said. "When you go, leave the lighthouse door unlocked. Tomorrow morning, I'll sneak into the barn. When you're ready to make the drive to your sister's house, back your truck in there, and I'll hide in the truck bed."

"Better idea," she said. "I already have a Hyundai Sonata parked in the barn. Excellent space in the trunk and the back seats fold down so you could crawl through."

Whether he curled up in the trunk or in the bed of her truck, the drive to Narcissus wouldn't be a pleasure cruise. "I'm guessing the Sonata has a better ride than the truck."

"Not nearly as bone jarring." She took a set of keys from her pocket, detached a key fob with the curvy Hyundai logo and handed it to him. "Can I call you?"

"Calls and texts should be okay." He waved his cell phone. "This is a burner."

She reminded him, "Woodburn was able to trace you the first time you called me on a burner phone."

"I think he overheard my part of our conversation on a bug planted in the house. Not by tracking the phone. Besides, I have a better idea." He reached into a jacket pocket and pulled out a small case. "Practice wearing these earbuds. And try different ways of fastening the microphone to your clothes so you can talk back to me."

"This is like something a spy would use. For espionage."

"Just remember. We're the good guys, and the good guys always win."

In the movies. No matter what peril they faced, the sultry heroine and dashing hero would triumph. He hoped, for once, real life would follow that script.

LATER THAT NIGHT, Liam stretched out on the sleeping bags and blankets of his makeshift bed in the lantern room at the top of the lighthouse. His muscles ached from the incredibly long day of running, climbing and hiding. His physical stress couldn't compare to the way his emotions battered his mind. Worse than the fear and rage he felt for himself were his feelings for Ava. An incredible woman, she was strong and beautiful, and he wanted to know her better. At the same time, he regretted coming here and putting her in danger. He didn't deserve her attention when he couldn't even promise that he hadn't killed Stuart. His guilt if anything happened would be overwhelming.

Ironically, he was the only witness to the murder. Somehow, he had to remember. The therapist he'd hired to help him recall his memories had suggested a form of focused meditation when he went to bed. With eyes closed, Liam concentrated on sensations he experienced before losing consciousness on the boat. Sprawled on the cushions in the stern lounging area, he'd felt the heat of the afternoon sun and the spray from the twin motors. Stuart had been trying to convince him to purchase this cabin cruiser for the Deep Dive fleet, but Liam had disagreed. This was a luxury yacht. Too fancy.

Gradually, he emptied his mind of all other thought. Stuart's voice faded into a blend of noise from circling gulls and splashing waves. Liam kept his eyes closed, regulated his breathing and waited for his indistinct memories to take solid form. His thoughts were uncensored, fanciful. As he often did, he imagined a mermaid perched on a rock, singing softly and combing her long, brown hair. Then came a deep, soft stillness.

This was new. Liam forced himself not to waken and break the spell of imagination and memory. He heard the sound of an outboard motor and knew another boat was approaching. Though he didn't move or rouse himself, he could see it in his mind's eye. An inflatable like a Zodiac. He recognized the sounds of the inflatable hooking up to the dive platform where the twin motors rested in silence. Another person was coming aboard.

Liam's pulse raced. His muscles tensed. Finally, he would see the murderer.

Anticipation heightened his senses. The moment blasted his meditative state. He returned to reality. Too soon.

He bolted to his feet. Shattered bits of memory scattered around his feet as he made his way to the windows looking out to sea. Out there, the answers were hidden. Someone else, not necessarily a scuba diver, had been on the yacht with him and Stuart. Was that mystery person the killer?

THE NEXT MORNING at about eight o'clock, Ava put the finishing touches on a huge breakfast of bagels, smoked salmon, cream cheese, sausage and omelet which she packed in a basket. Also included were bottles of water, juice, energy bars, a thermos filled with coffee and other supplies Liam had requested. When she stepped outside, she blinked at the welcome burst of sunshine. On a day like this, it was hard to imagine murder and danger. She paused at the starting point of a steep path that descended to the narrow, sandy beach. Offshore were dramatic rock formations resulting from lava flows fifteen million years ago.

The three largest basalt formations, called the "sea hags" because they resembled giant silhouettes of stooped figures wearing ragged robes, were home to raucous colonies of nesting seabirds. Cormorants, gulls and white-chested murres competed for territory on the sea hags guarding the tide pools. Seal Rock provided a long, flat surface at the edge of the breaking surf for marine mammals who were already sunning themselves on this fine, clear April day.

Ava moved on. She inhaled a breath of salty air and hummed as she approached the tower. The mic and earbuds had been working beautifully, and she used the device to let him know she'd arrived. "Lower the rope, Rapunzel."

"Don't compare me to a fairy-tale princess."

She chuckled. "If the glass slipper fits..."

"And what does that make you?"

"Obviously, I'm the fairy godmother."

The knotted rope slithered down from the lantern room. She tied it to the basket handle, and he pulled the food and supplies up to his lair. Though he was close enough to hear her if she shouted, Ava had gotten accustomed to the unexpected intimacy from their wireless walkie-talkie. In a normal tone of voice, she asked, "I understand why you need binoculars, but why the hammer and screwdriver?"

"To repair the latch on the door to the lantern room and also on this hatch." He hauled the basket inside. "Mmm, coffee. Maybe you are a fairy godmother, after all."

"I texted my sister first thing this morning. Departure time is one fifteen."

"I'll be waiting in the barn."

She imagined him checking his Casio G-Shock dive watch and making a mental note with a quick nod of his head. Her memories of her former professor—and her slight obsession with him when she was a student—became more clearly defined as they spent more time together. Liam hadn't physically changed much from six years ago, still lean and muscular. Maybe his biceps were bigger. It was hard to tell without seeing him shirtless.

As she strolled away from the lighthouse and went to the cottage, her memory replayed a day when she and the rest of her class were on Liam's boat, changing into wet suits. While he gave instructions for the tactical dive, she'd been stealing glances at his tanned upper body and muscular arms. He looked healthy, exactly the way a man should look. Not too heavily muscled. Definitely not too skinny.

And now, finally, she'd kissed him for real. Last night was different from that shy, long-ago kiss on the boat. Last night had been passionate. Tender at first, then quickly progressing to ferocious. She'd felt how excited he was and how much he wanted her. His desire had little to do with their investigation and everything to do with untamed, unbridled lust of a man for a woman. *Wishful thinking?* She entered the cottage through the back door, stepped into the kitchen and sank into a chair at the table.

Her first priority was to get control of her imagination before she saw Rachel. Her sister had always been able to read her emotions, which was why she'd texted a couple of messages about dropping by for a visit rather than calling and betraying the urgency in her tone.

If Ava turned bright red and stammered every time Liam's name was mentioned, their association would be revealed. The best way for her to control a difficult situation had always meant intense organization. She prepared lunch for Liam and made cherry and macadamia nut cookies to take to Rachel's. Considering her sister's baking obsession, bringing baked goods was like carrying snow to a polar bear or chocolate to Hershey, Pennsylvania.

With less than an hour to go before departure time, she sat at the rolltop desk and reviewed Liam's notes on her laptop, trying to decide what sort of questions she ought to ask her sister. Mainly, she'd focus on Stuart's ex-wife. How much did Holly Louise Whitcomb inherit after her husband's death? And what about her son, Oliver?

According to Liam's notes, Holly had an unshakable alibi—an Alaskan cruise—for the afternoon when Stuart was killed. Oliver had been hanging out with friends but couldn't account for the whole afternoon. Also, if Holly or Oliver had approached the boat in scuba gear, it still didn't explain how or why Liam had been rendered unconscious. Forensic tests done at the time didn't reveal the presence of drugs in the beer or sandwiches, which really didn't prove that he hadn't been dosed. Disposing of tainted food on a boat in the middle of the Pacific wouldn't have been difficult.

"Ava."

She heard his voice in her ear. She sighed and said, "I'm here, Liam." *Here for you.*

"Ava, look out the window." His voice came through the earbud. "I'm using the binoculars, and I see a yellow Jeep Wrangler pulling into the parking lot in front of the cottage."

She bolted to the window in the dining room. She knew only one person who drove a Wrangler. "My brother. Michael."

"Why is he here?"

"I don't know."

She couldn't think of a single reason for him to return to Lincoln County. Too many of the folks in Narcissus had been cruel when he was released from prison. Though he'd been cleared of all charges, they viewed him with suspicion and treated him like a murderer instead of a wrongly accused man.

According to him, the move to Pendleton where he lived in a small cabin and worked at a ranch was to escape memories of his murdered girlfriend and friends who betrayed him. Always a quiet guy, his years in prison made him reclusive…and dark. Some said he'd turned cold, that all his emotions had frozen. Ava didn't believe it. She'd heard him laugh. She'd seen the devilish glint in his eye when he played a practical joke on her. When he got out of the Jeep and slapped his tan cowboy hat on his head, she was happy to see him. Her handsome brother with his sharp blue eyes and sandy hair was one of the people she truly loved.

She dashed for the front door, flung it open and ran to him. He caught both of her hands and whipped her in a wide circle. Instantly, she was transported back in time to when she was ten years old and her older brother took a day off work to be with her. After their father died, Michael Donovan was her chosen male role model.

He set her down on the ground, stepped back, looked into her eyes and frowned. "What's this I hear about you getting hooked up with an accused murderer?"

She gaped. "What?"

"Dammit, Ava. You always did have a thing for bad boys."

Chapter Eight

Listening to the confrontation between Ava and her brother through his earbud, Liam was taken aback. Never before had anyone accused him of being a bad boy. He'd always worked hard and done well in school. He earned a doctorate by the age of twenty-four and was now a tenured professor at U of O. The documentary about his shipwreck recovery expeditions near the Strait of Juan de Fuca compared him to Jacques Cousteau and Indiana Jones. Both were adventurers and educated men, just like him. His cringe turned into a grin. Cousteau and Jones were definitely bad boys. Just. Like. Him.

Sure, he'd picked up a shady reputation for being a treasure hunter—a modern-day pirate. And he'd gone through a phase when he rode a badass Harley, wore leather jackets and drank tequila. He'd been proud of the rep, which probably made him more of a nerd than a real outlaw. Nothing wrong with being a "bad boy."

He heard Ava make a comment to that effect. "You're right, Mikey. I like bad boys. How could I not? Take a look at my brothers."

"Don't put this on me," he said. "You should have learned from the lousy examples set by me and Barry. Be smart, Ava. Don't hook up with a guy who isn't good enough for you."

Silently, Liam agreed. He peered down from the high lighthouse windows at the siblings who faced off in the parking area at the front of the cottage. The brother was a tall, lean cowboy. Ava, dressed in cargo shorts and a white button-down shirt under a khaki anorak, looked like she ought to be on a safari somewhere.

"Oh, yawn," Ava said. "I've heard this lecture before."

"You're right, sis. And I'll say it again. I never liked the condescending way you were treated by Portland Jimmy the lawyer. Then there was that street artist who didn't contribute a nickel toward rent—he was a waste of flesh. Not to mention the guy who claimed to be a descendant from Chief Joseph."

"Stating the obvious, Mikey boy. This is none of your business."

In the nuance of her tone, Liam heard sisterly irritation. His own sister spoke the same way to him. She'd been sympathetic when he was arrested and had set him up with a good lawyer, which was more than his dad had done. An acclaimed virologist, his father was too busy saving the world to worry about his son, who ought to be able to handle something as mundane as a murder allegation by himself. Not that Liam expected his dad to do anything. After Liam's mom died when he was thirteen, Dad pretty much resigned from his parental duties.

"I worry about you," Michael said to his sister.

"Somehow, I doubt that you drove all the way from Pendleton to criticize my former boyfriends."

"Rachel called me," he said. "She's concerned on account of that professor you had a crush on when you were at the university."

"No idea what you're talking about."

"Liam Brody." Her brother's voice rumbled like a volcano about to erupt. "I'm talking about Dr. Liam Brody, the guy in the newspapers who is accused of murder. Rachel said you wanted to date him six years ago when you took his class, but he was too old for you, not to mention he was your teacher."

"What's with you guys?" she grumbled. "All I did was send Rachel a text telling her that I wanted to drop by her potluck this afternoon before I had my regular weekly appointment with Georgina."

"Right," he said, "and she texted back, asking if you'd heard anything about Brody. And you replied 'w/e.' I guess that stands for *whatever*. She knew you were hiding something."

Apparently, Ava resented her sister's conclusion, because she let loose with a fusillade of hostility—none of which included actual profanity—aimed at both brother and sister. Liam stifled an urge to chuckle. He would have given a lot to have his family worry about him as much as her brother and sister obviously cared about her. Though not happy about being characterized as the next loser boyfriend destined to ruin Ava's life, he'd like to meet the rest of the Donovan family in person.

When Ava ran out of words, her brother said, "I'll give you a ride to Rachel's house."

"Another thing," she said, "you and our snarky sis were so busy finding fault with my possible choice of a mate that you missed the headline. You're as blind as a couple of big-eared bats. From what's been reported in the paper and on TV, the case against Liam is totally circumstantial."

"So now it's *Liam*, is it?"

"Missing the point, butthead. He's in the same position you were."

"Not hardly." Liam heard Michael scoff before he continued. "I got scooped up by a couple of cops who weren't gentle about throwing me into custody."

"Jessop?" she asked.

"Matter of fact, Jess-hole was front and center. I still have the scars. After he and his sadistic buddies locked me up and assigned me an inexperienced public defender, I never got out on bail. You know that's how it went, Ava. I was convicted before I appeared in court. The trial was a sham. I never had a chance of beating the charges."

"Oh, Michael." Her voice broke, and Liam heard her sniffle. "I'm so sorry for what happened to you."

"Your professor has a respectable job, important friends and a wealthy family. He's been handled with care, and I'm guessing he has a high-class, expensive lawyer, probably hired a private investigator. Brody was granted bail. He's been spending this time before the trial at his home. So far, he's gotten a damn good deal."

"What if he's found guilty?" she asked in the same shaky voice. "What if he's innocent and goes to jail? Just like you."

"Not doing himself any favors by skipping out on bail."

"Shouldn't he do everything he can to find the truth?"

Liam listened as the silent pause grew longer. Finally, Michael said, "I understand. No innocent man should ever be incarcerated. But I'm warning you, Ava Caitlyn Donovan, don't get involved with this guy. You'll end up being hurt."

Though Liam wanted a chance to rebut Michael, he didn't want to make his plea to Ava through their walkie-talkie device. Her true feelings showed more in her body language, and seeing her physical reactions helped him understand her. Better he should wait until they were alone face-to-face to tell her that he would never intentionally hurt her.

He watched while she and her brother talked about family things, including their mom's current good health, Barry's latest breakup with a girlfriend and Rachel's third-grade daughter winning a spelling bee. Finally, Ava sent her brother on his way with a promise to meet him at Rachel's house. She needed to drive herself because she was going to see

Georgina after. When Michael left, Liam watched his yellow Wrangler drive away on the narrow road leading back to the route through the Siuslaw National Forest. He threw a burner phone, his laptop, water bottle and energy bars into his backpack before descending the knotted rope to the floor.

Though he hadn't noticed watchers in the surrounding forest, Liam took care and dodged behind cover on his way to the barn behind the cottage. Ava had left the side door unlocked, and he darted inside. The old structure, with the high, gambrel roof, a spacious loft and wide double doors, was more ramshackle than the other buildings on the property. Several of the weathered boards had rotted away, leaving gaps. In the early 1900s when the lighthouse was built, the barn must have been used as a stable for horses. Later, it made a convenient storage space for cars, trucks and other equipment.

Parked at the front was a four-door Sonata. Liam spoke into his mic. "I'm in the barn."

"Be right there," she said. "Did you listen to everything my brother said?"

"Being called a 'bad boy' is kind of cool."

"Yeah, neat-o." Her voice oozed with sarcasm. "Mikey also admitted that he understood why you wanted to investigate. You know, it might not be a bad idea if we got—"

"See you in a minute." He purposely interrupted, guessing that she was about to suggest they recruit her family to help investigate. No way. When he wrote his *Fugitive on the Run Handbook*, one of the cardinal rules would be: no family. The last thing he wanted was to get the entire Donovan clan accused of being accessories.

AVA LUGGED AN insulated bag filled with food, juice drinks and water. She also carried a sleeping bag and a tarp to the garage where Liam would hide in the trunk of her Hyundai for their trip to Narcissus. Her sixteen-year-old Toyota Ta-coma truck would have provided a more comfortable hid-ing place if she'd installed the cover over the cargo bed, but she'd been using her truck to transport construction equip-ment and junk to the dump. Cleaning it up and putting on the cover might look suspicious. She could practically hear Jessop's scratchy voice demanding to know what she was hiding. *Nothing much. Just an escaped fugitive.*

Seeing Michael and hearing him fuss about her former boyfriends made her both happy and sad. Cheerful because she truly loved her family and was glad they cared. Miser-able due to the secret she was keeping from them. Liam's presence loomed larger and more dangerous than an elephant in the room. Bigger than a wooly mammoth. How could she keep denying his presence?

At the barn, she pulled open the double doors, went in-side and closed the doors again. Liam stepped out of the shadows behind the riding mower. Though his jaw was out-lined with stubble and his thick dark hair looked like he'd combed it with a turbo-drill, his easy grin told her that free-dom agreed with him.

"Sleep well?" she asked.

"Surprisingly, yes." He stepped up beside her, opened the rear passenger door of the Sonata and started placing her stuff inside. "The rhythm of the surf is a lullaby for me."

"You miss your dive boat."

"Damn right, I do. These weeks while my travel has been restricted feel like years. When this is over, I want to take a long trip, maybe to Cozumel. Ever been there?"

"Never have." But she'd heard about the incredible scuba diving along the Mesoamerican reef system, the languorous heat, white sandy beaches and palm trees. She'd spent very little time in tropical climates—so different from the rug-ged Oregon coast. Traveling there with Liam, diving with him, sailing with him sounded like a fantasy come true. "Maybe someday."

"Soon."

"You're awfully confident."

"Visualizing a positive outcome keeps me sane."

"Right." She'd never thought of him as the type to make a vision board. Liam seemed more like her, basing his plans on research and knowledge of the past. "Do you believe in happily-ever-after?"

"I need to. Especially now."

Leaving the passenger door open, she took the sleeping bag and circled to the rear and opened the trunk. After she smoothed the tarp and the unzipped bag inside, she unloaded a small stash of food and water bottles. Stepping back, she peered into the small but cozy nest. "Are you going to fit in there?"

"I'll make it work."

She scrutinized him from the top of his six-foot-two-inch height to his broad chest and shoulders to his extra-large boots. "If we clear out the back of the truck and put the cover over the bed, you'd have enough room to stretch out."

"And it's the first place anybody would look."

So true. She tried another suggestion. "If you're too cramped, the seats in the back fold down and make the trunk larger. The latches on each side are broken, so you can reach them from inside the trunk and put the back down."

"Got it," he said as he climbed into the trunk, folded his long body and closed the trunk over his head.

The rear of the Hyundai bounced while Liam shifted his position. Doubtful about the viability of pulling this off, Ava shook her head. This scheme felt unpracticed and haphazard. They'd never get away with it. Speaking in a normal voice which would be picked up by her mic, she said, "We should rethink."

"It'll work. Can you hear me through the earbud?"

"Loud and clear."

The jostling from the trunk stilled. "Ready," he said.

She opened the barn door, drove out and closed it again. In minutes, she was on the two-lane road through the old-growth forest, leaving the coast behind. Last night's rain had renewed the moss-covered trees and undergrowth of ferns. New leaves on hemlock, alder and maple wore a brilliant green. The towering Sitka spruce, some over three hundred years old, reached up and touched the clouds.

Though Ava loved the drama of crashing waves and screaming gulls at seaside, the primordial forests of Oregon gave her a sense of peace and calm. The winds that shrieked on the coast turned to whispers in the forest, offering reassurance that all was for the best. Nature would always take care of itself.

She heard Liam's voice through her earbud. "I've got a couple of things for you to focus on when you talk to your sister. Number one is Oliver Whitcomb, the seventeen-year-old son."

"Holly's son. That makes them Holly and Ollie," she said. "You don't really think he killed his father, do you?"

"It's possible. I've gone diving with the kid a couple of times. He's quiet and smart. I like him, and he doesn't seem like a killer. But I need to consider everybody as a suspect. Oliver might be responsible for drugging me."

"Why?"

"He and his father could have been plotting together. More than once, I've caught Stuart trying to sell artifacts we rescued from shipwrecks. He might have recruited his son to help funnel the artifacts to a fence. All they needed was to get me out of the way."

"Are you saying that you were actually the target of the assault?"

"They didn't want to kill me," Liam said. "Stuart invited me to come onto the yacht. We were a long way offshore when I passed out. There were no other boats in sight. Not sure how long I was unconscious, but it was at least a half hour. Plenty of time to shove me overboard and get me out of the way."

"Which means you weren't meant to be murdered."

"Correct."

She shook her head. His logic didn't add up. "Why would Stuart get his son involved? What did he hope to gain by drugging you?"

"If Ollie planned to kill his dad, I made a convenient fall guy to be blamed for the crime."

Though she'd only met Oliver once or twice, Ava found it hard to believe this young man—a typical teenager—had the smarts or the devious intentions of a criminal mastermind. "Why would he want to hurt his father? How is this related to missing artifacts? Or to drugs?"

"Not an airtight theory."

"More holes than a colander," she said. "Why do you think Rachel might know about Oliver Whitcomb? Her oldest kid is in third grade."

"Your sister works in a pharmacy," he said. "She hears a lot of gossip and might have information about drugs."

"She's an assistant, not a pharmacist. And I seriously doubt she'd have better, more accurate information than the forensic people who tested the food and drink on the yacht and did a tox screen on you."

Ava drove along the coast on Highway 101 for a few miles before turning onto the river road that led to her hometown. She'd reviewed the information Liam collected and hoped he'd come up with better theories than blaming Oliver. "What else should I ask Rachel about?"

"I'm looking for motivations that wouldn't be included

in police data. Was Holly dating? Maybe she has a jealous boyfriend. What about other people who hated Stuart? Who benefits financially if he's out of the way? What about his sister, Serena?"

"I doubt she'll be at a potluck hosted by Rachel. Not high-class enough for her."

"But she dated your brother Barry."

"Occasionally, she goes slumming with the likes of the Donovans."

She heard him chuckle. "According to Stuart's will, Ollie inherits his shares in Deep Dive, and Holly is the executrix which puts her in charge."

"I saw that in your research. You still maintain the majority share of the stock, but if you sell, you need to pay her off for the sale of the boats and equipment. That could add up to serious money."

"That's the kind of gossip I want to hear," he said. "I'm guessing that Stuart is one of the very few murder victims from Narcissus. People have got to be talking about him. Were there special reasons that Holly and Ollie or anybody else wanted Stuart dead?"

Entering the city limits of Narcissus, she slowed to twenty-five miles per hour. The last thing she wanted was to be cited for speeding by Jess-hole or any of the other local cops. This former lumber town had definitely seen better days. Several shops on Main were boarded over with graffiti-marked particleboard. An Open sign hung in the door of the bakery, and the twinkle lights outlining Fresh Daily were lit. Through the windows of the corner diner, she saw a couple of guys in flannel shirts who could have been great-grandsons of original Narcissus residents. The pharmacy where Rachel worked was closed on Sunday as was a tiny bookstore and an antique shop. Mack's Lumberjack Tavern with blinking neon signs in every window had several cars parked in the slanted parking spaces.

When she stopped at the one and only stoplight in town, she looked over and saw three men standing on the sidewalk outside the tavern and smoking. One of them leaned down and stared into her Sonata. Her gaze met his, and she gasped. "Tancredo," she said. "I think he recognizes me."

He signaled for her to pull over. "He wants me to park. Should I see what he wants?"

"Not now," Liam said. "Give him a smile and a wave. Then drive on."

"Agreed." It was like he'd read her mind. She didn't want to get entangled with this guy. Feigning confusion, she waved and tapped the accelerator. The light hadn't changed.

Moving with a speed and agility she didn't expect from a gray-haired, wizened man, Tancredo crossed the sidewalk, hopped off the curb and grabbed the door handle on the passenger side. The door was locked. He yanked on the handle. With his other hand, he slapped the glass.

"Pull over, Ava Donovan," his gravelly voice commanded. "I want to talk to you."

His palm flattened on the window. He was missing his fourth finger and pinkie.

Chapter Nine

Ava had no choice. If she followed her instincts and drove away at top speed, she'd hurt Tancredo's good hand and make an enemy for life. She shouted, "Let go of the door. I'll pull over to the curb."

When he stepped back, she rounded the corner and parked at the curb. In her ear, Liam spoke in a quiet but tense voice. "Get away from him as soon as you can. He's dangerous, possibly involved in illegal drug smuggling."

Though she didn't know Tancredo very well, she'd never liked the guy. He exuded the sneering superiority of a boss who—for some unknown reason—considered himself to be better than everybody else. From Liam's research, she recalled the suspicion of illegal drugs. In a way, smuggling made sense for Tancredo. As the harbormaster of a mid-size port, he had the necessary access for shifting goods and cargo from one ship to another. He'd been considered a suspect for Stuart's murder and investigated by the police. According to Liam's notes, he had a solid, believable alibi.

As soon as she parked, he rapped on the window. "Unlock the door."

Again, there was no way to avoid his request without appearing suspicious. When he opened the door of the Sonata and slipped inside, he brought a stench with him. The stink of sweat that stained his long-sleeved cotton shirt mingled with the odors of dead and decaying fish, oil and garbage. His long gray hair crawled out from a filthy baseball cap and hung in greasy tangles around his grizzled cheeks.

Ava just couldn't force herself to smile. "I haven't seen you in a long time."

"Hardly recognized you with the short hair." He wheezed and coughed. "Glad I did. I've got a question for you."

When he closed the door, shutting himself in beside her, she felt trapped. "If you don't mind, make it quick. I'm in kind of a hurry."

"Rushing to meet with Georgina, eh? Never thought I'd see the day when the high-and-mighty Solomon family lowered themselves to talk to a Donovan girl."

"Surprise, surprise." How did he know so much? The rumor mill in Narcissus and nearby Newport must be operating at full tilt if the men who spent their weekend at the Lumberjack's Tavern were talking about her and Georgina.

Speaking through the earbud, Liam whispered, "Ask him about the quarter-of-a-million-dollar loan he made to Stuart."

She turned her head to scrutinize the old man who didn't look like he had two nickels to rub together. "The Solomons aren't the only ones with money. I heard that you made a very large cash loan to Stuart."

He squinted at her. "Now, where would you hear something like that? One of your bigmouth brothers?"

"Is it true? A quarter of a million? I thought Stuart's family was rich."

"He and Serena squandered their inheritances." His lower lip stuck out in a frown. "Stuart bought that fancy cabin cruiser—the boat where he died—before he got around to paying me back."

"Why did you make the loan?"

"He was supposed to do a job for me."

A job? That could be anything. She tried to pry deeper without seeming too interested. "Did you get your money's worth?"

"Maybe. Maybe not." His voice turned hostile, almost threatening. "What's it to you?"

"Just curious." She backed off, not wanting to anger him. "I like to know things."

"You were always the smart one in your family," he said. "Little Ava went to college and met a professor. Liam Brody. I heard he's in touch with you."

Who would tell him that? "Let me guess. You've been talking to Deputy Jessop."

"I knew you were smart." He wheezed again, and she realized that the noise represented laughter. "I need to get a message to Brody."

Inadvertently, she glanced toward the back seat. If Tancredo knew Liam was so close, he'd tear out the seat cushions to get at him. "What's the message?"

"Strictly business, little girl." He stared through the windshield at the quiet streets of Narcissus on a Sunday. "His dive boat is moored at Newport. It's an older craft but well maintained. I've been aboard a couple of times."

"No," Liam said through the earbud. "He's never been aboard with me."

"Have you, indeed," Ava asked being careful not to accuse him of lying.

"With Stuart Whitcomb," Tancredo said. "I can vouch for the seaworthiness of the boat, and I've had a couple of offers from people who are interested."

"Why do they think Dr. Brody's boat is for sale?"

"Bargain hunters." He gave another grotesque laugh. "Some people think he might need quick money for his legal defense. They expect your favorite professor is going to jail."

"What do you think?"

"I don't care if he's guilty or not. Not my problem. All I want is to get some of my money back. Tell Brody I'll handle the sale for a 25 percent commission."

"That's a little steep."

"Yeah, and he's in no position to complain."

Liam spoke quietly through the earbud. "Ask for names. Who wants to buy my fleet?"

Though she wanted this conversation to be over, her voice stayed calm and steady. "If I should happen to see or hear from Professor Brody, who should I tell him is interested in purchasing his property?"

"Peter Quincy mentioned the possibility. And Serena Whitcomb." He downed the window of the Sonata, stuck out his head and spat on the sidewalk. "I'd demand cash or a cashier's check from that bitch. I don't trust her."

"What's your problem with Serena?"

"I hate the damn Whitcomb family," he said, dragging his shirtsleeve across his mouth and inadvertently giving her a close-up view of his three-fingered left hand. The remaining digits and thumb were filthy. Grime crusted beneath the nails. "Their grandpappy cheated mine and drove him out of business. The Tancredo family—my folks—should have been rich lumber barons. Instead, I had to get a job at the mill. I should have owned that damn place. It's where I lost my fingers."

"I didn't know your family had such deep roots."

"My grandpappy sank into a funk after he lost the business. Died young. Some say he killed himself. The rest of my kin scattered and moved on. I blame anybody named Whitcomb."

This old grudge sounded like a motive to her. "You must have been pleased when Stuart was murdered."

"You can tell Brody thanks from me." He flung open the car door. "Don't be a stranger, Ava Donovan."

As she returned to the route leading to Rachel's house, she put down the windows and allowed the breeze to blow away the smell of Tancredo. A bitter man. A hostile man. But was he a murderer? "Seems like Tancredo would want to keep Stuart alive so he could get his investment repaid."

"He's a tough nut to crack," Liam said. "Why was he on my dive boat?"

"Your partner must have invited him."

"If he hates the Whitcomb family as much as he says, why make a loan to Stuart? Why talk to Serena about selling my dive boat?"

"It's about power," she said. "I can imagine a scum bucket like Tancredo lording it over Stuart and demanding his money. The same for Serena."

"That fits," he said. "I've been doing business with Tancredo for years, and he loves to give citations for breaking rules. This is the first I've heard about his grandfather and the feud with Stuart's family. I probably should have paid more attention to the old guy."

"Same here."

At the outer edge of town, Ava drove past the three huge buildings for processing raw lumber. Two had closed down. One remained open and manufactured particleboard. The chemical stench of the process hung in the air. Her father used to talk about his days at the mill when he made a decent salary and could support his wife and five children. He died not long after he was laid off from that job. Long ago, Narcissus thrived. Not anymore.

"Almost there," she announced to Liam as she turned onto a smaller two-lane road. "How are you doing back there?"

"I'm okay. Eating your excellent macadamia cookies."

She took a left and then turned right and then to the end of a block lined with one-and two-story rectangular houses in various colors of wood siding popular in the post–World

War II era. The unimaginative architecture was saved from being boring by flourishing trees and gardens. Double rows of daffodils and narcissus, namesake of the town, marched across the front yard of Rachel's two-story, sky-blue house.

A couple dozen people milled in the front yard, including Michael, Barry and her other brother, Jerome. Rachel's grade school kids chased three other boys who were slightly older. Ava recognized several other people who were standing around and chatting.

"Fish Finley is here," she reported to Liam.

"I'd like to hear what he's going to say as a witness."

The crowd parted, and she saw her sister talking to a tall, slender woman with wavy, blond hair tumbling to her shoulders. She wore purple and yellow activewear topped by a matching jacket. "Holly Louise Whitcomb. She's here."

Ava checked her reflection in the visor mirror and fluffed her bangs. She'd be able to ask direct questions and get answers straight from the horse's mouth.

HIDING INSIDE THE too-small trunk, Liam listened to a cacophony of voices, punctuated by the laughter of children and the sound of the Hyundai's back door being opened and closed. The Sunday gathering of the Donovan clan and their friends exploded like the launch of a space rocket. He heard Ava ask, "What are you all doing out here in the front yard?"

"Waiting for you," said a man whose voice he recognized as Michael. "About time."

"We're getting ready to play touch football," a youthful male explained. "The front yard is bigger than the back and has the sidewalk running down the middle to separate the sides."

Michael added, "Rachel won't let us play in the back because we'll mess up the tables with the potluck."

"That's right," said an authoritative woman, probably Rachel herself. "We'll leave you footballers to it. Anybody who would rather eat and be civilized, come with me."

"I brought cookies," Ava said.

"And I appreciate your effort," Rachel said. "Listen, I'm sorry Michael is being a jerk. I didn't tell him to bother you at the lighthouse."

"It's okay. Gave me a chance to explain my opinion on Dr. Brody."

"Which is?"

"Innocent until proven guilty," she said firmly. "I don't think he killed Stuart, and there isn't substantial evidence to convict him."

"Come on, Ava. I know you used to like this guy, but he's guilty, guilty, guilty. He and Stuart went out to sea, then Stuart got clobbered and died. Did I mention that nobody else was on the boat?"

"Dr. Brody was unconscious." Ava piped up to defend him, and Liam was proud of her. He didn't seem to have much other support. She continued, "While Liam was out cold, the murderer could have sailed up and boarded or gotten close on a scuba dive."

"Oh, sure. Maybe the killer rode a dolphin. Or an orca."

"When Dr. Brody woke, he tried to revive Stuart, and he called the Coast Guard. If he killed Stuart, why not just dump the body overboard and sail back to the marina?"

"Who can understand the mind of a murderer?"

Another female voice chimed in. "Ava makes a good point. If Brody meant to kill Stuart, he could have easily gotten away with it. No need to call the authorities."

"Good to see you, Holly Louise," Ava said. "I'm sorry for your loss."

Liam concentrated hard, trying to catch a hint of Holly's emotional state in the tone of her voice. Was she in mourning for Stuart? They'd been married for nearly sixteen years and were parents to a son. Would she miss her ex-husband? Liam knew for a fact that Stuart hadn't been faithful or thoughtful. For a long time, he and Liam had shared a part-time assistant. A salty old widow named Maxine, she was the only person who remembered anniversaries and birthdays for Stuart. What was her last name? Gallo, Maxine Gallo. She'd bought the presents, sent the cards and the occasional bouquets of red roses when Stuart took off for a weekend without his wife on board.

Had Maxine Gallo been contacted by Liam's overpriced attorney? She knew both owners of Deep Dive better than they knew each other, which wasn't to say much. Liam and Stuart hadn't been the sort of friends who shared intimate secrets. The first he'd heard of Stuart's divorce was *after* he'd served Holly with papers. She must have been angry with him. Did she hate him? Want him dead?

"I always liked Liam," Holly said. "He was a real gentleman. Good sense of humor. And not bad to look at."

"I've heard that before," Rachel said. "From Ava."

"Of course, I liked him. He was a terrific professor."

"And not bad to look at," Rachel teased. "Am I right?"

He heard Ava clear her throat before she jumped in with both feet instead of politely tiptoeing around the edge of the topic. "What do you think, Holly? Did Liam kill Stuart?"

"Of course not," Holly said.

"Who did?"

For a moment, Ava's blunt question put an end to their chat. In the trunk, Liam listened with bated breath. He hoped the uncomfortable silence wouldn't last too long.

"Off the top of my head," Holly said, "I can think of a dozen people who wanted my ex-husband dead. People he insulted or cheated or lied to. They've talked to me because, obviously, I'm not the head cheerleader of the Stuart Whitcomb Fan Club. Let's start with Charlie Tancredo.

My dear ex-husband borrowed a bunch of money from him, off the books."

"Wait," Ava said. "Why would Tancredo kill him before he got paid back?"

"Stuart made it clear that he wasn't going to pay. After he died, Charlie came to me, and I promised to work something out when I've gotten my payoff. I feel bad about my son racing around in a fancy cabin cruiser bought with Tancredo's money."

Ava spoke up. "That's very fair-minded of you."

"And I don't want Tancredo as an enemy," Holly said. "If you're looking for motives, you might as well count me. Oliver will inherit the stock and I'll be his executrix because my dumb ex-husband never changed his will."

"Who else?" Ava asked.

Holly rattled off several names. "My ex wasn't a likable guy. He always wanted everything to be in perfect order. Actually, he demanded it. My therapist said he had OCD—obsessive-compulsive disorder—and I think she was right."

Liam had to agree. Stuart was a stickler for details—a trait he called "perfectionism." OCD was far more accurate. He actually enjoyed the detailed paperwork required to keep track of their inventory. Liam often found him humming while he hunched over a notebook or ledger.

Holly continued, "Then there are all the husbands and boyfriends of women he dated. Long list. A couple of them showed up at the house and popped him in the nose. The police have records because, of course, Stuart insisted on filing charges."

"Wow," Ava said. "I had no idea. Was there anybody else? Anybody who stands out?"

"The husband of your benefactor. Peter Quincy."

"Really? I know he runs a competing salvage business, but I never thought exploring shipwrecks was a cutthroat business."

"Quincy and Stuart were a couple of pirates. Draw your own conclusions."

Liam wished they had been questioning Holly under oath and could compel her to explain everything she knew about the connection between those two swashbucklers. Quincy was suspected of working with Tancredo and drug smuggling for northern cartels. Could he also be fencing artifacts from Deep Dive salvage operations?

The rest of the conversation with Stuart's ex-wife turned to local gossip and congratulations on Rachel's third-grade daughter's win in the spelling bee. After Holly moved away, Rachel did a "tsk-tsk-tsk."

"What?" Ava asked.

"Poor Holly! She's still hung up on that slimebag ex-husband. Did you notice? She still wears her wedding-engagement ring set. Platinum and diamond."

"I noticed. Big sparklers. It's got to be worth a lot."

"Over twenty-five thousand," Rachel said. "That's what Holly told me."

"Doesn't really go with the workout clothes."

"Uh-oh." Rachel swore under her breath. Still loud enough for Liam to hear. "Here comes trouble."

"Serena Whitcomb," Ava said for Liam's benefit. "What's she doing here? Rachel, did you invite her?"

"Do you think I've lost my mind? Come with me, sis. You and I have to stop her before she crashes headlong into Holly."

That face-off sounded like a potential disaster to Liam. He doubted anything good would come from these two women meeting. Selfishly, he thought their conflict might put a new perspective on the murder.

Chapter Ten

Ava managed to drop off her platter of macadamia nut cookies on one of the picnic tables on the patio before she fell into step with her sister. Together, they marched across the backyard to protect Holly from Serena Whitcomb. As they approached the shady maple in the corner of Rachel's neatly landscaped property, all three Donovan brothers stepped up to flank them, standing in support of Holly Louise.

Rachel spoke first. "I'm surprised to see you, Serena. Our little neighborhood potluck doesn't seem like your kind of party."

"You have an awfully short memory." Though she was average height, Serena looked down her nose at all of them. With her black hair styled in graceful tresses, her complexion perfectly tanned and her fingernails professionally manicured, she was polished and impressive. "When I dated Barry, I was here every week. I even gave you my housekeeper's recipe for enchiladas."

Sheepishly, Barry said, "Sorry to hear about Stuart. We all came to the memorial service, you know. How are you holding up?"

"I'm all right." Ava glimpsed a flicker of sadness in Serena's expression before she pinched her lips together and glared at them with her dark brown eyes. "If you really cared about my brother, you'd never invite his bitter ex-wife to your gathering."

"Not so bitter," Holly snapped. "I'm going to inherit more than you."

Rachel wrapped her arms around Holly—half to protect her and half to hold her back. "She's been my best friend since fifth grade."

"What about me?" Serena stamped her little foot in her Gucci designer sandals. Her toenails were the same bright red as her fingernails. "I've lived here for three generations."

"But you went to some fancy-pants prep school in New York. We never bonded. And you're at least five years older than I am."

Ava could see tempers rising. Hoping to cool the situation, she stepped between the two feuding women. "Why don't you come with me, Serena? We can get a plate of food and some iced tea."

"Don't try to push me around, Ava. There are a few things I need to say to Holly, and the brat won't return my phone calls."

Holly came at her. "I don't want to talk to you."

"Fine. We'll meet in court." Serena flipped open her red Birkin bag and reached inside. "I've got the paperwork right here."

Standing beside Serena, Ava was the only one who could see inside the purse that had probably cost more than her Sonata. She saw the small gun, probably a .45 like hers but metallic. The weapon looked far more lethal than her bubble gum pink Glock.

Before Ava could say anything, Serena snapped her purse closed before handing off the paperwork. Her eyes narrowed to laser-focused slits. Barry stepped up beside her and took her arm. With a pivot, he spun her away from the others and aimed her toward the buffet table. "Let me get you something to drink. You must be thirsty."

Because threating people was dehydrating? Serena's response to her ex-boyfriend went from outrage to seductive as she placed her long, slim fingers on his hand. "I'd like a martini."

"I'm sure you would."

While Barry escorted her away, Ava watched with concern. The gun in the Birkin worried her.

"Mission accomplished," Michael said. "That's why nobody messes with the Donovan family or their friends. Holly, where's your son?"

"Out front, playing football with the rest of the teenagers. At least, I hope he's playing. Oliver has been depressed since his father's murder."

Michael took charge of Holly. "Do you want to talk about him?"

She nodded. "It's been hard for him to lose his dad."

Ava's youngest brother, Jerome, glanced between his two sisters. "Are you guys okay?"

Ava wondered if she ought to mention the gun. She knew other people who carried weapons but not to a potluck on a Sunday afternoon. What did Serena have in mind? Surely, she wouldn't open fire here. She wasn't homicidal. Was she?

She nodded to Jerome. "See you tomorrow at the lighthouse."

"Cool. We need to go over specs on the plumbing. How many new bathrooms in the cottage and where should we put them?"

"I'll have answers for you tomorrow."

While she strolled back toward the patio, Ava heard Liam's voice in her ear. He had a ton of questions, but she couldn't begin to answer his concerns until they could talk face-to-face. She allowed Rachel to direct her toward the array of potluck dishes. Ice-filled coolers held soft drinks and beer.

"On the kitchen counter where the kids can't reach," Rachel said, "I have Pinot Noir, Zinfandel and Chardonnay from our fine local wineries."

"I'm not drinking," Ava said. "As soon as I leave, I have to check in with my—what did Holly call her?—my benefactor, Georgina."

"I don't envy you that meeting. I mean, your work at the lighthouse is very cool, but Georgina and her snooty family creep me out almost as much as Serena and the other Whitcombs."

"After I complete the renovation, Georgina is going to be looking for someone to manage her bed-and-breakfast. You'd be a natural for the job."

"So true," Rachel said, not bragging but stating a fact. "I bake, I clean and I have impeccable taste. But I already have a job."

"Do you ever think about going back to school to become a pharmacist? Sooner or later, your boss is going to retire and you could take over."

"Thanks for your opinion, pushy pants. Just because you're my sis, you don't get to call the shots for me. Unless you want me bugging you about settling down and having babies."

"You like working in the pharmacy, don't you?" Ava hoped to ease into the topic of drugs. Her sister was sharp and intuitive. Rachel would recognize a direct inquiry for what it was—an attempted interrogation. "And you already know so much about various prescriptions and their side effects."

"Sorting and preparing the dosage is similar to following a recipe for baking," Rachel said. "But I wouldn't like the responsibility of monitoring somebody else's medicine."

"Especially now, when so many people are addicted."

"That's the truth. Even here in our puny, little town." Rachel exhaled a sigh. "I spend half my time verifying prescriptions from doctors in Portland and Salem. A lot of people have to be cut off."

"Anybody we know?"

"Ava Caitlyn Donovan! I can't believe you asked me that. I'm a professional. I respect boundaries."

"Sorry. Just curious."

"Between you and me, addicts don't come to the pharmacy to get their fix. Good, old Charlie Tancredo is apparently dumb enough to loan money to Stuart. Also, Tancredo is a prescription drug pusher."

Good to know. It was another loose end for Liam to report to his attorney.

INSIDE THE TRUNK, Liam shifted positions, flexed his shoulders and back. Ava's conversations with various locals didn't interest him until she approached Fish Finley, who had been working regularly at the lighthouse as a subcontractor. Liam conjured a mental image of Fish with puckered lips like a parrotfish, a slender frame and a shaved head. Fish was a disappointment to him. Liam thought they had a decent relationship, but Fish signed up on the prosecution's side to testify about an argument he'd overheard between Liam and Stuart.

In his quiet voice, Fish introduced Ava to his fiancee. "Her name is Bonnie, and we're getting married. Show her the ring, honey."

"Congratulations," Ava said. "Have you set the date?"

"Better be soon," Bonnie said with a giggle. "Otherwise, I'm going to start showing. I'm four months pregnant."

"Double congratulations. You both look very happy."

"That we are," Fish said. "Hey, I didn't know you and Liam were friends."

"I took a class from him in college. We're not that close."

Not that close? Liam dismissed his irritation at her brush-off comment. She couldn't tell anyone about their relationship, not until they concluded their investigation. The cramped space in the trunk had begun to heat up and tighten around him. The air felt stuffy. He wished he could climb out and walk around, head up his own investigation.

"I helped with some of those classes," Fish said. "I always liked being with Liam on the boat. He never talked down to me, never treated me like I wasn't good enough."

"You are good enough," his girlfriend said. "You're the best."

Once again, Ava was blunt. "I heard you were going to testify at the trial. Is that true?"

"Wish I'd never made that agreement. Don't seem right."

"Why is that?"

"I don't think Liam is a killer, but I know what I heard. I've just got to tell the truth."

"You'd better be sure about what you overheard." Ava's tone sharpened. "Otherwise, it's perjury."

"No way," Bonnie said. "My man always does the right thing."

Liam wasn't so certain. He bent his elbow and tried to reach the back of his neck where sweat prickled. Tomorrow when Fish showed up for work at the lighthouse, he'd have another chance to dig out the truth.

After Fish and Bonnie made their excuses, Ava whispered into her mic. "Not sure if you can hear me, but it's my impression that Fish is lying about what he heard. Or putting a weird slant on it. Something strange is going on with him."

"I think you're right. How soon can we leave?"

"Getting uncomfortable?"

"How soon?"

"I'll go right now. Sit tight."

As if he had a choice? Liam twisted onto his side and silently reviewed the new information they'd learned. Holly had spouted half a dozen names of jilted boyfriends and spouses who had reason to hate Stuart, but Liam doubted any of them had committed this complicated murder that required drugging him, boarding the boat and assaulting Stuart without having him fight back. Both Tancredo and Holly had also mentioned the quarter-of-a-million-dollar loan to Stuart who was expected to perform some kind of service. And there was Rachel's not-too-subtle accusation about the harbormaster of the Newport docks pushing illegal prescription meds. Though Liam's attorney had deposed Tancredo, he hadn't been considered a suspect because his alibi was good.

Making progress. Liam's instinct to pursue his own investigation had been validated. Now he needed to get a message to his legal team: interview Tancredo in depth, check his finances and his access to prescription drugs. Holly had reminded him of the former assistant for Deep Dive who knew many of Stuart's secrets. Maxine Gallo needed to be interviewed.

And Liam would talk to Fish Finley. It was no big surprise that he'd heard Stuart and Liam arguing. Like many partners, they had disagreements that had never turned violent. What was Fish going to tell the prosecutor? Was he lying?

So much to do and so little time to do it. Liam squeezed his eyelids closed and shut down his brain. He couldn't think anymore. His limbs cramped tight. Though he didn't feel particularly heated, his entire body was sweating. This must be what suffocation felt like.

His consciousness shifted, and he inadvertently slipped into the meditative state where his memories came clearer. He imagined hearing the sounds of gulls and the lapping of waves against the hull of the cabin cruiser. His last memory had been the putt-putt of an outboard motor approaching. In his mind, he was aboard the boat right before Stuart was killed.

The vision of that day was sharp but disjointed, like seeing reflections in a broken mirror. A piece of sky mingled with the deep gray of the Pacific. Liam caught a glimpse of Stuart. His face twisted in anger. His voice grated as he argued with another man. Another voice. Liam couldn't tell if it was his own voice. Or someone else.

What were they saying? Something about how Stuart had to return what he'd taken. Accusing him of being a scavenger without honor.

Liam jolted back to reality, heard the door to the Hyundai open and close.

"It's me," Ava announced.

His vision of the death scene dissipated and vanished. So close, he was so close to remembering exactly what had happened before he passed out. He felt the car dip as she got behind the steering wheel and started the engine.

"Turn on the air conditioner," he growled. His throat was sore. His voice, hoarse. "Now. Full blast."

"Cranky," she said. "I've never actually locked myself in the trunk, but I'm guessing it gets stifling and hot. Does it smell like oil or more like a spare tire?"

"Air conditioner," he repeated.

When he felt the car lurch forward and zip quietly through the streets of Narcissus, he released the latch that held one of the rear seats in place and collapsed it forward. He stuck his head through the opening and sucked down a gulp of air.

"Sorry I didn't get a chance to talk to Ollie," she chirped. "He was standing in the front yard, watching the sloppiest football game I've ever seen. The kid looked depressed."

"It's okay. You did a great job getting people to open up."

"We have a problem, and I'm not sure what to do about

it." She glanced over her shoulder into the back seat. "I saw something. A gun."

"Where?" He crawled halfway into the back seat but stayed low so he couldn't be seen through the windows. "Who had the gun?"

"Serena. She was carrying it in her purse. A small, gray metal pistol."

The idea of suspects running around with weapons bothered him, but there wasn't much he could do about it. If Deputy Jessop hadn't been such a jerk, Ava could have gone to him for advice. "What about Marshal Woodburn?" he suggested. "He made a big deal of checking your Glock. Maybe if you told him, he could pay Serena a visit."

"I guess I could call him," she said. "Or I could talk to Barry. He used to date Serena, might have even been the one who helped her purchase a weapon. You know, for protection."

In the back seat, Liam reached into the insulated bag she'd packed and took out a water bottle. He unscrewed the top and chugged half. "Can't stay in the trunk. Take me somewhere near Georgina's house and drop me off. I'll get close enough to listen."

"What if you can't hear me?"

"I trust you to ask the right questions," he said. "You're good at this."

"When I was working as a teaching assistant at the university, I figured out how to ask questions and probe for answers. I learned pretty quickly how to identify which answers were lies or a cover-up."

"Which was how you figured out Fish was hiding something."

"His comments about truth-telling sounded a lot like 'the dog ate my homework,'" she said. "I wonder why he'd volunteer to give phony testimony."

The most obvious motive would be a payoff. Somebody could be bribing Fish to lie about an argument he overheard. If he could learn the identity of the payer, they might be on their way to unraveling the murder.

He unfastened the latch on the other back seat, pushed it out of the way and rolled into the rear of the car. *Sweet relief.* Not a lot of space, but the back seat of the Hyundai was luxurious when compared to the trunk. Lying with his back on the folded-down seats, he stretched out his legs. "There's a lot of forest around here. I can find someplace to stay hidden."

"I'm sure you can. When I was a kid, Rachel and I used to sneak around and spy on these crusty people when they had fancy parties."

"Crusty?"

"As in *upper crust.*"

He imagined Ava and her sister creeping through the verdant underbrush like a couple of wide-eyed woodland imps watching the crusty people who probably resembled his wealthy, intellectual, aloof family. His Los Angeles–based sister represented the socialite branch for the Brody brood, and she worked tirelessly on volunteer projects funding the medical research their father pursued. Liam avoided the events she planned and the blind dates she arranged for him. He identified more with the hardworking, energetic Donovan family, who genuinely cared for each other.

"I have a question," Ava said. "How should I get Georgina and her husband to talk about the murder?"

"You didn't have a problem at your sister's house."

"That's different. I don't want to be too blunt with the woman who is signing my paycheck."

He understood what she was saying. She didn't want to blurt out questions that would offend or would cause Georgina to view her with suspicion. "Keep the focus on her. Everybody likes to talk about themselves."

She nodded. "What else?"

"Use your position as an archeologist and historian," he advised. "Tell her you're looking for more information about the history of the area and the lighthouse."

"Actually, I would like more personal stories that I could put together into a book for the tourists who come to stay at Georgina's B and B."

"You took my nautical archeology class," he reminded her, "and we studied shipwrecks, including the *New Carissa*. Georgina's husband runs his salvage business from Newport, and you can talk to him about the famously dangerous coastline."

"Got it."

When Ava guided the Sonata off the two-lane road at the edge of town, he sat up and peered out the window. The old growth forest surrounding the Solomon family's compound formed a towering wall of trees with moss-covered branches and trunks. He glimpsed a nearby creek, shimmering in the sunlight. Blue jays, magpies and crows swooped through the trees, no doubt waiting to scavenge the leftovers from the four nearby mansions.

Ava parked beside a fat, horizontal log bordering a turn-around. "You can see Georgina's house from the top of that hill. I'll be back here to pick you up in about an hour."

"I'll be waiting."

Glad to be free of the suffocating trunk, he opened the door and stepped into the cool, idyllic forest, hoping she'd find significant information for their investigation and happy that they would have more time together later.

Chapter Eleven

Unsettled by the problematic issues she'd uncovered, Ava tried to focus on the details she needed for this meeting. Afterward, she could call Marshal Woodburn and warn him about Serena's gun. And she could talk to Liam about Tancredo, his loan to Stuart and the job he needed done. Then, there was Fish to consider.

Right now, she had to talk to Georgina. First, she'd share an update on the current progress. Then, she'd ask pertinent questions, using the blueprints of the cottage, about the plumbing issues. How many new bathrooms and where should they be placed? Finally, Ava would offer her opinion on integrating lighthouse history into the bed-and-breakfast setting, including a possible tourist book or booklet. She also had paperwork on the project budget and expected completion dates. Most of all, she reminded herself as she walked up the sidewalk to the front door, Ava wouldn't lose sight of her real reason for being here which was, of course, the investigation.

Georgina might be able to shed light on the motives for Stuart's murder. She and Ava didn't always agree, but Ava had come to respect the other woman's sharp critical eye and most of her opinions about style and taste. Mrs. Solomon Quincy knew a whole different set of Narcissus residents.

As she pressed the doorbell, Ava whispered into her mic, "Can you hear me?"

"Loud and clear," Liam replied. "I'm not as close as I'd like. Surveillance cameras are all over the place."

"Be careful," she said under her breath.

The heavy oak door swung wide, and Georgina, looking expensively groomed as usual, welcomed her into the largest of the four Solomon houses, built in a sort of cul-de-sac with acres of wooded privacy between them. The exterior of Georgina's three-story house—once owned by the lumber baron patriarch, George Solomon, himself—featured a natural stone tower beside the impressively carved, double-door entryway. A huge sunporch occupied the other side of the entrance. Clear fir tongue-in-groove siding, which was stained light gray, covered most of the house. The architectural design featured dozens of windows, many with leaded glass, and window frames painted hunter green. All topped off by a slate roof.

The interior showed opulent craftsmanship with polished paneling, wainscoting and arched ceilings—some painted and others supported with beams. Many of the built-in shelves, fireplace mantels, staircases, pillars and doors showed off woodworking skill and hand-carvings similar to those at the lightkeeper's cottage. Rustic and yet sophisticated at the same time, most of the carving was done by one artist during the 1920s and '30s. Ava thought he deserved a plaque commemorating his contribution to this northwestern mansion.

Though she appreciated the overall effect of elaborate styling from the plaster cupids of the early 1900s to the sleek 1930s Art Deco, to the mid-century modern, she had a hard time convincing Georgina that the lightkeeper's cottage shouldn't be as ornate. After all, this house belonged to an extremely wealthy man while the cottage was meant to be a dwelling for a commonplace worker and his family.

At a table in a library/office that opened onto the sun deck, Ava spread color samples in shades of white. "I'm trying to match the color that was first used in the entrance and dining room in the 1890s. We don't have color photographs to go by, and the description just says it's white."

Georgina balanced a pair of gold frame readers on the tip of her nose and pursed her lips as she considered the variety. "Some are cool, almost bluish. Others are pale yellow."

"These are all from the Benjamin Moore Historical Collection line. It's impossible to be totally accurate because these walls have been painted over several times. For the sake of consistency, I think we should stick to a palette."

"Orange," Georgina said. The color mimicked the thick, curly hair piled on top of her head in a purposely messy bun with tendrils falling around her cheeks. Casual but stylish in an upper-crust way, she wore a flowing, ombré mauve, silk blouse over snug white capris that showed off her slender legs and the glow that came from a tanning booth rather than exposure to the sun. No tan lines on this lady. No freckles, either. Her full lips spread in a feline grin. "Definitely orange and green."

"A perfect combo to complement mid-century modern designs," Ava said, "but maybe not right for the lightkeeper's cottage. I used to hate my parents' green shag carpet."

"Do you think the palette should be more muted?" Georgina twisted her gold cuff bracelet. "So boring, Ava."

"And not necessarily historically accurate. Some rooms during the late 1800s when the lightkeeper's cottage was built were dark purple or bright gold."

"So, I'm on the right track with orange."

Ava shrugged. "Several descriptions of the colors mention a cozy, rosy atmosphere inside the cottage. One writer talks about bringing the sunshine indoors. The palette, I think, should lean toward warmer colors like red and yellow."

"Which make orange."

"That's a lovely bracelet," Ava said. She'd seen 1920s illustrations of similar designs with rows of tiny gold pyramids alternating with rows of roses. "Do you mind if I ask where you got it?"

"A gift from my hubby. He tried to tell me it was antique, but I'm guessing he picked it up in a secondhand store. Peter is awfully practical and very cheap."

"Mind if I take a photo?" Ava could show it to Liam, and he could verify if the bracelet was actually antique and had come from a salvage operation. *Possibly illustrating a connection between Peter Quincy and Stuart.* She snapped the picture using her phone.

Georgina pointed to a creamy white sample. "That one."

"Good pick." They wouldn't get started with the painting until they were approaching the last phase of renovation. "We need to prepare these colors and wallpaper samples for the National Historical Society before actually making the changes and purchasing furniture."

"Shopping," Georgina said with obvious relish. "I can't wait to get started on that part of the process."

"We can do a lot of that online and by visiting specialized furniture stores and shops that can repair the pieces worth saving."

"In terms of the cottage, what are you working on right now?"

Solving the crime of the century? Instead of being blunt, Ava introduced the topic Liam had suggested. "Plumbing. We need to go over the blueprints so you can indicate where you want more bathrooms and bathtubs."

The practical decisions took a solid ten minutes to decide on a speculative basis. Balancing the historical cottage style with a modern B and B. When Ava felt like she had enough information to keep Jerome and his renovation crew busy, she introduced another topic. "I was thinking of putting together all my research and more interviews for a small, illustrated book about the lighthouse and the area. We could feature the lightkeeper's log written by Elizabeth Mayes in the 1920s."

"Marvelous!" Georgina gestured expansively. "I'll be your coauthor. And we absolutely must have a section about the Solomon family, starting with my great-great-grandpa George."

"At the same time, I could put together a historical display for the cottage, using the office with the wonderful rolltop desk."

"You know I expected to renovate that office into another bedroom for paying guests," Georgina said. "But I'll consider making it a historic setting."

"I think the Historic Landmark Board would appreciate the attention. And we could use the lightkeeper's logs for advertising."

"We'll see. Now, talk to me about schedules."

Ava pulled out a schedule with weekly goals and projects. "Right now, it's mostly demo and deconstruction."

"You've told me before, but what's the difference?"

"Demo is short for *demolition* and pertains to big jobs, like tearing out plumbing and replacing flooring."

"Like that god-awful linoleum in the kitchen."

"*Deconstruction* means taking things apart carefully, refurbishing them and replacing them. That's what we're going to do with the staircase so we can preserve the original carving." Ava introduced the topic of murder. "One of the subcontractors I've hired will need to take time off when the trial of Dr. Brody gets underway."

"Hasn't that proceeding started? Seems like we've been talking about it for weeks."

"It takes a while to gather evidence. What have you heard about the murder?"

"Not much. Stuart was cremated, you know. Wanted his ashes scattered at sea or some such nonsense. His mother and sister put together a memorial service that was poorly catered with few floral remembrances."

Harsh criticism. "I don't know the family. Are you close to them?"

"His mother never recovered from the humiliating divorce. Not Stuart's fault, of course, but she complains constantly about how none of the men in the family have properly supported her. Serena is much the same. Whining and moaning, she's furious that Stuart never changed his will and left his shares in the salvage business to his ex-wife and son."

"She never remarried, did she?"

"Hah! As a Donovan, you'd be among the first to know."

"Why?"

"Your brother Barry is the only man she's ever loved."

Ava's jaw dropped. She was shocked that Georgina Solomon knew gossip about her family. "I thought their relationship was over years ago."

"I've heard that the romance never really ended. Barry is quite handsome. He reminds me of that actor who plays a vampire in those movies set in Washington state."

"Really?" Her brother would hate the comparison.

"Of course, you wouldn't notice. You're his sister." Georgina casually studied the schedule. "When will you start working on the lighthouse tower?"

Ava dragged her attention back to the project at hand. "Not for a couple of weeks."

"That's what I'm excited about. I can't wait until the beacon is shining from the top of the lighthouse."

She wouldn't be too thrilled to know that Liam was currently hiding out in the lantern room. "I'm interviewing experts to repair the brick and stucco exterior."

"The damage can't just be painted over, can it?"

Ava took a deep breath and explained. When first built, the forty-eight-foot tower was pristine white, topped by polished glass, a metal widow's walk and a rotating beacon. Years of exposure had taken a natural toll, causing ragged chunks of stucco to separate from the bricks. Then came damage from Ava's nemesis—graffiti vandals. They marked the walls with garish scrawls and splattered paint without rhyme or reason. Their damage would require a great deal of work to erase or replace.

She heard a door slam in the rear of the house. "Company?"

"That's just Peter." Georgina raised her voice. "We're in here, sweetheart."

"Finally," Liam said. When Ava heard his voice in her ear, she jumped. Until now, he'd been silent, lurking in the woods and watching.

He continued, "You can stop talking about color swatches and actors playing vampires. Peter Quincy could be central to our investigation. Consider him a suspect."

Ava looked up as Quincy strode into the study. He didn't look like a killer. Quincy wasn't particularly attractive—not like her brothers or Liam—but he was well-groomed with light brown hair and a tidy goatee. His smile displayed perfect teeth. His forehead was smooth, unmarked by wrinkles. Blue eyes matched the color of his woven shirt with the sleeves rolled up to show his muscular forearms. When Peter Quincy married Georgina, who was eight years older, he fell into a great big pot of money, and he'd made good use of his fortune. He stepped up behind his wife's chair and leaned down to kiss her cheek.

She spread the color samples across the table in front of him. "Which do you like best?"

"They're all white."

She snatched up the one she'd chosen. "This one. Right?"

"If you say so." He nodded across the table. "Ahoy there, Ava."

In her experience, people who lived near the shore and used nautical language were either eighty years old or pretentious. She placed Quincy in the latter category. "Good afternoon."

While he sized her up, she saw a laser flash in the depths of his blue eyes. Either he considered her a threat or he didn't trust her. Either way, she'd be smart to heed the warning flare. Nervous, she broke eye contact and stared down at the notes, blueprints and color samples spread across the table. She might be imagining danger because of Liam's suggestion, but she didn't think so. Her survival instincts were usually reliable.

Forcing herself to meet his gaze, she tried to get the conversation rolling. Remembering Liam's advice, she said, "You two look happy together. How did you meet?"

Staying seated, Georgina gazed up at her husband. She laced the fingers of her left hand with his, and Ava noticed the gleam of her heavy, gold wedding band. Not as flashy as the diamonds worn by Holly Whitcomb in memory of her murdered husband but probably just as pricey. "You tell the story, sweetheart. You're more glib than I am."

Glib like a con man? Pasting an encouraging smile on her face, Ava listened to the story of Quincy spotting Georgina in Lincoln City during the November King Tide when the surf runs high. She was splashed by the spray of frothy waves crashing against the bridge, and he rushed forward to rescue her from the next onslaught. He pursued her relentlessly until she agreed to marry him.

"When I see what I want," he said, "I go after it. Nothing, and I mean nothing, stands in my way."

His single-minded determination worried Ava. What if Stuart had gotten crosswise with him? "Does the same attitude apply to your business?"

"I can be aggressive," he admitted.

"And he has quite the temper," Georgina said as she gazed up at him. "He's a deeply passionate man."

Ava cleared her throat and asked, "When were you married?"

"Five years ago in June," Georgina said. "I was thirty-seven and people in my family were already calling me a spinster. Can you believe it? So archaic. Don't you agree? You must be close to that age yourself, Ava."

"Twenty-seven."

"It's different in my family," Georgina said. "If I don't produce an heir, the purest branch of the Solomon bloodline will die out. Not really a valid concern. I have lawyers to handle inheritance issues."

Quincy added, "And now you have me."

"Anyway," Georgina continued, "I wasn't really looking for a husband. That's when Peter showed up."

"Good timing," Ava said, glad that her super-fertile sister and brother Jerome had already produced a batch of heirs if there had been any kind of Donovan fortune to pass down. "I hope Serena Whitcomb has that sort of good luck."

"Serena?" Quincy's smooth forehead creased. "What's her problem now?"

"You know," his wife chided. "She's not married and probably won't inherit her brother's shares in his salvage business."

"Either way, it's not a problem. I can work with Serena or with Holly. I'm sure either of those ladies will be happy to sell their half of Deep Dive to me."

In her ear, Ava heard Liam's calm but angry comment. "That bastard will never take over the business I built. If I go to jail, I'll sink every boat before I sell to him."

His hostility toward Quincy made sense to her. Georgina's husband was a competitor, and Liam didn't like to lose. Ava studied Quincy as he smoothed the neatly barbered hair on his chin. She said, "Sounds like you're planning to expand your operation."

"Sometimes, bigger is better." He grinned at Georgina. "Isn't that right?"

"I'm a fan of expansion."

"Don't get me wrong," Quincy said. "I liked Stuart, and he did okay with Deep Dive. But he wasn't a smart businessman, didn't take full advantage of the possibilities."

She had to wonder if he was talking about smuggling from Canada or fencing stolen artifacts from shipwrecks. "What about Liam?"

Quincy shook his head. "He's more interested in the discovery of shipwrecks. I could double or maybe even triple the profits."

His idea of taking over Deep Dive seemed hostile and creepy, but it didn't provide him with a motive for murdering Stuart. Quincy was a turkey vulture, diving down to pick at the bones of Stuart's livelihood. His plan to take over the business gave Quincy a reason to make sure Liam was convicted and spent the rest of his life in jail.

"My darling." Georgina gazed into his eyes. "Ava and I are going to be writing a book about the lighthouse, and she needs to interview some of the locals. Who would you suggest?"

"Charlie Tancredo. He runs the Newport docks and his family has been here for a really long time." He gave his wife a peck on the cheek, stood up straight and stared at Ava.

"I'm busy all day tomorrow but meet me Tuesday morning at Tancredo's office. I'm sure he'll have some stories to tell."

"I'll be there," she said.

Liam whispered into her ear. "Not by yourself. Too dangerous."

Ava agreed. Quincy or Tancredo or both of them could be murderers.

Chapter Twelve

As soon as Ava had dropped him off in the forest, Liam took advantage of the narrow, winding stream to wash off the stink of running, hiding and nearly suffocating in the trunk. He peeled off his jacket and shirt, wishing he'd thought far enough ahead to bring soap and toothpaste.

That was another instruction to include in his *Fugitive on the Run Handbook.* Also, he'd give obvious hints about evading the police, starting with how the good ones—like Marshal Woodburn—were always smarter than you expected. And how vital it was to have people you could trust like Ava. Using her as his touchstone, he could create a network from her family who would do anything to protect her. Also, there were former friends he could turn to. Maybe Fish Finley. Maybe Maxine Gallo. In his handbook, he'd devote an entire chapter to hygiene, starting with "Always be ready to wash yourself before you start to smell like roadkill."

Kneeling on a flat rock, he plunged both hands into the rushing water that came from snowmelt from Mount Hood and the Cascade Range. He gasped, splashed his face and gasped again. Too ice-cold to be considered refreshing, the shock quaked through his brain and got him thinking. Liam needed a plan to deal with newfound information.

Soon as possible, he'd establish a method of communicating with professional people who could dig deeper. Contacting his attorney or any possibly sympathetic law enforcement officer like Woodburn was out of the question. Their jobs obligated them to arrest him on sight and turn him in. His best bet was reaching out to Wyatt Willis, the private investigator he'd hired. The PI could set up an interview with Maxine Gallo and anybody else who would know about Stuart's unscheduled absences when he could have been smuggling or fencing salvage or showing Tancredo around the dive boat. Also, Willis might be able to figure out why Tancredo made that loan. What did Stuart have that was worth a quarter of a million?

Other issues revolved around drugs. Was there any truth to the rumors about Tancredo pushing prescription medication? If he had connections with drug smugglers from the northern border, was Quincy also involved? Were they a team? What about Oliver Whitcomb? Liam had spent time with Stuart's son when he was younger, but he barely knew the teenager. Much as he hated to think Oliver might have drugged him, the young man could be taking meds to deal with depression. He might be drug savvy. But why attack his old buddy Liam?

He shrugged back into his clothes while he listened to Ava's conversation with Georgina concerning bathroom fixtures and kitchen renovations at the cottage. Obviously, their designs wouldn't go back in time to the original 1890s stove and appliances, but Ava argued for blending modern upgrades with the retro-style of the early half of the 1900s.

Her self-control impressed him. Though she made her position clear, she listened to Georgina and treated her with kindness and respect. No doubt, Ava's life-long dealings with her large, contentious family gave her excellent negotiating skills.

He had taken a position at the top of the ridge overlooking Georgina's house when he heard Quincy enter and join the women. *Finally.* Liam hoped he'd hear details more relevant to the murder. At the same time, he'd noticed something or someone moving among the trees nearest the house.

Disguising himself behind the shadow of a moss-covered western hemlock, he watched as the shape took form. *Charlie Tancredo.* His grungy beige jacket and brown baseball cap blended with the surrounding forest. Tancredo crept through the trees, coming closer to the house and the office near the sun deck where Ava sat with Georgina and Quincy. In his left hand, the one with all the fingers, he held a handgun.

While listening through the earbud to Georgina chat about her first meeting with her adored husband, Liam watched Tancredo move closer with the stealth of a dark predator. What the hell was he doing? Threatening Ava? Or was he after Quincy?

Liam had guessed that Tancredo and Quincy were partners, but that assumption might be way off base. Through the earbud, he heard Quincy propose a meeting with Tancredo, who reacted to the mention of his name. He backed off and headed toward the road.

Inside the house, Ava was saying goodbye. Liam kept her in sight until she was safely behind the steering wheel of her Sonata and driving away from the house, then he bolted through the trees and down the hill, returning to their designated meeting spot. He got there just as she pulled over. Liam flung open the back door of the Hyundai and dove inside. Breathing hard, he said, "We've got to get away from here quick. You're not going to believe what I saw in the—"

"Yeah, yeah, tell me later. Right now, get in the trunk. I don't want to take a chance on anyone seeing you."

"Agreed." He pulled down the seat and hid himself in the Hyundai's rear compartment but left one of the seats down. If anyone caught sight of Ava's car, they wouldn't see him, but he could still breathe. Claustrophobia had never been a problem for him in the past, and he figured these feelings of suffocation came more from his current helplessness than from a true psychological phobia. What the hell could he have done if he saw Tancredo take aim? Could he have stopped him? Being a fugitive meant he couldn't fight his own battles, couldn't even show his face. Until now, he hadn't been the sort of man who hid in the trunk and let others take risks.

When he thought of Ava facing Quincy and Tancredo at the marina without his protection, every muscle in his body tensed. He suppressed the urge to lash out, to punch something or…someone. Yes, he needed her help to investigate. But no, he refused to deliberately put her in danger. Her safety was a hundred times more important than the charges against him. If she were hurt or arrested, he'd be weighed down by a painful guilt that tortured him more than prison.

Through the earbud, she asked, "You heard what Quincy said, didn't you?"

"Yeah."

"He wants to acquire your business."

"Yeah, I heard."

When Quincy had been bragging about how he intended to take over Deep Dive, Liam had seethed. His search and salvage operation had never been designed as a profit-making endeavor. He and Stuart earned just enough money to cover expenses and minimal salaries, mostly because Liam chose their clients based on factors other than the final payoff. He and Stuart might have argued about the need to take on more jobs, but they agreed on the mission of their business: salvage, preservation and education. They didn't sell everything. Locked in the basement of his house, Liam stored several rescued objects that were waiting to be claimed by rightful owners.

When the Sonata emerged from the forest and drove onto a stretch of highway on the coast, he released some of his tension. The knot in his gut loosened, and he almost relaxed.

Through the back seat windows of the car, he watched the afternoon fade into twilight. A light rain began to fall. Ava lowered her window and inhaled the salty air. He saw her bend her arm and reach up into her thick, curly hair. "I'm taking out the earbud," she said.

"Fine with me."

"And unfastening the mic."

He did the same, slipping the small devices into his shirt pocket. More loudly than necessary, he said, "Can you hear me?"

"Of course, I can. You're shouting."

"You did a great job with Georgina. And earlier at Rachel's house. You've got a talent for investigation and interview."

"Thanks."

She sounded relatively happy. Much as he hated to burst her bubble, he said, "Tancredo was outside the house, watching through the window."

"What?"

"He had a gun."

"A gun? I can't believe it. He couldn't have been after me. I agreed to help him, to make his connection to you. As if that's ever going to happen. Was he after Quincy?"

Liam only heard every other word. Hearing her real voice with the window open was more difficult than their connection through the walkie-talkie. He wanted to talk things over with her but decided to wait until they could be face-to-face. "We'll talk about Tancredo later."

Ava took the turn leading into the Siuslaw National Forest. When they got closer to the lighthouse, he heard the coastal version of a watchdog—barking from the California sea lions mingled with cries from the gulls and nesting cormorants. The Sonata jostled along, circled the lightkeeper's cottage and aimed for the garage. At the big double doors, Ava jumped out to unfasten the latch and drove inside.

He emerged from the back seat, stretched and looked around the ramshackle barn. Enough light spilled inside through missing boards that he could clearly see the sit-down mower and two ATVs parked near the six horse stalls at the rear. Though the barn had been necessary in the early 1900s for housing the horses, hay and wagons, the building had outlived its purpose. Sooner or later, a decision would be made about whether to restore the barn or demolish it.

Ava pulled the door closed and approached him through the shadows. "Do I need to worry about Tancredo?"

"Short answer? Yes."

She drew a check mark in the air with her index finger. She was so cool, so casual that he had to be impressed. In a calm tone, she asked, "What about Quincy?"

"Should you worry about him? Oh, yeah." He hoped to convince her to ease off on her involvement in the actual investigating. "This is a major problem, Ava. Tancredo is obviously dangerous. He was creeping around with a gun in his hand."

"Why come after me?"

"He wants to get the money he loaned to Stuart. For some reason, he's decided that you know something about it."

"Doesn't make sense." She shook her head. "I barely knew Stuart."

"But you knew me. I was your professor way back when. You were the innocent, beautiful student. And I was the dirty old man."

She shot him a disbelieving glance. "You're only six or seven years older than I am."

"Six, but who's counting. Everybody in Narcissus is talking about you and me. Us." And he refused to be the reason she was threatened. "Tancredo thinks so. And that's why Quincy has a grudge against you. He came right out and said that he wanted to take over Deep Dive."

"Not fair," she said emphatically. "I'm getting blamed and shamed. And I'm not having any of the fun."

"Here's the thing," he said. "I'd appreciate your insights when we go over the new information you uncovered, but I don't want you physically involved in the investigation."

She shrugged. "I have a few objections. But okay."

"And I'm going to find another place to hide as soon as I can." He hated to leave, but he took a step away from her. "I'm going to go now. I'll add the new details to my notes."

She offered. "You can use my laptop."

"But I already have my computer set up in the lighthouse."

She tilted her head, gazed up at him and dropped the cordial mask he assumed she'd been wearing all day. A playful smile lifted the corners of her mouth making it look as though she had a secret. Her blue eyes sparkled. "Instead of your computer, we could use mine. You can stay in the cottage with me. We'll update the files together."

Much as he wanted to take her up on that offer, the stakes were too high. Not only was Deputy Jessop on red alert but her brothers were suspicious and Quincy might feel the need to check on her. If any of them found Liam in her house, she'd be in serious trouble. On the other hand, it didn't seem right to leave her alone and unprotected in the cottage. "I should go through the house with you right now. To make sure nobody's hiding inside."

"I didn't see any cars in the parking lot at the front or on the side." She yanked open the back door and started unpacking the stuff she'd brought with her. "I think it's okay. The main thing is to make sure nobody sees you. I want to avoid that nasty problem. I'm not a thrill seeker."

"I'm not talking about thrills. Swimming with sharks is a thrill. Confrontations with people—enemies and friends—are a whole different kind of risk."

"I get it," she said. "Humans are the worst."

"I've been thinking, Ava. We were lucky today. Nothing big went wrong, but we can't count on luck. There's no way I'm going to let you meet with Quincy and Tancredo by yourself."

"Excuse me?" She straightened her spine. Her teasing grin tightened into an angry line. "Did you really say that? You won't *let* me meet with them?"

"Those two guys are bad news. I don't want you to get hurt."

"I can make decisions for myself."

"I didn't mean to imply that you couldn't." Though he hadn't intended to provoke, her reaction was predictable. He had no right to tell her what to do, even though he was trying to protect her. Should he apologize? Would it do any good?

He reached toward her, gently touched her shoulder and allowed his hand to caress all the way down to her fingertips. "I have a better idea. For what we should do tonight."

She pushed his hand away and glared at him. "This better be good."

"We can work on my computer," he said. "In the lantern room at the top of the lighthouse."

"I'll do it."

Her answer had come quickly and impulsively. He'd expected more difficulty in calming her down but was willing to take the win. "Are you sure?"

"How could I say no? Ever since I came to Cape Absolute, I've wanted to see the view from the widow's walk. Sure, I could have dragged the ladder inside and figured a way to get up, but it seemed unnecessarily dangerous. Like I said before, I'm not a risk-taker."

"Give me fifteen minutes and come to the lighthouse."

"Make it forty-five," she said.

"Why?"

"It'll be sunset."

"You won't be disappointed. I've figured a good way for you to get up there."

She gave him a skeptical—but not outraged—look. "Are you promising a thrill ride?"

"You bet I am." He hoped that was a promise he could fulfill. Keeping her safe was all that really mattered.

Chapter Thirteen

Ava carried her cooler and other supplies toward the back door of the cottage. Though the sea lions and birds kept up their racket, she'd grown accustomed to their noise after living here for two and a half weeks. Her ears were attuned to any sound that might be unusual. The engine of a car or a motorcycle. A human-sized creature tromping through the forest. The whisper of conversation or the beep of a cell phone.

Likewise, she watched the play of light and shadow in the trees and down the hill toward the edge of the surf. She saw no sign that anyone was nearby, didn't sense the presence of a spy or an intruder. Still, she stayed alert. Liam was right to be concerned about someone staking out the cottage or spying on the lighthouse. Also right about the trouble that being observed could cause for both of them. She paid attention to what he said, but decisions were up to her alone. She would decide how involved she'd be in the investigation.

In the cottage, she carefully relocked the back door, dropped the leftovers in the kitchen and swept through the first floor, checking to see that no one had messed with the front door locks that hadn't been updated in the past thirty years. The entryway seemed okay, but papers on the rolltop desk in her office had been shuffled around. At least, she thought they were in different configurations. She remembered leaving a small yellow spiral notebook beside her computer. Or had she done that last night? Was she imagining the intrusion? Her laptop appeared to be untouched. Even if it had been turned on, she was password protected.

A floorboard creaked, and she looked in all directions, seeking the cause. The air was still. Silence surrounded her. *But I heard a sound.* And it rattled her. Groaning and scratching noises weren't unusual in an old house. Still, she reached for the lower desk drawer where she kept her pink Glock. Just as quickly, she pulled her hand back. Arming herself wasn't a rational idea. Even if Tancredo and Serena were packing pistols, Ava doubted her ability to defend herself with the Barbie-style Glock. To say the least, she wasn't a good shot.

If only Liam were here. Digging into her pocket where she'd put her earbuds and mic, Ava thought she could activate the walkie-talkie, but if he didn't have his receiver turned on, he wouldn't hear her. She stood very still, held her breath and listened. *Nothing.*

On high alert, she proceeded through the rest of the house and up the staircase to the second floor. Her suspicions might be nothing, but she worried. If an intruder accessed the sensitive information on her computer, they'd know she was working on the investigation into Stuart's murder.

Upstairs, she saw no sign of a disturbance until she entered her bedroom suite. In the center of her cream-colored chenille bedspread, she saw the yellow spiral notebook that belonged downstairs on the rolltop desk. *Left there as a warning.* Someone wanted her to find it. They wanted her to know she wasn't safe in the cottage. They could sneak inside. *I need to get the locks changed.*

She snatched the notebook, flipped it open. On the first page, in spikey handwriting she immediately recognized was a note: "Ava, you should get the lock on your front door upgraded."

Exactly what she'd been thinking. On the next page, he'd written: "I changed my mind about your boyfriend. No innocent man should go to jail. See you tomorrow A.M. I'll help."

Her knees gave out, and she collapsed onto the bed. Her brother had easily made his point by sneaking into her house and writing her a message. She really hoped he hadn't talked to the rest of the family about Liam. He wouldn't, would he? No way, Michael was smarter than that. Still…

She hit his cell phone number, and he answered immediately. "I picked your lock, Ava. It's amazing how many useful skills you pick up in prison."

"You scared me half to death."

"Good. That was my plan, sis. You need to take this seriously. Stuart was murdered, as in dead, and the person who did it is still out there, wandering around."

She was glad he agreed with her. "It wasn't Liam."

"I sure hope not because then I'd have to kill him for leading my sister on. And I don't want to go back to jail."

"See you in the morning," she said.

"I can come over tonight if you want."

"Not necessary."

She disconnected the call, rolled off the bed and shuffled into the bathroom. Tonight she intended to stay with Liam at the top of the lighthouse. This was their time. It might be their first, last and only chance to be alone. When she'd invited him to spend the night at the cottage, her motives hadn't been wholesome and innocent. From their brief kisses, he'd made it clear that he wanted more…and so did she.

She glanced in the mirror over the sink and groaned. The light rain had turned her naturally curly hair into a dark brown frizz ball, but her lips looked dried out. The mascara she'd been wearing at the beginning of the afternoon smudged down her cheeks. Repair work was necessary.

She jumped into the shower and washed away the nervous sweat of the afternoon. Clad in a towel, she worked a pinch of styling cream and a glob of mousse into her hair to control the curls. Then she padded barefoot through her bedroom to the closet. Somewhere in the back of her mind, she recalled Liam's favorite color was bright red. Or was it pink? She flipped through a selection of hanging shirts, finally selecting a soft coral blouse that buttoned up the front, making it easy to take off and display the lacy red bra she wore underneath. Since she'd be climbing around to get to the lantern room at the top of the lighthouse, she chose slacks in a chocolate brown that wouldn't show dirt. Completing her outfit were strappy, red sandals that were really more comfortable than they looked, plus the platforms added a solid four inches in height, which was always welcome for a shorty like her.

Checking her reflection in the old-fashioned full-length mirror in her bedroom, Ava decided she looked okay. Not glamorous unless she left the top three buttons of her shirt undone. But she was cute and ready for…something.

She glanced at her phone, wishing she could call her sister and ask for advice. Rachel was brilliant when it came to analyzing a relationship and figuring out what to do. What would she say about Liam? On the plus side, he was educated, financially solid and ruggedly handsome with a sexy smile. The big negatives were annoyingly obvious. He was charged with murder. And he'd skipped out on bail.

In the back of her mind, she heard Rachel's voice, speaking softly. She'd say, *You already know what you're going to do, Ava.*

"Do I?"

Follow your heart.

That would be Rachel's advice. And she would be one hundred percent right.

From the moment when Ava recognized Liam in the kitchen, she'd made up her mind that she wanted to act on the attraction she'd felt toward him when she was a student. They had chemistry. She trusted him, wanted to help him even if it messed up her career, and she instinctively believed in his innocence. Liam Brody wasn't a murderer. He was a good, decent man who needed her help to move forward with his life. Maybe, just maybe, she needed him as well.

In the kitchen, she refreshed Liam's supplies, making leftover meat loaf and cheddar sandwiches, selecting wine, adding fruit and more of her macadamia nut cookies to the insulated bag. She checked the vintage 1930s clock hanging over the back door. Time to go.

With the hood on her anorak flipped up, she hoped to preserve the minimal styling to her mop of hair. But when she stepped outside, the hood was unnecessary because the rain had stopped. The clouds thinned. Gulls and white-chested murres swooped through the skies to catch their last bit of food before the nocturnal hawks and owls took over on predatory night patrol. Again, she looked toward the forest and then to the shore, making certain she wasn't observed while she made her way across the fifty yards to the lighthouse.

Inside, Liam peered down through the hatch, thirty-seven feet above her head. "Fasten the bag to the rope. Just like before."

Following his instructions, she watched as their dinner and two bottles of Zinfandel ascended to the upper floor. After a pause, the rope slithered back down. Attached at the end was a triangular arrangement—a flat board about twenty-four inches wide fastened to the rope with nautical knots she recognized as Liam's handiwork. The contraption looked like a crude swing.

"Sit on the board and hang on," he said. "I'll pull you up."

Doubtful about this device, she asked, "Are you sure this is going to work?"

"You don't think I'm strong enough to lift you?"

She frowned. "I'm heavier than I look."

"This isn't about muscles. I've rigged a pulley system. Hop on."

Trying not to visualize herself in the hospital with two broken legs, Ava mounted the wooden swing. "I'm ready."

Her red platform heels swung off the floor. The curved walls of the lighthouse tower wrapped around her as she dangled, slowly ratcheting up a few feet at a time and swaying from side to side. The last time she'd been on a swing was years ago, and the sensation of weightlessness felt strangely titillating. He'd promised a thrill ride, after all.

Liam hauled her all the way up and through the rectangular hatch where he pulled her toward him. "Put your feet down," he said. "You're here. And you're taller."

"Platform heels." The short woman's best friend.

While he closed the hatch and fastened the bolts that held it in place, she looked around. They were standing in an enclosed, circular room where the mechanical equipment used to keep the light revolving were housed. A ledge ran below the windows. After it had been refurbished, the huge magnifying lens would be mounted in the center. Right now, before repairs, the space stood empty.

Liam had made himself at home. A sleeping bag spread out against one wall and a couple of crates served as chairs and tables. Smiling, he came toward her, caressed her cheek and tilted her head up toward him. "I have something I need to say."

"So do I." Light from the windows above them shone in his thick, dark hair and turned his gray eyes to silver. She mimicked his caress, gliding her fingertips down his cheek to the stubble on his chin. "You go first."

"I appreciate everything you're doing, and I trust you to make good decisions. At the same time, I've got to take a more active part. I can't spend these few days of freedom hiding in the trunk of your Sonata."

"I understand. But more involvement on your part sounds like a risk."

"For both of us," he said. "There are questions I need to ask. Fights I need to fight. You've done a great job of digging out gossip from the good people of Narcissus and getting me familiar with Georgina and her jerk of a husband."

"Stop." She placed her index finger across his mouth. "I'm not backing out. I need to be part of your investigation."

Outside, the wind whistled around the lighthouse. Liam took her to a narrow door and held it open for her. She stepped onto the metal widow's walk that encircled the top of the lighthouse. The heavy rain clouds lifted, and she gazed to the west. Skies of gold and red and magenta reflected in the rolling waves of the Pacific.

A good omen. Red sky at night. Sailor's delight.

Chapter Fourteen

Nothing stood between Ava and the sunset except a waist-high metal railing. She held tightly, anchoring herself. Perched near the top of the lighthouse, she was over forty feet off the ground on a cliff that towered another thirty feet higher than the shore. Behind her was the forest and the cottage. From where she stood on the widow's walk, she and Liam couldn't be seen, except by the birds and boats far out to sea. The horizon—lit by golden hues—rippled endlessly from north to south. Waves rushed toward the massive rocks below and crashed on the narrow, sandy beach in a mesmerizing rhythm.

Long ago, when she was a little girl, she imagined magical palaces where princesses danced all night in ornate ballrooms, and every day brought a new parade of exotic animals like elephants and tigers. The vast world spread before her, unlimited and exotic.

She glanced over her shoulder at Liam. "Is it safe to be out here in the open?"

"Facing the west, we're hidden. The lighthouse stands between us and the cottage. And the cliff juts out far enough that no one can watch from the forest."

"You've been out here before?"

"Late last night and early this morning. This is my first

sunset." He placed the basket holding the food and wine she'd packed against the wall by the door and stood beside her at the railing. He stretched his long arm into the sky as though he could catch one of the soaring, swooping gulls. "When I'm at sea, this is my favorite time of day. The chores are done, and the sun goes down. Darkness settles, then comes the moon and stars. And I feel part of it all."

The glow from the sunset reflected on his face. A gust of wind swept his hair back from his forehead as he stared into the distance. He belonged out here with the sky and the surf. "Did you always want to be a sailor?"

"A swashbuckler," he said.

"And how did your parents feel about that occupation?"

When he shrugged off her question, she realized how little she knew about his background. And she needed to know. Last night, she'd thrown herself at him with very little real understanding of who he was, other than the obvious: handsome, intelligent and courageous. Also, she knew he came from wealth and grew up in the Pacific Northwest.

Once again, she probed. "Your mom and dad must have wanted something special for you when you grew up."

"We never talked about it. Not all families are like yours, Ava. My Brody kinfolk are among the crustiest of the upper crust. Most of them live back East. We're detached. I've met my aunts, uncles and cousins exactly three times, once at my mother's funeral. She died from a brain aneurysm when I was thirteen. My father was so wrapped up in his work as a virologist that he didn't have much inclination to spend time with me and my sister."

"I'm sorry."

"Can't complain," he said. "Nobody smacked me around or locked me in the basement. And they happily paid for just about everything I wanted. My sister runs the Brody Foundation based in San Francisco, and she organized the legal team for my defense."

"What about your father?"

"We haven't spoken."

"But you were arrested. You're facing trial."

"Not his problem." A thread of sadness wove through his words. "One thing I learned from him was to take care of myself."

She'd always envied rich people. Not anymore.

THINKING ABOUT HIS family curdled his blood. He refused to waste time worrying about his relationship with his father or, more accurately, the lack of one. His family history needed to stay in the past. Those distant relatives had never gone out of their way to hurt him. Well, maybe once or twice, but they weren't malicious. Brody family disagreements arose from financial conflict. *It's only business.*

He closed his eyes and leaned against the wall while those words repeated and echoed in his mind. He'd heard the voice before but couldn't identify the speaker. Once again, he flashed on that day on the yacht with Stuart. Lying helpless across the cushions in the stern near the dive deck, he tried to move but his limbs were too heavy. He struggled to open his eyes. Felt a shadow move over him. *It's only business.*

Clearly, he heard Stuart's voice. *Changed my mind.*

Forcing one eyelid to open, Liam managed to squint. Saw an inflatable boat bobbing in the water. The motor went silent. There were sounds of a scuffle.

As quickly as it had come, the vision vanished. Poof!

"Liam, are you all right?"

He gazed toward Ava outlined in the colors of the sunset. "I'm fine."

Too bad he couldn't use the memory fragments inside his head as evidence. He needed proof, needed to know for sure that he wasn't a murderer. Only then could he seek a more fulfilling commitment with Ava.

He wrapped his arm around her slender waist and pulled her close. Her nearness warmed him. In her tall wedge sandals, the top of her head came up to his chin. They fit together very well. Her curves pressed into his body, filling the empty spaces. The sweet, clean fragrance of her hair teased his nostrils, and he was glad he'd taken the time for an ice-cold bath in the forest so he'd smell more like pine resin than sweat. He wanted to be even closer to her, to taste her lips and feel her breasts rubbing against his chest. Her invitation to stay in the cottage tonight became a serious temptation, even though he knew the timing was wrong for them to sleep together in a desperate act of passion. He couldn't help wondering if her sheets were satin and her mattress was firm and her nightgown was filmy. So tempting but not yet.

"I'm lucky to have such a loving family," she said, picking up the conversation they'd dropped before the scattered remnants of his vision interrupted. "True, they drive me up the wall, but they're as much a part of me as my ears or my arms."

"Or your heart." Liam reined in his desires. Right now, he needed to be smart, logical and focused on their investigation. "You mentioned you had something to tell me."

"Don't be mad," she said.

"What is it?"

"Remember that loving family we were just talking about? Well, sometimes they overstep and stick their noses where they don't belong." Her shoulders rose and fell as she huffed a sigh. "Michael broke into the cottage while we were at Georgina's house. He swiped a notebook off my desk and took it upstairs to the bedroom where he left a note telling me to upgrade my lock on the front door."

Not happy about her brother's intrusion, he asked, "What does he want?"

"He's had second thoughts about you and wants to help. The note said it's not right for an innocent man to be incarcerated, and Michael knows from personal experience what that particular brand of injustice feels like."

"Does he know I'm with you?"

"I haven't told him, but he suspects. He wants to meet tomorrow morning, and I'd like to introduce you. Your decision, Liam. What do you say?"

He hesitated for a moment while pluses and minuses balanced on a scale. The possibility of pluses won. "I say welcome aboard. We need all the help we can get."

"I'm not sure what he can do."

"We'll think of something." He already had a good idea how the presence of Michael Donovan could solve the problem of having Ava face Quincy and Tancredo at the Port of Newport. Michael could accompany her. Those two wouldn't dare threaten her while her tough, ex-con brother protected her.

"You'll like him," Ava said with unshakable certainty. "You and Michael remind me of each other. You're both loners, both tough guys—"

"Bad boys?"

She nodded. "The main difference is that you're a sailor, and he's a cowboy. After his release from jail, he moved to Pendleton where he works on a ranch. Do you like horses?"

"I went to the Kentucky Derby once."

She chuckled. "I'll have to take you to the Pendleton Round-up in September. It's one of the oldest rodeos in the country."

Her comment surprised him. Making plans for the future? Their future together? Somehow, in spite of all the suspicion and doubt, she believed he wouldn't be in prison and they'd still be with each other. He wished he had her confidence.

After a quick kiss, he separated from her, took a step forward, looked over the railing and pointed to the cliff below. "That looks like a path going all the way down to the shore."

She joined him and leaned out so far that he was compelled to grasp her arm above the elbow. No fear of heights from Ava. "Looks different from this perspective. It's a narrow, rocky trail. Not a terribly difficult descent, it comes out on the beach not far from Seal Rock. From there, it's a short walk to the dock."

"The dock?" He brightened. "I can't see a dock from here."

"It's tucked under the cliff, well protected from incoming surf."

"Do you have a boat?" He'd welcome a way to move around the coast without hiding.

"Not even a canoe."

The dock couldn't be seen from the cottage or from the edge of the cliff. Not a bad place for a secret meeting. Tomorrow morning, he could talk to Fish Finley on that secret shore after Fish arrived for work at the cottage. Liam brightened at the thought of investigating outdoors instead of hiding in secret passageways, trunks of cars and the isolated room at the top of the lighthouse. "I know Fish has a little motorboat."

"He's come to work by sea a couple of times." She frowned. "You aren't thinking of talking to Fish, are you? He's testifying for the prosecution. Not on your side."

"We'll see." Liam shifted to another branch of their inquiry. "When you were with Georgina, you noticed her cuff bracelet. Did you snap a photo?"

"Got it right here." She dug into the pocket of her anorak and took out her phone. Before she showed him the bracelet,

Ava turned to the west and snapped a succession of photos capturing the golden sunset below the dark purple clouds. Then she handed over the phone and sat with her back leaning against the whitewashed wall below the beacon windows. She pulled the basket with food and wine closer and reached inside.

Liam concentrated on the screen that displayed a three-inch gold cuff with an intricate Deco design featuring rows of pyramids alternating with curlicue roses. "Expertly cleaned up. You can still see the detail."

"That's correct, Professor. In class, you told us that gold coins and jewelry retrieved from shipwrecks suffer less deterioration than most other metals. I've used that rationalization to always buy gold jewelry."

"This pattern is similar to goods we salvaged from a merchant ship that sank in the 1920s. Quincy gave this to his wife, right?"

She nodded.

"The property from this salvage operation was returned to the owners of the ship and their insurance company. And Deep Dive was paid a substantial fee for the find." He looked from the screen of her phone to the brilliant sunset, hoping there might be an innocent reason for Quincy to have this bracelet. "I hate to think Stuart took this bracelet from our inventory and gave it to his buddy."

"I can't believe that would happen," she said. "Don't you keep records of artifacts?"

"Of course." And Stuart kept the records. Detailed records, written by hand and entered into the computer. "I trusted him."

"Where do you store the objects you salvaged?"

"Some are in my basement. Others are kept in a secure warehouse."

"How secure?"

Some of the objects they found were valuable, like the bracelet Quincy had given to his wife. A high level of security was required, and Liam had been using this warehouse for years, ever since he made significant finds in the Strait of Juan de Fuca. The space was temperature controlled and windowless with locks on the area belonging to Deep Dive and also at the entrance where guards were on duty day and night.

"Very secure," he said. "The only ones with access are me and Stuart. Once a year, we take inventory."

"Comparing the objects in storage against Stuart's listings."

"When I was arrested, the police checked the warehouse. They found nothing missing."

She suggested, "Maybe because Stuart never wrote things down in the first place."

I'm a fool. He cursed himself for believing in his partner and not taking the time to have an independent third party record their inventory. "Stuart must have given the bracelet to Quincy in exchange for... I don't know what."

"Doesn't matter," she said. "It's evidence that Stuart and Quincy were in cahoots."

"Cahoots? Who are you? Some kind of noir detective like Sam Spade?"

"I used the word correctly. It implies a partnership for nefarious purpose, and I like the way it sounds. Cahoots. Cahoots."

He smiled as he returned her phone, but his anger and disappointment didn't fade. In a quiet voice, almost as though he was talking to himself, he said, "I didn't want to believe that Stuart was cheating me. But here's proof. He gave or sold this piece to Quincy. And he invited Tancredo onto the dive boat when I wasn't on board."

"Sorry," she said.

"We'd been partners for eight years and friends for longer than that. I remember when he got married and when his son was born. I crewed on his yacht, and I thought Stuart was amazing."

"We all make mistakes," she said as she lifted out a bottle of Zinfandel and showed him the label. "From a Willamette Valley winery."

"I like a good red."

"I thought you might." She whipped out a corkscrew. "Growing up, I didn't know Stuart well, but he had a reputation in Narcissus for cheating and lying and going through a new girlfriend every week. Stuart's sister hated her brother's infidelity and compared him to my brother Barry."

"Serena, right? The woman with the gun in her purse."

"Sticky Serena the Human Saran Wrap, that's what my sister called her because she was clingy. Rachel didn't much care for Stuart, either. I remember how furious she was when Holly told her she was pregnant."

"Are you saying your sister didn't approve of an unmarried pregnancy?"

"Nothing so close-minded. Rachel expected Stuart to break Holly's heart, and she didn't want her friend to be hurt."

"Was she right?"

"Not at first." Ava handled the corkscrew with easy expertise to open the bottle with a subtle pop. "Right after they got married, Holly lived the life of an Oregonian princess in a sprawling mansion with a full-time maid and a chef. Stuart took her on a trip to Europe, then to the Bahamas and he was totally gaga over his baby boy."

She took two plastic wineglasses from the basket, handed them to him and poured the glistening, red liquid. Ava held up her glass for a toast. "To innocent men."

"And the women who believe in them."

The wine tasted of cherries, earth and spice. The flavor aroused his palate. Liam wasn't much of a drinker, but he liked his wine.

Ava made a yum noise that was unintentionally sexy. "Anyway," she said, "Holly had a happy ending for a while."

"Few and far between."

In his experience, "happily-ever-after" only occurred in the endings of rom-com movies. He turned his head and gazed into her big beautiful blue eyes. He'd gladly settle for "happy right now."

When he inclined toward her, she tilted her chin to receive his kiss. The last golden rays from the setting sun warmed them and drew them closer. He set his wineglass down and reached for her. This kiss required both hands. With one, he traced the ridge of her spine down her back to the fullness of her hips. The other hand slipped inside her coral shirt. When his fingers touched her bare torso, she gasped and gave a wiggle that encouraged him to reach higher and brush his fingertips against the soft, delicate underside of her breast. Another quick intake of breath. Her skin felt hot and smooth. Still balancing her wine, she shifted position until she was sitting on his lap with one arm coiled around his neck.

She nuzzled his throat, nipped at his earlobe and kissed his cheek. "You're fuzzy," she whispered.

"And you're satin."

He kissed her again, tasting the earthy flavor of the Zin. She threw back her head and downed the rest of her wine in one glug. In a carefree gesture, she tossed away her plastic glass and slanted her lips across his. The kiss was hard, passionate. She drew him into her until he was drowning, happily abandoning any pretense of intelligence or logic.

The raucous cries of gulls had faded at the end of day, and the gentle murmur of the surf serenaded them. Their high perch on the widow's walk, facing toward the ocean and away from the cottage, kept them safe from observation. No one could see them but the diving, swooping birds. They were alone in a private, intimate world.

But they weren't.

The world hadn't stopped turning. He was still a fugitive, accused of murder and looking at a life behind bars. In spite of the fierce urge to make love to her right here, right now on the widow's walk, he needed to regain control. If he didn't get them back on track with the investigation, he'd lose his ability to make sense of the evidence. *I don't want to go to jail.*

Summoning every ounce of willpower, he lifted her off his lap and set her down beside him. She gasped for breath. Her cheeks flushed bright red. Regretfully, he said, "We can't."

Though her gaze turned as predatory as a blue-eyed tigress, she agreed. "Certainly not."

"I need to update my data."

She bounded to her feet. "I'll get your laptop."

Good thing she didn't expect him to move quickly. It'd take a few minutes before he was able to stand.

Chapter Fifteen

The next morning at half past seven, Ava tried not to think of her dream deferred and unfulfilled. Last night, she'd imagined that her budding relationship with Liam would blossom to a more intimate level—a nice way of saying she wanted to have sex with him. But he'd sidestepped her obvious advances. In retrospect, she told herself she ought to be glad. If they waited until his future was more secure, they might have a chance at something deeper and more serious than a frantic, one-night coupling. Already, she'd waited six years for him to notice her. A few more days were no big deal.

She left the cottage while the blushing sunrise colored the skies above the giant boulders close to shore and the incoming tide. With her earbuds and mic in place, she spoke to Liam when she reached the path leading down to the rugged, sandy beach. "Are you sure it's safe for you to come outside?"

"Nothing is a sure thing, but I'm ready to give it a try."

Still, she couldn't dismiss the ever-present threat from Jess-hole and the manhunt she'd heard about on the news last night. The TV reporters made Liam sound like a mad-dog supervillain, but the accompanying photo showed a handsome hero, which somehow made him more horrible in a Jekyll-and-Hyde sort of way. Hiding in secret places hadn't been easy for him, but stepping into the light could be worse. "It's risky."

"I'll meet you at the dock under the cliff."

Climbing down the path, she picked her way through rocks, beach grass and prickly shrubs to the hard-packed sand where a couple of sea lions waved to her from their long, flat rock near the breaking waves. Her descent took only a few minutes. At the bottom, she gazed up at the lighthouse towering like a beacon of hope. An unlit beacon. How appropriate for her current mood!

Standing at the edge of the water with morning sunlight dancing on the waves, she turned her head and watched him hike down the hillside. As soon as his boots hit the sand, he strode toward her with long strides, wrapped his arms around her and nuzzled her earlobe. His two-day growth of stubble scratched her cheek. He whispered, "I like being out here with you. With the wind and the waves..."

"And the squawking gulls." She stepped out of his embrace, grasped his hand and pulled him toward the overhanging cliff where the short dock bridged over the water. "We're not safe yet. We need to make ourselves less obvious."

"Fine by me."

"Michael is going to meet us here around eight o'clock, which means he could arrive at any moment." She took out her earbuds and deactivated the mic. "What have you been doing this morning?"

"I followed up on a call I made last night to Wyatt Willis, the private investigator I used before. He'll do some poking around. His first project is locating Maxine Gallo."

"The assistant," she remembered.

"I have some specific questions for her about the inventory of salvage we've collected and stored at the warehouse." He removed his earbuds and mic. "I also have questions about Stuart's shares in our partnership."

"And you need to know what happens to Deep Dive if you're convicted and go to jail."

He cringed. "Don't remind me."

She didn't regret her words. He needed to keep the stakes in mind. "What are you going to talk to my brother about?"

"Anything he might know about Holly, Ollie and Serena."

"They sound like a trio of folk singers."

"Mellow." He walked past her to the short wooden dock where no boats were moored. "I like this tiny marina. Did it get a lot of use when they were first building the lighthouse?"

"Not really, large ships or tall sailboats wouldn't try to maneuver through these rocks. This is more of a dinghy dock." She grinned. Being outdoors with him made her cheerful in spite of the danger. "What do you want Michael to find out about the threesome?"

"Why does Holly still wear her wedding ring when she's been divorced for years? How much does Oliver know about the drug scene in Narcissus? If Serena inherits her brother's share of Deep Dive, what is she going to do with it?"

Ava frowned. Michael wasn't a particularly social person, definitely not a gossip like her sister. "You might be asking the impossible. Michael isn't a chatty guy. And if he approaches Serena, she might glom onto him as a substitute for my other brother Barry."

"Mostly, I want your big, strong brother to act as your bodyguard."

She scoffed. "I'm not in danger."

"Tell that to Jessop when he threatens you."

Irritated, she stalked toward the dock and slapped the top of a waist-high, rugged piling. "I can handle Jess-hole."

"With your little pink Glock?" He walked to the end of the dock and peered into the water. "To tell the truth, I'm more worried about Tancredo and Quincy."

"Quincy was quick to suggest I talk to Tancredo as a

source for local legends," she said. "Why else would they want to meet with me?"

"To find out what you know about me and about Stuart's murder," he said. "I don't trust those guys, and I'd feel a hell of a lot better if your brother stood at your side."

She had to admit that Michael had an intimidating aura. After spending years in prison, he'd developed a flat, menacing stare that could look right through you. Without speaking a single word, he conveyed ice-cold intensity. "Okay, Liam. I'm guessing you have another theory about the murder. Let's have it."

He shrugged. "I need confirmation from the PI, but I've heard that Tancredo has connections for fencing illegal salvage."

"Like Georgina's gold bracelet."

"And Newport is a natural location for smuggling."

"So you think Quincy and Tancredo were in cahoots with Stuart." Under her breath, she repeated the ridiculous word. "Cahoots, cahoots."

"Here's my theory. Stuart invited me out for a boat ride to get me alone. He drugged me with some nearly untraceable concoction that he got from Tancredo."

"Why?"

"Tancredo had loaned Stuart a bunch of money and wanted to get it back. To do so, Stuart needed to get me out of the way so he could take over Deep Dive and expand into the illegal salvage business with Quincy."

"Wait." She held up both hands to stop his narrative. "I like this theory better than your idea about Stuart and Ollie drugging you. This time, you think Stuart intended to murder you so he could make more money. Doesn't track because the Whitcomb family is loaded. For that matter, Quincy married wealth. He's not hurting."

"Greed is an interesting phenomenon," he said. "What

most people consider filthy rich, others find lacking. Stuart might have wanted more. The same goes for his sister."

"The upper crust," she murmured.

"Back to my theory." He gave a professorial gesture. "I was unconscious on the boat with Stuart at the helm. Quincy boarded, probably using an inflatable boat. Instead of killing me, they argued. Quincy is famous for his bad temper. In a rage, he whacked Stuart and killed him."

"Which leaves him adrift in the ocean with one dead man and another unconscious."

"Thinking on his feet, Quincy tosses the murder weapon overboard and leaves, knowing the police will assume I'm the killer and will end up in jail."

She hated to admit that he might have solved the mystery without her help and focused on the part of his theory that still seemed off-kilter. "How does Quincy profit from Stuart's death and your incarceration?"

"I don't have that part worked out." Liam stepped off the dock and onto the sand. He peered into the shadows from the cliff. "What do you think, Michael? Any ideas?"

Ava watched her brother emerge from the dark and come toward them. What was going on here? She hadn't told her brother that Liam was sleeping in the lighthouse. Her plan had been to introduce them and carefully evaluate whether these two volatile men would be able to work together without exploding. Only then would she admit to a relationship with the fugitive.

Michael had taken that choice away from her. Somehow, he'd crept down here without being seen. Or maybe he'd arrived early and had been waiting for them, confident that they couldn't hear his approach over the rustling of the surf, the screams of the birds and the barking sea lions.

"Back off, Michael." She snarled at him. "Why are you here so early?"

He barely glanced at her. His hard-edged gaze rested on Liam as he came closer. Somehow, he managed to not look clumsy walking across the sand in his pointy-toed cowboy boots. He halted a few feet away. "Answer my sister's question. How does Quincy profit?"

"My guess? He needs help from Serena."

"Yeah," Michael said, "that's the way I'd call it."

Ava glared at one, then the other. Neither Liam nor her brother cracked a smile. A well-matched pair, both stood over six feet tall. Both were lean with wide shoulders and narrow hips. Liam's hair was darker, but he and Michael both had angular features and stubborn jaws. If they worked together, they'd be formidable. If not...

"I don't understand." She threw up her hands in surrender. "How can Serena help Quincy?"

Liam kept his focus on Michael while he answered her. "In spite of being detail oriented, Stuart never changed his will when he divorced Holly two years ago. The way it's set up now, his son inherits his estate—properties, investments, trust funds and tangible purchases. Holly is appointed to act as trustee and executor. He split his 49 percent ownership in Deep Dive between his son and his sister. Serena wants it all."

"I'm still confused," Ava said. "I don't understand how Quincy fits in."

Liam explained. "In addition to being greedy, the upper crust sticks together. I'm guessing that even though Serena and Georgina don't like each other, they'll work together for profit. Quincy can manipulate both of them. Serena doesn't want to run Deep Dive. Once she has all of her brother's shares, she can sell them for an inflated price to Georgina's husband. Combining Deep Dive and his own salvage business makes Peter Quincy the main guy in that business for central Oregon."

"He's right." Michael nodded like a handsome cowboy bobblehead. "You're not as dumb as you look, Brody."

"He's a PhD," she said. "Of course, he's intelligent."

"Now isn't a time for book smarts, little sis. We need street smarts, and the ability to think like murderers and criminals."

"There's one more piece to this theory," Liam said. "In order for Serena's minority ownership to be useful, Quincy still needs to get me out of the way. Another murder would be suspicious. But if I go to jail…"

He left the thought hanging and Michael finished it. "In jail, you couldn't interfere with their plans."

"Exactly."

When Liam reached out for a handshake, Michael stared at his fingers for a long five seconds before accepting the gesture. Expecting them to be friends was too much, but Ava hoped they'd be able to work together.

AFTER AVA AND her brother Michael hiked up the path to the cottage to meet the work crew headed by her other brother Jerome, Liam got comfortable in the shadows under the cliff. He'd brought along his laptop in his backpack but didn't take it out. Last night, he'd spent too many hours hunched over his computer, honing his theory and trying not to think about how much he'd rather be sharing his makeshift light-house bed with Ava. He sprawled, kicked off his boots and dug his toes into the sand. A dose of sun and surf would help him regain his balance before his meeting with Fish Finley.

He intended to deny any affiliation with Ava or her broth-ers, but his mere presence near the lighthouse made the con-nection. Even Fish—who wasn't the swiftest guppy in the tank—could draw that obvious conclusion. What would he do with that information? What were the odds that he'd sup-port Liam?

On the plus side, he and Fish had developed a comfortable work relationship over the years. With Deep Dive, Fish earned a decent hourly wage plus overtime and insurance benefits, even though he was part-time. After a dive, Fish came along with the rest of the crew for beer and burgers. He was friendly. And loyal.

And yet, he'd agreed to testify for the prosecution. That was the minus. If this conversation turned out wrong, Fish might report to Deputy Jess-hole. Why? Either he secretly hated Liam or he intended to sell the information to the highest bidder. Most likely, the latter.

Might have been smarter and safer to call Fish on the phone for this chat, but Liam wanted personal contact. When he and Michael Donovan confronted each other in person, they created a more intense bond. No guarantee they wouldn't argue in the future. But they shook hands and silently pledged trust. It was understood that they both wanted whatever was best for Ava. He hoped to make the same kind of connection with Fish.

He stood and stretched, brushed off the sand and strolled to the dock. At the end he sat and dangled his bare feet in the cold water. As the sun rose higher in the skies, a gang of dark brown California sea lions lolled in the sun, flapping their fins and occasionally barking. The spotted harbor seals—less sociable creatures—glared and ignored their whiskered cousins.

Liam had a couple of strategies in mind.

First: if the meeting went well, Fish might be convinced to come to work tomorrow at the lighthouse on his motorboat. Having water transport and diving equipment opened up all kinds of possibilities. Using the water, Liam had a way to follow Ava and Michael to the docks in Newport and avoid being seen.

Strategy number two: if Fish had been paid for his testimony, Liam could double the cash involved to make sure Fish would be on his side.

Number three: a long-term goal for Fish—especially since he was starting a family—might be to have permanent employment. Liam could offer that. With Stuart gone, he was shorthanded at Deep Dive and salvage jobs were piling up.

A trio of sea lions slipped into the water and glided to the beach where they waddled at the edge of the breaking waves and made noise. Liam took their performance as an announcement that Fish was on his way down the path. Leaving the dock, he returned to the sandy beach but didn't put his shoes on.

Though he'd seen Fish less than two months ago, there was a significant change in the skinny young man with the shaved head and the pouty lips outlined by a scruffy goatee. His shoulders were high, and his backbone stiffened. He wasn't smiling.

Liam approached and held out his hand. "Thanks for showing up."

Fish gripped, shook and released. His gaze was unwavering. "I didn't tell Bonnie I was going to see you. I'm pretty sure she wouldn't like it."

"Bonnie is your fiancée," Liam said, grateful that Fish hadn't spread the news about their meeting to anybody else. "Congratulations."

"We're going to have a baby."

"Congrats, again."

"I'm pretty sure she'd want me to turn my back and walk away. But Ava is my boss's sister, and I can't afford to lose this job."

"Money is tight. I get it."

"Do you know how much diapers cost? And car seats and cribs and formula. Man, it's a small fortune. And Bonnie wants a house with three bedrooms—one for us, a nursery and a home office for her so she can do her crafts and her podcasts."

If Fish went unchecked, he'd continue to babble like an artesian spring. Liam rested his hand on the younger man's shoulder and said, "Maybe I can help."

"What do you mean?"

"Suppose somebody offered you a payment in return for your testimony. Not saying that's what happened. This is hypothetical."

Fish pursed his pouty lips and nodded. "Suppose they did."

"Why do you think they'd do that?"

"They're out to get you, Brody. They might have offered me four thousand bucks. In a hypothetical way. And I'm not going to lie. You and Stuart argued. All the time."

"I've got a temper," he admitted, but there was a big difference between an argument and a death threat. "What did you overhear?"

"You were fighting about safety procedures. As usual." Fish had an unusual way of chuckling, expelling small bursts of air in a glug-glug-glug noise. "You're always on us about bringing along newbies or checking our air gauges."

Which was why Liam bought health insurance for all his employees and required them to have regular checkups to make sure they were fit to dive. "I'm a safety-first kind of guy."

"Don't I know," Fish said. "Anyhow, you told Stuart that the next time he ran his tank too low you wouldn't help him out, wouldn't haul his ass back into the boat."

"Do you think I meant it? Really? Do you think I'm a murderer?"

"Hell, no."

"Why are you testifying against me?"

Fish shrugged his narrow shoulders. "This is still hypo-thetical, right?"

"Sure."

"I might have agreed on account of I'm desperate for cash. What's the harm? Everybody knows you're not a killer. No way will you be convicted. I mean, they let you out on bail."

"Who gave you the money? Hypothetically."

"Everybody speaks well of you, man. You've got a ster-ling reputation."

"I want a name, and I'll pay you double the hypothetical four thou."

"Serena Whitcomb. That's eight thou, right?"

Chapter Sixteen

Liam couldn't claim to be surprised. Learning that Serena Whitcomb had paid Fish to testify for the prosecution fit neatly with his reasoned-out theory of the murder. Serena would do anything in her power to make sure Liam went to prison and lost control of Deep Dive.

He gave Fish a nod. "I appreciate your honesty."

"It's all I can do. Can't perjure myself." He puffed out his cheeks and tried to look solemn. "I won't tell a lie on the witness stand. I heard you and Stuart arguing, but I also know you didn't mean any real harm. Like when you get really mad and tell somebody that you're going to take them out into the middle of the ocean, tie them to an anchor and feed them to the sharks but before you do…"

Fish was off and running with one of his long-winded monologues, leaving Liam to wonder about Serena's motives. How could she agree to Stuart's murder? *Not a good look for the rich lady.* But Quincy might have explained his assault on Stuart as an accident, a result of losing his temper and lashing out. Liam cut into Fish's narrative which showed no sign of slowing. "Does Serena think I killed her brother?"

"Who can tell?" He gestured helplessly. "Underneath all her fancy clothes and polish, she's a nervous woman. Changes her mind every ten seconds."

"Did you know she carries a gun in her purse?"

"Hell, no. I don't like that. Not at all."

Liam moved on to his final strategy of satisfying a long-term goal for Fish. "I want to offer you a full-time job at double the salary I was paying before. You start right now."

"But nothing's going on with Deep Dive."

"This isn't about scuba," he said. "I need an executive assistant."

"An executive, huh? Bonnie is going to like the way that sounds."

"But you can't tell her." Liam's voice was firm. "If you take the job, that's your first assignment. Don't tell anybody that we talked, and you're working for me. Can you do that?"

"You got it, boss." Fish gripped his hand and gave a vigorous shake. Though skinny, he had surprising strength. "Can I still work for Ava's brother on construction?"

"I wouldn't have it any other way."

Liam took out his wallet and pulled out five hundred-dollar bills. Another tip for his *Fugitive on the Run Handbook*: always carry cash, lots of it. "Here's a signing bonus. Now you work for me."

"Fair enough." The cash disappeared into his back pocket. "You're sweet on cute, little Ava, aren't you?"

"I am. But don't tell her. Or her brothers."

"I'll keep a lid on it."

Fish was strong, loyal and oddly perceptive. Couldn't ask for more in an assistant. For maybe the first time since he'd been arrested, Liam felt like he was in control of the situation. "Here's your first assignment. Ava mentioned your motorboat and said you sometimes use it to come to work."

"Not today," Fish said. "I took my Yamaha motorcycle because Bonnie needed the car."

"Tomorrow, bring your boat and moor it right here at this dock." He would arrange for them to motor over to Newport and keep an eye on Ava's meeting with Quincy and Tancredo. "Can you do that?"

"Aye, boss."

Liam liked the way they'd fallen into their usual relationship. He was the captain, and Fish was the crew. "Better idea. Can you take off at lunchtime, go home, get your boat and bring it back here?"

"Aye."

He wished his mic and earbud were active so he could tell Ava about his plan. They were another step closer to finding the truth. As if the mere thought of her had conjured her presence, he looked up and saw her running across the beach toward them.

AVA HADN'T WANTED to interrupt his conversation even though she expected it to go well. Like everybody else in town, Fish knew she and Liam were connected. When she told him that he needed to hike down to the shore near Seal Rock because someone wanted to see him, the first words out of his mouth were, *Brody. It's Liam Brody, right?*

She couldn't come up with a plausible denial, so she'd said nothing and smiled.

Fish smiled back.

From the casual look of the two men near the short dock, they seemed to be getting along. She hoped so because she was about to drop another bombshell. When she reached Liam, she gasped for breath. "It's Ollie," she said. "On his way."

"Here?" he asked.

"Yeah." Stuart's son had sounded angry over the phone. Now wouldn't be the best time to test the waters and find out how the teenager felt about Liam. "You need to step back into the shadows."

"That's probably wise."

She caught her breath and turned to Fish. "Did everything work out for you?"

"I'm an executive, but you can't tell anybody. Bonnie is going to be happy. So, yeah, I'm happy."

"I'm glad, Fish." Later, she'd catch up on the details. "I'd like for you to return to the cottage. Jerome has a project for you."

"You got it, Ava. And thanks." He dashed toward the path leading up the cliffside, waving a greeting to the curious, dark brown sea lions as he passed. They responded with raucous barking.

She whirled to face Liam, placed her palms flat against his chest and pushed him toward the cliff into the rock-strewn darkness where Michael had hidden. "Ollie suspects that I know where you are. He wants me to give something to you, says it's important."

"What is it?"

"He didn't tell me. And he's got to talk to you before his aunt Serena finds you."

"Am I missing something?" He stepped into the shade. "How is everybody figuring out that I'm here?"

"Small town osmosis. One person wonders. Another speculates and tells another. Pretty soon, the entire population of Narcissus is talking about how I'm harboring a fugitive." She didn't like the way things were turning out. "It's only a matter of time before we have another hostile visit from Woodburn and Jess-hole."

"Maybe I should meet with Ollie while I can." His smile bloomed with confidence. She could tell that something inside him had changed. "I'm encouraged by how well the talk with Fish went."

"Fish likes you. He knows you're a decent person."

"Am I? Because I keep having indecent thoughts about you and me."

Hidden under the cliff, the shadows spread around them and masked them from view and she felt safe enough to glide into his warm embrace. The cool sea breeze swirled around them. His lips tasted of sun and salt. She had to step back before her own indecent urges overwhelmed the need for caution. She cleared her throat. "What kind of relationship do you have with Ollie?"

"I've known the kid since he was born, literally. While he and Holly were still in the hospital, I visited and gave him an infant-sized sailor cap. When he was older, I took him trick-or-treating. Went to his Little League games."

"What about his teen years?" She thought of the foundations and charities where Liam volunteered. She knew that he sponsored trips for at-risk kids and also taught boating, swimming, fishing and snorkeling. "You seem to get along well with adolescents. Some people might say it's because you never grew up."

"What would you say?"

She avoided that touchy subject. Her long-held opinions about how rich kids were raised with too many advantages and too few responsibilities weren't really fair and ought to be kept to herself. "Tell me about Ollie. Were you 'good, old Uncle Liam'?"

"I hope not. He was a smart kid, and I never talked down to him. We were close. But when he was a teen, we grew apart." He spread his palms and gestured helplessly. "I didn't know what to do. Stuart and Holly were having problems, which were none of my business. But I felt bad for the kid, wanted to offer support."

"Did you tell him that?" she asked.

"I took him fishing, and we'd sit on the boat. We'd be mostly silent for hours."

"Is taking care of Ollie how you got the idea of volunteering with other kids?"

"Maybe." Liam shrugged. "I never felt like I reached him. Stuart was no help, never wanted to talk about his son. His solution to their widening estrangement was to gift Ollie with bigger and better things."

That pattern held true. Ava heard through her sister's gossip grapevine that young Oliver inherited a small fortune in property owned by Stuart. Though his mother was supposed to oversee these things until he turned twenty-one in a few years, Oliver already had access. "He has the boat, you know."

"Which boat?"

"The one Stuart wanted Deep Dive to add to the fleet. Apparently, he'd already purchased it. Now it belongs to Ollie."

Liam clarified. "The boat where Stuart died. The one he bought with money borrowed from Tancredo."

"Pay attention, sailor. We already figured out that Stuart bought the boat. Now we know it went to Ollie. He is the proud owner of a seven-year-old cabin cruiser with dual outboard motors, and I'm guessing he'll bring it to this dock because he specifically asked me to meet him here."

"Why use that boat?" Unreadable emotions flickered in his eyes. Sorrow? Melancholy? "Is it some kind of revenge because he hated Stuart? No, that can't be. When he was younger, Ollie worshipped his dad."

The father and son looked very much alike. When Ollie smiled—which wasn't often—he had Stuart's double dimples. Ava had noticed the resemblance at the funeral. Everybody in Narcissus had attended, and the mood couldn't have been more fraught. Holly shed copious tears as did several other women who claimed to be his one true love although none of them wore his wedding ring like Holly. The rest of the Whitcomb family held their tempers in check, remaining cool and aloof. No tears. No wailing. Not even from Oliver who spend most of the day staring at the toes of his Top-Siders and mumbling.

"I'm not sure what Ollie wants." She turned away from Liam; being close was too tempting. "He sounded angry on the phone. Angry and hurt."

"His aunt Serena paid off Fish to testify for the prosecution. She wants me in jail."

"How did you change Fish's mind?"

"Money talks. My purse is bigger and, therefore, louder."

She strolled down to the water's edge, moving away from Liam. He seemed calm and casual, unconcerned about the approaching danger. She stalked back toward him, entering the shadow to warn him. "Don't underestimate Ollie. He's seventeen, almost an adult."

"Capable of grown-up violence."

"And he's not coming to the lighthouse to see me. He's after you." She jabbed her forefinger into his chest to get his attention. Ollie had something he wanted to find out or wanted to say to the man who had been his father's partner and, for a time, his best friend. Though it might be appealing for Liam to talk with the teenager, Ollie was unpredictable and possibly hostile. "You can't trust him."

"At heart, he's a good kid."

"If you're wrong, you could end up in jail." She didn't want to cast doubts without evidence, but she had to convince him, to remind him of the danger. "Please, Liam, be smart. Stay hidden."

"I will." He caught her hand and raised it to his lips, brushing a light kiss across her knuckles. "I promise."

Though she appreciated the gesture, now wasn't the time for romance. She reclaimed her hand and gave him a no-nonsense scowl. "Leave your earbuds in so I can tell you when the coast is clear and you can return to the lighthouse. Until then, I'll be out of touch."

"I'll miss you."

She'd expected him to object and insist on overhearing her conversation with Ollie, but he made no such demands. Instead, he waved to her and stepped back into the deepest shadows behind the rocks. What was going on with him? Did he have some kind of plot in mind?

Overhead, the gulls and cormorants swooped through the haze that rolled across the sky and dimmed the midmorning sunlight. She concentrated on her breathing, which eased her anxiety as she slowly walked by the edge of the surf. At the far end of the beach, the cliffs receded into offshore rock formations that stood like sentries to guard this small cove.

When she first took up residence at the lighthouse, she felt secluded and protected from the rest of the world. Now she sensed an ominous threat coming closer and closer. The sea breeze carried dark secrets. The forest hid an ever-present danger. Not only was she worried about Liam, but she feared the unnamed murderer among them. Someone she'd met. A voice she'd heard. The phone in the back pocket of her cargo pants played a sea shanty ringtone. Caller ID read: Sis.

"Hey, Rachel. What's up?"

"What's up with you, babycakes? Already this morning, I've had three customers ask about you and your professor."

Aha! A chance to discover who was spreading gossip. "Was one of them Holly?"

"Matter of fact, yes. Holly and Serena Whitcomb and Hannah, the bartender at Mack's Lumberjack Tavern."

"What are they saying?"

"Holly always liked Liam, and she'll do anything to help. Serena blames him for her brother's death and wants to see him in jail. And Hannah…well, she has the hots for him." Rachel paused for a moment. "Holly agrees."

"Do me a favor," Ava said. "Ask her why she's still wearing her wedding and engagement rings."

Ava heard her sister pose the question. The next voice on the phone was Holly herself. "Stuart showed up on my doorstep and ordered me to sell the rings and split the cash with him. Can you believe that jerk? These rings are worth nearly a hundred thousand buckeroos. As if I'd share it with him. Hah! Being married to Stuart for sixteen years, I earned this jewelry."

"And you stuck the rings on your finger."

"I swore I'd never take them off. Since he's dead, I guess it's different. But I still like the idea of having a fortune at my fingertips." She gave an odd little giggle. "Oh well, nice talking to you, Ava. Here's your sister."

Rachel said, "I have another question for you, baby sis. Why did you invite Michael to stay with you at the lighthouse? Do you need him for protection?"

"Just for the sake of argument, what would you say if I told you I believed Liam was innocent and I'm investigating?"

"No, no, no, no you aren't. You're supposed to be the smart one in the family. How could you do something so silly?" Her volume went up. "Ava, the man is a fugitive. Stay away from him. If you help him, you're abetting."

"What if he's innocent?"

"That means somebody else is a killer," Rachel said logically. "They might come after you."

Not a pleasant thought. "Talk to you later, Rachel. Got to run."

While Ava watched, a sleek yacht with a dark red hull and a covered helm and cabin cruised into view and aimed toward the dock. Ollie had arrived.

Chapter Seventeen

Liam had questions for Ollie. The kid didn't owe him answers, but they'd been close at one time. Was he willing to play for Team Liam?

Hiding in the shadows under the cliff, he clenched his jaw and held himself back as he watched Ava and Ollie walk across the sand toward the path. The young man stood over six feet tall and moved with long, fast strides that caused Ava to trot in an effort to keep up with him. *Inconsiderate. And sloppy.* His baggy board shorts hung low on his skinny hips, and his faded Kurt Cobain T-shirt looked like grunge and probably smelled like teen spirit. How had this sullen punk emerged from the cute kid who dressed as a starfish for Halloween? A waterproof backpack hung from his shoulders—a reminder that Ollie told Ava he had something important to share. The pack wasn't big enough to hold a club or an oar or whatever was used as a murder weapon, but there was plenty of room for the drugs that were used to knock Liam unconscious.

Though he hoped the kid wasn't guilty of anything more sinister than being a teenager, he was suspicious. He hadn't spent the past couple of days hiding in a secret passageway, crammed into the trunk of a Hyundai and peeking down from the top of a lighthouse for nothing. Ava had advised him to stay unseen, and she was right. His real goal could be accomplished without speaking to Ollie or anybody else. Liam needed to find the truth.

His psychologist suggested that he might arouse more of his buried memories by placing himself close to the situation where the trauma occurred. And there sat the yacht where Stuart was killed—a floating crime scene. The cabin cruiser had a midsize cabin with the helm at the front. The galley, fridge, benches and table were tucked neatly under the hardtop. Additional space at the stern—between the covered cabin and the twin Yamaha F300 outboard motors—provided storage and more seating in case they happened to find a couple of women in tiny bikinis who wanted a ride.

The yacht hadn't been outfitted as a salvage vessel. For the purposes of Deep Dive, it was too small and too pretty. When Stuart welcomed him aboard this craft, named *The Reckless* by the previous owner, Liam immediately told him that the boat didn't suit their business. Yes, a cylindrical rack could be added for scuba gear and oxygen, but salvage work could be messy. Clearly, this cruiser hadn't been designed for that. This was a pickup yacht with a queen-size bed under the hull and a well-stocked bar in the galley. Liam had a fairly good idea why his partner wanted *The Reckless*. Good for Stuart, but not for him. There hadn't been a woman in his life before Ava, and she probably wouldn't be enchanted by this fancy-ass cabin cruiser.

He stepped out from the shadow and approached the dock where the boat was moored. While guiding the twin engine yacht through open water, Ollie had managed nicely. Stuart made sure his son had taken the required boating safety classes and received certification. No doubt, the teenager would make good use of this beautiful boat.

From the dock, Liam stepped onto the dive platform beside the rear-mounted motors and entered the outdoor seating area with gleaming white benches and long, waterproof cushions with dark red, beige and white stripes. The top of each bench opened to reveal more storage. Liam took a look inside, hoping he might find a wet suit and scuba gear. No such luck. He saw life jackets, water guns, a couple of boogie boards, hoodie sweatshirts and other teenager gear.

When he'd been on board with Stuart before the murder, the lighting had been different. On that cloudless, bright day, they cruised away from Newport in the early afternoon. Liam remembered the warmth of sunshine on his face and the top of his head.

Today, hazy clouds blanketed the skies, and the wind was a whisper. On the moored yacht, he went through the covered cabin to the helm where a captain's chair faced the wheel and the cherrywood dash which was equipped with the usual dials and switches, including a GPS navigation system and VHF radio. When he'd been with Stuart, he'd commented on the cleanliness and elegance of *The Reckless*. "But we don't need a luxury yacht in our fleet."

"You've got to think big," Stuart had said as he sailed away from the marina and headed for the open sea. "Suppose we're entertaining a wealthy, important client, and we need to show him that we're worthy of handling his business."

"It'll take more than polished cherrywood trim to impress." This clash had been consistent between the partners. Stuart had been far more ambitious, constantly seeking lucrative deals, while Liam dedicated himself to research and old shipwrecks. "We have as much business as we can handle."

"Think bigger." He had gestured grandly to the galley behind the helm. "Help yourself to food and beer."

"No champagne?"

"Sorry, partner. I'm not going to waste bubbly on you."

Liam stared through the windshield at the massive, offshore rock where gulls and cormorants and murres nested.

His last hours with Stuart weren't the makings of epic memories. *Same old, same old.* Their relationship had been tarnished by years of squabbling and fussing and undertaking inane projects and purchases. Like *The Reckless.* Liam had already spoken to the psychologist about this minor argument with his partner. Then, he'd described, in excruciating detail, the way he'd put together his lunch, consisting of a soggy, premade tuna salad sandwich, guacamole and chips. Also, a longneck handcrafted beer.

The therapist had pointed out that the tuna salad or the guac could have been dosed with any of the many "date rape" drugs that worked their way quickly through the system and wouldn't have shown up in the toxicology screen that took place hours after ingesting. Though appalled by how easy it was to knock someone out, Liam believed he'd been drugged. How else could he explain the woozy feeling that had overwhelmed him? The yacht had cruised farther from shore until they were surrounded by the rolling waves of the Pacific. The rhythm lulled him. His eyelids grew heavy.

Stuart had left the helm and joined him in the stern lounging area where they both sprawled across the cushions and nursed their beers. Had Stuart been eating anything? He didn't recall. The twin Yamaha motors were silent, and Liam had heard the waves lap against the side of the yacht. No other vessels had been in sight, and they'd drifted miles away from shore. He'd felt peaceful and relaxed.

His memories before he passed out had already been recalled, including his recent flash of the inflatable boat that had approached *The Reckless* and the argument between two men when Stuart said he'd changed his mind. On the day of the murder, Liam fell into an unconscious state, his mind went blank and he remembered nothing until he awoke and found Stuart's body. Bleeding from a head wound, he was unconscious and near death.

Hoping to fill in the blank space, Liam arranged himself against the cushions, imitating his position on the day of the murder. He closed his eyes and opened his mind to memory. The taste of avocado, the crunch of chips and the cool slide of beer down his gullet. What had Stuart said to him? Something about management and how the yacht would be an advantage when selling their services. "Besides," Stuart had said, "we deserve some luxury. We ought to be able to have some fun."

"Do you need money?" Liam remembered himself asking.

"Hell, no. I'm richer than you'll ever be."

"Then…why?" His voice had been weak. His words slurred. He'd only had one beer, not enough to be intoxicated. What was wrong with him? "Why do you want Deep Dive to buy this boat? Tax write-off?"

"Relax, buddy. You worry too much. Not important. It's only business."

Only business. That was Stuart's justification for everything.

Sitting in the boat at the dock, Liam's mind went blank, just as it had when he was at sea with Stuart. But now, he could take control. He kept his eyes closed, regulated his breathing and waited for his indistinct memories to take solid form. His thoughts were uncensored, fanciful. He imagined a mermaid leaping through the waves with her long, chestnut brown hair streaming behind her. She had Ava's eyes and her full lips. He heard the musical sound of her laughter. *A siren song.* This beautiful reverie was interrupted by the chug of a motor from the inflatable boat that docked at the rear of the cabin cruiser.

Someone else had joined them on the yacht. But who? Was this a planned rendezvous or a happenstance meeting? Must have been planned. They were in the middle of nowhere. Someone had come looking for them.

Stuart's voice echoed inside his skull. *I changed my mind.*

Was this a deal gone wrong? Liam struggled to hear more. The other voice—indistinguishable, garbled and loud—had argued, had told Stuart they had to do it his way. Their disagreement had grown more and more heated.

Liam remembered his need to respond. Instinctively, he'd wanted to defend his partner. Trying to reach out, his arm had fallen limply onto his lap. His legs splayed. He couldn't move. His head felt like it weighed a hundred pounds. His neck was too weak to support it. His tongue lolled. His mouth tasted like cotton.

The argument had expanded, louder than the surf and the cries of sea birds. A ferocious, roaring noise. *Help Stuart.* He had to help Stuart.

With a huge effort, Liam forced his eyelids to open. He squinted toward the covered cabin and saw the fight turn physical. A male figure in a black wet suit raised a heavy-duty, aluminum oar and swung it like a baseball bat. He hit Stuart at the back of his skull, then again and again.

Liam jolted awake, left the vivid memory behind as he jumped to his feet on the stern deck. The horror of his friend's death and his inability to stop the killer chilled him to the core. And yet, he felt a deep, abiding sense of relief. He spoke aloud, reassuring himself. "It wasn't me. I didn't kill him."

He had witnessed the attack on Stuart. Didn't know the identity of the murderer but had uncovered additional evidence. The man in the wet suit had approached on an inflatable with an outboard motor, similar to a Zodiac. Unfortunately, that fact didn't narrow the field. Many people at the marina had inflatable boats. *Deep Dive* owned two.

Concentrating hard, Liam tried to identify the man who attacked Stuart. They seemed to be nearly the same height and average build. In the wet suit, it was hard to notice his body type, and Liam hadn't seen his face. He seemed to have a business relationship with Stuart, which pointed toward Quincy or Tancredo.

He heard a voice in his ear. Ava spoke through the mic. Not a mermaid's song but a slightly panicked warning. "Jess-hole is here. He's already on the path, coming down to the beach. You've got to hide."

There wasn't time to leap off the boat onto the dock and run across the open beach to the shadows under the cliff. Liam went to the helm and opened the hatch leading to the bedroom under the bow. Not an ideal hiding place but it would have to do. Hoping Ava had her earbuds in, he said, "I'm in the bedroom under the bow on *The Reckless*."

AVA COULDN'T BELIEVE what she'd just heard through her earbuds. Why in the world had Liam gone onto the boat? What did he think he was going to prove? She came to a halt on the beach at the end of the path and called out to Jessop, who charged across the sand ahead of her, ignoring the friendly yapping from sea lions. "Deputy, please, wait for me."

He swiveled around. His pointy nose aimed in her direction. "Don't tell me what to do."

Desperate for an excuse to stop him, she blurted, "Search warrant."

"Doesn't work that way. You can demand a warrant before letting me into your house, but this is a public beach. I don't need your permission to search for the fugitive."

Ollie stepped up behind her. "But you don't have my okay to board my boat."

Jess-hole's eyes narrowed to slits. "I can't believe some damn kid is giving me orders. The both of you can go straight to hell."

She heard the heavy clomping from her brother descending the path and kicking rocks out of his way. On the beach,

Michael strode past her, nodded to the sea lions and went directly toward the deputy who rested his hand on the butt of his holstered pistol. In a deep voice, calm and yet somehow threatening, he said, "I strongly advise you not to swear at my sister."

"You don't scare me, Donovan. You're an ex-con. I can take you into custody."

"What's the charge?"

"Harboring a fugitive."

"You've got no proof."

Ava heard others joining them. Her responsible brother, Jerome, who had never been in trouble with the authorities, and Fish Finley climbed down the hill and charged across the beach to stand on either side of Michael. They made a formidable trio. Michael looked like an archetypal cowboy who could easily wrestle a 650-pound steer to the ground. After years of working construction, Jerome was muscular and tanned, wearing a hard hat. Fish, a shorter man, exuded a wiry strength under the black leather biker jacket he wore to lunch. Ava smiled to herself. All they needed was a chief with a feather headdress to be the Village People.

"Well, Deputy, I hope you brought a bus," Jerome said. "If you arrest Michael, you'd better arrest all of us."

"Me, too," Ollie chirped as he joined them.

Bursting with pride, Ava inserted herself as the peacemaker. "We all have a busy day ahead of us. If you're done here, Deputy, we'd like to get back to work."

Jess-hole cast an angry glance toward the yacht moored at the dock. He wanted to board, wanted to search. And if he found what he was looking for... A shudder twitched across her shoulders. In spite of their bravado and support, Liam was still in danger. The deputy could come back here with others and force the issue. They could tear the place apart until they found him.

For the moment, they were safe. She decided to take the win as Jessop retreated toward the path. The other men followed, and she stopped Ollie. Quietly, she asked, "Do you mind if I board your yacht? There's something I need to look for."

"No problem." He almost smiled. His cheeks flushed. "I'm on your side."

"Tell the guys I'll be up there in a minute."

Running across the sand toward the dock, anger churned in her gut. She didn't like being rescued by her big brothers and hated being threatened by Jess-hole. In addition, Liam's irresponsible actions really ticked her off. If Jessop had found him, all their efforts would have been overturned. They all could have been arrested. Why didn't he just stay hidden? Glancing over her shoulder to make sure Jessop wasn't watching, she stepped onto the stern deck beside the motors and scampered to the helm where she tapped on the hatch beside the wheel.

Forgetting she wore the mic and he could hear her every word, she shouted, "Liam, let me in."

He whipped open the door, grasped her arm and pulled her into the dimly lit bedroom under the bow. She stumbled. In a swift, smooth move, he used her forward momentum to guide her onto the queen-size bed with a dark blue quilt.

"Angry?" he asked.

Flat on her back, she glared up at him. The hazy sunlight through a small porthole shone on his huge, incandescent smile. "What's so funny?"

"Not a joke," he said. "It's truth. And it's good, really good. Ready?"

"Just tell me."

"I didn't kill Stuart."

Not exactly a big reveal. She knew he had doubts about his innocence, but she hadn't for a minute believed that he was capable of murder. No matter what form his amnesia took, he surely would have recalled a lethal outburst. "Well, of course you didn't."

"I wasn't sure." Lying on his side with his head propped on his fist, he reached with the other hand and caressed her cheek. "I've never actually blacked out before, but I've come close. And Stuart knew me well, maybe better than anybody else. He knew how to push my buttons."

"You cared about him."

His voice softened. "I miss him, Ava. I never mourned my friend."

Clearly, Liam had undergone a transformation, but she wasn't sure how or why. "What changed?"

"I remembered." He rolled onto his back beside her and stared at the low ceiling. "My psychologist suggested that I put myself into situations similar to the murder, close my eyes, try to meditate—which is something I don't do very well—and let my mind wander."

"What did you see?"

"A guy in a black wet suit clubbed Stuart with an oar. I wanted to help but I couldn't move. Felt like my arms and legs were weighted down. Then I passed out again."

"But you saw the killer?"

"Right."

"Don't keep me in suspense." She shifted position so that she was hovering over him. "Who was it?"

"I don't know. Didn't see his face. In the wet suit, he looked average height and build. Nothing unusual about him."

"You are the most infuriating man I've ever known." She climbed on top of him, straddled his hips and planted her fists on either side of his head on the pillow. "You have to stop taking risks. Get off this boat. Go back to the lighthouse tower. Tonight, we can figure out what we should do next."

"Doesn't matter. I can turn myself in to Woodburn right now."

"What?"

"I didn't commit murder. The truth will come out."

She didn't think of herself as a cynic, but life had taught her that good didn't always triumph. Michael had spent several years in prison for a crime he hadn't committed. "I don't want to pop your happiness balloon, but—"

"Let me have this moment."

He flipped over on top of her and held her down while he kissed her. Unwilling to release her righteous rage, she struggled. The friction of their bodies rubbing together drove coherent thought from her mind. He was strong, dominating. As an avowed feminist, she shouldn't like it. But she did. Her anger turned too quickly to passion. His tongue did amazing things inside her mouth, and his hands skimmed across her body, touching one erogenous zone after another. She wished she could abandon herself to these feelings.

Not now. Ollie could come back to the boat at any moment. They could be discovered. Liam could be arrested.

She shoved him off her. "No, and I mean it."

"Later?"

"Not making any promises." She straightened her windbreaker as she climbed off the bed and pressed her back against the paneled wall beside the porthole. "I'll let you know when it's safe to go back to the lighthouse. In the meantime, get off the boat."

"Bossy."

"You bet I am."

"Do you know the best thing about knowing for sure that I'm not a murderer?"

After that incredible kiss, she doubted he was about to go high-minded and moralistic on her. "What?

"You," he said. "I don't have to feel guilty about my attraction to you. There's no barrier between us. I don't have to hold back. The truth set us free."

"I'm not following your reasoning."

"All along, I've been telling you that you deserve better. Bad boys, con artists and cheats aren't good enough for you, Ava. As a man accused of murder, I had to accept that I had no right to approach you. But now…"

He left the words dangling, and she completed the thought. "You think you deserve me because you're not a cold-blooded killer."

A goofy grin spread across his face. "Sounds weird to say it that way, but yeah."

"You're not setting the bar real high, are you?"

He grasped her arm again and gave her a hard, quick kiss. "And you deserve me."

"Lucky me." She dug into the large side pocket of her windbreaker and pulled out a small, leather-bound volume. "As if your ego needed any more boosting, you'll be happy to know that Ollie remembered the time you spent together. He even smiled when he talked about your fishing trips. And he left you a present. A daily captain's log from Stuart."

"I'll be damned," Liam mumbled. "I should have thought of that sooner. He was always writing lists and keeping logs. This could be the evidence we need.

"Exactly." She tossed the book onto the bed. "It ought to make for interesting reading."

Chapter Eighteen

After a morning spent hiding among the rocks under the cliff and sneaking into the forest when Jess-hole returned with two other deputies and a search warrant, Liam had watched *The Reckless* cruise away from the dock. He'd wanted to thank Ollie for believing in him. The kid had really come through, and Stuart's captain log might provide the evidence they needed.

In the early afternoon, he got the all clear from Ava through his earbuds. Though tempted to hop onto Fish's motorboat that was parked at the small dock under the over-hanging cliff, he retreated to his hideout in the lighthouse tower. Stretched out on his belly on the sleeping bag, he un-fastened the thick rubber band holding the book closed and gave his full attention to the pages in the dark blue, pocket-size volume with a gold anchor emblazoned on the cover. On the first page, written in Stuart's elegant script was the date—January 1 of this year—and the words: *Captain's Log.*

Liam flipped through the unlined pages, which had no particular rhyme or reason for the lapses between dates. Sometimes, there were three entries on consecutive days. Sometimes, ten days passed between notes. Only about twenty pages had been used from January until the mid-dle of March, the day before Stuart died. On each recorded page, he had written the date, location, temperature and a sentence or two about the day's business. On some pages, there was only a name—usually a woman, a place and a time. No need to explain the purpose of these meetings with the ladies. Nonetheless, Liam would pass on these references to Willis, his private investigator. One or more of Stuart's girlfriends might provide a lead.

Carefully, Liam turned the pages and read, remembering the tail end of his nearly twenty-year friendship with Stuart. On January 8 at their first yearly meeting to discuss plans for Deep Dive, they had argued. Loudly. That might have been the day when Fish overheard him threaten Stuart with bodily harm. Stuart's note for that day: "LB is a bilge rat. If I had the $, I would buy that sucker out."

LB had to stand for Liam Brody. He smiled as he ran his fingers across the perfect cursive writing, which Stuart told him resulted from years in a private academy practicing penmanship. The term "bilge rat" instead of something more obscene also came from early training. Stuart seldom swore. Though definitely a manly man, he'd been excessively tidy. As personality disorders went, OCD wasn't a bad one. Liam had taken advantage of his partner's need for order and left all the cataloging of salvage items and artifacts to him—a decision that might have come back to bite him on the bum.

He reread the final entry: "Must repay the loan. Tomorrow, I must convince LB to join my clandestine op or to sell me his shares."

Finally, Liam had the real reason why Stuart had taken him into the middle of the ocean on his new cabin cruiser. But the entry didn't mention drugging him. If Liam hadn't agreed to participate in the "clandestine" operation—which had to involve smuggling objects they recovered as salvage— and had also refused to sell, what was Stuart's game plan?

Liam got off the sleeping bag and went to the lighthouse

windows. Though the glass hadn't been cleaned in years, he still had a spectacular view of the endless Pacific horizon. Leaving Stuart in charge of their inventory had been a mistake. Faced with treasures that had been lost for years, the temptation had been too great. Most of the objects they recovered weren't worth much, but some were valuable. And they were right there for the taking. If Stuart didn't record the piece in his ledger, there was no evidence that it existed. He was able to smuggle whatever he wanted with a low probability of being discovered.

Standing at the window at the verge of the cliff, Liam continued to study the captain's log. Using an old-fashioned pen-and-paper notebook instead of writing on a digital tablet or computer suited Stuart's compulsive nature. Many times, Liam had found him with pen in hand as he worked on lists and entries. After he recorded the bits and pieces of salvage, he gave his lists to an office worker, someone like Maxine Gallo, to put into a computer file.

Dammit, Stuart, what were you thinking? For the first time since he'd found the body, Liam felt the sting of regret. He'd never have the chance to set things right with his partner. Never again would the two of them argue. They'd never stand on deck watching a western sunset while sharing a fine Pinot Noir. Or go clamming. Or fishing. *I miss him.*

The investigation took on a new purpose. Solving Stuart's murder meant saving Liam from wrongful accusation, and it also meant justice for his partner who might have been annoying as hell but didn't deserve to die.

He reread the January 8 entry. Why did Stuart comment that he didn't have enough money to buy out Liam's shares? The Whitcomb family had major wealth and lots of property. Stuart often bragged about his riches. Liam never doubted him, but the minute he'd mentioned smuggling to his lawyers and the private eye, they dug into Stuart's bank accounts and investments. He appeared to be solid.

Other evidence indicated Stuart wasn't as fiscally sound as he'd once been. Rather than arranging for a rendezvous at the luxurious Heathman Hotel in Portland, he'd opted to take his date to a cheesy little motel on the beach. Holly's engagement and wedding ring were another example. She'd told Ava that he demanded she sell the rings and split the cash with him. Holly said he sounded desperate which was why she refused to cooperate and kept her jewelry for revenge, flashing those diamonds every chance she got.

On the other hand, Stuart had recently acquired *The Reckless*, an expensive cabin cruiser. How had he paid for it? More than likely, he'd used the money he borrowed from Tancredo. Was it some kind of trade or a deal worked out with the people who were fencing salvage for him? Liam's private eye had informed him that Stuart's records were clean and showed no apparent association with smuggling or fencing operations. *Nice work, Willis.* The PI had stayed on the job and kept in touch with bits of info. Maxine Gallo could be the source of more details about his finances. Had Willis made contact with her?

Liam activated his laptop using the portable charger, intending to type another email to Willis about Maxine. Might be a waste of time. How could that salty old dame know more about Stuart's finances than his lawyers, the prosecuting attorney and other law enforcement investigators? It was possible, totally possible. Over the years, Liam had learned that sometimes the least likely people had the most information.

A new email from Willis gave him a fresh burst of hope. The PI had tracked down a fence in Portland who did business with Quincy over the years and had receipts and records showing salvage that had been recovered by Deep Dive. Proof! Liam's suspicions were confirmed. He responded to

Willis, telling him to inform his attorney of the evidence. *Thank god, his computer and electronics were encoded and couldn't be traced because he was leaving a wide trail.*

An immediate return email gave an address and phone number for Maxine Gallo in Nye Beach where she had a storefront shop selling ceramics and hanging macramé holders. Name of her shop: Knots and Pots. According to Willis, Maxine refused to talk to anybody but Liam, preferably in person.

Did he dare to take that risk?

His knee-jerk reaction told him to go to Nye Beach and pursue the investigation on his own. Law enforcement had bungled the case. As soon as they decided he was the killer, they didn't bother to dig deeper. *Not true for all of them.* Marshal Woodburn had shown himself to be competent and critical of the investigation. Might be smart to hand Stuart's captain log over to him and let the professional detectives follow up on these leads as well as following up with the fence in Portland. But his gut told him that Maxine had more information about Stuart. She knew his secrets. Liam needed to see her.

He sent another email to Willis, along with the promise of a sizable bonus for his outstanding investigative work. Three words summed up his plan: *I'll visit Maxine.*

Before he left the relative safety of the lighthouse, Liam wanted to read the entire log and glean whatever evidence he could. There were several notations of meetings with PQ, Peter Quincy, and CT, Charlie Tancredo. Apparently, Stuart quarreled with them as often as he fought with Liam. His problem with Tancredo revolved around impossible demands from people he called "the Canadians" who might be part of a north-based drug cartel.

"Damn it, Stuart," he muttered. "Why would you get involved with drugs?"

The interactions with Quincy seemed less dire and more profitable. Not that fencing stolen salvage and cargo wasn't criminal fraud. Such transactions violated maritime laws and restrictions. If they'd been found out, Deep Dive would have lost everything from swim fins to sonar equipment.

Liam stared at the pages in the captain's log, trying to make sense of Stuart's deeds and motivations. His thoughts ping-ponged between anger at Stuart and confusion about why he'd gotten involved with smugglers and fences—people who were clearly not the type of companion usually associated with the eldest son of the Whitcomb dynasty.

The entry on February 2 said: "CT promises we'll have no trouble from the law. They leave us alone. We pay them well." No doubt, crooked officials could be bribed to ignore a minor smuggling operation. Deputy Jessop came to mind. He'd be the first in line with his hand out.

But Liam had become well-acquainted with law enforcement over the past weeks, and he didn't believe they were all corrupt. Not to mention that the U. S. Coast Guard would be part of an investigation into international smuggling and possibly the FBI. For some unknown reason, Tancredo thought they had immunity. And he'd given Stuart a substantial loan. Why? To what purpose?

Trust no one. Suspect everyone.

Right now, Liam's best alternative seemed simple: *Keep investigating.*

Maxine Gallo awaited him in Nye Beach, only twenty miles away by motorboat. Though he doubted she'd turn him over to the law, visiting her shop represented a huge risk. Nye Beach—a combination of quaint shops and seaside condos—nestled in the historic part of Newport. People in that area knew him. But he couldn't stay away. Maxine might be able to provide the last piece of evidence to exonerate him. He hoped she could shed light on Stuart's false inventory records. Or she might be able to explain how he physically removed the objects from the dive boat, where he kept them and how he transported them to the end destination.

Quincy had to be involved in that process. And maybe Tancredo. The harbormaster might have been on board the dive boat while working on a "clandestine" job with Stuart and Quincy.

After Liam talked to Maxine, he figured it was time to contact his attorney and turn himself in to the police. With the captain's log, testimony from the Portland fence, indications of fraudulent inventory records regarding salvage and—last but not least—potential narcotraffic from Canada, his investigation raised questions about Stuart's murder. The police inquiry would need to be re-opened. Liam knew he'd be in trouble for violating bail, but that was nothing compared to murder changes.

He stood at the smudged window at the top of the lighthouse, looked out to sea and considered. *Should he voluntarily surrender to the police?* Thus far, he'd been lucky. He hadn't been discovered, and Ava hadn't been charged with aiding and abetting.

Second thoughts rose up like a tidal wave. Why risk the trip to Nye Beach? *Why not turn himself in right now?* Within an hour, he could be back in custody and on his way to jail where he'd wait until the charges against him were dismissed. His high-priced attorney was on speed dial. All it took to end his fugitive peril was the touch of a button.

He wasn't ready give up. Liam had a deeply compelling reason to see Maxine and wait until morning to contact his attorney. That reason had a name: Ava Donovan.

He didn't want to leave with unspoken words hanging between them. There could be no misunderstanding. His connection with her went deeper than any danger he might experience, deeper than the threat of prison. His mind filled with images of Ava. Running across the beach past the sea lions and the gulls. In the kitchen of the cottage wearing flannel pajamas. Hiding with him in the secret passage. He grinned as he remembered her ascent to the top of the lighthouse wearing her crazy, red, platform sandals. The glow of sunset colored her cheeks as she stood on the widow's walk.

The shape of her face was perfection. Her primrose blue eye shone with a gentleness that reflected her compassionate self. Her lips were made for whispering into his ear. Didn't matter what she said, every word soothed him and aroused him.

Tonight, he would fulfill the desire that had been building inside him since he first saw her. He couldn't wait to gather her sweet, slender body in his embrace, to run his hands over her smooth skin and tangle his fingers in her curly hair.

Though he never would have asked to be charged with murder and driven to Ava for help, he was glad about the way things had turned out. She'd changed him. In a few short days, she'd given his life meaning and made him a better man. Tonight, he'd show her how grateful he was to have her back in his life. And he wouldn't let her leave him again.

He gazed beyond the rock where the gulls, cormorants and murres nested to the rolling Pacific waves. The sea was relatively calm, waiting for him and for Ava. Below the edge of the overhanging cliff, the dock was hidden. Fish's motorboat was moored and ready.

Liam stepped into the sunlight prepared to wrap up this investigation. Tonight would be his reward.

Chapter Nineteen

Heading north along the coast, Ava sat beside Liam in Fish's turquoise blue, nineteen-foot-long fishing boat that was clean with equipment neatly stowed but still smelled of fish. Though the outboard motor maintained a steady pace though calm seas with winds of only five to ten knots, the chill Pacific frothed around them as Liam guided the small craft toward Nye Beach. The ocean breeze brought ruddy color to his sharp cheekbones and the stubborn jut of his jaw. His steely gaze studied the swells of the waves as they rode past forestland, rocky shores and seaside towns.

She harkened back to the time when they'd first met six years ago, and he'd directed his maritime class on a salvage expedition. Whether steering a humble fishing boat or captaining his dive ship, her former professor was more comfortable on the sea than the land, but she couldn't help wondering if they were sailing into disaster.

She tossed her head and leaned into the rush of wind through her hair. "Tell me again, Mr. Fugitive. What are you going to do if approached by an officer of the law?"

"Surrender peacefully. I'm ready to turn myself in." He snugged an arm around her waist, pulled her close and planted a swift kiss on her mouth. "Don't think about what might happen, Ava. Concentrate on this moment. This is where we're supposed to be, you and me. It feels right, so damn right. Have I ever mentioned how much you remind me of a mermaid?"

Not a fantasy that appealed to her. Ava liked having legs. "What changed? Why aren't you hiding anymore?"

"With Stuart's captain's log, the testimony of the fence in Portland and my returning memories, my attorney has enough new evidence to demand further investigation. The trial will have to be postponed, maybe indefinitely."

She understood his reasoning, but he'd left much unsaid. "With all that new information, do we really need to take this trip to Nye Beach to meet with your former assistant?"

"Maxine Gallo worked more with Stuart than with me. She might be able to shed light on his fake inventory lists. Also, she hinted that she might have more information."

"Couldn't you just call her?"

"I trust Maxine, but I'll know more if I talk to her face-to-face."

She understood what he meant. Body language and facial expression were invaluable indicators. She'd known from the moment she saw him that Liam wasn't a murderer. As if she'd recognize a killer when she saw one. "How can you spot a lie?"

"I'm told the nose grows really long."

"Cute." She groaned. "And how do you tell the good guys from the villains?"

"The good ones don't come at you with knives drawn."

"Here's something I've never understood," she said. "I have a friend who can tell at a glance if a guy is wealthy or broke, no matter what he's wearing or what he says."

"You've got to look deep into his eyes. The rich dudes have dollar signs."

"But you don't."

"Maybe I'm not as rich as you think."

More likely, wealth didn't matter to him. Liam didn't run his life based on his bank account which was why Stuart could swindle him. She continued their game. "What do you see in a murderer's eyes?"

"A tiny skull and crossbones." He grinned. "Now I've got a question for you. Look into my eyes and tell me what's there."

She twisted around so she could see his face while he continued to monitor their forward progress through the waves. Golden rays of sunlight spilled over him. The glow reflected in his sexy gray eyes. Instead of a skull and crossbones, she could have sworn that she saw a radiant valentine. "A heart."

"Really? I hoped there would be something X-rated."

"You're so naughty."

"Guilty."

While his sea captain's gaze stayed fixed to the course ahead of them, his grasp of her tightened. The hand at her waist stroked upward over her rib cage until he cupped her breast. Her back arched as she leaned toward him, wanting more. His thumb flicked her taut nipple, and she gave a gasp of surprise and delight.

Step by step, inch by inch the walls of restraint erected between them began to crumble. He was a good man, not a murderer. Liam would fit perfectly with her loud, loving family. With no more need to hold back, she was free to enjoy these amazing sensations she'd fantasized about for years.

Though she wanted to ignore the dark cloud on their horizon, she had to face the shadow. When he turned himself in, he'd be taken into custody. She wouldn't be able to see him or talk to him. After these days of being intensely connected, his absence would leave a terrible void in her life. "I don't want you to go."

"It won't be for long. I'm coming back for you, Ava. We've

been given a second chance, and I don't intend to waste it. And tonight…" He kissed her again. "Tonight is for us."

She snuggled against his chest. The warmth radiating from his body lit a fire inside her. She felt cozy and sexy at the same time, and she prayed he wouldn't be arrested on the sidewalks of the little seaside town before nightfall. "First, I should take care of business."

"By all means."

"I ought to call Peter Quincy and tell him that I'm not going to go with him tomorrow to see Tancredo."

"Good idea. Sever that connection. At best, Quincy and Tancredo are sea slugs. At worst, they're murderers."

Staying in Liam's embrace, she took out her phone and made the call. As expected, she got Quincy's answering machine. Speaking loudly so she'd be heard over the whir of the outboard motor, she canceled their meeting at Newport, giving no other reason than "something else came up."

When she ended the call, she frowned at the phone. "I hope Quincy's dirty deeds won't affect my relationship with Georgina. Do you really think he's the one who murdered Stuart?"

"Not sure," he said. "Stuart's last entry in his captain's log on the day before he was murdered said he planned to meet me and Quincy on the fancy new boat. The two of them wanted to convince me to sell my shares in Deep Dive to Stuart. He and Quincy would form a new salvage company. There was no mention of drugging or violence."

"Why did you pass out?"

"The way I figure, Quincy must have decided to take matters into his own hands. He laced my food with some kind of drug he got from Tancredo. Then he approached in his inflatable boat."

"You remembered the boat."

"But I don't know if it was Quincy or Tancredo who

boarded *The Reckless*. Could have been both. I heard a loud argument. Didn't recognize the voice. In my last vision, I saw a man in a black wet suit whack Stuart with an oar."

"Quincy is known for having a hot temper," she said.

"Tancredo as well."

"Poor Georgina." She gazed toward shore as they passed the entrance to the Port of Newport where Liam's dive boat was docked and Tancredo was harbormaster. The arched bridge—part of Highway 101—spanned the entrance to Yaquina Bay. "She seems truly fond of Quincy. And he's attentive to her."

"Is there a name for a male gold digger?"

"I think it's a gender-neutral term." And she had something else to consider. "Georgina isn't going to be happy with me if I'm partly responsible for putting her husband in prison. I might be out of a job."

"I wouldn't worry about it." His busy hand at her waist slid lower, and he gave her bottom a gentle, affectionate pat. "Your boss wouldn't want to be married to a murderer."

He spoke with a confidence Ava didn't feel. Though Georgina was respectful of history and the environment, she came from a family of heartless lumber barons who were responsible for horrendous working conditions and vast deforestation. "The Solomon family wasn't exactly known for fair play and high moral standards."

"We don't know for sure that Quincy is the killer. There are unanswered questions about Tancredo. Why did he make that quarter-million-dollar loan to Stuart? He gave Stuart a task, but I don't know what it was. And there's the whole issue of drug smuggling. If Tancredo was involved with a northern cartel, he might have struck the fatal blow to preserve his criminal empire."

Ava preferred that scenario. She squeezed her eyes closed, trying to erase her casual thoughts of murder. How could she be so easygoing while thinking about the death of a person she knew? This wasn't a board game. There had been real blood. Real violence.

On a bluff jutting into the ocean, she spotted the Yaquina Head Lighthouse. She pointed toward the iconic silhouette. "One of the most photographed light towers on the Oregon coast. This used to be called Cape Foulweather. The lighthouse is ninety-three feet tall, almost twice as high as Cape Absolute."

"Did you do research there?"

"Frequently. Yaquina Head was decommissioned in the 1930s but has been carefully restored and is fully operational, still using the originally Fresnel lantern. The light doesn't revolve. Instead, there's a signature beam—on for two seconds, then off for two, then on for two and off for fourteen before starting the sequence again."

"You've done your homework."

"That's kind of my thing."

Thoughts of Elizabeth Mayes, the widow of Cape Absolute lighthouse, scrolled through her mind like an old-time movie. Similar to Stuart, Elizabeth had written of her activities, hopes, plans and regrets in her daily log. Maybe Ava should do the same. Keeping a journal while she did renovations on the lighthouse might be a good idea, especially if she decided to put together a book about the project.

Liam veered into a small inlet where the rough sea went smooth. Houses and condos perched on the cliff overlooking the water. "Fish gave me the name of a guy who owns a house in this cove. As it turns out, I know him, too. He doesn't mind if small boats moor at his dock for an hour or so."

"An hour? We're not going to be at Maxine's shop that long, are we? I promised Fish we'd return by six o'clock."

"Plenty of time," Liam said as he cut the motor, expertly

guided the boat to a mooring place and hopped onto the pier. He took her hand to help her come ashore before he tied the bowline to the cleat. "We'll be back to the lighthouse a few hours before dark."

Her cell phone showed over two hours before they were due back which should be plenty of time. She made a quick call to Michael at the lightkeeper's cottage. Of course, he didn't answer. Though taking care of her older brother wasn't really her responsibility, Ava wanted to show her appreciation for his help and protection. She texted him a note about dinner. Probably they'd pick up a pizza. Even though her number one focus was spending time alone with Liam tonight, Ava never ever forgot her family and friends.

She picked her way along the narrow path at the foot of the cliff where coastal grasses, weeds and lupins sprouted among the craggy rocks. A rough wooden staircase with a handrail led to street level. Nye Beach represented a historic part of Newport where quaint, eclectic storefronts, coffee shops and specialty restaurants lined the sidewalks below two-and three-story apartments with views of the boardwalk and the beach. On a Monday in April, the long, wide swath of packed sand wasn't crowded. Dogs chased in and out of the water. Kids built castles and flew multicolor kites while their parents set up lawn chairs to watch the waves.

When Ava paused to take in the scene, Liam laced his fingers with hers and gave a squeeze as though they were a typical couple out for a stroll instead of a couple of lawbreakers wanted by the police. His touch felt familiar and natural, giving her a pleasant sense of well-being. She gazed up at him. Three days' growth of stubble gave him a rugged look, but he didn't seem scruffy. He appeared to be relaxed, like a guy on vacation.

They mingled with tourists on the sidewalk and easily located Knots and Pots. The name of the shop was written in fancy, old-fashioned script, and the front window displayed several hanging planters in a literal rainbow of colors ranging from fire engine red to deep purple. When they stepped inside, a bell jangled loudly. A tall, broad-shouldered woman with wild, curly hair—also in rainbow shades—popped out from the rear of the shop. Hard to miss her; she dressed in stripes and paisley over tie-dyed leggings. Her handsome, weathered face showed her age, but she bounded toward them with the robust energy of a young athlete.

"Good afternoon, Professor." She flung her arms wide and gave him a bear hug. "Gotten yourself into a mess of trouble, haven't you? I figured, sooner or later, you'd come to me."

He hadn't expected such an enthusiastic greeting. He was, after all, a fugitive. Associating with him could cause her trouble. "Are the cops watching your place? Looking for me?"

"As long as you're with me, you're safe."

He wanted to believe her. When he introduced Maxine to Ava, the assistant gave her another all-encompassing hug, followed by the obligatory family connections. "Donovan, eh?"

Surprised, Ava said, "I didn't know you were familiar with Narcissus."

"You betcha. I'm a local, too. Third generation." Maxine combed her fingers through her wild, colorful hair. "You're the baby sister. With those three handsome brothers and your sister, Rachel, who always wins blue ribbons for her pies and cakes. How's your mom? She does crafts, doesn't she?"

"Jewelry," Ava said, looking over Maxine's wares. "She'd love your shop. How did you get into macramé and pottery?"

"It belonged to my great-aunt Marie. When she passed away and left me this building with the shop and apartment included, I decided to move in and keep the family tradition going."

Maxine guided her to a glass case near the cash register and pointed out secondhand jewelry and handmade pieces. Ava's gaze caught on a gold brooch with a Deco pattern of pyramids and roses, which was similar to the design on Georgina's bracelet. "An interesting piece of jewelry. Is it antique?"

"Hmm." Maxine swiveled her head and turned her attention to Liam. "What do you think, Professor?"

THE GOLD BROOCH came from the same salvage operation as the cuff bracelet Quincy had given to his wife. Before they arrived at the shop, Liam had wondered if Maxine would take his side in this tangled situation. Unfortunately, the chunk of stolen jewelry seemed to put her in Stuart's camp. "We both know where that brooch came from."

Her voice took on a falsely innocent tone. "Maybe I've seen this style before."

"Why did you want to meet with me?"

Again with fake naivety, she said, "Why do you think?"

He had neither the time nor the inclination to play guessing games. Maxine had always worked more closely with Stuart than with him. Though Liam thought she hadn't approved of the deceptions Stuart pulled and the lies he required from his assistant, she partnered up with him. Unlikely as it seemed, Ava would have pointed out that Maxine and Stuart were in cahoots.

"I was wrong about you," he said. "I believed you were honest. Sure as hell didn't expect to find out that you were working with Stuart to plunder the salvage we collected. That brooch was stolen from a vessel that sank in the 1920s."

Maxine's artistically drawn eyebrows pulled down in a scowl. "I'm not a thief."

He didn't bother with an argument. "At the very least, you owe me an explanation."

"Fine."

She stuck out her chin. Though not an attractive woman, Maxine had a presence. He wished he could trust her. "Let's hear it."

"I kept that brooch to insure cooperation from Stuart. If the cops came sniffing around, I could flash the jewelry and tell them where it came from. You gotta believe me. I wouldn't think twice about throwing him under the bus."

Liam sensed there was something more she needed to tell him. "And?"

"And I kept something else, too. I have copies of the handwritten ledgers he used—the accurate ledgers as opposed to the fraudulent records of artifacts and objects. I can compare them with the original lists you and the others compiled when you collected salvage."

"You kept an accurate inventory," he said.

"I was a better assistant than you realized."

Those lists and documents proved Stuart's fraud and pointed to other motives for his murder. "How long was this going on?"

"Quite a while," she admitted. "I quit almost a year ago. Also, I have the name and address of the fence in Portland who Quincy was working with."

Liam already knew about Quincy and his Portland contact. "Dammit, Maxine. You should have told me at the time when all this was happening."

"Okay, that was probably a mistake. Sorry."

Anger built inside him. She and Stuart had been cheating him and their clients for years. "Why?"

"Excuse me, Mr. Fancy-Pants, but it didn't seem like a big deal. We didn't take much, and Stuart let me keep some of the pieces, like that brooch. He paid me something on the side to keep quiet about what he was doing. And I liked the bonus." She gestured flamboyantly to her empty shop. "This place isn't exactly a gold mine."

"After I got arrested, why didn't you come forward with this information? The fact that Stuart was engaged in fraud gave a lot of people motive to want him dead."

"Never thought of that." Her eyes widened. This time, her surprised innocence was real. "Oh, God, Liam, now I truly am sorry. I never thought you'd be arrested. Anybody with two brain cells would know that you didn't kill Stuart."

Her vote of confidence came too late. "Who did? Who's the killer?"

Her thick shoulders lifted in a heavy shrug. "I've got no clue."

But she knows something. "I can understand why you didn't want to reveal your part in the scam. Even if it was nothing more than petty theft, you could be charged." He studied her expression, noticing how she avoided looking directly at him. "You're a smart woman, Maxine. Did it occur to you that a rich man like Stuart had no reason to steal trinkets? Why take the risk?"

"I think he got a kick out of doing it. Stuart was an interesting man. He had the soul of a pirate and the detailed penmanship of an eighteenth-century office clerk."

"Do you have the ledgers?"

The jangling bells at the front door announced the arrival of a new customer, and Maxine called out to the woman who entered. "Make yourself at home."

"The ledgers." Liam growled. His patience was at an end.

"Hush, now. I don't want to miss a sale."

He grasped her arm and turned her toward him. With an effort, he kept his voice low. "I'll buy every pot, every knot and every philodendron in this store if you tell me what you're hiding."

"Who says I'm keeping a secret?"

"You don't have to be afraid, Maxine. Stuart is out of the picture. He can't hurt you or get you in trouble."

She scoffed. "Stuart Whitcomb never scared me."

"Then, who?"

"Tancredo."

Chapter Twenty

In the apartment above the store, Liam stood at the window and looked down at the foot traffic on the sidewalk in Nye Beach while he and Ava waited for Maxine to close her shop and join them. Her living space showed as much pizazz as her clothing and hairstyle. Predictably, the decor featured several hanging plants and wall hangings with polished agates and crystals woven in the strands of jute. The patterns for chairs, tablecloths and drapes ranged from wild roses to purple polka dots, to a design that looked like frenzied static.

Ava paced between the kitchenette and the entrance. She'd shed her lavender rain jacket. Somehow, she made a loose-fitting, striped blue shirt and high-rise white jeans look sexy. Or maybe that was just his interpretation.

Bursts of energy exploded from her, and he knew she was watching the clock, counting the minutes and not wanting to be late returning Fish's boat. Or feeding her brother. Her ever-responsible attitude warred with the sultry glances she lobbed in his direction, reassuring him that she was also thinking of the time they'd spend together tonight. Nearly as anxious and eager as he was to take their relationship to the next level, her every movement seemed sensual.

He stepped into her path to block her progress, and she halted midstride. Her forward momentum was such that she bumped into him. When she rested her palms on his chest to steady herself, he took advantage of the moment to embrace her and kiss her forehead. He inhaled deeply. Her curly, brown hair smelled like a garden of fragrant lilac and mint.

"Don't worry," he said. "We'll get back before dark."

"How can anybody think in the midst of this chaos?"

"Are you talking about the details of Stuart's theft or the decor in this room?"

"Both." She fidgeted in his arms. "It's amazing that Maxine was efficient enough to manage the business at Deep Dive."

"She was actually good at her job."

"Even better than you imagined." Ava tilted her head back and sighed. "After she was done with her administrative duties, she had a whole side occupation selling stolen artifacts."

And he was still furious. "When she hands over those ledgers, it's going to open another can of worms. Quincy is involved. He's going to be in serious trouble."

"As long as he stays on Georgina's good side, she'll make sure he has an excellent lawyer."

She squeezed against him. Her breasts flattened against his chest, distracting him from what she was saying. He took a moment to get back on track. "Repeat."

"The important question," she said. "Did Peter Quincy murder Stuart Whitcomb?"

He nodded. "Say more."

"If Stuart threatened to blab about fencing the salvage, Quincy might have wanted to make sure he couldn't tell anybody. Also, Quincy is famous for his hot temper."

Liam gave another nod. Her reasoning fit one of his prior theories that Quincy met Stuart on the boat with the intention of both of them talking to Liam and convincing him to sell his shares in Deep Dive. A phrase popped into his head. "Changed my mind."

"About what?" she asked.

"In one of my visions, I remembered Stuart saying those words. He changed his mind about something."

"Which might have made Quincy angry enough to strike out." Her forehead wrinkled as she considered. "I hate to say it, but Georgina's husband looks pretty good as a suspect."

"I'm not going to be too quick to judge." Maxine had more to tell them about Tancredo. "If Quincy and Stuart wanted to talk to me, why was I drugged?"

When he heard the apartment door open, he gave Ava a peck on the cheek and turned to face Maxine. Her large body wilted under the stress of the situation, but her multicolored hair was energized in an outburst of spikes and curls. When she stomped across the room and flopped onto a colorful love seat, a round orange cat who clashed with the purple polka dots leaped onto her lap and yowled.

"My poor, sweet Melon Ball. You're hungry," Maxine said. "And so am I."

"I wanted to order pizza to take back to the lighthouse," Ava said. "I'd be happy to get you something."

"A meatball sandwich and a calzone," she said. "The phone number for the Italian place on the corner is on the fridge."

While she went to place their order, Liam sat opposite Maxine, leaned forward and stared into her eyes. "I'm not leaving here without those ledgers. I'll try my hardest to keep you out of trouble. My expensive attorney can help. He needs to earn his retainer."

"You always played fair." She grinned. "Not like Stuart who was a terrible horndog, a liar and a cheat. Still, the man had lovely handwriting."

"Tell me about Tancredo."

"People don't pay much attention to the grungy, three-fingered harbormaster who smells like rotten fish. He's always there, always keeping an eye on things. The marina clients with their fancy yachts ignore him unless they have a problem. I'm guessing they consider him beneath them. And the commercial fleets, like Deep Dive, give him his due without realizing that Tancredo is a truly dangerous bastard. For years, he's worked with the drug runners from British Columbia. They're every bit as dangerous and lethal as the cartels in Mexico." She visibly shuddered. "As soon as I found out Tancredo was involved with Quincy and Stuart, I backed off. Quit my job and never looked back."

"How did you find out?"

"I had a message for Stuart. When I contacted him on the dive boat, I learned that Tancredo and Quincy were with him. I don't know for sure if they were picking up drugs for distribution or making an exchange of some sort. Frankly, I didn't want to know."

Liam had heard that Tancredo was on the boat without his knowledge. "Why wasn't I on board? Where was I?"

"Teaching or out of town. Stuart was no dummy. He always made sure you wouldn't catch a whiff of his wrongdoing."

All the sneaking around meant Stuart knew about Tancredo's drug contacts. Liam could almost understand the way Stuart dabbled in criminal activity. Fencing and theft were like a game to him. As Maxine suggested, it seemed harmless. Not as though he'd stolen a pirate chest full of gold doubloons. Drug smuggling was different.

"I've heard," Liam said, "that Tancredo provided drugs to people on the street."

Maxine shifted her bulk and Melon Ball adjusted his position, nudging her hand so she had to stroke his fur. He started purring as loudly as a motorboat. "The harbormaster isn't a drug dealer. He likes his job too much to risk it."

"I was drugged before Stuart's murder," he said. "Probably with something similar to date rape drugs, like Rohypnol. Whatever I was given absorbed quickly into my system and didn't show in a tox screen. It knocked me out. I didn't have any memory at first. Little by little, things are coming back to me."

Maxine shook her head. "I'm so sorry, Liam."

"Could Tancredo have been responsible?"

She and Melon Ball harmonized on a groan. "Yeah, Charlie Tancredo could easily lay hands on those kinds of drugs."

Liam was still having trouble visualizing the unkempt Tancredo as a wily villain. "What about the quarter of a million dollars he loaned to Stuart?"

Taken aback, she narrowed her gaze and stared. "Are you sure about that?"

Liam had found it hard to believe the first time he'd come across the loan in his preliminary research of suspects. But Tancredo himself confirmed the loan when he talked to Ava. And Holly was aware of it. A quarter of a million.

Ava bustled into the front room from the kitchen and grabbed her lavender raincoat. "Okay, I ordered three pizzas, two meatball sandwiches and four calzones."

"That should do it," Maxine said. "For me and my sweet Melon Ball."

"I'll go pick up the order," Ava said.

Liam offered, "Give me a minute, and I'll come with you."

"You stay here and finish your talk. You don't need to rush." She slipped into her coat. "I still haven't been able to contact my brother, but I called Fish and told him not to wait for us. He can take my Sonata from the garage."

He watched her dash out the door. From the time he knew her as a student until now, he'd admired her ability to multitask and organize. He wondered how that talent would play out tonight when they were finally alone.

Maxine loudly cleared her throat in a blatant attempt to get his attention. "Tell me more about this loan from Tancredo."

"The first time I heard about it was when my attorney and private eye collected data on Stuart's finances. The actual cash was difficult to trace, but the valuation was there among his assets."

Her eyebrows lifted. "I'm not altogether sure what you're saying."

"Bookkeeping isn't my strong suit," he admitted. "All I know is that Stuart used a large chunk of the loan to buy his cabin cruiser, *The Reckless*."

"I've got it!" Maxine slapped her thigh and Melon Ball jumped down. "Tancredo wasn't talking about money. Stuart had something else of his, something worth a huge amount of cash."

"Drugs?"

"Bingo." She bounced to her feet. "Now I understand. Somehow, Stuart had taken control of a valuable stash. Tancredo's merchandise."

"No wonder the harbormaster wanted him dead."

Finally, he had an answer that made sense. Stuart had been involved in double-crossing Tancredo and stealing his drug supplies. A strong motive for murder.

BACK IN FISH'S MOTORBOAT, Ava stashed the pizza feast from Bella Trattoria—minus a meatball sandwich and calzone for Maxine—in a cabinet at the helm. The food would be cold when she delivered it to her brother, but that was why microwaves were invented. As she had predicted, their meeting with Maxine ran long, and she was glad she'd told Fish to take her spare car keys from the rolltop desk and use her Sonata to drive home.

The extra time spent with Maxine Gallo had been well worth it. The flamboyant former assistant had given Liam copies of Stuart's fraudulent inventory ledgers. She'd kept the originals in the wall safe for Knots and Pots. More than the paperwork, she'd clarified the three-way axis with Stuart, Quincy and Tancredo.

While Liam expertly guided the motorboat away from the dock near Nye Beach and headed for the open sea, she reviewed the details. "Let me see if I've got it right," she said. "Stuart partnered up with Quincy, who is also in the salvage business, and the two of them siphoned off pieces of valuable freight they recovered from sunken ships."

"Stuart created a fake inventory. Certain items were never delivered to our warehouse."

"What kind of volume are we talking about?"

"Not much." He shrugged. "Both Deep Dive and Quincy's Salvage are small-time businesses. Neither of us have the heavy-duty equipment necessary for reclaiming large consignments and shipping containers."

As far as she could tell, Stuart had been taking a big risk for a relatively small reward. "Some of your finds were remarkable. Like the gold, Deco-style bracelet and brooch from the ship that went down in the 1920s."

"Not a bad haul," he said. "The jewelry was locked in a safe and belonged to some of the passengers on board. Claims were filed by heirs and estates when we recorded the salvage. The total paid by an insurance adjustor was slightly more than a hundred thousand."

"That's significant."

"And unusual," he said. "Even though maritime archeologists and anthropologists like to think of themselves as seafaring versions of Indiana Jones, we seldom recover valuable sunken treasure. Maybe only once or twice a year. I wonder if that shipwreck from the 1920s was what tempted Stuart."

"Maybe he just needed money. Holly thought so." Ava couldn't believe Stuart was broke but understood that wealthy families, like Stuart and Serena Whitcomb, often had excessive spending habits. "Your people did the research, is that true?"

"Like a lot of people, Stuart is rich with assets, but he's not liquid. Doesn't have cash in his back pocket. That's why he ran into trouble when he lost Tancredo's drugs."

This part of the story confused her. Did Stuart steal the drugs or lose them? Or was it some kind of loan? "Tell me what happened."

"Maxine and I put our heads together, and this is what we came up with." Cruising due south along the coast, the incoming tide rolled gently and the wind was calm. "Drug distributors from British Columbia used Tancredo as a dispersal point for their shipments. When it wasn't safe for them to come ashore and deal with him directly, they dropped off their cargo in an underwater preselected location, not too hard to locate with the kind of sonar we use at Deep Dive."

"How big are these packages of drugs?" she asked.

"The size could vary from a carry-on bag to a steamer trunk. The contents would have to be carefully packed and sealed to keep out moisture."

"Seems like a simple procedure. They drop it off. Later, Quincy or Stuart go out and make the pickup using their sonar equipment to guide them to the right location."

"Simple." He agreed. "Until something goes wrong."

"And Stuart loses track of a quarter-million-dollar shipment of illegal drugs."

She and Liam batted around theories of what might have happened, ranging from an outright theft by Stuart to an incorrect record of the location, to a sonar or GPS malfunction. Liam concluded, "It might be that I was using the boat for another project and Stuart couldn't get it alone."

"I don't think we'll find out unless Quincy or Tancredo tells us."

"That's not going to happen."

She leaned back in her seat and tilted her head toward the late afternoon sun in the west. The saltwater breeze cooled her skin. The low-pitched rumble of the motor created a subtle background of sound. Zipping across the waves, she enjoyed a feeling of weightlessness as though floating.

As their investigation drew to a close, her tension eased. She exhaled a long sigh and relaxed. Surely, they'd uncovered enough evidence to clear Liam of the murder charges. Though they didn't know who had come aboard *The Reckless* and bludgeoned Stuart, it had to be either Quincy or Tancredo—men with criminal intent and lots of motive.

When their little motorboat neared Cape Absolute, her gaze fixed on the lighthouse. In spite of the scrawls of graffiti, the tower stood tall and proud at the edge of the cliff. The ever-present seabirds soared from their rock and swooped above the waves. They were almost close enough to hear the barking of the sea lions. She felt like they were coming home to a special place for her and Liam.

"I'm glad this is almost over." She scooted closer to him and glided her hand down his muscular arm. "Everything turned out well."

"And it's about to get better."

He enfolded her in his arms, lowered his head and nuzzled her cheek. His stubble was scratchy, and she giggled before she flung her arms around his neck and kissed him hard. Though preoccupied with guiding the boat safely to shore, he returned her kiss. The ocean winds swirled around them, but he was hot, flaming hot. She pressed the length of her body against him, needing a full connection. Her leg straddled his thigh.

"Ava, my bright star," he whispered in a husky voice. "I've wanted this for so very long."

"Yes," she responded, unable to come up with anything

more intelligent. Now wasn't the time to be smart. Now was about pure sensation. "Yes, yes."

In a wide swoop, he circled the massive offshore rock and cut the speed so he could maneuver in the narrow space between the rock and the shore. The sound of the motor faded to a gentle putt-putt-putt. He glided the boat to a perfect stop beside the short dock.

Before they ran aground or crashed into the wood pilings, he leaped out and tied the line to the cleat. Just as quickly, he was back in the boat beside her. He gave long, lingering attention to their kiss. Tearing open her lavender rain jacket, he hauled her closer to kiss and fondle. With every touch, her body came more alive. She trembled when he nibbled at her earlobe.

More than anything, she wanted to be alone with him, to give him everything he wanted and to take his attentions in return. With huge reluctance she pulled away. Her unfocused gaze centered on his rugged features. Breathing hard, she stammered, "I—I—I gotta f-f-feed Michael. He's probably starved."

"Your brother can wait."

But she couldn't. "Open that cabinet. Give me two of the pizzas. And a calzone."

"Wait for another minute and I'll come with you."

"Bring the rest of the food." If she didn't go now, she never would. And she couldn't disappoint Michael. She'd been making dinner for her brothers since she was a kid. "Let me dash up to the cottage. I'll meet you back at the lighthouse."

She slipped the backpack with her phone over her shoulder, grabbed the food and jogged across the sand to the path leading up to the cottage. At the brink of sunset, many of the sea lions had already abandoned their rock to forage for dinner and find a warmer place to sleep. Likewise, the nesting birds were settling in for the evening.

She and Liam weren't much different from the other animals. Creatures of habit. Tonight, they'd create their own special ritual for making love. Slowly, they'd discover the secrets of their bodies. Then, in a rising crescendo, they would fulfill their mutual longing and desire.

It would be epic.

Charging up the hill, she was breathing hard as she approached the lightkeeper's cottage. In the side parking area, she saw Michael's yellow Jeep Wrangler and another vehicle. The classy, gray Escalade had vanity plates that read: MSTR Q.

Under her breath, she whispered an out-of-character curse. "Damn you, Peter Quincy."

Chapter Twenty-One

Ava couldn't believe Quincy had come here. On their way to Nye Beach, she'd left a message on his phone telling him that their scheduled meeting for tomorrow was canceled. He had no valid reason for showing his face at the lighthouse. Damn, damn, double damn, hell.

Put a lid on it. Growing up and dealing with the frequent frustration of three brothers and a sister, Ava had made a rule for herself. No swearing. Otherwise, every other word out of her mouth would be profane.

Quincy was here. And she needed to deal with him. She glanced toward the path from the beach. Liam hadn't yet appeared. Should she run back and tell him? But she'd be wasting precious time. Michael was in the house with the man who might have murdered Stuart.

Setting down the pizza boxes, she took the phone from her backpack. Her fingers hovered over the screen. Marshal Woodburn's phone number was in her contacts. She might need him for backup, but when Woodburn showed up, he'd have to take Liam into custody. A phone call to law enforcement would signal the end of the greatly anticipated, well-deserved evening in her beloved fugitive's arms.

Her first move: check out the situation and get accurate details. It was possible that Quincy and Michael were sitting and talking while they shared a beer. Circling the house, she crept up to the windows in the parlor with the big-screen television. She heard the broadcast of the Seattle Mariners baseball game. This early in the season, hopes ran high for a brilliant year. Michael had already lectured her about how the signature team for the Pacific Northwest would come through and win the World Series.

Hoping everything was normal, she searched through the construction clutter, spotted an empty ten-gallon bucket, which she hauled to the windows and flipped over. She climbed on top and peeked inside. Her brother and Fish Finley were lying on the worn carpet with hands tied behind their backs and ankles bound with gray duct tape. For a moment, her heart stopped. Were they okay? If Michael had been injured, she'd never forgive herself. She'd dragged him into this mess.

Then she saw Fish wiggle his shoulders. Michael's eyes were closed, but he was also moving. She didn't see blood. Didn't notice any kind of injury.

A gravelly voice rumbled behind her. "Step down from that bucket. No funny business."

"What have you done to them?"

She looked over her shoulder and saw Tancredo with a pistol clenched in his good hand. His presence scared her far more than an appearance by Quincy. Georgina's husband was a creep and a gold digger, but he cultivated a gentlemanly attitude as befitted the lord of the Solomon manor. Clean and well-dressed, he didn't strike immediate fear into her heart.

On the other hand, Tancredo with his stringy gray hair and grizzled jowls, looked like he'd crawled out of the sewer. Though he stood several yards away, she could smell the stench of rotted fish.

He growled and spat. "Your boys are going to be fine.

When they wake up, they won't remember what hit them. Didn't feel a damn thing."

Exactly what had happened to Liam. "You drugged them."

"You're welcome." He wheezed a chuckle. "If I hadn't knocked them out, they'd be witnesses, and I'm not stupid. I can't leave anybody behind to send me to jail."

It didn't bode well for her that he wasn't making an effort to hide his identity. Ava feared she was expendable. Looking down at the phone in her hand, she pressed the call signal for Marshal Woodburn. "What do you want from me?"

"Get down off that bucket and turn around so I can see your pretty face."

She did as he said, angling her arm behind her back so he wouldn't see her phone. She doubted Woodburn would answer but hoped his voice mail would record her message and alert him to where she was and what kind of danger she was in. Instead, someone else picked up and told her she'd reached the US Marshal Service.

Speaking loudly so her phone would pick up her voice, Ava said, "You don't scare me, Charlie Tancredo."

"Then you're a fool, Ava."

"How dare you come here to the lighthouse and threaten me. You must know there are people keeping a watch on this place, people like Marshal Woodburn." She desperately hoped her loud message was getting through. "They're looking for Dr. Liam Brody."

"What kind of game are you playing?" He took a step toward her. "You got something in your hand. Show me."

"Get away from me, Tancredo." She stepped back, putting more distance between them. "Don't point that gun at me."

"Show me your hands."

He grabbed her arm with his three-fingered hand and shook her. The phone fell to the ground. With his waterproofed, steel-toed workman's boot, he stomped the screen.

Swerving his lanky body with surprising agility, he flung her to the damp ground and aimed the barrel of his handgun at her head.

Instinct told her to close her eyes. To curl into a ball and bury her head in her arms like a child afraid of the boogeyman. But she refused to die like a coward. Ava didn't look away. Her jaw set, and her eyes focused. If she was about to die, she wanted to see the bullet coming.

He squeezed the trigger. The shot exploded.

Though she felt no pain, Ava froze. Her ears rang with the reverberation of the gunshot.

She stared at Tancredo. His baggy pants hung low on his scrawny hipbones. His filthy jacket that had once been beige was unbuttoned. Underneath, he wore a black wet suit.

"Come out, Professor," he yelled. "I want to see you now. Or the next shot goes right between her big, blue eyes."

When Liam walked around the corner of the house with hands raised, her pulse fluttered and her breath caught in her throat. She wanted to believe he'd rescue her, but it was more likely that he just signed his death warrant.

In a totally calm voice, he asked, "Where's Quincy? I see his car but don't see him."

"I don't need him. That joker has been out to hornswoggle me from the get-go."

"Did you steal his car?"

"Don't need his damn luxury vehicle. I came here in my inflatable. That boat gets me around just fine." He waved his gun in Liam's direction. "You, of all people, should know that."

"You killed Stuart."

"Shut the hell up," Tancredo yelled.

She watched Liam's face change expression. He went from rage to comprehension and back to anger. "It was you on *The Reckless*. Finally, I recognize your voice."

Ava scrambled to her feet and ran to him. She pressed

herself against him so tightly that she could feel the interplay of muscles in his chest and breathe in his masculine scent. Everything about him was so right. Together, they were near perfection.

Tancredo made his wheezing cackle. "I knew you'd remember. It was only a matter of time. The amnesia from those drugs doesn't last forever, and I saw you watching while Stuart and I were going at each other."

"You shouted," Liam said. "I heard your words grate in the back of your throat before you bludgeoned him. I witnessed the murder."

"Real clever, Professor. Give yourself a gold star." His lip curled in a sneer. "Stuart Whitcomb got what he deserved. Payback was long overdue."

Ava remembered Tancredo's grudge against the Whitcomb family. He blamed the grandfather for cheating Stuart's ancestor out of what should have been his rightful inheritance. The harbormaster must have been nursing that hostility his whole life. He even blamed Stuart for the loss of his fingers. "Is this about what happened to your grandfather?"

"That and more. This was about the loan."

"The drugs," Liam said. "Call it what it was. Not an aboveboard loan but lethal narcotics. Somehow Stuart swindled you out of a significant amount of illegal drugs."

"I'm not sure if he meant to cheat me or if he just wasn't good at handling the sonar equipment." Tancredo gestured with the gun. "Go that way, down to the shore. We're going to take a little cruise."

Ava didn't like where this story was leading. "What do you want from us?"

"Your boyfriend is going to have a chance to play the hero," he said. "We're going on a treasure hunt. We'll go to the harbor, pick up his dive boat and head out to sea."

"To retrieve your lost shipment of drugs," Liam said.

"Figured it out, did you? You're a hell of a lot smarter than Whitcomb. I should have hooked up with you instead of your partner. You're going to get into your boat, read the GPS data and take me where I want to go."

Ava couldn't believe this. Was that supposed to be a compliment? As if Liam would agree to help Tancredo and drug runners from the north. His sick appreciation disgusted her. When he waved his gun again, Liam refused to move. She felt his muscles tense and prayed he wouldn't do anything that caused Tancredo to attack.

Gently, he moved her away from him and turned to face Tancredo. "Why the hell do you think I'd help you?"

"If you don't, Ava will pay the price. She'll die slowly. My first shot will tear off two fingers on her left hand. She'll share my pain."

More than the pain, she feared Tancredo's cruelty. He'd kill them both. In her mind, their only chance came from staying alive as long as possible, hoping that Woodburn got the message and came racing to their rescue. "Let's go, Liam."

Tancredo wheezed a laugh. "You heard the lady. She goes first down the path, then you follow. Me and my .44 Magnum will bring up the rear."

Forcing herself not to falter, she struck out toward the path leading down to the beach. The steep, rocky incline wasn't easy to descend in the semidarkness as dusk fell, and she moved cautiously. Somehow, she needed to talk to Liam and tell him not to resist. She'd summoned backup and had to believe Marshal Woodburn would be here.

But Liam had ideas of his own. He moved up quickly behind her and caused her to stumble. As he helped her up, he whispered, "When I give the signal, run like hell for the far end of the beach. I'll deal with Tancredo."

"You can't take him. He's got a gun."

"Run as fast as you can. Don't look back."

Desperately, she said, "I won't leave you."

Gunfire blasted behind them, and Tancredo yelled, "Break it up, you two."

He shoved away from her. "You can do this. I love you."

No, no, no, no. This wasn't supposed to happen this way. They were supposed to spend a splendid night together and declare their intentions.

She staggered forward. When she reached the bottom of the path and her feet hit sand, the few sea lions on the rock set up a racket, distracting Tancredo. The gulls circled and cried out as they watched the drama.

Liam called to her, "Go, Ava. Now."

Without thinking, she burst into a sprint. Her back prickled, and she feared she'd be shot at any moment. She heard Liam struggling with Tancredo. Faster, she needed to go faster. She dodged to the edge of the surf where the sand was firmly packed.

In the distance, she saw the inflatable boat Tancredo had hauled ashore. His timing was bad. The incoming tide lapped at the edge of his craft.

She heard a loud moan, someone crying for help. And she turned toward the rocky shore. A long, weathered driftwood log rested near the hillside. A person sprawled against it. His blood-covered hand reached toward her and then fell to his side.

She recognized Quincy. A harpoon from a spear gun stuck out from his upper chest. Tancredo must have shot him and left him there to bleed out. Her horror faded to silence when she spotted the handgun on the sand beside him.

Quincy's head slumped forward onto his chest. Barely conscious, he was too weak to move, but his gun might be their salvation. She dashed toward him and scooped up the weapon, which was much bigger and harder to handle than her neon pink Glock.

Unsure of how to handle the weapon and wishing she'd taken lessons on marksmanship, she spun around. Down the beach, she saw Liam and Tancredo locked in a hand-to-hand struggle. The heavy weapon hung loosely in her hand. She couldn't fire at Tancredo without endangering Liam.

Instead, she aimed at the sky and let go with four shots. The noise echoed across the Pacific like thunder. Both combatants turned toward her.

Liam took advantage of the distraction to deliver a ferocious blow to the old man's jaw. Tancredo's legs crumpled, and he went down. Liam ripped the gun from his good hand.

She raced toward them, watching as Liam lowered the barrel of the gun to aim at the scrawny chest of the grizzled, old harbormaster. She flung herself into his arms.

Not taking his eyes off Tancredo, he kissed the top of her head. "We won."

"I love you, too."

But they wouldn't spend tonight together. Marshal Woodburn led a posse of law enforcement officers onto the path and down to the beach. He took charge of arresting Tancredo and summoning ambulances and EMTs to help Quincy as well as her brother and Fish. After he disarmed Liam and took her gun, he regretfully cuffed Liam.

"Sorry, Professor."

"I never meant to be this much trouble."

"Sure you did." Woodburn grinned and smoothed his thick, gray mustache. "Was it worth it? Did you find what you were looking for?"

He gazed into Ava's eyes. "Everything I wanted and more."

Three weeks later...

THE MURDER CHARGES against Liam were dropped, but he was still under house arrest for violating his parole. He'd pleaded guilty and fully expected to be sentenced with a heavy fine and community service for his days as a fugitive. No price was too high. The time he'd spent with Ava changed his life for the better.

Marshal Woodburn didn't bother with handcuffs when he drove Liam from the jail to his mid-century modern home in the hills outside Eugene. "You can't ever tell anyone I admitted this," he said, "but I'm proud of your investigation. Your evidence put Tancredo out of business, and the harbormaster rolled over for the DEA and exposed a ring of narcotics dealers and smugglers."

Liam nodded. "My goal was justice for Stuart, but I'm glad for the more far-reaching benefits."

Quincy's injury put him in the hospital for two solid weeks, but he didn't seem to have permanent damage. And Georgina had taken him back. Charges against him were still pending, and he'd probably never use that fence in Portland again. With help from Liam's pricy attorney, Maxine's involvement in fencing had been pretty much erased in exchange for her ledgers filled with proof of wrongdoing.

Fish Finley had been running Deep Dive for the past three weeks, ably assisted by Oliver Whitcomb. Both were turning out to be great assets, capable of keeping things operating when Liam got back to work at the university or went far afield to do research.

He stretched his shoulders and gazed through the windshield at the spring landscape. Fresh green leaves of trees and shrubs were highlighted by blooming rhododendrons in vivid purple, yellow, white and orange. Fluffy clouds hung low over the peaks of the wooded Cascades. The incredible, natural beauty of the land surrounding his home excited him, but the joy surging through him came from a different source. Finally, he would see Ava. He'd hold her in his arms. Tonight, they would finally—finally!—make love.

She'd been quick to forgive him, though she'd been

charged with aiding and abetting a fugitive and pleaded guilty. Her sentence—expected to be a hefty fine and parole—would be decided later. She'd visited him twice in jail before they decided it was too frustrating to see each other and not be able to touch. He had planned for this reunion, including the purchase of a perfect diamond engagement ring that Woodburn had kept safe for him. For hours every day, Liam practiced how he would propose to her.

Paused at a stoplight, Woodburn said, "I want you to know, Liam, that you really aren't a criminal mastermind and local law enforcement isn't completely inept. With the possible exception of Jess-hole."

"You knew about his nickname?"

"I know about everything."

Liam immediately understood. "You were watching while we solved the crime. You gave me a chance to prove my innocence."

"And if you tell anybody, I'll deny it." He reached into his jacket pocket and produced a small velvet box. "I expect you're going to need this before you see Ava."

"Is she waiting at the house?"

"Couldn't keep her away. She said something about serving you a dinner that was cooked by her sister, Rachel, the blue-ribbon baker."

"Great." Food wasn't the first thing on his mind.

"I'll stop by tomorrow to hook up your ankle bracelet. Don't leave the property."

With Ava here, he had no other place he wanted to be. As they cruised through the forest surrounding his house, he saw her on the front porch. She waved with both arms and charged at the car as soon as Woodburn parked.

He caught her on the fly and held her. Overwhelmed, he absorbed the moment. Finally, they were together, the way they had always been meant to be.

Though he'd intended to wait until after dinner when the sun was setting behind the mountains and a soft breeze tickled the leaves, Liam didn't make it any farther than the front porch. He dropped to one knee. On the flat of his hand, he held the velvet box. Gently, he opened the lid and took out the ring.

She pulled back her hand. "Wait."

"Something wrong?" His throat was dry. "What is it, Ava?"

"We have to wait until after Christmas."

"Why?"

"The renovations will be done by then. I want to get married in the lighthouse."

"I wouldn't have it any other way."

He slipped the ring on her finger.

* * * * *

MISTAKEN IDENTITIES

TARA TAYLOR QUINN

For my two siblings, the one I lost and the
one I am so lucky to spend my life knowing.
Chum, you are always loved and never forgotten.
Scott, I cherish every single memory we make.
I love you, little brother.

Chapter One

Anxiety slid through her like a snake. One Savannah Compton mentally beheaded as she neared the airport turnoff. She watched her rearview mirror as much to find a clear path to get over as to remind herself that the make and model of the black sedan that had kept distance with her since she'd left the Grand Rapids neighborhood was as common as they came.

And the woman behind the wheel bore no resemblance to the driver of the blue SUV that she'd thought she'd seen a few times the day before.

Being a partner in a nationally renowned firm of experts that spent a lot of time fighting crime took its toll. One she'd handled without a blip until her partner and friend, Dorian Lowell, had been kidnapped the year before. The medical expert had been found unharmed and had come through harrowing days lost in the mountains, running from high-powered killers, managing to keep a newborn baby safe the whole time.

But that kidnapping…plus, just months before—Dorian being taken off her normal hiking trail, just around the corner from her home, to be found days later unharmed. Savannah still had moments of residual stress.

Mostly when she felt her most vulnerable, emotionally

alone, as she did pulling into the Grand Rapids, Michigan, airport on her way to San Diego, California.

Not back to the Sierra's Web home office in Phoenix, where she'd spend a day or two with the friends who'd become her only family. Or on to another job. Her norm.

No, she—savvy, smart, sophisticated expert lawyer that she was—had decided to fly off willy-nilly into an abyss layered in darkness. Beneath the glaring California sun.

Alone.

Kelly Chase, the firm's expert psychiatrist, had official names for the butterflies that swarmed Savannah's stomach when she let herself think about certain things.

Or when she imagined she was being followed.

And if Kelly had been with her right then—or even knew what she was about to do—her friend would most definitely understand the slight presence of paranoia continuing to ride on Savannah's shoulders as she dropped off her rental car and headed into the terminal.

Certain that the black sedan had been at the rental return two down from her.

After Dorian's kidnapping, all seven of the Sierra's Web partners had reached a mutual agreement to undergo training for things like noticing tails and awareness of their surroundings in general. They'd pledged to visit the gun range on a regular basis, too. Savannah had been first to vote. To sign up. And to master the course.

And the whole thing had made her afraid of her own shadow sometimes.

Thankfully not all that often. She had it under control. Went days or even weeks without a single moment of anxious discomfort.

But when she was out of her comfort zone…

The airport wasn't the problem. She flew almost as often as she drove. Once inside, Savannah dropped off her bag, headed through her priority security line, and stopped for a glass of wine before heading to her gate. Without once looking over her shoulder.

Where she was headed, what she was about to do wasn't the most logical choice she'd ever made. Far from it.

She remembered backward two and a half decades, to the murder and kidnapping that had changed everything—a terror Dorian's much more recent abduction had brought back full force.

It didn't take an expert psychiatrist or even an expert lawyer to figure out that moments of anxiety were to be expected and dealt with accordingly.

Maybe all it took was an acknowledgment of the seven-year-old girl she'd once been, who still lived inside her. The one who'd held on to what was, refusing to let go while moving forward with absolute focus, one step at a time.

Fear wouldn't win. It wouldn't rob her of joy. Of life.

Or of the chance to see her baby sister again.

No matter how big the two of them had grown.

The timing wasn't up to her.

The determination, the refusal to quit, the never-ending search…those had been within her control. Choices she'd made. They were part of the person she'd become that day so long ago.

And why there was no choice but to board the plane when her flight was called, in spite of her tension, then buckle herself in.

And wait.

"Seriously, Isaac. I've been doing these guest lectures since way before you came on board. There's no reason for you to tag along…"

Behind the wheel of the black limousine in which they were traveling, undercover FBI special agent Isaac Forrester figured himself as the driver of the situation, not the follower, but sent the beautiful, soft-spoken, wise-beyond-her-years suspect a shrug and easy smile. "Much less inconvenient standing in the wings hearing about women's studies than appearing in front of your father to explain why I wasn't standing in the wings," he said to her.

"Daddy doesn't have to know."

But somehow the older man would—know, that was. Every movement his daughter made. And, more recently, every movement her bodyguard made as well.

He'd suspect his cover had been blown. Except that there was no way the powerful businessman would leave Isaac alone with his precious Charlotte, let alone charge him with keeping her safe, if Eduardo Duran had even a hint of an inkling that Isaac wasn't who he said he was.

But to that end, he didn't have a second to waste. He'd been in Duran's employ as personal protection director and lead personal guard for Duran's only child since late fall— a long two months—and could feasibly continue on far into the spring. But he had no intention of being that bad at his job. He'd spent nearly a year in and around the transplanted Salvadoran, building trust, laying groundwork so that when Duran's previous personal protection director had suddenly had to leave his post, Isaac had been the obvious choice to step in.

"Please, Isaac?"

Stopped at a light, Isaac turned to see Charlotte's big brown eyes staring at him with more than just a casual desire to not have her bodyguard attached to her back during the morning's university lecture.

Every nerve in his body shot to attention, every muscle honed, as, light turning green, he pulled into a small cul-de-sac not far from their destination. And pinned his charge with a look most often reserved for the interrogation room.

To her credit, Charlotte didn't look away. Or even seem to blink. Her long dark hair pulled into its usual bun gave her unlined face no cover.

And as hard as he looked, he saw no subterfuge there.

They had proof that the woman's unique coding signature had been used on a suspicious bank transfer from a US investment group to an untraceable source outside the states.

With three doctorate degrees at twenty-five, one of which was in information technology, Charlotte had already made a name for herself in the field with a program she'd written to help monitor generative AI use and inconsistencies.

She swore, though, that she had no interest in a career in technology. Her true love was ethnography and autoethnography—or, as she put it when breaking it down in her lectures to undergrads, studying individual cultures and how women's personal experiences connected with a global picture of social meanings and understandings.

Studies that were mostly above his pay grade. Or typical intellectual pursuits, at the very least.

Isaac's brain didn't trust anything Charlotte Duran said. His gut, though... When she met his gaze so sincerely, she reminded him of the little sister who'd once adored him.

And had grown to hate him.

"Tell me what's really going on," he said. They were early for her lecture. Early everywhere, always, so he had a chance to check out the surroundings to his satisfaction.

She knew he'd take the time to sit there until she grew nervous about being late and opted to talk.

And could be, in that very second, concocting some smoke screen to distract him.

"I plan to feel really sick right as the event is starting— something I ate—and slip out the side door before anyone in the audience is aware that the lecture is about to be canceled."

She was telling him she was going to ditch him, whether

he liked it or not? The woman was scary smart. Intelligent enough to know that he was far better at, and more knowledgeable of, his game than she'd ever be. That he had skills she didn't even know about.

Which told him that it wasn't him she was running from.

Or...that was what she wanted him to think she was telling him.

"And you were going to go where? To do what?" he asked. Curious, engaged in her determination in spite of himself.

She continued to hold his gaze as she told him, "I was going to wait in the women's restroom in the lobby of the dormitory half a block away and make my way back to the auditorium in time to meet up with you and catch my ride home."

"To what end?" He had to know.

He *wanted* to know, too. Two months living in the woman's back pocket and he still didn't have a workable profile of her.

He hadn't found an iota of hold-up-in-court evidence to arrest her and, through her, bring down one of the largest international criminals around. Eduardo Duran had ties to everything from arms dealing and illegal art sales to large-scale shipping thefts.

"Arnold Wagar is going to be there."

Another name on Isaac's list. He forced himself to continue to appear relaxed as he tuned in with every sense he had.

"To report on your lecture to your father?" He didn't for one second think that was the reason. But because he had no idea why on earth a banker who had ties to a high-profile, disgustingly wealthy international criminal would be at a women's studies lecture, he played ignorant. Hoping to find out.

"No. To see me."

Ah. Forcing his breathing to remain normal, Isaac fought the urge to grab the woman's hand and try to convince her that if she came clean, he could help her.

No way he was risking his cover. Not without the ability to guarantee her father would be locked away for the rest of his life.

Nor was he in the habit of making promises he didn't intend to keep.

"My father told me last night that he expects me to marry the man," Charlotte said, her brown eyes seeming to darken further as she slowly shook her head. "I'd do almost anything for my father, Isaac," she said then, her voice not quite breaking but sounding like it might at any second. "My whole life, it's been just him and me." Her gaze implored him to understand.

He wasn't sure if she was honestly seeking to have him see the relationship or hoping that he'd agree not to see things that could hurt her beautiful life.

"He was always there for me. Always. Every Christmas he spent with me. Whether at home or traveling, we were together. There was always a tree. And he always managed to get me the one thing I wanted more than anything but hadn't mentioned. When he was in town, we ate together, at least one meal a day. And when he was gone, no matter how important his meetings, even with heads of states, he called me every morning and every night." She barely took a breath as she continued to unload on Isaac, who didn't take his eyes off her. "I got my first doctorate degree in technology because that was what he wanted," she said then, stabbing at Isaac with another piece of the proof that showed him the truth of what so many knew—without giving him tangible evidence to take to court.

Duran had been one of the first to use Bitcoin, a highly technological form of payment, and had grown even wealthier from the intricate tunnels of virtually untraceable means he'd used to amass his fortune there.

Untraceable unless, say, the daughter who'd devised them gave them up.

"I've agreed to live at home, for my supposed safety and his peace of mind, even though I'm technically free to move out at any time. And agreed to a bodyguard when Daddy explained that he'd rest much easier if I'd do that for him. I do most of my various work projects online, as I did a lot of my schooling as well, also for security purposes. And I let his people—you now—vet the few real friends I have before inviting them into our midst. I have never once even tried to sneak out to party. I don't do drugs. And the few times I've actually liked a guy enough and he liked me enough to put up with my father's overbearing protectiveness, I always insisted on condoms during sex…"

TMI. Issaac almost looked away at that one. Thankfully his nearly forty years, and two decades of police work, had prepared him to keep a steady expression no matter what he heard.

"But this…" Charlotte's gaze was definitely moist when she paused, wringing her hands for a second before clasping them together. "I will not marry a man I don't love," she said. "Not even for Daddy. I don't care how decent and kind and rich he is. I don't even care that he adores me. The thought of Arnold Wagar's hands on me makes my skin crawl. The man's practically old enough to be my father." Wagar was only four years older than Isaac's thirty-seven, but who was counting?

"And besides—" Charlotte finally looked away, her gaze pointing out the front windshield "—I'm not even sure I want to *get* married," she spoke into the silence of the car, surprising Isaac. "I'm beginning to realize that I've been under Daddy's thumb for so long, I'm not ever sure I know what *I* want."

In the two months he'd been walking practically hand in hand with the only Duran offspring, he'd never seen her show a moment of doubt. Of weakness. Or vulnerability.

She was sass and teasing and brimming over with confidence. The perfectly well-adjusted child of a very bad man.

A man Isaac had yet to be able to arrest.

He'd found a lot of substantive evidence that he and his team were on the right track. As had other teams before them, both foreign and domestic, including the CIA. But now that Duran was a US citizen and a very important piece of forensic work had pinpointed Charlotte's technological coding signature, Isaac had been charged with doing what no others before him, including Salvadoran compatriots, had been able to do.

Bring down an international nightmare.

Even if it meant taking the precocious twenty-five-year-old genius down with him.

HAVING GRADUATED WITH a law degree at twenty-two, Savannah was used to relying on her mind for all important learning. She was a critical thinker. Made decisions based on logic, not emotion. But when she heard the announcement that the nonstop flight she was on from Michigan to San Diego was suddenly making an unscheduled landing at the Denver airport, she nearly allowed her fear to convince her to cancel her secret plans.

What was she thinking? Flying off to San Diego without a word to anyone? Lying to her best friends, who were the only family she had, about taking a long overdue vacation to cruise the Bahamas in an expensive suite for which she'd paid months before—and that was currently sailing empty on a very large ship filled with revelers. Her would-be vacation mates.

But while ordinarily the lie would have been a shock to her system, in the one instance before her, it was not. From the age of seven, she'd lived with one particular lie. A matter of life and death, as proven by her father's murder.

A lie put upon her by the people who little-girls-whose-fathers-had-died were taught to trust above all others. Her mother. And the police.

National statistics, she'd been told, understanding even then what that meant, showed that in the history of witness protection not one person who followed all guidelines was breached. They were all safe. She and her mother and sister—in absentia—were in the program for being associated with a witness on a case, but her father had been a witness. And he'd broken protocol to stop by Nicole's daycare and tell the one-year-old goodbye...

She thought that the flight was perhaps landing to tend to someone with an emergency. Though, looking around her, she couldn't see anyone in distress—nor had the attendants made any announcement about a medical emergency. Normally they would call for any medical personnel on the flight who could possibly assist until the plane was on the ground. Savannah was fully engaged in talking down her own paranoia by the time the wheels actually did touch down.

"Ladies and gentlemen, we need to ask all of you to leave your belongings and deboard the plane as efficiently as possible, starting with row one." As soon as she heard the steward's voice, Savannah pulled her purse onto her shoulder and reached for her phone, finger on Kelly Chase's speed dial icon. Just in case.

In the event she had a full-blown panic attack and needed her friend's expert advice.

Or...more likely...there'd been some kind of report of a

bomb or other dangerous material on the plane. Sierra's Web would be able to access accurate information within minutes, which would put a stop to Savannah's over-the-top anxiety.

She never should have lied to her partners.

But how could she tell them that she'd had a hit on her own familial DNA, submitted under an assumed name and a fake email, which indicated a sibling match. She couldn't confess without possibly putting herself, her partners or, just as bad, her sister in harm's way.

Until she knew that Nicole was safe—hopefully having been sold in a black-market kidnapping to a desperate but loving couple who'd tried every other way to have a child—Savannah couldn't let anyone know who she was. Or who Nicole was, either, for that matter.

Witness protection protocol, and the best hope of keeping them both safe, demanded it.

Which meant when she got to San Diego, she couldn't approach her sister. Or even let it be known that she knew who Nicole—going by the name of Charlotte Duran—was.

All passengers had been led to an empty gate area at the far end of the terminal. There were bathrooms just across the hall for their use. They were instructed not to leave the area or risk missing what was expected to be a very quick reboard process.

Phone still in hand, Savannah took a seat along the back wall. She needed to be able to see any and everything that might be taking place among the members of her flight—crew and passengers alike.

Were any of them suspicious looking?

Or watching her suspiciously?

Had there been a bomb scare? That's why no one had been allowed to bring their carry-on luggage?

A man about her age, dressed casually in shorts and a but-ton-down shirt, sat across and down from her, turning to the woman next to him—his wife, Savannah surmised, based on the identical wedding rings—and proceeded to spend the next full minute or more detailing a fairly complicated plot devised by someone to steal all of the valuables from the bags the passengers had been ordered to leave behind. The tale grew so far-fetched, and yet television worthy, with every counterpoint his wife brought up to his suppositions that Savannah might have been distracted from her own uneasiness long enough to rediscover her calm. If not for the two uniformed law enforcement officers she'd noticed taking away first one and then another of her fellow fliers.

Had they been surly looking characters, she might have felt relieved—safer, even. But so far the four parties she'd seen led away had been an elderly gentleman with a cane, a woman with two little children, a guy in professional dress who looked to be in his twenties, and one of the flight crew. None of them had returned.

Two middle-aged women, obviously traveling together, were approached by one of the officers.

Had all the people being carted off come from some other airport, just transferring planes in Grand Rapids? Could be there was a problem with transferred luggage. They all had to have something in common. Maybe they'd already been on the plane when she and the others in Grand Rapids had boarded…

"Miss, can you come with me, please?" Savannah's head swung toward the deep voice. She'd been so stuck on the two women being escorted away to her right that she'd missed the officer coming up her aisle on the left.

"Me?" she asked, heart pounding, phone in hand. She didn't know any of those people. Hadn't done anything.

Except be the recipient of a report from a public DNA family-finder source. And then use a public computer in Grand Rapids, logged in only as an anonymous guest, to look up the address that the donor had permitted to be given only to a close familial match.

She stood when the officer stopped in front of her, waiting, and followed him down the terminal to a smaller hallway.

Savannah hadn't made the choice to have her information known to anyone when she'd submitted her DNA. No way. After more than a decade with Sierra's Web and in courts all around the country, she knew far too much about the criminal portion of the world to put her information out into the ether. She'd submitted anonymously.

Had checked the database without any expectation of finding something. Had done so just to rule out the possibility, so she'd quit thinking about it.

A little work from there had gained her the rest. Only because this person, a woman who called herself Charlotte Duran, had permitted her information to be shared.

Savannah had discovered that the woman's father was a successful businessman with a conglomerate of companies he'd amassed through buyouts over the years.

"I haven't done anything wrong," she said the second she was shown into a small room with a table and chairs and asked to take a seat.

She didn't sit. "I'm a lawyer," she said next, keeping the understatement in that message to herself. "And don't intend to say anything until I call my own attorney."

It wasn't like her to start out on the defense. At all. The reminder came a little late. Still, she paid it heed. If she'd somehow triggered something to someone from a quarter-of-a-century-old murder just by looking up an address she'd been given, she had to be at the top of her game.

Not losing it.

On the other hand, if there'd been a bomb scare—or any

other type of threat, for that matter—she and her firm of
experts might be able to help.

Savannah took a seat at the table.

Chapter Two

Isaac wasn't at all surprised when he got a summons to report to Eduardo Duran's home office. He'd made an executive decision that morning, doing the job he'd set out for himself—to build trust with the daughter to get to the father. He'd taken Charlotte to the lecture and had whisked her offstage immediately afterward, citing a potential safety risk, getting her to the car and heading off the lot before Arnold Wagar had had a chance to get out of the audience and out to his car.

And he'd ordered her not to answer her phone. That one had been a no-brainer. Her father had told her, explicitly, to do whatever Isaac said to do. Charlotte was off the hook.

Isaac had, in one small move, won more of the young woman's loyalty than he'd been able to gain in more than two months of guarding her every move.

Facing the wrath of a man he despised was a small price to pay for the large step toward putting a man he believed to be a cold-blooded killer, among other heinous crimes, away for life.

Isaac had seen names on accounts that all disappeared into the same ether. Had recognized one of them as a hired assassin.

He stood ready to give a detailed account of the bogus

threat he'd supposedly seen in the theater that morning because he couldn't use the true threat—a forty-year-old man buying his way into illegal wealth while sacrificing a young genius. He waited in front of Duran's impressively large solid-wood desk, in his standard black pants and jacket, hands on top of one another at his beltline. His gun was invisible beneath the suit coat but fully accessible to Isaac.

A position of docility and readiness at the same time.

The older man, in his usual suit and tie—blue that afternoon—remained seated and, with a nod, dismissed his own protection detail. Isaac caught a hint of the steps of two of the men he—as head of protection detail—managed, on the soft carpet behind him. And heard the heavy pine door close with an authoritative click.

So it was going to be personal.

And Isaac had some kissing up to do. He couldn't afford to lose the job. It wasn't like his little trust-building exercise that morning was going to bring Charlotte Duran running in to confess all of her and "Daddy's" illegal deeds once Isaac was back at his Washington, DC, office.

"Have a seat," Duran said, his tone all business but…more respectful than Isaac had expected. With no obvious hint of animosity in verbiage, delivery or even body language. The man nodded toward one of the two oversized wooden chairs on either side of where Isaac stood.

Bracing himself for the unexpected, not relaxing his guard even a little bit, Isaac sat. Elbows on the arms of the chair, hands on his thighs.

"I have reason to believe that someone is poking around in my daughter's business," the man started in, and Isaac nodded, remaining silent out of seeming respect. Waiting to hear what the man had to say.

While trying to guess how Duran was going to bring the conversation around to Wagar. And, more, how he'd attempt to manipulate Isaac's support in his plan to see his daughter married to the man of his choice.

The latter was most important to Isaac. He'd be skating a slippery slope. To hold on to his job—and his cover—with the man who was, for all intent and purposes, his boss, he'd have to agree to Duran's mandates. And to continue to build the loyalty that was his surest bet of doing his job and making the world a safer place, he had to protect Charlotte from the unwanted attention.

"I'm a powerful man." Duran's tone had grown darker.

A reminder issued.

"This gives me the ability to provide my only offspring with the best of the best. But it also makes her vulnerable to any number of evils lurking in this world."

A pot calling the kettle black, if ever Isaac had heard one. He had no trouble maintaining his facade. He'd faced more than his share of wealthy, powerful despicable men in his decorated career. Including a politician who'd greased a lot of homegrown hands, but ones in other worlds as well, before Isaac had been finally able to get evidence that the man couldn't buy his way out of. His compatriots had come swarming like flies to testify against him rather than be caught in his web.

"My intel says that a client of a woman is looking to prove that my Charlotte has a biological relative here in the States. This woman, Savannah Compton, is a lawyer, a partner in a firm of experts out of Phoenix—Sierra's Web. Further investigation shows that the firm has worked with various law enforcement agencies around the country, including the FBI..."

Isaac's outward demeanor didn't change. But he was suddenly thankful for the jacket, which hid the fact that he was sweating. Wagar out; nationally renowned firm of experts in.

He'd never personally worked with Sierra's Web, but he'd certainly heard of them. And had to call his superior immediately to warn the firm away from the Durans lest they lose over a year of work and create untold future risk to national security.

A call he couldn't make while maintaining the cover that would allow him to prevent, or at least greatly lessen, that risk.

Which made it a hell of a lot harder to sit there. One client out to scam a wealthy man versus arms dealing? He'd get the firm off Duran's back.

And maybe win himself a gold medal or two with the older man.

"I had a law enforcement friend of mine call the firm. They claim that Ms. Compton is on vacation. My friend talked to another one of the partners, someone she worked with personally, who swore that Savannah is not working a case for Sierra's Web."

So much for the phone call. "Did your...associate...believe that?"

"She did," Eduardo Duran said. "She worked a particularly tough child-abduction case with the firm and has an excellent rapport with them. She went on to say that this Savannah hasn't been herself in the past year or so, which is why the partners were all relieved when she booked the cruise."

A partner gone rogue. From burnout?

Or buyout?

Either way, while the woman posed a potential inconvenience to Isaac, she wasn't the problem he'd at first thought.

Rogue, he could handle.

Maybe even use to his advantage if the woman's supposed threat created a way for Isaac to get more access to Duran's day-to-day business dealings. He would need to be present during Charlotte Duran's classified conversations, for instance.

His mind spun with possibilities as he listened to the older man's theory that the expert lawyer was working a case outside the firm, probably because it had criminal overtones and she'd known the firm wouldn't agree to take it on.

"The phone call I received this morning indicated that this Compton woman's client is intending to mooch millions from me through Charlotte."

Millions. Even if the lawyer made just a quarter of that, it was one case, a week or two, that would pay Ms. Compton far more than she'd make in a year or two at the firm.

"I assume you're issuing a payoff with a stringent non-contact order and nondisclosure document attached to it..."

"I was going to. Changed my mind until I know more," Duran stated, but the furrow in his brow did not bode well. "I had an *interrogator* at the Denver airport this morning. Savannah Compton isn't on her way to board a cruise. She's on a flight to San Diego. One that had an impromptu lay-over in Denver. During which she claimed that she'd taken a short leave from her firm, and from her career, to vacation at the ocean."

"So your intel was wrong." Which led Isaac to wonder why he was taking part in this conversation. What did Duran really want from him?

How was he being manipulated?

And did the man own the entire country? Who had large enough clout to bring down a plane to question one passenger for his own personal business?

"No. My information was spot on," Duran said. "I had a search engine designed to pick up any search of this address and alert my team in real time when it happened. This time we got lucky enough to have a camera nearby," he finished, turning around a thirty-two-inch screen to show Isaac a grainy security-camera image of a woman in expensive-looking gray slacks and an orange sweater seated at a computer screen. Obviously, Isaac was to assume that the woman was Savannah Compton. A man like Duran would have verified that before bringing a lower-level employee like Isaac into his confidence.

When Duran enlarged the image, Isaac could see the Duran address, listed under Charlotte's name, in the search field.

"Charlotte owns this place?" Isaac's question was probably not the first one he should have asked.

"I have right of occupation for life," Duran told him, sliding his screen back around. "I moved her here when she was in her teens. She had dual citizenship as her mother was American born and traveled back and forth between the States and our home in El Salvador to take care of the elderly grandparents who raised her. Charlotte favored her mother in looks and had always yearned to live in California. When she turned eighteen, she sponsored my own citizenship."

That part Isaac had known.

"And what about her mother?" While he had no idea why Duran was being so uncharacteristically forthcoming and had his guard up, with full sensory reinforcements, he couldn't waste the chance to learn more.

Every fact, no matter how seemingly insignificant, had a place in the puzzle. One tiny piece could join everything else together. Or be the glue that held things in place so the entire picture could be seen.

"Amy died in childbirth, God rest her soul. She was such a beautiful, loving, gentle woman…"

For a second there, Isaac stared. The genuine grief on Duran's face shocked him. Until he reminded himself that the man was so successful because there were parts of him that were truly likeable. Authentic.

Proven by the millions he gave to children's charities every year.

And the way he doted on his daughter.

Never missing a Christmas…

"Her grandparents both passed within a year of Charlotte's birth, and Amelia had no other family," Duran said then, his demeanor returning to the hard, businesslike persona with which Isaac was most familiar. "Both of her parents were only children and were killed in a car accident when Amy was ten. So, you see, there's no way my daughter could possibly have a close biological family member. This is an attempt to get to her, convince her that her heart's desire to have family on her mother's side is coming to fruition, to worm their way in to my fortune through her."

"So why not get more from this morning's questioning?"

"When my contact called, relaying what was going on during the airport meeting, I had them let the Compton woman go. She's not going to be truthful. Which means we're going to have to let her get close enough to figure out who she's working for and what their game plan might be."

And that was where he came in. The point of the meeting became clear. "How close do you want me to let her get to Charlotte?"

"I don't want her anywhere near my daughter."

The man would have someone else dealing with the Compton woman, he translated.

"Am I to approach her if she's in our vicinity?"

Duran stared him the eye. Isaac held on with no effort at all. "I leave that to you," the boss said with a nod. "I'm trusting you with my daughter's life. And I trust you to handle this threat to it, if the occasion arises."

Isaac nodded back. Discussed a couple of minor details with the man regarding what Charlotte was to know about the situation—nothing at all.

And then took his leave, with the man's last words of trust still ringing in his ears. If he'd heard correctly, and he had no doubts that he had, Eduardo Duran had just ordered him to kill Savannah Compton if the need arose.

Another piece of information that fit perfectly into Isaac's portfolio on the criminal.

Added to all the others that would never stand up in court.

SAVANNAH HAD NO idea what law enforcement had really been after in Denver. Bomb scare. Terrorist on board. Or something as simple as a suspected stowaway. What she did know was that as soon as she'd identified herself and her position within Sierra's Web, she'd become one of them.

As much as one could be from the outside looking in.

Sierra's Web had worked with the Denver FBI office. And probably the local police as well. They were known. And as soon as she'd let them know she was on vacation, heading to the ocean for some much-needed R & R, they'd let her go.

Maybe if she'd said she was working, they'd have filled her in more. As it was, she took the Denver stop as a mental note to self to get herself in check.

Just because she was going to try to see her baby sister, to ensure, if nothing else, that Nicole—using the fake name of Charlotte in the DNA database—was well and happy didn't mean that she was opening an old, very dangerous, can of worms.

If she contacted the woman personally, maybe. Attempted to speak with her, even, possibly. Which was why she didn't intend to do either of the two.

She was keeping it smart. Following the rules that had long ago been embedded into her. Being safe.

She'd overreacted. And was done with that.

She was going to San Diego knowing full well that she would absolutely never be able to tell her little sister who she was or let Nicole know where she'd come from, what had happened to their family.

But for her own peace of mind, her own broken heart, and for her mother, too, she had to make sure that the tiny little love they'd lost had grown up healthy, happy, and was living a good life.

Just knowing, finally, that she was alive and well...

Then maybe, just maybe, she'd be ready to move forward with her own life. Five of the seven of her best friends and partners had all found love over the past couple of years. They were starting families of their own.

Even Dorian.

Yet Savannah felt no closer at all to opening her heart to more than their enduring friendship. It was like she was still caught up in post-college euphoria, unable to live more deeply, while they were all growing up without her.

And just as she was feeling her own lapse, becoming aware that she might be stagnating, possibly missing out on the best part of life, she got a DNA hit on the Family Finders website? It had to be more than just a coincidence.

More like providence—or her mother—hitting her over the head with her need to get moving into her future.

That apparently meant letting go of the past.

Seeing Nicole, knowing she was well and happy, might be the only chance she'd ever have to be able to do that.

To that end, Savannah ignored the irritating sense of foreboding, of being watched as she waited in baggage claim in San Diego for her travel bag and then loaded it into her rental car. She refused to give rein to the thought that someone was staying behind her on the road as she followed prompts from the car's mapping system to the address she'd typed in. Only watched her rearview mirror for lane changes and safe-driving protocol.

She was doing something just for her. Finally taking care of herself. The mission was a healthy one. And she was not going to let life's past occurrences steal the chance away from her.

And if, by chance, Nicole wasn't healthy and happy?

The doubt crept in. She shook her head at it, would not borrow trouble from a future that may never materialize. The present was right there. Being lived. She deserved the right to give it her all.

And when the present moment took her past the more than ten acres of manicured lawn that bore the address she'd typed in, she slowed, took in all she could, peered anxiously for any sight of human habitation but didn't stop. She had no reason for being there.

It wasn't like one knocked on a ten-foot-high wrought-iron gate to sell something. Or schlep for charity.

But...wow.

She'd searched the address on a map site before she'd booked her flight to San Diego. The photo had shown a rural, albeit oceanfront, property with what looked like a small house behind a mass of trees.

Most definitely not the mansion in the distance that had to be worth millions.

Shaking her head in shock, she sped up as she left the property behind her, hardly able to take it all in.

Was the Family Finders entry some kind of cruel joke? Had someone hacked their system?

Had she just been fooled into thinking Nicole was actually alive and well?

Or unbelievable as it seemed...was that really Nicole's home? Had her baby sister landed in the lap of luxury? Maybe been adopted into a wealthy family?

Nicole was only twenty-five, but it was possible she'd invented something that made millions. Or married money.

Savannah drove by a few more times over the next hour, just looking. Hoping for some kind of sight of a young woman she'd instantly recognize as her sister. But she gained nothing but an increased sense of paranoia, to the point that the last time by, she was paying more attention to the car trailing behind her than to the grounds she was there to survey.

And let that fear drive her to seek out the closest hotel—a lovely beachfront property that reeked *luxury*—and get a one-bedroom suite with a balcony overlooking the ocean. On a floor high enough not to have any worries about someone breaching her space.

Savannah needed Hudson, their tech-expert partner, to do a deep dive for her, matching one of the many Charlotte Durans that had come up on her own somewhat-educated search of the name to the address she'd retrieved from the Family Finders secure match page. Hud and his team used a lot more than common search engines to ferret out information.

She couldn't call Hud. Couldn't call anyone.

This quest of hers...she was on her own.

Somewhat fitting, really, considering she was clawing her way out of a past no one knew about to find a future she couldn't see.

Chapter Three

The second Isaac finished his guard-duty shift, leaving Charlotte's safety in the very capable hands of her in-house protector, Emmajean Smith, he was out the door.

Emmajean, who slept in a room adjoining Charlotte's, was not a woman Isaac trusted with any confidences at all—she was wholly dedicated to Eduardo Duran—but he trusted her with Charlotte's life. The woman would die herself before letting any harm come to Charlotte.

And Charlotte, desperate to avoid any contact with a very determined Arnold Wagar, had claimed a migraine and retreated to her room late that afternoon. While Isaac felt a strong surge of sympathy for the young heiress where a potential forced marriage was concerned, he didn't like the idea of her spending hours at her computer doing God knew what while he had no access to find out.

Eduardo Duran had made one mandate quite clear to Isaac when he'd hired him on as personal protection director—unless the house was on fire or under attack, no male bodyguards were to have access to his daughter's personal suite while she was there.

At first, he'd thought the man had been protecting his daughter's virtue. Had found that to admire about him. He'd later figured out that the *stay away* order had come from Charlotte, as part of her agreement to remain living at home.

And with today's reveal that Charlotte owned the home, he was beginning to suspect the young woman more and more.

Eduardo Duran's daughter was not top of his mind, however, as he got in his undercover personal Range Rover and drove the short distance to La Hacienda—a five-star hotel not far from the Duran property. He'd been on the phone to his team in Washington the second he'd secured himself privately outside of Duran's office that afternoon.

Needing everything they could find on Savannah Compton.

They'd come up with surprisingly little. Other than the professional photo and bio on the Sierra's Web internet site, which Isaac had accessed himself with one quick search, they'd found almost no other information. Her address wasn't published—apparently something that Arizona law allowed in certain circumstances. None of the Sierra's Web partners, Savannah included, had any social media accounts discoverable by the FBI.

She had no police record. Not even a parking ticket.

He was the one who'd lucked into the only extremely valuable piece of information he had—the license plate of her rental car.

A simple search of the footage from the Duran estate's security cameras had shown him a new silver sedan driving slowly by the property multiple times that day. Clearly someone getting the lay of the land. The fact that it had been followed by a familiar-looking black sedan had been a pretty good clue as well. Duran's people were on her hard.

Getting the license plate off the footage had taken a quick request to the forensic lab in Washington, but his response came back with information from the rental car company, confirming the car's current renter to be Savannah Compton and, as a bonus, the name of the hotel the car had been registered at as well. He didn't ask questions on that one.

If Isaac hoped to learn anything about the Durans from the woman—perhaps gaining access to some elusive email address even, which could crack open the whole case—he had to act quickly. Duran hired the best of the best, and if he wanted the Compton woman gone, she would be.

He almost felt sorry for the expert lawyer, even if she *was* working for a scammer. As legends-long files filled with circumstantial evidence could attest, getting on Duran's bad side was most definitely not a good idea.

There was always the possibility that she didn't know that. Perhaps someone thinking they were related to the Durans through Charlotte's mother had hired her with legitimate intentions.

A second cousin, perhaps? There'd been no one biologically closer.

Could be a best friend, even. Someone who, as she aged, was thinking about the American-born-and-raised Amelia and, for her friend's sake or even her own, wanted to connect with Charlotte.

No matter the Compton woman's reason for allegedly flying to San Diego in a hunt for Charlotte Duran, Isaac had been given a very small window of what could be a huge lead. No way was he going to pass that by.

If Duran found out he was seeking out the woman he'd been told to stand down from—unless he had reason to kill her, of course—he'd handle his boss with a very quick and confident lie about some danger he'd thought the expert lawyer posed to Charlotte. And challenge Duran with a charge that he was tying his personal protection director's hands—in a way that he knew would have Duran giving him a bye on the indiscretion.

His current challenge was how to actually gain physical

access to his person of interest. He was dressed in expensive but casual dark pants and a lightly striped gray button-down shirt as he parked his vehicle and walked into the lobby of the hotel.

Showing himself to her was risky. She'd recognize him if she ever actually got close enough to Charlotte to see him with her. But he had a plan there, too. He was at the hotel posing as a member of the local wealthy set—a businessman, into acquisitions, he figured. Enough like Eduardo to hopefully get her to ask questions about the area's most successful entrepreneur.

And later...he could be seen as a friend of Charlotte's. And her father's. At least that was how he intended to play it. If he did his job right, she'd never get close enough to Charlotte for an actual conversation to take place.

He'd been undercover for more than a year, bodyguard for a couple of months. What was one more character to keep track of?

The opulent, gold-plated lobby wasn't overly crowded. One glance around gave Isaac a comfortable sense of who was and wasn't there.

No Savannah Compton.

The second floor, a balcony of sorts, was open to the lobby below and was swarming with people. Happy hour was happening in the locally popular bar. He'd done his homework and intended to hang out there for a bit, have a glass of local beer, maybe avail himself of some of the freshly prepared hors d'oeuvres, while he got a real-life sense of his surroundings.

Had time to survey hotel staff and security measures.

And figure out who he could convince that he was Ms. Compton's fiancé and then charm into calling her downstairs so he could surprise her with his early return from deployment.

STILL IN HER travel clothes, Savannah sat at a table for two in the corner of the busy open bar, sipped wine, and enjoyed being completely invisible to the throngs of people happying their way through the hour around her. She was completely alone—without being alone.

And was completely relaxed for the first time since she'd signed on to her Family Finders account to see that she had a biological match in the United States.

With her back to a brick wall, no one could be behind her, following her. She was surrounded by merriment.

And there was a very good-looking, well-dressed man riding up the escalator from the lobby. Dark hair, cut short enough but not too short, clothes that seemed made for his body, and...well...the best build she'd seen in...maybe ever. She acknowledged the thought with the caveat that she was on her second glass of wine. She wasn't going anywhere that night, except to her room. Eventually to bed.

No matter what her purpose for choosing San Diego was, she was on vacation for the first time in years. Had left her Sierra's Web cell phone in the desk drawer of her office. Needed to "let go," as Kelly had put it.

Savannah's plan was to find a future. Enjoying a little eye candy seemed like a baby step to that end. Completely out of character, so that covered the *letting go* part.

Still, she'd have looked away, except that the man was alone and seemed more focused than ready to party. Like maybe he was meeting someone?

Curious, she watched to see who it was.

Until he disappeared behind the crowd before exiting the automated staircase and was lost from view.

Suddenly feeling lonely, Savannah thought about calling Kelly, just to check in. All her partners had her personal cell number. And all had made a pact not to contact her unless she 911'd them.

Nicole was definitely an emergency.

And the reason Savannah couldn't call any of them.

If they knew she wasn't on the cruise there'd be questions. She'd have six experts needing to know why. Ones who'd all failed to follow up with a friend in college who'd been struggling. Sweet Sierra. Who'd died in part because her friends hadn't been adamant enough about getting answers from her.

None of the partners were going to make that mistake a second time. They'd solemnly sworn the promise to each other the day they'd opened their firm.

And there was no way she could have a nationally renowned firm famous for uncovering hard-to-find answers, getting even a hint that one of them had a secret, scary past.

If someone stumbled back too far…

No.

Savannah's little trip to San Diego was going to be buried like the rest of her childhood secrets. If she was successful, maybe the "vacation" would actually be a coffin in which her past would finally be laid to rest, once and for all.

"Mind if I sit here?"

So startled out of her intense self-reverie that she sloshed wine over the side of her glass, Savannah had to do a double take when she saw the owner of the charming masculine voice. Her candy from the escalator.

Providence again?

Giving her a push out of the stagnant bubble in which she'd been living all of her life?

Or maybe even just a weirdly timed distraction to get her through a minute or two?

"This isn't a come-on, I swear," the man continued, his dark eyes seeming to wrap her in a quiet sincerity in the loudly happening room. "You just seem to be…quietly enjoying that glass of wine…and after the day I've had, I'm finding little energy to stand at the bar and make idle conversation."

Ready to smile and probably nod, Savannah's response was cut off as the man kept talking. "Not that you aren't... well...worthy of a come-on... Oh, God, you're waiting for..."

"No!" Savannah blurted before the man could dig himself into such an awkward hole that he bolted. "I'm not. And please, sit. I'd rather not look as though I'm waiting for..." She let her words trail off as his had.

And sipped from her glass as he ordered some craft beer and appetizers, feeling a smile blooming inside her as he asked her preference and included her in his order. She'd been going to get her own to take up to the room. "It's the least I can do," the man said, waving at the table as the waiter left. "Since you've taken pity on me."

He smiled. She smiled back. Without any inner voice warning her to stop. To be careful. To look behind her.

"My name's Isaac, by the way," the man said, holding out his hand. "I live close by, work in acquisitions."

She took the proffered palm, tingling at the warmth that shot through her at the contact. "I'm Savannah."

And I'm so far from any sense of home I don't know that I'll ever find my way back.

ISAAC GOT NOTHING from the encounter except an unsolicited and completely unprofessional jolt to the groin. He was working, undercover, playing a part, and human.

Savannah Compton—not that she offered her last name at all during the next hour they spent together—looked him straight in the eye, unwavering, as she'd told him that she was in San Diego on vacation. Planning to enjoy the ocean, the beach, and soak up San Diego's year-round sunshine and balmy temperatures.

She was engaging, seemingly relaxed, as though she

hadn't a care in the world. And emitted a husky laugh enough times that it got to him.

In a purely male way.

When she switched from the water she'd opted for while they'd eaten back to a fresh glass of wine, he nursed his second beer—in spite of warnings to himself that one hour of her time had taken its toll on him.

It had been a long time since he'd been alone with a woman socially, who didn't know what he did for a living. One who seemed to be enjoying his company in a completely nonprofessional sense. His choice, that.

And maybe not his best one. Clearly he needed to get out more. And needed to extricate himself from the unintentional consequences of the situation he'd created.

He stayed because he couldn't get up and go away with nothing. He wasn't made that way.

And he hadn't yet figured out why he was failing. The woman appeared to be beating him at his own game. Playing a part, giving up nothing.

Did she know he worked for the Durans?

Was she somehow gleaning something about them through him?

He almost always managed to get seemingly innocuous information out of those he interviewed and have it be exactly what he'd needed from them.

The fact that she had him questioning himself intrigued him almost as much as it irked him.

Playing to his plan, he went into more detail about what he did for a living. Using a tactic of *give some to get some.* He didn't get any. Even when he point-blank asked what she did for a living.

"Right now, I'm on leave from doing anything," she told him with one of those distracting chuckles.

She told him she traveled a lot. Didn't specify that it was for the job.

He talked about college, allowed that he'd gone to the University of Michigan. And she countered with the fact that she'd made a lot of good friends in college.

She asked him nothing. Not where he'd grown up. How long he'd been in San Diego. Nothing that he could capitalize on with turnabout being fair play.

"Did you graduate?" he asked her then. He had not. He'd been at wits' end with his little sister, Mollie, seeing the trouble she'd been heading toward, and had entered the police academy instead. And then the DC police, until he'd made enough of a name for himself.

By bringing down a major dealer.

And sending his baby sister to jail for a stint, too.

Then he'd gone back for his degree in criminal justice and joined the FBI.

"I did," Savannah nodded, her words coming slowly, counter to his racing thoughts. Her brown eyes pools of pleasure, glinting with the lowered lights. Happy hour had ended. Tables were filled around them, but with couples, or parties of three and four, conversing quietly among themselves.

When the toe of her shoe lightly brushed the side of his calf, he told himself the touch was accidental.

And wished it hadn't been. Would have liked to have been able to transport himself to another world where he could have capitalized on the mistake by rubbing her back. Maybe taking her hand.

"You ever been married?" The question was not work related. In any way.

She shook her head. "No." The answer came immediately. With maybe a hint of regret?

A real reaction? One he could file as information that

might fit together with something else that could come to mean something?

Had there been someone?

Could be who she was working for? An old love come back to haunt her?

"You?" she asked, her first direct question of him.

He shook his head. Looked her in the eye as he delivered a real truth that also fit his cover. "I'm married to my job."

He'd done the family thing. Had messed it up royally.

The job he got right. And to that end... "What did you study?"

She shrugged. "I bounced around."

She'd glanced at her wine. The first sign that she was hiding. Reinvigorated, feeling more like himself, Isaac asked, "What's your degree in?"

He knew the answer to that one. Waited to see if she'd tell him the truth. Or how she'd lie. Either way, she'd be telling him something useful to his professional profile of her.

"Various things."

He leaned in. Moved his hand a little closer to hers. And then, feeling slightly skanky, slid it back to his glass, taking a sip to cover the slip. "Like what?"

Savannah shook her head. Sipped her wine and covered his hand with hers. "You really want to sit here and talk about classes I took more than a decade ago?"

So he could deduce that she was in her early thirties. Something he already knew. Sierra's Web had formed shortly after they'd all graduated from college. Isaac started to sweat as he forced his mind to stay on task—and off the feel of those soft fingers on top of his hand.

He glanced up at her for a deductive assessment and got caught by those brown eyes, grabbing his as though he was some kind of lifeline. And heard himself practically groan out a solid truth. "What I really want to do right now, I can't," he told her. "Something tells me you aren't the kind of woman who hooks up for a one-night stand, and I'm not the kind of guy who takes advantage of any woman."

Not in a sexual sense.

Her gaze didn't waver. Nor did she appear the least bit embarrassed. "What if I want to be that kind of woman?" she asked him. "Just once. Maybe not a one-night stand, but a fling? You know, the fling I met on vacation?"

He couldn't help but smile. The woman had enough confidence to take a rejection and turn it into a proposition. He liked that. In any other situation, he'd have been all over it.

Until it hit him. She was working him to get to Charlotte. She knew who he was.

Was using the oldest trick in the book to get her "in."

Sex.

He'd just been played for a fool.

And while he kept the smile in place, played along with her, he made a very clear, though silent, promise to himself and to her.

It wouldn't happen again.

Chapter Four

She wasn't going to see him again. Savannah knew when
she and Isaac left the bar together—parting at the escalator
that would take him downstairs, across from the elevator
that would take her up—that their agreement was to leave
any future association up to fate. Rather than exchanging
contact information, they made a choice designed to say a
forever goodbye.

They'd determined in the midst of flirtatious smiles that
if they were meant to have a fling, they'd run into each
other again.

She almost hoped she could see him one more time. Just
to thank him for being a truly decent guy. Not accepting her
very out-of-character invitation, but rather choosing to be a
friend. Just sitting with her through a couple of lost hours.

Almost hoped, but not quite. That impromptu break with
him had been a godsend. She'd been feeling so adrift. Alone
and unfound.

But the wine, the shared food, the intriguing conversation had somehow cleared her mind. Shown her the path that
was awaiting her.

The trail to her freedom, her future.

And by noon the next day, she was executing the plan.
She'd been on hold since she'd been seven years old, had

lost her father and had her baby sister snatched out of her life. Had been wasting away in the chasm of not knowing.

But no more. The decades-long efforts and prayers she'd been putting out into the universe had borne fruit. She had a name. An address. All she needed was to see Nicole. To replace the image of the one-year-old little dark-haired baby holding her arms out to her with that of a healthy and thriving twenty-five-year-old woman doing just fine without her. Then Savannah would be free to move forward into a future that could possibly include a house she lived in with family that lived there with her.

And the damned dark ghosts that her mind kept telling her were behind her, watching her, following her would become mere cars on the road again.

Since driving by the front of a massive estate wasn't likely to give her a sister sighting, Savannah had decided to try to get her glimpse of Nicole from a vantage point that allowed her to hang around as long as she liked, without fear of being followed or noticed. One that, with the newly purchased high-end, high-tech binoculars at her side, would allow the close-up view she so desperately needed.

She waited for the skipper she'd hired to get them into a position on the ocean waters that would allow them to drop anchor with the back of Charlotte Duran's estate in full, if distant, view. Savannah breathed in ocean air from a seat on the deck of her rented boat, more relaxed than she'd been in...years.

A lot of the clarity had been gained from spending a couple of hours completely outside her real life, with a kind stranger who'd treated her like a viable dinner companion.

It was almost as though she'd been able to see herself through his eyes—and in doing so, had seen her potential. Had seen the life that was there for her to live. The life she'd been missing.

The grown-up lives her partners had all been finding.

Other than Savannah giving directional coordinates to the woman at the wheel, the two hadn't spoken. Her chauffeur was being paid to get her there and back and didn't ask questions.

Which also added to Savannah's state of inner tranquility. She didn't have to *be* anybody. Or tend to anyone, either. There were no expectations of her, no advice to give, no case studies to make, no duties for her to perform—other than to see her sister from afar. Hell, she didn't even have to make her bed. It was being done for her.

For a few short hours or days, she could just watch, wait… and breathe.

And for the first day, that was all she did. Watch. And wait. Sitting out on the ocean on her own personal cruise. Until the sun started to set and her skipper—Suzanne, she'd said her name was—advised that they needed to head back.

Savannah had talked to the young woman some. Enough to know that her father owned the marina. That she'd grown up on the water and was working at the marina while she was in college. Getting a degree she didn't want or need, simply because her father had required it before allowing her to run day cruises for hundreds of tourists at a time for a living.

A woman who knew what she wanted.

She'd studied economics while Savannah had spent hours with her binoculars, watching a small beach backed by lusciously green, perfectly manicured lawn. To the right, a gazebo with a fireplace and outdoor table and living room seating for at least twelve. To the left, closer to the house, was a large swimming pool, with plenty of cool decking and loungers, gated in black wrought iron. Leaving at least an acre of largely unadorned lawn in the middle.

For parties, Savannah imagined as she put her surveillance glasses away for the trip back. In her mind's eye she saw the empty grounds she'd been staring at filled with tables and chairs, soft lighting, a buffet table with servers making certain they kept the flies off the food. There were casually though expensively dressed people of all ages sitting at tables but also milling about. People standing with drinks in their hands as they conversed in small groups.

At one point there was a white runway in the grass—with white chairs in rows on each side of it—that led to a gilded outdoor arch. During that imagined episode her sister came down the aisle in a white dress.

In her peaceful state of mind, Savannah spent the evening up in her suite, ordering room service, got a good night's sleep, and the next day, as Suzanne zoomed them back out on the ocean, she pictured toddlers in that vast green Duran grass. Maybe twins. Girls. Running almost faster than their chubby little legs could carry them, with the soft grass cushioning one as she fell.

She and Nicole were orphans with no other relatives, who'd been robbed of the chance to be family to each other, but they could still each have biological family in their own individual lives.

As the boat slowed, nearing their anchor spot, Savannah knew that if she saw Nicole surrounded by family, she'd be able to go, to be on a plane to Florida yet that night, to spend the rest of her vacation lounging beachside on the opposite coast of the country she and Nicole shared.

Goal in mind, she watched the Duran property from afar, completely silent as Suzanne studied for the next couple of hours.

And then, heart pounding, Savannah sat up straight, frozen in place lest the binoculars giving her sight moved at all, obstructing the view. The couple—Nicole and her husband?—exited the double French doors at the back of the house together. Was Nicole really married, then? California marriage records were public, but she'd have to submit a request by mail or visit each country recorder's office to obtain access to them. Or put Hud on it.

Her stomach knotting against a swarm of internal butterflies, she scarcely allowed herself a full breath so as not to lose even a second of sight. Until the couple continued to walk—and stepped onto that luscious spread of green grass, heading right in her direction!

Half a mile away, but with her view...they'd be right in front of her.

Palms sweating, she wiped one, then the other on her beige capri pants, wobbling the binoculars as little as possible and never taking her gaze away from the slowly walking pair.

Look up! she silently implored the woman who seemed inordinately fond of the ground beneath her feet. Savannah would have thought the woman was looking for something, except that the steps were too in sync with each other, and without pause, to be giving their owners opportunity for search.

And then, one second to the next, it happened! The face lifted, eyes gazing out toward the ocean, and Savannah gasped. Those eyes...she couldn't make out the color, but the round shape...blending into a petite nose...she knew them!

Could've been looking at a photo of her mother or, around the eyes and nose, herself...

"You okay?" Suzanne's voice penetrated through a barrier of seemingly cotton-stuffed ears.

"Fine." She found her court voice. None other was forthcoming. "Just found what I was looking for."

Her voice, hearing it, the need to use it, grounded her for a second. Until the woman moving closer looked up again, and it was as though she was looking straight at Savannah. Seeing her. Meeting her gaze.

Tears flooded her eyes, and she had to blink them away.

Couldn't lose one second of her time with Nicole, breathing in every aspect of the moment, knowing they were all she was ever going to have. Willing the couple to walk all the way to the beach. To stay a while.

Nothing else existed. The boat rocking gently with the waves only meant that she had to brace herself and keep the binoculars focused. No smells, no sounds registered. Just the woman, dressed in a short denim skirt and black sleeveless top, with some kind of black open footwear, coming toward her.

The couple was close enough for Savannah to notice that the man was older. Or had a receding hairline and dyed his hair gray. His skin seemed less youthfully smooth than Nicole's, and he wore wire-framed glasses.

And...were they fighting?

The man—a father-in-law maybe—reached for Nicole's hand, pulled it to the crook of his elbow and when he let go, leaving it there, she returned her appendage to her side. Was staring out toward Savannah.

As though calling out to her. Savannah heard the call, felt the pull, with such force she took a step forward.

Realized she was still on the boat.

And just a speck in the distance to her sister, if Nicole could see her at all.

But she could see...far more than she'd expected to. Disbelieving elation turned to working focus in a heartbeat as Savannah's expensive lenses showed her the sharp shake of her sister's head, followed by the male hand—from a suited body that was heavier than was meant for the shirt—reaching for her again. Grabbing Nicole's hand. More roughly.

And her sister snatching it back. The man turned to Nicole, speaking what looked to be quite sharply based on his body language, the sharp movement of his head. She was talking then. Her jaw movement left no doubt about that.

Then the man was speaking again, rubbing a hand down Nicole's long dark hair, and it was as though Savannah could feel the touch on her own matching dark strands, over her shoulder and down her side and back.

She shuddered, watching as, a second later, the man kept a hand of ownership on Nicole's body, even when the younger woman turned away.

And looked out at the ocean again.

Facing Savannah.

Who didn't need to see the way her little sister's face scrunched...the broken movement of Nicole's torso...to feel her tears.

And Savannah's fate was once again sealed by situations beyond her control.

She had no idea what came next. What she could do.

But there was no way in hell she would be catching any flights that night.

Nicole might live in surroundings that made it appear that she was thriving, but Savannah's baby sister clearly was not happy.

Nor did she look safe.

Savannah couldn't leave her like that.

DURAN HAD ORDERED him to leave Charlotte alone with Wagar on the lawn. Isaac had his own job to do. And while that required his undercover persona to stay employed, he didn't follow Charlotte outside, but he did keep watch from an upstairs room in the home. A better vantage point because he could see the entire backyard at once from above, so anyone trying to get access would be immediately visible.

As Charlotte stood with her back to him, mid-lawn, having rebuffed Wagar, Isaac felt another bout of compassion for the younger woman. No matter what she might've been involved with, she'd grown up under a very powerful thumb. Without Duran, an orphan.

Meaning no one else to turn to.

Didn't forgive an adult choice to cross the line between lawful and criminal. He'd take her down when he found the proof to do so.

Her shoulders hunched, and he glanced up, feeling as though he was intruding by staring at her, and was immediately hooked by a glint out on the water. Above sea level. It was stationary. And constant. A pinprick of light seeming to point straight at him.

Cursing against the time it took him to get his digital binoculars, he had them up and focused within seconds of being back at the window.

And then, while using the camera function to click photos as quickly as he could, he stood with only his eyewear sticking through the side of the opened curtains as he stared at the woman standing on the small-range center-console boat, binoculars covering her eyes.

Savannah Compton.

Another person was on the boat with her. Female. Blonde. At the center console, reading.

A skipper. But more than that, too?

An accomplice?

Her client?

The woman who was going to pose as a member of Charlotte's dead mother's family?

Using a woman was a good move.

Made by someone who knew a lot more about Charlotte than Eduardo suspected?

Questions posed, hanging there without answers.

He needed answers.

The Compton woman, or her client, posed no immediate physical danger to the younger Duran. They needed her alive, not dead, and were so far out that without powerful lenses, the heiress wouldn't even be able to see the lawyer out on the ocean.

But the lengths the woman had gone to to spy on Charlotte did not bode well. Was she planning to approach the house by water? Risky.

Worth it for the millions she hoped to gain?

He'd arrested people who'd put themselves on death row for much less. Three zeros less.

And from there? What would the plan be? Wait for Charlotte to appear?

Had Compton been out there the day before?

After their impromptu "date" two nights before, he'd spent the next day watching out for her car on the road. Keeping Charlotte within sight at all times.

He hadn't once glanced at the ocean. Charlotte had had a closed student-only lecture, a private lunch with a women's organization at which he'd stood trying to make his tall, broad form invisible in the corner. She'd had dinner at home with her father—with Wagar as a guest.

From which she'd excused herself before dessert and retired to her suite. On Emmajean's watch.

He'd spent more than an hour resisting the urge to head back to La Hacienda's mezzanine bar, just in case. And had gone to bed, relieved that Compton hadn't made an attempt to approach Charlotte and disappointed that he hadn't seen the lawyer all day, even in the distance. He couldn't find out what he didn't know without some kind of move from her.

Which he was currently witnessing.

Down below, Charlotte walked away from Wagar, causing the man's hand on her lower left back to drop, and when the older man followed after, she turned, said something to him, and stepped out onto the fifty yards of sand that led to the water's edge.

Lenses back over his eyes, he glanced up at the boat in the distance. Saw the lawyer just as he'd left her, visually cataloguing every move Charlotte made.

It didn't take him knowing what was going on—that Wagar was determined he was going to be her husband and Charlotte was equally determined he would not be—to figure out that the wealthy twenty-five-year-old was not interested in her father's plans for her marital future.

If he was the one in the boat, he'd be forming a plan right then and there. You used the weak link, the blemish in a relationship, a bone of contention to separate powers. And Charlotte, a woman in tune with women's needs, had just shown another equally astute woman her vulnerability. The way to draw her away from her loyalty to her father.

At least long enough to get what she wanted from her. To use her and leave her feeling like a fool.

So, he had Compton's way in. Big picture. How that would translate to actual contact remained to be seen.

He snapped a couple more photos. Looked at the small screen to preview what he could.

And…wait… Lenses back up to his eyes, Isaac focused to the left of Savannah Compton's boat. Another boat, smaller. A fishing vessel. Tucked into a cove completely visible to Isaac but mostly obscured from Savannah Compton. And while there was a pole mounted on the boat with a line in the water, one of the two figures dressed in dark pants and what looked to be wetsuit tops had his own power-driven lenses. And seemed to be dividing his time between the Duran beach—Charlotte—and the larger vessel—Savannah.

Duran had made it clear he had people watching the expert lawyer. And if they were that close, that up on her movements, Isaac was going to have to be much more careful regarding his own contact with her.

He could do it.

Taking on different personas—throwing on a mustache, a wig, dyeing his hair with rinse-out color, cowboy garb with heeled boots—had become second nature to him.

While Isaac's mind began to spin with possible scenarios—starting with another happy hour that night—he stiffened as the second person in the boat reached down toward the boat's bottom.

With a quick glance to see Charlotte still on the beach, the lawyer standing at attention, her binoculars pointed in Charlotte's direction, and then back to the two men in the boat, Isaac was vetoing his disguise idea. Savannah knew him as…

No! He saw the gun rise too late. Standing alone on the third floor of the mansion, horror filling his gut, he watched the second fisherman's hand jerk with the force of the blast. Watched as Savannah Compton fell to the floor of her vessel.

And ran for Charlotte.

Chapter Five

Lying on the floor of the cabin cruiser, Savannah felt the sting in her upper arm but didn't dare move even the inch or two it would take to get a look at the sleeve covering it. Had no idea how much blood there was.

There'd been a wave, the boat had rocked, she'd been off-balance, had side-stepped, and the next thing she remembered was diving for the floor the second she'd heard the blast and staying there, frozen, as Suzanne, keeping low, had gotten the boat roaring at top speed out of the area. Driving with one hand and her eyes barely above the boat's edge.

Her arm didn't feel ripped apart, but she'd heard that gunshot pain wasn't always immediate. She didn't feel moisture and figured that for a good thing. Surely if there was gushing, she'd know.

The entire trip back, she calculated, considered, listened intently.

And stayed rational.

Listening as Suzanne radioed from the boat that there'd been a shot fired, giving the coordinates. Hearing a return conversation minutes later, stating that police in the area were checking residences closest to the area.

By the time they'd moored the boat, an all-clear had come from the area. Only a couple who'd been out at the beach at the time of the gunfire had even heard the one shot. And both were fine.

Nicole was fine. Savannah catalogued the news.

As soon as they'd docked, she realized there was only a tiny smear of blood on her sleeve, along with a shard of the plexiglass that had hit it. It wasn't until more than an hour later, when she was back in her suite, that she became a shivering mess.

A piece of the windshield had shattered at the bullet's impact. Hitting her.

And it could have been the bullet itself. If the wave hadn't hit when it had...

She could have been killed!

At the marina, Suzanne, her father, the police had all figured the shot as coming from someone on land, aiming at something else on land. A squirrel. Snake. There'd even been a couple of leopard sightings. Deputies had been dispatched to go over the lush, treed cove area from which the bullet had come, inch by inch. Looking for the dead animal. Or signs of poaching.

Savannah had had her day's ride comped.

She'd paid anyway, leaving another day-trip's worth of pay for Suzanne. The girl had taken the whole thing in stride. Had seemed quite proud of herself for her ability to captain the boat and her fare safely to the dock, with little real damage.

She'd apparently watched Savannah on the floor, too. Had kept track of her breathing, with no sign of blood.

And had been eagerly talking to the small crowd that had gathered around her when Savannah had climbed into her car and driven back to the hotel.

But once in her room, panic hit.

With two words repeating themselves over and over.

Witness Protection. Witness Protection.

She'd broken protocol. Looking up Nicole. Coming to see her—even from a distance.

Nicole was fine, she reminded herself, pacing.

But that bullet…had it been meant for her? Not some poor rodent in the wrong place at the wrong time?

Just seemed way too coincidental that she was the only one hit by a seemingly stray bullet at the exact time she'd been standing there spying on Nicole.

What kind of danger had she put herself in?

Once in, there was no way out. She knew that. Had been told over and over. Especially in her teens when she'd figured enough time had passed and she and her mom could start looking. When she'd been so filled with her ability to be right that she'd once tried an internet search on her own only to have her mother walk in from the kitchen and see her.

She'd heard from the witness protection marshal who'd been summoned to her home an hour later that if whoever her father had been about to blow the whistle on knew that she was going to bring up the past, that she believed Nicole was alive, she'd be living on borrowed time.

She'd never looked again.

Not until after her mother's death.

With her stomach churning and her heart pounding, she wore a path in the lush carpet from bedroom, through the double doors, past bath to living area, over to the windows lining the whole space, back again via the view. Making a circle.

Repeating the process over and over.

Thoughts reeling, one after the other. None of them coming together.

Until she stopped at the window, looked out at the ocean, and knew. If she was on borrowed time, she was. There was no taking that back.

She'd been feeling like she was being followed for the past year. Maybe now she really would be.

But Nicole was in trouble—an abusive husband or boyfriend, most likely—and Savannah couldn't die without trying to help her.

She wouldn't be able to live with herself, either in her current life or any afterlife, if she abandoned that sweet baby holding her arms out for Savannah to hold her.

She couldn't abandon Nicole.

She couldn't help her if she was dead.

So there had to be a third option.

She'd have to hire someone...and do it in a way that no one knew the person was attached to her. Which meant she had to find out as much as she could about her sister to know how best to have a conversation with Nicole without alerting whoever had killed their father. Only then would she know who to hire.

She might've only been an expert in the field of law, but more than a decade with Sierra's Web had taught her a lot. She'd never seen herself going it alone without her partners, but she could.

And for Nicole, she would.

No way was she going to contact her best friends, who'd been her family for her entire adult life, and bring potential danger to them.

She just had to figure out what she *was* going to do. How she could stay alive long enough to help Nicole, not get her hurt—and hopefully to have her own future as well.

Staying in her suite wasn't the answer.

Leaving it didn't seem like such a good idea at the moment, either.

And yet, aside from standing there with nerves that were still jittering, she felt as though she was finally taking charge of her life. Facing it all.

Not giving in. Or giving up, either.

Rubbing her arms, she touched the small cut on her arm and, with sudden fear rendering her weak, took a step back.

Before stopping. And forcing herself forward again.

A bullet could probably plow through a cabin cruiser's windshield. But not as probably through soundproofed double-or triple-pane acrylic windows, which she suspected she was standing in front of. Hotel liabilities were legal nightmares. And the surest way for an establishment not to have to deal with them was prevention.

Which was why guests in most hotels couldn't open the windows in their rooms. Less chance of falling out. And less chance of an intruder accessing the space. Soundproofing had become a privacy issue, most particularly at luxury hotels. Guests not only wanted their own comfort not to be disturbed by other guests but also expected a level of privacy as they held their own conversations.

And liaisons.

She needed to have whatever meetings she had in her hotel room.

Good. First bullet point for her plan.

Before the second had a chance to form, the hotel phones—one on the large workspace, one in the living area, and one on the nightstand over by the bed—began to ring.

Had they found out where she was staying?

Savannah's gaze moved between the three ringing phones. Back and forth.

As she stood rooted to the floor and started to shake.

Answer.

Seated in his car at La Hacienda, Isaac listened to the phone ring two, then three times. He'd been told by Duran's head of security that the Compton woman had gone back to her hotel. At the same time the man had denied all responsibility for his team having had anything to do with the shot that had been fired at her.

Savannah's car was in the parking lot.

Happy hour had just ended. His timing was purposeful.

Isaac was there to attempt to cash in on his earlier, seemingly unplanned personal association with Savannah Compton long enough to find out what she knew about the Durans—nothing more.

But his gut still tightened when he couldn't get her on the phone. Suspecting the worst.

From everything he knew—but couldn't trace back to Duran with enough solid proof to hang him—the man's hired goons didn't generally hit and miss. An untimely ocean wave giving the smallest rock to her cruiser had been to blame. The expert lawyer had escaped one bullet headed straight at her. Chances were, she wouldn't be so lucky a second time.

Ring six. How many more would he get before the hotel's service picked up to record his message for the guest in room 11029? *Answer.*

He wasn't going to leave a message. Didn't want the recording to exist.

Holding his phone with fingers tight with tension, he glanced around one more time, just to ensure that he was alone. No eyes on him.

Duran trusted him. But he wouldn't put it past the man to have all his employees watched now and then. Just to be sure. A guy didn't get to the billionaire's stature without layers of stringent protection in place.

Just like the layers of untraceable transfers of moneys and contraband that supported the criminal's wealth. The invisible manpower for the dirty work.

Ring eight.

"Hello?"

Settling back in his seat, Isaac smiled. Getting into character. Doing it so well, he felt like a guy initiating a second meet after an enjoyable first one. "Savannah? It's Isaac..."

"ISAAC?" SINKING DOWN to the sofa, weak with relief, Savannah let herself fall back two nights to the time out of time that had given her the clarity to move forward with her life.

She wouldn't let herself be deterred from the urgent business at hand. But if a moment or two of distraction from the persistent and irritating anxiety getting in her way allowed her to proceed with the same logical thinking that had given her more than just a glimpse of her sister, then she had to take that time.

"How did you find me?" she asked, settling back with warmth flooding through her at the thought that he'd enjoyed their time together enough to try.

"You aren't going to believe this...and...well... I'd rather talk in person. I want you to be able to look into my eyes and know I'm not some creep..."

His recalcitrant tone had her smiling. Something she so very badly needed in that moment. "I find it hard to believe that I'll ever be thinking that," she said.

"So you'll meet me in the bar?"

No. She wasn't leaving her suite. Drew a blank as to any normal sounding reason as to why that was and blurted, "I just washed my hair. It takes a good hour to dry."

Not her best work.

But it sufficed.

Until he said, "You'll look like some of the other people milling around down here, like you just came in from a dip in the pool. There's a party going on, spilling out onto the beach."

In another lifetime, she'd have suggested they meet there. The happy-hour crowd had worked well for them.

In another lifetime...

"You could come up here," she said, prompted by all the emotions she was fighting in her current lifetime. Top of the list suddenly—not being alone. Just for a few. And then, hearing herself, quickly added, "I have a suite. Bedroom door firmly closed," and got up to close said double doors—would have locked them for good measure if she could have done so from the outside.

She'd pretty much invited him the other night.

Of course, three glasses of wine had been partly responsible for the ill-advised invitation.

The man was the only nonemployee she knew in her current, very narrow present. And he'd liked her enough to find her after they'd left hanging the possibility that they'd see each other again.

She'd be lying to herself if she didn't admit that every time she'd been in the lobby the day before—and that day, too—she'd looked for him. Just in case he'd come back on the chance of seeing her again. "And I have four phones and a can of pepper spray in case I feel threatened," she added, humor in her tone as she delivered words that were also true. She kept the multiple self-defense training certificates to herself.

Unless the man came up with an illegally carried gun—something that wouldn't make it past hotel security to get on the elevator—she felt pretty confident she could hold her own.

And when Isaac chuckled, sending shivers through her, and said he was on his way up, she made a run for the bath to wet her hair.

Thanking providence for saving her from herself one more time.

ISAAC'S STEPS WERE quick and sure, adrenaline flowing as he made his way to the access he'd just gained into what could turn out to be the unexpected flag on Duran's horizon that broke open the case. Sometimes it only took one mistake, one unsolved little problem.

And the fact that Eduardo Duran had had somebody shoot at the woman that afternoon, just half a mile from his estate, told him that she was a problem.

One that was far bigger than the older man had let on.

Which made Isaac all that more eager to find out why. Who was she representing? And why was that person such a threat to the billionaire?

Yet as he got off the elevator at her floor, adjusting his jacket over the dress pants and button-down shirt, readying himself for a professional introduction—albeit one that would only sprinkle enough particles of truth over the cover to give him the appearance of complete transparency—he slowed for a step or two.

Ostensibly to prepare, but it wasn't the speech he was about to give that had his focus. He'd enjoyed the couple of hours he'd spent with the expert attorney. Had left feeling... good. Had slept well that night. Would have liked to have left the memory alone. Something he could call up now and then when he felt a little too much...alone.

On Christmas, for instance. Those that he wasn't working.

Instead, he was about to obliterate the little screenshot of a supposedly unplanned tête-à-tête with another farce. One that wasn't going to be nearly as fun.

One that was going to wipe the smile, the look of welcome off Savannah Compton's compelling face. And replace it with...

A flash of Mollie's shocked, hurt gaze shot across his mind's eye. Followed by a couple more long-ago, but never forgotten, expressions attacking him from his little sister's eyes. A second of disbelief that settled into disgust-laced resentment. It had been fifteen years, and his little sister, his only family, hadn't spoken to him since.

While the reminder hit his gut with a familiar pang, it was well-timed, preparing him for the moments ahead. No matter how much you liked or cared for someone, no matter that feeling of connection, being on opposite sides of the law would keep you forever apart.

At least when the "you" was Isaac.

And the other side of that, when someone you trusted took information you gave freely and used it to stop you from breaking the law, you didn't hold them in high regard. When the "you" was Mollie.

But not Savannah Compton. He couldn't believe she trusted him.

Unless, in the next few minutes, she came clean with him. Told him she was there to make contact with Charlotte Duran. At which point, he would be the only one lying to keep secrets. The only one killing any semblance of trust between them.

Because he still couldn't tell her who he really was.

Either way, *vacation fling* was off the table the second he knocked on her door. A bit of regret hung over him. But his knock was firm.

And when she answered the door—with her hair so wet it appeared as though she'd really been in the process of washing it when he'd called—he didn't lean in and deliver a kiss to her cheek.

In spite of his strong inner urge to do so.

He smiled, though. Met her gaze with a long one of his own, an act, and...uncomfortably very real, too, as he allowed that much of a connection between them to continue to live.

If his plan was going to work, he needed her to trust him.

And the way he felt inside—wanting, personally, to be

worthy of Savannah's trust, to continue to hold it—was one of the hurdles he was going to have to overcome to get the job done.

Hundred, thousands, maybe millions of people's lives had been negatively impacted over the years by Eduardo Duran's illegal activities. He couldn't let his own personal feelings get in the way of saving future millions from the same fate.

And while she was just flirting with a man that had nothing to do with her purpose in town for the moment—and while that increasingly irritated part of him wanted to be just a guy she met in a bar—the reality was that as soon as she heard what he'd come to say, she'd become a player in the deadly game.

Whether she told him so or not.

Savannah broke eye contact first. "Make yourself at home while I dry my hair," she said, nodding toward the living area. "There's wine there if you want to pour a couple of glasses."

Playing his part, he took up the bottle, uncorked it. Set one filled glass on the coffee table in front of the sofa and took the other with him to look out at the darkness over the ocean, broken occasionally by the light of a ship. He heard the blow-dryer shut off but didn't turn.

Just waited.

He needed her to make the next move so he could best determine his own. Did she want to continue the flirtation?

His own "truth" could come out as a caveat to that.

At which time she'd accept the business proposal he was there to present, and the flirtation would die a natural death.

Or was she, the expert lawyer, just needing to know how he'd found her, and when he told her, she'd order him out?

In that scenario the task in front of him would be more difficult.

He heard her approach, glanced over as she stopped a

foot to his right, looking out alongside him. She sipped from her glass.

He took his first sip, too. Waiting.

"So, how'd you find me? A first name, the hotel…"

Glancing at her, he gave her kudos for an expression that, while congenial, gave nothing away. Nor did her tone.

She seemed…not at all upset to have been found.

Which spoke more to the flirtation scenario, not the lawyer.

Out of time, he chose to go that route.

"I wasn't completely honest with you the other night." He started right in, his tone filled with regret that was prompted by the part he was playing but came from a place deeper inside him. The part he had to find a way to stifle once and for all.

He looked over at her, waiting for her to meet his gaze, which took a couple of long seconds. And then he said, "I do work in acquisitions, sort of," he told her. Then shrugged and added an actual fact. "I buy and sell privately, for myself. Stock, mostly. And not always successfully." A piece of information that had not been meant to escape.

What the hell?

"But my actual job…is working for the owner of one of the world's most successful conglomeration of portfolios…" A vague way to describe Eduardo. One that fit. Nothing about the man's dealings were clear cut or easily understandable. He mastered in stealth, in hiding, in making it impossible to know exactly what he was doing.

She'd taken another sip of wine. Was facing the window again. Seeing the sedately lit hotel grounds below, as he'd done? The small groups of people, mostly couples, who came and went along the softly glowing pathways that wound around and down to the beach? Into the darkness.

He couldn't get the read on her that would help guide him.

He was just getting ready to dive in further when she said, "And this has to do with me, how?"

Ah. Her tone had cooled.

He didn't want to lose the warmth. "I work for a man who lives near where your boat was shot at today," he said, concern marring his brow, urgency in his tone. "I'm a bodyguard, Savannah. And personal protection director for the household," he added with a note of humility. "Which is a fancy way of saying I'm the head bodyguard who is in charge of, and responsible for, the rest of the bodyguard staff."

She'd turned slowly to face him, eyes wide, mouth open.

"The police came to the house to ask questions. I was called in to assure the owner that everyone under our care was fine. I asked to remain present for the remainder of the interviews so that I could prepare my staff for any possible safety measures we might want to put in place..." He poured on the sense that he could serve and protect. "During the ensuing hour, we were asked if any of us knew a Savannah Compton."

When she turned sharply toward the window, he touched her shoulder gently. "I didn't know it was you, of course, and said no." He explained what he had to get out there and then quickly added, "They were asking just to make certain that no one in the household—an estate that was within shooting distance of your boat with a strong enough rifle—had it out for you. They were looking for suspects. In order to keep you from further harm."

With a quick look back at him, she nodded and quickly faced the window again, her wineglass more an ornament in her hand than a beverage she was consuming.

Because she'd switched to working mode?

Had left personal territory for professional?

Or because he'd frightened her?

Based on the frown marring her features, the tightness around her lips, he suspected the latter.

And even while that had been his goal, the idea that he might have succeeded didn't feel great.

"As they were leaving, one of the officers mentioned to me that you'd been staying at La Hacienda, had taken the boat out from there."

His words brought her glance back to him. This time she didn't turn away. She took a sip of wine.

And he knew that he was on the cusp of succeeding. That she was falling into his plan. And his faith in the idea grew. He decided to push harder. For the job. Always for the job.

But for another, very different and unfamiliar reason, too. He cared, personally, that she stay safe.

Chapter Six

Savannah sipped wine. She controlled her breathing. Managed to maintain outward calm. But her insides were quaking.

What in the hell had she done?

She'd heard that the police were going to question nearby residents, to make certain that all was well. She'd pictured a knock on the front door, a question along the lines of *Is everything all right here?* and a quick wave goodbye.

The local police had clearly thought they were dealing with a possible illegal shooting of a rodent, a poacher, or a somewhat foolish target shooter who needed more practice.

But...putting protection staff on alert?

Thinking she was truly in imminent harm? She'd suspected, of course. And had been hell bent on getting her paranoia under control.

But what if...

She'd brought the monster out of hiding.

She couldn't stop him from gunning for her. It was too late.

Like Pandora's box.

She was there. Had exposed herself to powers that be in the waters behind Nicole's house. Had her sister been told then, too? Had she answered the door to police?

After already having what had looked like a horrendous episode in the garden?

Did Nicole know she'd had a sister? Did anyone retain that kind of memory function from the age of one?

Mariah would know.

When thoughts of her child-life expert friend and partner nearly brought tears to her eyes, Savannah straightened her shoulders. She was strong.

Had always had to be.

For Nicole, she'd beat the fear. And anything else that came barreling her way.

Coming somewhat out of her fog, Savannah glanced over at her guest, realizing that he'd been silently watching her. She tried to think back to the last thing he'd said. Something about being told that the victim of the shooting had been staying at La Hacienda.

And said, "So on a hunch that Savannah was an uncommon-enough name that there wouldn't be two of them registered at La Hacienda, you took a chance, called the hotel, and asked to be connected to my room." Her lawyer mind was nowhere near working up to speed, but at least she'd woken it up.

"No, I did an internet search on the name Savannah Compton, recognized you from the photo that popped up alongside the first listing, and then called the officer who'd left her card back for identity confirmation regarding this afternoon's incident."

Right. He was in private protection but, with a good reputation, could feasibly work in cooperative conjunction with law enforcement.

Or...with a flash of jealousy another possibility occurred to her. He'd said "her" when referring to the officer. Had she been even half alive, the woman could have been taken with him. Could have emitted some sign that she'd be open to further conversation...

As Savannah had.

Which pissed her off. It wasn't like she was some needy person who couldn't get a date. And she was acting like an inexperienced girl meeting the high school quarterback.

But then, Isaac definitely had a way about him. The man oozed compassion. Charm. The fact that his body was perfectly proportioned, and he had looks that could stop an octogenarian in her tracks was like a bonus to the rest of what he brought into a room...

"From there, I vacillated," the man started to talk again when Savannah failed to respond. "I had no business contacting you, the way I'd come by the information. As soon as I was off duty, I drove over here, checked out happy hour, thinking maybe I'd run into you again..."

"I didn't go down."

Obviously, Savannah. Good one. You sound real smart now. An intelligent expert, to be sure.

He'd have read about Sierra's Web. The firm's internet presence was the only thing that came up with her photo.

"But I kept thinking...if you really were in danger... I'm trained to prevent physical bodily harm to those who could be targets..."

Her heart lurched, and she stared at him. Couldn't pull her gaze away from his deep brown-eyed silent communication.

His eyes were telling her things that it was far too soon in their relationship to say.

"I know you have a world of experts at your disposal, bodyguards on staff..."

She nodded. But didn't speak. She had to hear what else he'd been about to say. He was that compelling to her.

"I just... I'm right here, right now...off duty for the next twelve hours...and had to reach out..."

Savannah took a long sip of wine. To keep from eagerly letting down her guard, asking the man to spend the night, wrapping her arms around him, and getting lost.

"I'm on leave from the firm," she told him instead. "I needed some personal time. And since the police told me they thought the shot was someone shooting a rodent in the swampy woods there at the cove or maybe intending to do some target shooting, I haven't called anyone for help."

All true. Just minus other truths.

There were things she couldn't tell him, couldn't tell anyone, for their own safety. But she would not lie to him.

When he took her hand, she held on. Let him lead her over to the couch. And when he set down his wineglass, she did hers as well.

Ready to get lost for a few hours. To experience the euphoria, the forgetfulness she could access. To sleep.

And wake up in the morning stronger. Better able to figure out how to go about ensuring that Nicole was all right.

Even if it meant putting herself in further harm by continuing to keep surveillance on Nicole until she could figure out a way to make certain that someone knew her younger sister might be struggling at home.

She didn't have to have direct contact. Just had to know who she could somehow alert anonymously...

Isaac hadn't spoken. Was watching her.

She liked it.

And said, "I don't know your last name."

Just didn't make good sense to spend the night with a man, even a bodyguard in good police regard, without knowing his full name.

"Forrester."

She liked that, too.

But wasn't so fond of the way his expression suddenly

changed. As though he'd just then made up his mind about something.

Was he about to ditch her?

It would be a first, but why not? She'd never been shot at before, either, until that day. Nor had she ever lied to her partners before the past week.

Or even thought about, let alone been tempted to embark on, a one-night stand.

Taking both of her hands, Isaac looked her in the eye and said, "I have more I need to tell you."

Oh, God. He was married.

"I work for a wealthy man," he said.

She'd figured as much. The coast along Nicole's property was dotted with multimillion-dollar estates. And only someone with a lot of money would have a personal protection director on staff. It didn't take an expert to figure that out.

Which meant that Isaac would have already figured her for having done that particular math.

He was still frowning as he said, "Because of what he does...acquiring businesses that can't afford not to be bought out..."

A nice way of saying his employer was a corporate raider? "He's involved with hostile takeovers?" she asked.

With a raised brow and a half nod of acknowledgment, he said, "He's made some enemies. And with you having been in close vicinity to the waters his daughter sails out to on a regular basis, combined with the fact that, from a distance, the two of you share size and coloring, and with him having just completed a less than friendly takeover from someone who threatened to make him hurt..."

His voice trailed off, and she saw where he was going.

But something else entirely was making her blood race, her heart pound. Could the providence she'd thought had put her in touch with Isaac to begin with really be at work? In a much larger way?

A man known for being hostile in business. An older man refusing to take the no Nicole had been firmly and clearly stating. Her eventual tears, as though she had no way out. A daughter who resembled Savannah in build *and* coloring?

Had the man she'd seen making Nicole cry been her little sister's adopted *father*?

And even more fantastic...

Did Isaac work for Nicole?

Hardly able to breathe, she stared at the man sitting there holding her hands... Did Isaac *know* her baby sister? Swallowing back tears, finding her court face by sheer force of will or sisterly love, she waited until she could trust herself to speak with only fear evident in her voice and asked, "You think I'm in danger?"

Isaac's head tilting slightly to the side and back, almost like a nod, the way he was looking at her...

"You think I should leave town immediately." She couldn't.

And if Isaac worked for Charlotte, her chances of keeping watch over her sister without being noticed were nil... unless she told him the truth.

He was a bodyguard. He could protect himself.

In a world where crimes were traceable.

Whoever her father had been about to testify against, whoever had murdered him and then burned his corpse had had friends in high enough places that there hadn't been a single suspect in her father's murder.

Or a single clue to Nicole's disappearance.

Thoughts falling into an eerily calm place, Savannah entertained them one by one.

Women had one-night stands all the time. Just because she never had didn't mean she couldn't.

Telling anyone who she was, most particularly someone close to Nicole, could not only put that person in danger but could get her sister killed.

It took her a second to get out of the clear succession of thoughts racing through her to notice that Isaac was shaking his head.

"I think it's only fair, before I say more, that I tell you who I work for," he said. "I've seen from your firm's website a lot of the kinds of cases you've done, the wealthy people you've worked for, and I'm sure what's published there is only a smidgeon…"

She nodded. Alert. Waiting.

As though her life depended on what he would say next.

Because, in more ways than one, it did.

"It's no secret around here," Isaac said, drawing out her internal agitation almost to breaking point. She sipped her wine, praying for a hint of its calming spirit to spread through her. "Everyone sees me out and about with…"

Using a tactic that had been getting people to talk to her since college, she raised one brow as he paused. Staring him straight in the eye. No panic lurking in the conglomeration of intense emotions roiling through her.

"I work for a man named Eduardo Duran. Have you ever heard of him?"

Savannah calmed. Just…sat, all thought, no feeling. Not in that second. She'd made the right choice to come.

Frowning, she shook her head. An honest response. Which brought sensation back. In barely containable force. While her heart pounded blood through her veins with such force she could feel it. The pounding in her chest. In her temples.

Eduardo Duran. Charlotte Duran.

Isaac, the man she'd met by chance at a hotel happy hour—and she'd definitely chosen the hotel by chance—

worked for her sister's family! Worked on the estate where she'd seen Nicole that afternoon.

Arguing with her father?

Was there a woman in the picture, too? A mother? Had the couple bought Nicole as a toddler?

Had Nicole been told anything about her biological mother and sister? Was that why she'd put her DNA in the Family Finders database?

Nicole had to have been calling out to her. Needing her.

And love had carried the message.

No matter what Isaac Forrester, concerned bodyguard, advised her to do, no matter the risk to her life, there was no way she was going to disappear to protect herself.

Until she knew that Nicole was okay, she wasn't going anywhere.

Most particularly not when she finally had her in. A man in her life who had no idea she was Nicole's sister—probably didn't even know her sister's real name. A man who could tell her about Nicole, giving her a chance to make suggestions to him, a way to make a real contribution to her sister's future happiness.

A man who, in any other situation, she could be falling for.

A man she believed she could trust.

Evil had ripped Nicole out of their lives all those years ago.

But love was going to win.

Chapter Seven

The woman was far craftier than he'd given her credit for. Ignoring the pit of disappointment in his gut, Isaac watched Savannah's response to his big reveal, figuring he was going to have to change course.

If he didn't know better, he'd sit right there and believe wholeheartedly that the expert lawyer on leave to do dirty work truly had never heard of Eduardo Duran.

And if she was that good...

His job just got one hell of a lot more challenging. Damn good thing he was a seasoned faker.

"Duran's a powerful man who's made a lot of enemies. People who can't find justice through proper channels..." The words, unpracticed, flowed smoothly from the persona of a bodyguard pretending to be personally concerned for the welfare of a lovely woman in distress in whom he had interest. "From what I heard in the household security meeting we had this afternoon, Duran feels certain that whoever shot at you took you for his daughter, Charlotte."

"Household security?" Savannah's voice had just the right amount of fear to convince him she was only who she thought he believed she was. "I thought you were the boss."

And he suddenly understood the trepidation coming at

him. It *was* for real. She'd had him pegged as the lead man on staff.

"I head up the personal protection detail," he told her. "But I'm under the jurisdiction of household security. Mr. Duran has a twenty-four-hour armed security detail guarding the property." He'd hoped to play things easier, but he was going to have to pour it on thick. "They call the shots where the rest of us are concerned."

He needed her to agree to his offer, once he got that far. His gut—and Duran's reaction that afternoon—were telling him that the lawyer could lead him to someone who knew more than Duran wanted them to know.

The weak link that would be the man's demise.

Isaac needed Savannah Compton alive long enough to lead him to it.

You want to protect her life regardless. The voice newly popping up inside him was an irritant. One he was going to have to shut up.

He'd give his life for another's every day of the week. But when one crossed to the wrong side of the law, as Savannah had, as he suspected Charlotte had, there were sometimes unforeseeable and unavoidable consequences that one undercover FBI agent working alone couldn't avert.

And here came the bigger news. "Household security is on high alert. And you are on the radar. Mr. Duran's head of security and closest confidant is uncomfortable with how close you were to the property. He has since learned that you bought a pair of binoculars in town yesterday morning."

He saw her throat move with the difficulty of her smile and did a quick mental check. Was he pouring it on too thick? Should he have held back?

Since when did he question himself in the middle of an operation?

Squeezing Savannah's hand, Isaac looked her in the eye. "You need to get out of town, Savannah."

She'd started shaking her head before he'd put the period on the sentence. "I can't, Isaac," she whispered, her gaze worried as she looked up at him. Holding his hand as tightly as he held hers.

As though they were evenly matched at their game.

He almost, for a second there, felt sorry for her. She had no idea who she was dealing with. In Duran. And in Isaac.

She opened her mouth as though to speak, clearly hesitated, studying him as though ascertaining whether to touch him and then, with another tight swallow, said, "I'm here... to find...someone. I'd been given information that led me to believe this person is staying on the coast, somewhere along the stretch where the Duran estate is located. I was out on the boat all day yesterday, too. Watching properties along the coastline. I...can't leave until I know they're okay."

She was good. Better than most. He was almost enjoying the parrying back and forth. Maybe he would have if innocent lives weren't at stake.

And she'd made a major mistake, too. Two of them. Duran was onto her. Had been before Isaac had ever heard of her. And on that boat that afternoon, she'd gotten too close.

Bending his head a little closer, he held her gaze and said "No one's worth losing your life over" so softly that the words didn't travel across the room.

She nodded silently. Steadily holding eye contact. As though begging him to read between the lines.

For a moment there, he second-guessed Duran's information about the lawyer's intent. She was an impressive adversary.

He took heed. Of her skill and his own emerging weakness where she was concerned. He wouldn't be caught with his pants down again.

"Who?" he asked, compassion and concern filling his voice and his expression.

When she shook her head, he relaxed a few muscles. He was beating her at their far too dangerous game.

"I want so badly to tell you, Isaac," she said. "I do." Her gaze implored him. "But I can't."

His own frown showed utmost concern. A lot of which was real.

"Why not?" He had to decipher truth from fiction and figure out what she didn't want him to know.

What she was hiding.

Or rather, *who*.

Who was paying her to be there?

Who'd hired her?

Afraid that Duran already knew, Isaac had to get Savannah to talk to him to better his chances of keeping her alive.

"Because if I tell you, I put your life at risk." The widening of his eyes was completely sincere. She'd surprised him with that one. And again, when she covered their clasped hands with her other hand, holding the bundle against her knee as though she was hugging it.

Making him far too aware of the warm flesh of her thigh beneath her lightweight pants.

Until he figured out that had to have been her intent. This woman, too beautiful, too smart for her own good, wasn't above using her sex appeal to win.

Something he'd never been called upon to do.

But would if he had to.

"I'm pretty sure that whoever shot at me today was just after me," she confided, not hiding what appeared to be very real fear in her gaze. "I've suspected someone's been following me for the past year..."

His mind scrambled to fit that in with what he knew. Tried to find the logical way it fit into what Duran had told him.

Couldn't.

Until he realized that whoever had hired her to get to Charlotte Duran probably wasn't the expert lawyer's first dark client. For all Isaac knew she'd been working dirty under the table for years. He'd had no time or ability to do any kind of deep dive on her.

Silently chiding himself for not having figured it out sooner—anyone after Duran would know to hire an experienced accomplice—he stayed silent. Keeping his gaze glued to hers. Making it as difficult as possible for her not to tell him more.

"I don't think whoever shot at me today was a poacher or target shooter. And I don't think it was someone thinking I was Duran's daughter—you said her name was Charlotte?—either."

As hard as it was for him to sit there playing the concerned new love interest who was also a bodyguard, Isaac forced himself to do it. Even rubbed the thumb of the hand she held along her leg. Encouraging her to trust him.

Trust *them*.

"And I don't think it matters whether I stay in San Diego or fly to Greece—the people after me are going to find me."

She'd played it too far. "That makes no sense," he said, working hard to keep all irritation—and disappointment—out of his tone. Making certain he remained in character.

Always playing the part.

And when she looked away from him, he called her back. "I know you and your firm have worked a lot of high-security cases, Savannah. You've got a nationally renowned firm of experts in pretty much every field around you all the time. Surely if you've been followed, one of them would have known. At the very least, you'd have reached out for someone to check, just to make sure. Your firm has partnered with law enforcement for years. You could have had access to security cameras."

When she dropped his hand, reached for her wine, he figured she'd realized she'd made a mistake. Was recalculating. Buying herself time to figure out how to recover.

They both wanted something from each other. He needed to know who she was working for and why—strongly believing she was his key to cracking the Duran case. And she wanted his access to Charlotte to use Duran's daughter to squeeze him.

For money. Or as Isaac was beginning to suspect, for something much more threatening to Eduardo Duran than cash.

Question was, who wanted what they wanted more?

"A year ago, one of our partners, one of my best friends, was kidnapped," she said, surprising him again. He took note of the tactic she'd used on him twice in one sitting. Would be better prepared the third time she tried it on him.

Showing concern again for a few seconds, he then looked away long enough to take a very small sip of wine before taking her right back into his circle of focus. "Was she...killed?"

It wasn't like the firm would have put it up on the website if she had been. The woman's photo would likely have just quietly disappeared.

Savannah's head shake relieved him. Bringing on yet another moment of warning from within him. He couldn't care.

Not until later. When the job was done and he could take his couple of days to himself to debrief.

"No," she said, her tone growing stronger as she took another sip from her half empty glass. "She was rescued a couple of days later, scared but unharmed. But ever since then... I've been...struggling with bouts of anxiety." Her gaze fluttered, meeting his, away, and then ultimately back again.

Showing...shame?

Damn. Savannah Compton had missed her calling becoming an expert attorney. Didn't matter how many high-
powered cases she'd won. She was a consummate actress.
Inarguably the best he'd ever met.

"I talked to Kelly about them—she's our psychiatry partner. They're normal, based on what we all went through that
weekend, and something I've worked to get past. I've been
telling myself, until tonight, that that's all it was. Me being
paranoid. And refusing to let the fear make me believe things
that aren't true."

Isaac almost sat back at that one. Talking about being
convinced of untrue things while lying to the face of someone she was pretending to have a personal interest in…the
woman was almost diabolical.

If there was any way she made it through current events
alive and on the right side of the law, he should ask her to
work for him.

Except that he could never afford to pay her. Most particularly since being the partner in a hugely successful national
firm didn't seem to be compensating her to her satisfaction.

She was so good, he'd even consider that Duran had been
lying to him when the crook had warned Isaac about the
lawyer, except that he'd been right on target.

She'd arrived. Had clearly had eyes on Charlotte Duran.
Isaac had seen those binoculars and where they'd been
trained with his own eyes. And had recorded images of her
spying from that boat in the event that he somehow convinced himself he'd seen wrong.

No one with legitimate interest in someone spied on them.

And Eduardo Duran might be a fiend who disgusted Isaac,
but Isaac also knew, more than most, just how attuned Duran
was to everything going on around him. How accurate.

He paid big for the knowledge.

It was part of the reason he'd been able to live freely when he was, internationally, a wanted man.

Isaac knew better than to disrespect the man's intel.

Savannah's glass clinked loudly as she put it down on the table, drawing his attention back to her face. Worry lines had formed, but she was still looking him in the eye as she said, "Say something."

"Who do you think is following you?"

She shook her head. "That's the part I can't talk about." The deep sorrow in her voice matched that shining from her gaze. "I wish I could, Isaac. More than you'll ever know. But I can't."

If he didn't know better, he'd think he was talking with an abused woman on the run from her abuser.

To the point that he wanted to go hunt the guy down and arrest him before he killed him himself.

She lost some of his respect for taking it that far.

"Just give me a name."

"That's just it," she said. "I don't know."

Seriously? His look of incredulity couldn't be hidden. Or faked.

And she took his hand again. He was prepared that time. Wasn't going to fall for the sex card as he listened to her say, "I know this sounds strange," she told him. "I just... I truly don't have any idea who it is. I really thought it was paranoia. Or hoped it was. Until today. Whoever it is knows I'm here. And he's after me."

Boom. As good as she was, she'd played right into his hand.

"Won't you be bringing this same danger on whoever you're here to find?"

"I hope to God not."

His impression of her acting lowered a notch. Because

there was a hole in her logic. He let go of her hand to grab his wineglass. Couldn't appear too eager.

Hard to get was more what the current seconds were calling for.

"You tell me you can't tell me what's going on because you'll put me in danger, but then you tell me you don't know who's after you, and you're looking to connect with someone—who you also can't identify to me."

If she was as desperate to use him to get to Charlotte as Duran thought she was, she'd have to find a way out of that one.

She leaned in, her gaze completely serious, and fully focused on him. "I know...something. Have known for years," she said. "I don't know who. And the person I'm looking for—I have no intention of making contact. I don't want anyone to ever know I looked. I just need to...see for myself."

He got chills. She was that on target. In the space of seconds, she'd managed to climb her way out of the hole she'd dug.

"So let me help," he said, going in for his win, holding up a hand as she started to object. "I'm not saying I help you look for or find whoever you're here to see. I give you my word I won't even try to find out. Just let me help keep you safe while you go about looking."

Her chin trembled. Her eyes grew moist.

Isaac resisted an instinctive need to pull her into his arms.

"Duran's going to be watching you," Isaac told her. "Or his men are. As one on the inside, I can help you escape their notice. Say I thought I saw you across town when I know you're at the beach, that kind of thing. Not those exact details, of course, but..."

He rushed his speech purposely to let her know how badly he wanted to be there for her. To play the fool to her sexual come-ons. To seem like he was falling for the idea that there was something special to them, a *love at first sight* type of thing that had drawn them together from his supposed innocent hello the other night.

"You aren't safe here," he continued. "Duran's people know you're staying here, and as easily as I got through to you, you can bet they'd have an easier time. We'll need to move you someplace safer. And get you a different car to drive…"

When tears filled her eyes, he stopped. He couldn't help himself. He had to admire her technique.

And when a few minutes later she leaned forward, laid her forehead against his chest, and whispered an incredibly heartfelt sounding "Thank you," he kissed her hair.

Chapter Eight

Savannah liked Isaac Forrester. As in *liked* liked him. *Woman to man* liked. More than she'd been drawn to anyone in the years since her close friend, Sierra, had been murdered during college. Sierra—Sierra's Web. She and her partners had all been close with Sierra. Had fought to have her disappearance investigated. And had been the reason her murder had been solved. All of them, Sierra's friends who'd become family to her, working together.

They'd been a team ever since. And there she was, leaning on a total stranger.

Keeping secrets. All over the place.

Not calling home.

Because she was going home. Rescuing the seven-year-old girl who'd been locked in no-man's-land since the day her father had been murdered and her baby sister had been kidnapped.

She might've been fighting for her life in a very real, physical sense, but that fight wasn't what prompted her to lean on Isaac Forrester. It wasn't what drove her.

Nicole did. Needing to know that her sister was okay, being able to finally free herself of the guilt—being loved and cared for while her baby sister, who'd still been breast-feeding and needed their mother far more, who'd been completely helpless, had been in the hands of murderers—took precedence over everything else.

Including her fondness for the man who'd almost literally fallen into her lap two nights before.

Providence.

It had to be.

Not only had the man awoken the woman who'd been frozen inside her for her entire adult life, he worked for her *sister*. Or at least for the family.

Her "in" had been given to her. A sign that she was on the right track.

At the very least, a fortuitous set of events that she absolutely could not ignore.

But before she actually left her hotel room with the man who told her he had a place where he knew she'd be safer, a place no one at the Duran estate knew existed, she excused herself to the restroom. And on her phone, set her thumbs to flying over the on-screen keyboard.

Life at Sierra's Web and in court had taught her that if things seemed too good to be true, they generally were.

Except that she'd almost been killed that day. Nothing good about that.

She'd seen her sister being pressured. Unable to get away. Crying. No good there, either.

To think, even for a second, that Isaac could have had anything to do with any of that as a way to manipulate her into the hands of Nicole's kidnappers—into the hands of whoever had been determined to silence her father—well, it just didn't make sense.

He had her. He hadn't needed to manipulate her in such grand measures.

Paranoia was not going to win over good sense.

Several links popped up on her search. All ammunition to kill the enemy of fear in her mind.

She read each one.

Flushed the toilet she'd been standing by. Washed her hands.

Isaac Forrester was exactly who he said he was. With an impressive display of law enforcement endorsements. She'd recognized one of them. Sierra's Web had partnered with the sheriff on a familial child abduction case the previous year.

Looking at herself in the mirror, seeing a woman she hardly recognized with dark hair, dry again, hanging freely around her and eyes that glowed with purpose. Imagination or not, she saw more life in them than she'd ever seen before.

A product of the adrenaline flowing through her.

She was finally on the cusp of completing her life's quest.

And had a gorgeous, hard-working, impressive guy standing by her, offering to have her back as she did so.

One who'd been honest with her. He needn't have sought her out that night. Or told her the truth about what he really did for a living.

He'd chosen loyalty to her over loyalty to his career in letting her know that she was on Duran's radar, that her life was definitely in danger there. And was going to be continuing to do so, helping her escape the sights of Duran's security until she was back home.

Because it was the right thing to do. Saving lives always came before career advancement.

Which was why she had to continue to keep her decades-old secret. By speaking outside of witness protection, she could put Isaac's life in further danger.

Watching her eyes cloud, she stood there, in front of the mirror, with doubts plaguing her. Was it selfish to accept his offer of help? Would mere association with her endanger him?

If that were so, she couldn't go home, either.

Shouldn't be at the hotel, putting staff and other guests at possible risk.

Could never be around another human being…

Stop. The command came from within. Carrying a load of frustration, of determination with it. She would not entertain anxiety-induced thoughts.

She'd been honest with Isaac about the dangers. Had told him more than she'd ever told anyone about her secret mission.

It had been twenty-four years.

And whoever had killed her father had no way of knowing what a seven-year-old child had known about her father's death. Hadn't known how precocious she'd been. What she'd figured out on her own, leading her mother and investigators to tell her the truth to prevent her from asking questions or talking to too many people and putting herself in danger.

As long as she kept that piece to herself, she'd be fine.

They'd all be fine.

She had to believe that.

And opened the bathroom door with a grateful smile on her face.

WHEN HE HEARD the click on the door lock, in the alcove between the suite's bedroom and living areas, Isaac quickly shoved the burner phone he'd just used into the inner jacket pocket he'd pulled it from the second Savannah had left the room.

He was back on the couch, sitting forward, elbows on his knees, hands folded when she appeared. A ready stance.

And a nonthreatening one.

"Have you had a chance to change your mind?" she asked, calm, contained as she took the seat she'd vacated next to him. Still meeting his gaze straight on.

If they weren't playacting, they'd be talking without

words. Making it more challenging to get a read on her. How did the woman ooze sincerity with just a look?

He might have just taken on one of the toughest assignments of his career.

"Not at all," he told her. "To the contrary. I think you should pack. I have a place we can go to." He kept hold of her gaze even when his libido was telling him it was time to look away. His professional instincts were guiding him, and when he was working, they always took precedence. "I'm on call twenty-four seven, but I have most nights to myself. And an apartment not far from here where I usually stay…"

Her frown didn't surprise him. "You think it's wise for you to take me to your apartment?"

She'd played right into that one. "Hell no," he said and added, "I don't think it's wise for us to be seen together at all." When he saw the disappointment cross her expression, he knew he had her. And hit his end note.

The one he'd come there to play.

"When I became a bodyguard, I used some of my personal investment money to secure a small place outside the city. It's only minutes away but set in the woods, with a road that only services three other properties. It's small and old, which allowed me to afford it, but it's made completely of cement, has camouflaged surveillance cameras, and trees that keep it hidden from aerial view." He paused to take a breath but then continued right on. "In my business, you never know what you're going to be up against. I needed to know I had a place I could get to, get my charges to in the event we were under attack."

He thought he read admiration in the lawyer's eyes. Didn't allow himself, as she nodded and squeezed his hand before she went to pack, to dwell on that touch of her skin against his. Didn't matter how much he wanted to hold on. To pull her to him. To kiss her. He kept his mind firmly focused on details. The house had been designated for his use from the time he'd gone undercover. In case his cover was blown, and he had to disappear quickly. And was currently listed under the name of a deceased person in a sealed property record. But it was owned by the San Diego office of the FBI.

Was one of the bureau's safe houses.

And, as of his last phone call, was going to serve as a place for the bureau to house—and watch—a possible suspect involved with Isaac's undercover operation.

Any guilt lurking inside him for lying to Savannah about where he was taking her was somewhat appeased by the fact that he was doing everything in his power, pulling out all stops, to keep her safe.

From the danger she'd brought, and was continuing to bring, upon herself.

"A friend of mine just dropped off a car for you to drive," he told her as she rolled one bag out of the bedroom and told him she was ready. "We'll leave your rental here until morning, and then Dale, my friend, will see that it gets dropped off at the airport."

Nodding, she said, "Making it look like I left town. I like it." And then, giving him a look that he could only describe as suggestive, told him, "You're good."

He took a step forward, his gaze on her lips...and grabbed the handle of her bag instead. "I'll take this down the emergency exit stairs. Dale's going to meet me outside the door to load the bag in the car. Five minutes after I leave, you go down the same way. He'll give you the keys. I also asked him to pick you up a new burner phone. Just in case." He handed her a napkin. "That's the address of the house and a security code for the lockbox on the door."

Her mouth fell open, and he stopped, knew he'd made a mistake, had come on too strong, too much like an agent taking a witness to a safe house, and executed a quick mental reversal. "The lives in my care depend on my ability to keep them safe," he said, his tone softening. He had to allow his gaze to dwell with hers again.

In that personal way they'd silently established.

And again felt a pang of regret in his gut.

And lower...hunger built.

Savannah's glance was long, searching, and he stood there, feeling like they were mating with their eyes, until she nodded and asked, "Will you be following me there?"

No. He was going to his small, completely sterile apartment to take a cold shower.

"Please?" Her imploring glance seemed so sincere...

Why? What was her plan? What did she expect to get out of him that night? Maybe a photo of him? Compromised? Something she could use to bribe him to give her access to Charlotte?

As the thought occurred, hit his gut soundly, Isaac saw the bigger picture. She'd known who he was the other night. Had turned on the charm.

Flirting.

Just as he'd thought. But not to get him to lead her to Charlotte. She wanted a way to *bribe* him to give her access. To better ensure her success.

Which meant that—

"Of course I'll follow," he told her, reaching out a palm to cup her face.

And to seal the devil's deal they'd just made, he bent down.

And placed his lips on hers.

SAVANNAH HAD BEEN kissed before. The first time she'd had sex was on prom night her senior year in high school. She'd dated throughout college, too. Until Sierra.

There'd been a man or two while she'd been on the road

for an extended period of time dealing with cases over the years. Pleasant experiences that both parties had known were going nowhere.

But as she drove the newish small blue SUV off the hotel lot, Savannah's body still tingled at the memory of that one brief touch of Isaac's lips against hers.

She hadn't completed her mission, hadn't yet said goodbye to the past to enter the road to her future. So how could the life ahead be there already?

In her experience, while the world provided a lot of good moments, there'd never been such a combination of determination and fate holding her up.

It was like Isaac had appeared ahead of schedule to show her what lay ahead, continuously calling to her, to give her the strength to get there.

Or maybe his arrival was divinely timed. Giving her something to hold on to while she let go of the past.

She wasn't building false hopes. Absolutely did not hear a possibility of wedding bells or even long-term bells ringing in her head. Didn't even want them.

But a future? One that could contain Isaac?

Her heart was opening to the idea.

His plan for her escape had worked like a charm. Easy peasy. She'd been looking over her shoulder as she drove, watching the mirrors religiously, and hadn't seen one vehicle that appeared to be on her trail.

Not even his.

But he'd called on the new phone she'd been given as she'd pulled off the lot to let her know that he'd be about five minutes behind her. He just had to make a quick stop.

For condoms?

She didn't ask.

Didn't suggest the bottle of wine she'd have liked to have,

either. To share with him. They had all night, and neither of them had finished the glass he'd poured for each.

There'd be no more wine. Not now that her moments alone in a hotel room to wallow were done. She was officially on her hunt. Had a firm plan to help Nicole.

Charlotte. Her sister identified with that name. Not Nicole. Savannah was going to have to get used to it. Every time Isaac said the name, it hurt.

She couldn't let that show.

"Charlotte," she said aloud to keep herself company as she drove in a darkness lit only by the electrically charged bulbs hanging in symmetrical lines along the way. "Charlotte. Charlotte."

She didn't hate the name.

Just hated what her sister not going by Nicole stood for.

A robbed life.

Four of them. The baby girl's. Hers. Their mother's. Their father's.

They'd been a perfect, completely normal middle-class family.

She'd just made her last turn, was looking for her destination half a mile ahead, when she noticed the car that turned in behind her.

Heart pounding, she was frozen by the fear that engulfed her.

Isaac had said that after the boating incident, Eduardo Duran considered her a risk. The binoculars. She'd been spying on his property.

Isaac was in Duran's employ.

By sheer force of will, she held the moving vehicle on a straight path, kept her foot on the gas pedal steady.

The house was supposed to be just ahead. If it was, did she turn in?

Keep going? Isaac had said there were a couple or three

more houses on the road. Which was it, two or three? Were they inhabited?

Did the road dead-end?

What a fool she'd been! Grabbing for the phone in her pocket, Isaac's burner phone, she let out a frustrated cry. He'd had her turn off her phone. Had said that Duran's people had top-of-the-line equipment and would be able to trace it. She'd taken out the sim card after that.

Oh, God, why hadn't she paid more attention when Hud and Glen had gone into detail about their work on cases? She'd always been so busy...had just wanted the results they'd had for her.

Hud's number wasn't programmed into the new phone.

But the burner rang. Just as the car behind her sped up, driving on the questionable shoulder of the road to come up beside her.

Her mouth opened, her throat froze. Flooring the gas, she sped ahead, holding on to the wheel with both hands, looking straight ahead. Bracing for a blast. For pain.

And heard a horn honk.

Not a gunshot.

With a quick glance around her, half thinking she might be hurt and dreaming, she saw the burner phone where she'd dropped it on the console.

It was still ringing.

And the caller ID was right there, visibly on the screen.

Isaac.

Chapter Nine

She'd gunned the gas.

Though Savannah was smiling five minutes later, profusely thanking him and seemingly at ease as she pulled her suitcase out of the back of the SUV and rolled it toward where Isaac stood at the newly opened door, he knew she'd been frightened when she hadn't recognized him behind her.

Which was why he'd called.

Yet she was playing the whole thing off as though it hadn't happened. Had pretended that she'd just missed the drive. She looked around the place with a pleasant expression on her face. Said it was cozy.

Rolled her bag into the room he suggested she take. He could hear her moving around in there, unpacking.

Because she didn't want him to know how afraid she was? Or had been?

On one hand, he didn't blame her. He'd never let fear show if it overwhelmed him while working. Or if he did, it would be his last day on the job.

On the other hand...what was she trying to hide?

As Isaac moved about the house, making sure the water was on, the refrigerator stocked as he'd been told it would be, and then securing every room to his satisfaction before walking around outside, he couldn't get Savannah's fear out of his head.

What was she so deathly afraid of?

A lawyer out to get bribe material so her client could squeeze Eduardo Duran…it just didn't track that she'd be that skittish. More likely, she'd tell her client that he'd have to find someone else to do the job.

There had to be more to the situation than he'd been told. By either Duran or Savannah.

Was she desperate for money?

That didn't make sense, either. Not with her firm's legendary success.

Or had someone she cared about needed medical treatment—another motive behind desperate actions? But that didn't fly, either. Her best friend was a medical expert with a plethora of experts working for her.

She'd said she was there to find someone. Charlotte. He already knew that.

But why?

What did her client think he could get out of the woman to hold over her father?

As soon as the question occurred to him, he was giving himself a silent verbal blasting for not having realized the possibility sooner.

She wasn't just after Charlotte in some general sense. She was after something specific.

One thing.

Savannah knew what it was. And so did Eduardo.

Which would logically conclude that Eduardo knew exactly who Savannah was working for.

And could possibly use her—force her—to help Eduardo get to her client.

He knew who she was. She'd tipped her hand with the

boating maneuver. And that was why she couldn't quit. Didn't matter where she went, he'd find her.

If the man had a secret that could ruin him, he'd stop at nothing, turn the screws on every powerful person for whom he'd ever done a favor or anyone who'd ever turned a blind eye to his business dealings and could be framed to put that secret to death once and for all.

From all Isaac knew about the man, he was certain about that much.

Savannah had to know at least part of that, too. It explained her almost irrational fear. She'd mentioned it earlier—he just hadn't picked up on it as real. He'd thought she was spinning her tale when she'd talked about a paranoia that had had her in its grip for the past year.

Since her friend's kidnapping the year before.

Did her business with Eduardo have something to do with that?

Was she protecting her firm, as she'd said she was? By not telling them what was going on?

Or had the not-telling-them part been a lie? Was she there on firm business?

That didn't make sense, either. With Sierra's Web's reputation, the FBI would have stepped up in a heartbeat to help.

Was someone blackmailing *her*?

Did Charlotte know her father's secret? Savannah's part in it?

He kind of doubted that part. The woman wouldn't have been so consumed by Arnold Wagar's advances if she'd had something of a life-and-death scope on her mind.

But... Eduardo's sudden announcement of a plan to marry his daughter off to the older man... Was Wagar somehow in on things?

And Eduardo was using his daughter to buy the man off?

Bothersome questions.

He needed answers.

And had a source right there. Savannah Compton. Who was determined to stay on his good side. Which gave him some advantage.

She'd given him much greater leverage with her earlier confession, magnified by the greatly accelerated speed out there on the road.

"You're set for the night, then?" he asked her, moving toward the door as she came out of the bedroom.

She froze. Only for a second. It was all the tell he needed.

"I've only seen the bedroom. Just made the bed with the sheets that were on top of it. Give me a second to glance around, in case I have any questions." She sounded reasonable. Capable.

Isaac admired her for it.

"You can view all of the surveillance camera footage on the television," he told her. "You'll see the icon on the screen. Passcode is already set." Ostensibly giving her access so she'd feel safe.

And reminding her that she had reason to need to keep watch on that footage.

"I know it's dark out here, but the shades are room darkening, too, so you can turn on all the lights in the place and they won't be visible from the outside."

Hating himself for playing on her fear, Isaac watched her make her way through the place, checking out the bathroom, running water in the kitchen sink, and thought about all the lives that had been shattered by Eduardo Duran over the years, the hits made at his behest, the arms and illegal drugs he trafficked. And felt his backbone stiffen.

He just had to keep his lips off her body.

When she opened the refrigerator, he said, "I had my friend stock basics. Feel free to use whatever is there. I'm assuming you aren't going to want to go out again tonight."

Unfamiliar home. Remote area in unfamiliar town. With darkness adding its own edge to the unknown.

He needed her to be afraid enough to invite him to stay. To have his extended presence be her idea.

And then, while she was still peering inside the refrigerator, he reached for the door handle and asked, "All good?"

Standing there with the door open, the interior light shedding shadows on her face, she nodded. Then, with a "Hey," turned, pulled out a bottle of wine, smiling straight at him, and said, "You can stay for a few if you'd like."

And he dropped his keys onto the table by the entrance.

SHE HAD PLANS to use the man. Savannah wasn't proud of that fact. Not a great way to treat a once-in-a-lifetime meeting.

A part of her hoped when all was said and done, he'd understand. And be willing to forgive her. Hoped that when she returned home, she'd not only have assurance that her baby sister was thriving but that she'd go with the connection she and Isaac shared intact.

Even if only to hold on to as a wonderful memory.

Proof that providence did provide.

As she held out her wineglass for Isaac to fill from the wine he'd just opened—the same kind she'd ordered at the bar the first night they'd met—Savannah's first thoughts were not on Charlotte.

They were on Isaac. And the kiss he'd given her just before they'd left her hotel room.

He hadn't even opened his mouth, nor she hers, and yet she'd felt as though they'd just been intimate.

She was there for Charlotte. Would lose her life if she had to in her quest to ensure her sister was safe and well. Nothing had changed there.

But in those moments, with darkness outside and someone from her father's deadly past looking for her, in addition to Duran's men, she needed Isaac to take her out of her headspace long enough for her to recharge.

Except that he took a chair in the living room, not a place on the couch they could share. And had taken a sip of his wine when she'd been holding hers for a toast.

They talked about their lives, their childhoods. She'd grown up in a one-parent home with no siblings. He'd had two parents until they'd been killed in a small plane crash, leaving Isaac, at nineteen, the sole caregiver for his thirteen-year-old sister.

A woman now grown, living on the opposite side of the country, and not good about keeping in touch.

He'd delivered the facts with regret laced in understanding.

And Savannah wanted him to join her on the couch. Wanted to scoot closer to him. Not due to attraction that time, but in commiseration.

Their circumstances were vastly different, and yet they were both orphaned with only a younger sister, from whom they were estranged.

The pain in that was intense. And a normal part of life, too. You couldn't change what was out of your control. "There are some times you just have to hurt," she said softly. "You loved. Choices were made, and you're forced to live with knowing that a part of you is out there somewhere but you can't ever see her. Talk to her." She took a sip of her wine.

He'd been watching her intently, but personally so, and his eyes narrowed as she delivered the last.

She put down her glass of wine. She'd had nowhere near enough. And she was through. She hadn't said the one she'd loved had been her sister, but she'd revealed too much.

Contemplating sex with the man was one thing, pouring her heart out another entirely. And unacceptable.

"You're talking about the person you came here to see?"

The shake of her head was instinctual. And she added, "I'm not here to see anyone." She'd already told him so, back at the hotel. She had no intention of making contact.

His brows drew together, but his position remained relaxed. And far too sexy. Those open hips, the bulge visible beneath the fly of his pants now that his jacket had fallen open.

Even the gun holstered at his hip.

A gun, sexy? Had she suddenly flipped into kink, too?

More like him being in legal possession of a gun made her feel safe.

He'd taken a sip of his wine. Set the glass on the coffee table, across from her. "I know you said that, but...you're here to find someone but not to see them?" he asked. She saw the frown on his face. Knew her explanation didn't make a lot of sense on the surface. Was afraid she was losing him.

And she shrugged. A lifetime of staying safe through secrets didn't just suddenly fade because she was attracted to a man with whom she was alone.

Or one she trusted.

She'd given every single one of her partners immediate legal access to everything she owned—had already given them her heart—and even they hadn't penetrated her code of silence.

He crossed his ankle over his opposite knee, took another sip of wine. A small one. When he returned the drink to the table, the liquid had barely dropped down on his glass.

She thought about moving to the chair next to his. Touching distance. Could tell by the smoldering look in his eyes that he was interested in her.

He'd kissed her!

So why...

"What are your plans for tomorrow?" he asked then. "I'm

back on duty at nine, guarding Charlotte, and need to be able to steer security away from wherever you might be."

She didn't want to think about danger. Security. Him leaving. But couldn't pass up the door he'd just pulled wide open.

"You don't work until nine? Charlotte sleeps in?" Had he been Savannah's bodyguard, he'd have to be present by seven, which was when she left her house every morning that she was in town.

Or was at work in her hotel room while out of town on a case.

"Her nighttime bodyguard is going off shift at that time." Which told her very little. "Every day?"

He shrugged. Leaving her to wonder if he was deliberately holding out on her or if the arrangement was permanent until it wasn't. Something that changed according to day, week, or month.

"Does she work?" she asked then—casually, she prayed. She was being polite, taking interest in his daily work. Showing some curiosity, too. Considering the young woman's wealth, it would be odd if she didn't.

And held her breath as she waited for the first real piece of news on her little sister's life. Only to receive another noncommittal lift of one shoulder. So what? Nicole worked some but not regularly?

Or was involved with charity work but didn't get paid? Based on the home she owned, it wasn't like she needed the money.

"I can't imagine..." she started and stopped, telling herself not to pour it on too thick yet buzzing with an adrenaline that had taken over her entire system. Could this be it? The conversation that would set her free?

Providence.

Isaac was watching her, engaging with her visually, holding on, as he had from the first moment he'd joined her at the bar. "Imagine what?" he asked as she took a moment to formulate questions.

"If she resembles me, that would mean she's...around my age...and...living on an estate like that... I mean, I do fine... have a nice home...but that place...and needing full-time security...a bodyguard staff... It must be tough." She chose each word carefully. Not wanting to blow the chance to do what she'd come to do but needing to maintain a sense of normal curiosity in Charlotte without seeming overly interested.

Isaac's head tilt seemed more casual than on guard as he said, "It's like anything, I imagine. You take the bad with the good."

"I just..." She kept her gaze on his, giving him honesty as she confessed, "I don't know that I could live like that. I'd think I'd feel...caged." A comment meant to segue into the tears she'd witnessed on her sister's face that afternoon.

Who better than one of the family bodyguards to be put on watch for any signs of domestic abuse?

Another shrug, one that was clearly sharper, told her to stop. Too much, too soon. As waves of disappointment crashed through her, she picked up her wineglass. Allowing herself to reassess the choice to be done with it.

And horror struck. Did Isaac already know about Charlotte's distress and was turning a blind eye to it?

The possibility hung there. She couldn't bring it in. Didn't believe it. The only way Isaac Forrester would allow a young woman to be mistreated would be if he was getting enough evidence to have her abuser taken away from her, not just warned.

He'd be in that house collecting evidence.

And clearly wasn't going to say any more about his boss's daughter at the moment.

"You don't have to stay if you don't want to." He'd been different ever since they'd moved to his house. Meeting her gaze, silently communicating his desire to be with her. But more distant, too. More reticent.

"I want to."

Three words. Spoken with feeling. They filled her body with warmth again. Reignited her desire to have him there. Reinstated her faith that they'd met for a reason.

"So why are you sitting over there, not talking, and I'm over here asking inane questions to get to know you better?" Good save. And truth, too.

"You're in my home for protection, at my invitation. I've offered to help you stay safe in any way I can. Seems wrong to take advantage of that situation."

Oh. An *old-fashioned* gorgeous hunk of man who wore a gun.

Running her tongue over her lips, more of a nervous gesture than come-on, Savannah crossed her legs as she said, "What if I want you to?"

Because she did. "No strings attached," she added.

And he stood up.

Surging with anticipation, dripping with desire, nipples hard, Savannah waited for him to finally join her on the couch. To get about the business of losing herself in the most incredible sexual encounter she'd ever imagined.

He took his holster off his belt. Set it on the coffee table. Slipped off his shoes. And then said, "I can't, Savannah. Not tonight. With everything that happened today. And tomorrow as yet unknown. I'd like to stay here on the couch, though, at least for another few hours, and then head home to bed in my apartment, alone, to get some sleep before I have to go into work. In case anyone is watching to see if I came home for the night."

She wanted so much more. And yet as she stood, still hungry for sex, she wasn't as unhappy as she'd have expected. He was going to stay.

Was watching out for her.

And that said a whole lot more to her right then than a guy who'd jump on sex just because he wanted it. No matter how sincerely offered.

Chapter Ten

No way Isaac was having sex while agents from the San Diego office were watching the house. But for some reason, when it had become obvious he wasn't going to get any information out of Savannah Compton that night, he hadn't been able to just put down his wine and walk out on her.

He could tell she'd been desperate not to be alone. He'd just known.

And so, turning on the inside camera aimed at the living area, he half lay on the couch and dozed until his watch alarm vibrated against his wrist, letting him know it was time to go.

He glanced in on Savannah only to make certain that she was there and that the covers were moving with her breathing.

He didn't let his gaze linger, didn't stare at her shoulders, bare except for one-inch silk straps, and kept his gaze firmly there and above as he left the room as silently as he'd entered.

And though he'd debated with himself, he hadn't turned off the camera before he'd left. Savannah Compton didn't seem like the type to walk naked around the living room, and he felt better about agents having an eye inside the house.

Just a precaution in case Duran's tracking abilities were impossibly brilliant. And the men the international criminal had hired found ways to land on a property invisibly and seep through walls.

All other points of entry were guarded, albeit surreptitiously. The FBI took their safe houses seriously.

Especially when they were holding potential suspects.

He drove away slowly, so as not to wake her up or draw any other attention to himself, and didn't turn on the headlights until he was a quarter of a mile down the road and passed what he knew to be a marker for a preset surveillance-tent site on the safe house property. The site was fully equipped with electrical hookup and internet connection. And when the house was in use, a tent with a couple of decent air mattresses was erected.

It didn't look like much on the outside, but the agents had everything they needed to do their jobs within. And traded off every four to six hours.

Although eager to get home to his boring little apartment, Isaac didn't even make it to the highway before his private Duran cell rang.

Dread filled his gut as he pulled the phone out of his inner jacket pocket, slowing as he drove to the side of the road. Expecting to see Emmajean's name on the screen, he came to an abrupt halt as he recognized Duran's.

Eduardo Duran had phoned that number exactly zero times in the months Isaac had been in his employ.

"Yeah," he said urgently. Thinking of Savannah. Had Duran done something to her the second he'd left the house? Was it over?

And his cover blown, too?

"Charlotte's gone."

Shock hit Isaac. Gas pedal to the floor, he flicked on the car audio system as he drove, dropping the phone into the seat. "Emmajean?" he yelled, to be heard.

And because he was pissed. Livid.

At himself. At Savannah. The distraction she'd posed. The possible part she'd played. Had she known? Was that why she'd asked him to stay the night?

"Where in the hell was Emmajean?" he demanded when no immediate response from his boss was forthcoming.

"In the bathroom." Eduardo's voice had lost some of its commanding strength. Isaac struggled to keep up. To read between lines he had and the many he didn't yet know.

"Who got Charlotte?"

"I was hoping you." Ah. The reason for the call.

And with that last statement, the man actually sounded... lost. Beaten.

It wouldn't last—Isaac knew that. Men like Duran didn't lose. Or give up.

They were captured. Or they died wealthy of natural causes.

Isaac's brain clicked into full focus. "Any sign of forced entry?" He had a job to do and was one of the best at it.

"My men are still checking. Emmajean came out of the bathroom twenty minutes ago and found her gone."

Isaac relaxed enough to take a full breath. "You're sure she's not in the house?"

"Full staff, security, household, and protection detail have been in every room, every closet. I've been calling her cell. It's not ringing here in the house, not on her charger. And she's not answering."

Didn't mean she'd been abducted.

And yet... Charlotte and her phone...the woman never let it out of reach. To the point of paranoia.

But to take her from her bed? On an estate that was armed to the hilt?

If someone was going to attempt to blackmail Eduardo Duran by taking his daughter, they'd have to be as good as or better than Duran's army.

Which meant frighteningly unpredictable.

And what better way to prove that, to break Duran, than to invade his most personal space?

Still, Isaac had to see all possibilities. "She might have left on her own."

"Her car's here."

"What about the rest of the fleet?"

"All here."

Still didn't mean she couldn't have left of her own accord. Except that unless Charlotte felt safe—as she had with her plan to hide out in a secure bathroom the other day—she never went five feet without protection detail. The need had seemed ingrained in her.

Breaking all speed limits, Isaac wasn't sure why Duran was still on the phone with him. The connection was still live.

Duran usually just clicked off when he was done with whoever he'd been talking to.

The Duran Isaac knew would be in a suit at his desk in a time of dire emergency, no matter the time of day or night, barking orders at his head of security.

Isaac was barking them at himself. Savannah Compton. Doubts hit for a second time. More solidly. Had she known the plan all along? Had keeping him with her for the night been the plan?

At the hotel or the house...either would have fit.

"Have they called the police?" he bit out, mind spinning with next possible moves.

Looking for suspects, clues he'd missed.

"It's too soon to bring them in. We need to exhaust reasonable means of finding her first." Duran's voice was small in the silence. "But I've already called in the best of the best in the private sector, and they're downstairs. You know her whereabouts and outside activities, the people who interacted with her far better than anyone else, Forrester. Get here."

The man was not himself.

Isaac almost felt sorry for him.

Eduardo Duran's daughter was gone, and he was breaking.

Isaac had found Duran's biggest weakness.

Just not soon enough.

Someone else had found her, too.

SAVANNAH SPENT THE early hours of the morning on the internet. Hud had set up all the partner's computers, including laptops and tablets, with complex firewalls and safety protocols so that they could travel and surf with relative anonymity. And while she couldn't control her current internet connection, she trusted Isaac.

And he'd trusted her enough that he'd left his system password on the table for her.

She'd found it within minutes of his leaving. Had heard him go. And gotten up immediately after. Until she had a chance to see the outside of the property in the daylight, to get a feel for where she was and how she might keep herself safe in the event her location was compromised while she was there alone, there was no way she'd be able to go back to sleep.

Thoughts of Charlotte had been consuming her since the second she'd awoken. The night before—the personal part, where forgetfulness with Isaac had come first—was better left in the past. She'd been scared. Not thinking clearly.

And while she was certain that she'd have immensely enjoyed a sexual encounter with Isaac Forrester, she was glad it hadn't happened. She had Isaac's attention. Was in his secret home. Which meant access to him. A chance to find out about Nicole. *Charlotte*. She couldn't blow the golden opportunity that had just landed in her lap by making it personal.

Risking a breakup.

If he was a one-and-done type of guy—and she'd offered a fling... Yeah, sex couldn't happen. She had to keep the thrill alive. The temptation.

She had to flirt.

But couldn't go all the way...

Most particularly as she took the time, used the skills Hud had taught her to do some deep diving of her own on Charlotte Duran. And found almost nothing.

No public records. No publicity photos from charity events.

No listing on popular people encyclopedia sites. And no hits using the social media hacks she'd been taught.

She'd found a university course with the name Professor Charlotte Duran as teacher, but no way to verify that it was the same woman Savannah had seen the day before. There'd been no accompanying photo. No teacher's biography.

And still, Savannah smiled. Nicole, a university professor? In women's studies? Talking about the need to be aware of cultural language in a global society? Their mom would be so proud...

Hell, Savannah was proud, and she didn't even know for sure that the two women—Professor Charlotte Duran and heiress Charlotte Duran—were one and the same.

It felt right, though. Maybe because she wanted so badly for it to be so. To know that other than the distressing personal issue she'd witnessed the day before, Nicole really was thriving. And not just financially...

The phone beside her on the table rang. Savannah jumped, the alert seeming deafening in the peaceful silence. Without touching the thing, she glanced at the screen.

Isaac.

Before eight in the morning. Four hours after he'd left her.

Calling before he went into work? The thought brought a smile, and she picked up.

"Hey, handsome..." She'd have liked the greeting to be solely powered by logical choice. Her decision to keep him on the temptation hook. The smile on her face—one he couldn't possibly see—gave lie to the wish.

"Where are you?" He didn't sound in the mood for sex. At all.

His short, staccato tone sent fear shooting through her. "At the house," she said, her focus on her surroundings, and she slowly got up from the table and moved toward the closest cement wall without window range. Shoved her back up against it. "What's going on?"

"Have you been there all morning?"

Was she being interrogated? Shaking her head against the absurdity of the thought, she said, "Yes." And as her gaze continued to take in what she could see of the house, she asked again, "What's going on, Isaac?"

"Are you alone?"

Realization dawned with enough relief to make her weak. His tension was on her behalf. "Yes. I'm fine," she assured him and tensed again immediately, too, as her mind continued to process. "You have reason to believe someone might be here with me?"

"I didn't know." Isaac's voice had softened some. "Listen, I'm sending someone out to watch the property. You'll be safe there. But I need you to promise me you won't leave. Not until I can get there."

With Isaac asking? "Of course." That had been a given. More than a decade with Sierra's Web had taught her that in a world of bad people, there would be one you could trust. And when you found that one, you worked together to combat evil.

Her life was endangered. She feared, after the previous

day's gunshot, that someone to do with her father's past had found her. And she knew for certain, after Isaac's confession the day before, that Eduardo Duran's people were after her, too.

She had no choice but to gratefully accept Isaac's help.

But wasn't going to do so without further information. "As long as you tell me what's going on."

A long pause fell on the line, finally prompting her to say, "Isaac?"

"I can't go into detail, but there's been a breach in Duran security, and I just needed to make certain that it didn't have to do with someone going rogue to get to you."

The initial tension in his tone...had been concern for her. And what did that mean, a breach in security?

"Should I be on the lookout?" she asked. "California's not an open-carry state. I don't have my gun." Didn't like the idea of being a sitting duck.

And didn't think the self-defense and knife-throwing training she'd done were going to serve her in her current situation.

"I'm guessing you're always on the lookout, but as long as you stay put, you're probably in the safest place you could be," he said, sounding more like the man she was growing to know so quickly. "My guy will be there within the next few minutes. As soon as he texts me the all-clear, I'll let you know."

"Thank you."

"Just trying to keep my promise to my vacation fling," he said then, his tone lightening considerably.

Letting her know he was no longer worried about her. Which eased her tension, too.

"What promise?" She didn't even have to work at sounding sexy for him.

"To protect you while you do what you have to do." There was no doubt of the warmth that had infused those last words.

Stumbling back to her computer, Savannah fell into her chair, her heart melting all over the table.

DARKNESS HAD LONG since fallen again by the time Isaac headed back out to the safe house. He'd been in touch with Savannah a couple of times, under the guise of checking in to make sure she was holding up okay, and had been receiving hourly reports from the agents watching the safe house and the living room inside it.

She'd kept the blackout curtains drawn all day.

An expected move from someone who was involved in criminal activity. And from a victim being hunted, too.

She'd made no attempts to leave—hadn't even opened the front door.

No one had slowed when passing the driveway, let alone attempted to access the property—or the expert lawyer.

But while the FBI's internet-usage access at the safe house could be somewhat monitored, Savannah's laptop had, so far, been completely unbreachable. The best tech in the FBI's San Diego office had been attempting to get in for most of the day and would continue to do so.

And if Savannah Compton had attempted to contact anyone or had been contacted by anyone, the burner phone Isaac had given her hadn't been used. They had just dumped the phone. They had a continual open trace on it, too.

He'd had her turn off her personal phone so that it couldn't be traced. Had watched her take the sim card out of it, of her own accord—reminding him that the woman was far more formidable an opponent than she appeared—but the bureau had been tracking it anyway. There'd been no activity.

She could have a third phone. Made sense that she did. One solely for the dirty job.

The woman was deceptively good. Playing the femme fatale for his sake, to lure him, and doing it so well he had to consciously stop himself from falling for her. And yet when it came to the job she was there to do, she didn't seem to miss a beat.

Even while locked up in a safe house.

She had to be communicating with her source somehow. If not by phone, then in that firewalled computer of hers. Which made her electronic device the number-one priority on his list of things to conquer that night.

Charlotte was still missing. Had been gone more than seventeen hours. Not something she'd have done of her own accord without at least notifying her father.

As much as Eduardo adored Charlotte, Isaac was pretty certain that Duran's daughter adored him more.

Or at least thought she did. During the months Isaac had been escorting every step she took off from Duran property, Charlotte's hero-worship of her father had been almost enviably evident.

He'd once thought his little sister looked up to him, believed in him, loved him in the same way. Having her in his life, his home, his heart had given him a lift he'd never have imagined. Her love had made him feel like Superman.

Stopping half a mile down from the safe house, he rolled down his window to speak with the agent stationed in the woods just off the road's shoulder. Heard a rendition of the same reports he'd been receiving all day.

House was quiet. Property was quiet.

No sign of the woman, other than occasional pacing to and from the living area.

Window up, Isaac touched the gas lightly, approaching the drive slowly. All signs indicated that Savannah was playing some kind of waiting game.

Forcing the rest of them to do the same.

Seventeen hours and no ransom note yet. No demands of any kind.

The good news, as Isaac had told Eduardo himself many times that day, was that Charlotte Duran's body hadn't been found. There'd been no car accidents. Duran's security had been making quiet checks all over the city. With the help, Isaac suspected, of an insider within the police department. It was reasonable to assume Charlotte was still alive. She was worth too much money for someone to just throw her away.

Taking her out of that house, getting by the levels of security had to have been a mammoth feat. One that could only have been accomplished by experts.

Not an effort one would undertake for nothing.

Turning onto the safe house property, Isaac started up the long drive, considering a revenge motive again, as he and his coworkers—FBI agents and Duran security in separate consultations—had done several times that day. Hate could consume someone to the point of doing whatever it took to avenge oneself. But just taking Charlotte from Eduardo didn't seem to fit that profile. The perp would need to twist the knife into Duran for utmost satisfaction. He'd need Duran to see him, hear him. To know from whence his pain came.

He'd need to take credit.

It was too soon for a missing person report, but there wouldn't be one in any event. Duran was choosing to conduct his own private investigation, hiring the best of the best in conjunction with his full-time security staff rather than getting police, FBI, and press involved. At least on an official level. Isaac had long suspected that the man had at least one law enforcement officer on staff under the table.

Outside of Duran's purview, the FBI agents and two agents from Isaac's team who'd flown out from Washington were searching for Charlotte. Being careful to preserve Isaac's cover.

They were too close to bringing Duran down to do anything that might blow the case.

But even with all the experienced feet on the ground, seventeen hours of collective efforts had generated absolutely nothing. Not a single viable lead.

No one even knew for sure if Charlotte had been in the house when she'd been taken. There'd been no sign of forced entry or struggle. The outdoor cameras had been blacked out, but only for a matter of minutes. No vehicle had been caught on video either in the driveway or out on the street. There hadn't even been a footprint in Duran's private beach—which was raked every night just before dark.

Isaac's theory was that they'd taken her by water. It was the only thing that made sense to him. No way had the front been breached without at least one of the half dozen security measures—including motion-sensor floodlights and a separate trigger that was turned on every night on the sprinkler system—being activated.

There were cameras at the intersections at both ends of the road that led to Duran's property. All vehicles on the loop had been investigated. And had been cleared.

Phone logs had all been checked, and Duran had also agreed to turn over all phones in his employ for physical investigation to the team of private detectives he'd hired, though Isaac strongly suspected Duran's head of security had confiscated a stash of non-registered devices before the phones had been provided.

Stopping his vehicle beside Savannah's, blocking hers from being seen upon approach, Isaac thought he saw movement, a small flash of light, from the side of one of the front windows. The dark curtain moving.

She was watching for him.

The unwelcome pleasant physical jolt that gave him kept

him sitting in his car, getting his head firmly back into the case.

Charlotte was missing. Whether the young woman was truly in danger or in on some ploy with her father, whether Savannah's client was involved or not, Isaac had to give the disappearance his full focus.

The slit of light showed again from the next curtain over.

The few minutes of blackout on Duran's security cameras ate at him, too. It could have been due to a power company surge as had been reported, but the coincidence of that timing was too much for Isaac to swallow. Someone at the house had to have shut down those cameras. Causing him to think that either Duran had had his own daughter kidnapped, to keep her safe until the Compton threat had been dealt with, or someone on Duran's security staff was double-crossing him.

Both possibilities were currently on Isaac's table. The first—Duran being behind Charlotte's disappearance—didn't track with the man's obvious distress. But a guy didn't get as far as Duran had, carry the power he carried without the ability to put on a good show. To be a chameleon and play whatever part was required by the current coup.

And if his goal was to protect Charlotte, he'd most definitely hire the best of the best to find her, to make the kidnapping look legitimate.

The second possibility—that someone in Duran's employ had gone rogue—weighed more heavily upon Isaac. Maybe because being a rogue employee himself, he knew how feasible the possibility really was.

Whether the employee was connected to Savannah's client—a planted mole—or had just chosen his timing based on the shooting event the day before, Isaac couldn't say.

He'd spent a good part of the day, in between other duties, checking out every single security agent and bodyguard in Duran's employ. Finding nothing. And getting a sick feeling that he was on the right track, too, with no way to explain the sensation.

It had prompted three calls to Savannah, though. He'd made the first one half worried for her safety and half suspecting that she'd been in on Charlotte's abduction. The second two had been partially out of suspicion but more to keep her actively waiting for him.

To keep her in place until he could get there and interview her face-to-face, while allaying her fears about the supposed security breach he'd mentioned earlier.

He had to get her to go about her business as she would have from her hotel room. To feel free to leave.

So that his agents could follow her.

And then hope that she led them to whoever had Charlotte.

Or, if not that, to whatever debilitating secret she and Eduardo shared. Because Eduardo hadn't been acting himself since the minute he'd mentioned Savannah Compton to Isaac. It all had to be connected.

He sat there staring at the house, getting his head in order, and without warning, experienced again the relief he'd felt each time he'd heard her voice answer the phone that day, giving him his own confirmation—in addition to those from his agents—that she was fine. His sensations were merely an unfortunate consequence of the job. A residual from the part he was being forced to play.

Undercover agents were human. And had to learn how to live with genuine feelings that were products of living realistically as someone else.

Learn to live with them. Not run from them.

He had to keep his eye on the final goal—putting Eduardo Duran and his multibillion-dollar illegal empire permanently out of business.

Being at the house, knowing that Savannah was right there, safe, available for him to question, Isaac suddenly wasn't as hell-bent to actually be back in her presence. It had been a long day. On only a few hours of sleep.

He'd taken on a lot of different roles during his under-cover-agent career but never one that had blurred lines be-tween reality and fiction as much as the current one was doing.

He could handle the situation. He *would* handle it. Just...

A bigger flash of light came from the front of the house. To the left of the windows. The front door had opened.

Savannah, in capri pants and a T-shirt, with her long hair loose and silky looking as it covered her breasts, stood there.

Ready to welcome him.

And, God help him, just the sight of her made Isaac hard again.

Chapter Eleven

He was back.

Savannah couldn't see enough in the darkness to tell but figured he was finishing a phone call while he sat in the drive. Was impatient to have it done.

She didn't recognize the eagerness with which she waited at the door, the pleasure it brought her to see Isaac finally getting out of his car.

She was used to living alone. Generally welcomed the rare full day she'd get at home every few months. Time to herself. Hours with no pressing responsibility. Able to move from activity to activity at her leisure. With no need for other human interaction.

But the current situation was not general to her.

And Isaac...she didn't know what he was. She just knew her spirits picked up a whole lot as he walked toward her, buttoning his jacket. Like he was getting ready to appear someplace important.

"Everything okay?" he asked as she stepped back from the door.

The question showed her how she must've looked to him. Like some lonely housewife or needy vacation fling, with so little in her life that his arrival was the day's event.

"Fine," she said. And, overall, it was. The day had proven productive. "I'm just glad you made it out."

She'd been waiting to have the one glass of wine that would help her sleep. To share it with him as they talked.

About Charlotte. Unlike the night before, she stood before him armed with a conversational plan. A way to find out what she needed to know. If she was lucky, she could be on a plane in the morning, and then, at least for a time, she could hire one of the firm's bodyguards to make certain that there was no longer anyone at her back.

Regardless of what Isaac said, it didn't make sense to her that Duran would bother with her if she just went away. And the other...the past ghosts...the same. While she was in San Diego, perhaps she posed a threat to whoever had taken Nicole. If nothing else. Maybe whoever shot at Savannah knew only about Nicole's part in the tragedy all those years ago. Someone who'd merely been a hired hand to kill her father but had found himself unexpectedly saddled with a toddler, too, and had seen her as a chance to make another buck. Or the shooter had just been the one who'd handled the human trafficking of a one-year-old child.

After a day to herself and her computer to keep her focused, she was thinking more like herself again. Logically. Not emotionally. Left brain, not right.

For the most part. Her reaction to Isaac Forrester aside.

To that end, she turned her back on the man as he came through the door. Speaking over her shoulder as she asked him, "You want a glass of wine? I waited for you."

"Sure." He didn't sound all that enthusiastic. He sounded... tired.

She reached for the opened bottle from the night before. "Did you get the security breach resolved?" She figured he must have or he wouldn't be there.

The breach must've been why he was so late visiting, too. She'd been about to make a bed on the couch for the night— to turn in early with the television showing security camera footage and a movie streaming on her computer—when he'd called to say he was on his way.

And...his coming out anyway, in spite of his long day, had put a smile inside her, to offset the doubts and distress.

It had also given her hope that any immediate danger, requiring his friend to keep a watch on Savannah's temporary lodging for him, had passed.

He'd taken the glass she handed him. Hadn't answered her question regarding the breach. Was standing there, watching her. Assessing?

Like he wasn't sure what to make of her?

She didn't think so. It was like he was taking her in. Absorbing her essence.

A ludicrous thought. She dismissed it. Wasn't going there.

She went to the couch instead. Took a seat next to the bedding she'd brought out. Left him to his chair choice from the night before.

Or not.

He sat on the couch. Not close. But there. Took a sip of wine. Laid his head back. Stared straight ahead but seemed relaxed. Or like he was in the process of becoming so.

Her heart lurched. The twelve hours he'd just been through had obviously not been easy. He needed some wind-down time. She certainly got that.

"You didn't have to drive all the way out here," she said softly, in case what he really wanted was to be home in bed. "You've had a long day and didn't get a lot of sleep last night." And, in spite of how she'd been acting around him, truthfully asserted, "I'm really fine. And can take care of myself."

Without lifting his head from the back of the couch, he turned toward her. His gaze moving over her face.

She felt like the sight pleased him. Gave him a somewhat

tired, understanding smile. "I was actually about to turn in when you called." The words were meant to free him to go.

"You kicking me out?" He wasn't getting up.

"No." She'd meant to leave it at that. But added, "I was glad you called." There were things she couldn't tell him. They seemed to prompt honesty everywhere she could give it.

Something else drove her to give him the silence he seemed to need. A feeling inside that they were meant to be connected. Even if just for the moment. Like he was in her circle of people she watched out for. And she was content to sit quietly and slowly sip wine with occasional long looks but no words between them.

Several minutes later, he said, "The security breach turned out to be no more than an electrical surge from the power company."

He was staring toward the ceiling as he spoke. And she felt for him. Putting in long hours, adrenaline pumping, having the weight of lives on your shoulders, only to find that everything was just a misunderstanding. She'd been there with Sierra's Web more than once. Had engaged her entire team on just such a case—an apparent stolen will and feared lost fortune—the year before. And while there was great relief in knowing that there hadn't been criminal activity or human suffering, it was still a bit frustrating to have spent so much mental and emotional energy for nothing.

Straightening enough to turn toward her, Isaac met her gaze and said, "I apologize for holding you up here all day. I just needed to make certain…" He paused as his look seemed to grow deeper. "That it didn't have anything to do with you. I promised you protection…"

"I'm here by my own mandate, Isaac," she said softly. "I brought this on myself, fully knowing that I could be putting myself in danger. If something were to happen to me, it'd be my fault, not yours." No way could she have him taking on responsibility for choices she'd made. "You didn't even know me until a few days ago." She said the words to absolve him of any responsibility for her. To erase the possibility of him bearing guilt for what could happen in the days ahead.

But the reminder hit home, too. She was trusting a man she'd just met.

Using him for her own gain.

And falling for him, too.

Not liking herself a whole lot at that moment, she wanted to pack her bags and go. To leave the home he'd so generously opened to her.

Until she had a flash of her sister at the back of her magnificent property, standing on her private beach and falling apart because a man wouldn't leave her alone.

"I know about guilt." The words came softly from deep within her. And she turned to face him, bringing her knee up on the couch, not far from his thigh. "Sierra's Web...we named our firm after a friend we all had in college, Sierra Wendel. She'd been physically abused, but none of us knew it. I was pre-law then, volunteering as a receptionist at the law clinic, and she'd come in, wanting to find information on evidence. She'd said it was for a class, but when I asked which one, she pretended like she hadn't heard me. I figured she was just preoccupied. Didn't ask any questions. Didn't push..."

"You were working, had a duty to your employer." He said the words as though he was the lawyer, not her.

"Right, but as a friend, living in the same dorm with her, I had a feeling something wasn't quite right with her. But she was kind of an introvert. Private. So was I. And I never followed up."

She stopped. Thought about Winchester Holmes, who'd been in love with Sierra though he hadn't admitted as much to any of the partners until the previous year, and the way her dear friend had beaten himself up over the years for not asking questions.

Straightening, feeling her resolve to be there for Nicole strengthen tenfold within her, Savannah said, "Sierra was murdered as an indirect result of that abuse, and if any of us had talked, even to each other, about our concerns, if any of us had acted on them, we probably could have saved her life."

Instead, the friends had been instrumental in solving her murder.

Isaac raised a hand, opened his mouth, and Savannah gave him a sharp shake of the head. "I know," she told him. "We all did what we thought best at the time, respecting her right to the privacy she was guarding so carefully, which is why I'm telling you...my choices are mine. I'm in town for my reasons. I'm purposely not sharing the details. My choice. You aren't going to change any of that. And I can't have you feeling guilty over anything that transpires because of my presence here."

She met his gaze full on again. Speaking as much with her eyes as with words.

Life. Death. Sex. Ghosting.

Whatever happened, she'd made her bed all by herself.

And told him so.

HE'D BEEN ABSOLVED of guilt. She'd made her bed. As he saw the pillow and blanket on the far end of the couch behind her, remembered her saying she was about to turn in, Isaac felt the irony of her words all the way to his bones.

She'd made her bed. And he had to lie in it. Pun intended for his own tired brain only.

Apparently she'd been intending to sleep on the couch instead of the bedroom she'd used the previous night. Because he'd been on the couch.

Good thing he'd used his phone to remotely turn off the inside camera when he'd pulled up to the house.

He'd made his bed, too.

He just hadn't gotten there yet.

Had been fighting his own sense of loathing at the idea of setting in motion the grand lie he'd planned. With the goal of getting Savannah to go about her business the next day in the hope that she'd lead agents to secrets that could put Duran away for life.

And if she led them to Charlotte, which he strongly suspected she would, all the better. He wasn't completely convinced his charge was in trouble. Though, considering Eduardo's distress, he was leaning more in that direction.

It was likely, considering the closeness of father and daughter, that she knew the big secret, too.

Which could have put her in danger.

So he needed to get Savannah out of the house and back on the business that had brought her to town watching the Durans from a boat on the ocean.

He had protocols in place, agents ready to protect her if need be. The FBI needed her alive, possibly to testify against Duran, depending on what she knew.

But as Isaac sat there in the low light, the quiet, catching whiffs of Savannah's light, somewhat spicy scent, he wondered if she was struggling as hard as he was with whatever was happening between them. He wasn't imagining the heat. It wasn't just coming from him. His was feeding off from hers. Maybe hers stayed lit by his. He was no expert on that subject.

But couldn't believe she was faking it all.

No one was that good. Not even him.

And that first night…she'd intimated that he could have come upstairs with her…and hadn't had any idea who he was.

He'd been the pursuer that night. He'd known who she was. Had been there specifically to meet her, to find out what she knew about Duran. And had come on to her for that purpose alone.

But as she'd said, she'd made her choices. Chosen the job she was on. She'd responded to his light flirting. Seemed to be enjoying their seemingly impromptu association.

As had he seemed. He'd made sure of it.

Leaning over, he laid his lips on hers. To get it done. Out of the way.

To admit that desire existed between them and wasn't going to just disappear by force of will. Or by calling off the jobs they were doing.

It was just a kiss. Meant to diffuse by taking away the mystery. The challenge. The curiosity. The sense that it couldn't happen. Was forbidden.

But when her soft lips accommodated his, he felt his body surge with heat, felt himself nearing a point where he'd hear the siren's call louder than his own determination, and he pulled slowly, regretfully back.

"Talk first," he told her. And without waiting for her response, not trusting himself to say no if she made any hint at an invitation to put talk off a little longer, he said, "Duran's security team have spent the day out looking for you. Tonight, in our final meeting, they were allowing the possibility that you'd left town. So, from that standpoint, you should be safe enough to go about your business tomorrow. I can't speak for whatever danger you might have brought with you…"

She licked her lips. Quickly, like they were dry. Not as a come-on.

That quick dart of her tongue turned him on anyway, and after a deep swallow, he kept talking. "I'd feel a whole lot better about it, though, if you'd let me run interference for you, as we'd originally planned. Letting you know where Duran's people are so you can be somewhere else, keeping my ears open to all conversations and letting you know if they're back to thinking you're still around..." Depending on what her client might say to whoever had ratted him out to Duran in the first place.

And if there was total radio silence? Did that mean her client had what he wanted?

Charlotte?

Did Savannah already know that?

Did she know if the professor was okay? Was a plan in place to make Eduardo suffer through silence before squeezing him for whatever they were after?

If so, Savannah would likely meet with Charlotte in the morning to say whatever she'd come to say, tell the secret she had to tell—assuming Charlotte didn't know it already—to be able to get a great deal of wealth out of Duran.

And if Savannah, thinking that Isaac's "friend" was no longer watching her, packed up and headed straight for the airport?

He'd have to make a quick, unscheduled trip to the terminal and find a way to convince her to stay.

More likely, if any of his stars aligned, first thing in the morning she'd lead agents to Charlotte.

Finding the missing woman was paramount in the moment. But it wouldn't be an end. Not for Isaac. He wasn't done until Duran was.

Even if it meant offering Charlotte and Savannah immunity to testify against the career criminal.

Any way Isaac looked at it, he needed more time with the expert attorney.

Had to continue growing their relationship.

And when she leaned into him, whispering a quiet thank-you before opening her mouth on his, he gave up being on duty and let the fire within burn him up.

Chapter Twelve

Savannah didn't forsake her purpose. Or her plan.

She didn't forsake herself, either. There were no promises between her and Isaac. His life was in southern California with the Durans. She was a fleeting moment there.

A vacation fling who meant enough for him to help her with her quest, without even trying to get tangled up in her private threads.

Yet passion had flamed between them. Unlike anything she'd ever felt before.

Life was too short, far too unpredictable for her to pretend she didn't feel it. Or want it.

When Isaac's tongue met hers, she welcomed the contact, shared it, giving as she took. And when he pushed her down to the couch, lying half beside, half on top of her, she wrapped her arms around him, holding him close.

There were no words. Not spoken ones. His gaze bore witness, though. With so much impact she became captivated. Staring at him as she reached a hand down to his fly, to cover the hard muscles and passion burgeoning there.

Retaining eye contact when his hand slid inside her pants and found her wetness. It pleased him. A lot. The intense darkening in his look told her as much as the hard pressure of his penis against her thigh did.

The visual communication went silent, briefly, when he pulled her shirt over her head. She shivered, with pleasure more than chill, as the air hit her skin.

And unbuttoned his shirt while he jerked the sleeves of his jacket down his arms.

The clothes fell in a pile beside the couch. Panties on suit pants. Briefs on bra. She caught a glimpse, but only one. She couldn't stop seeking out from his gaze the things they weren't saying.

Couldn't prevent herself from making visual promises that she knew she'd never be able to say. Their coming together was a blip in time, but that didn't mean she wasn't committed to it, to him, fully and completely.

For those moments, for however long they lasted, her heart was his.

When he entered her the first time and became a part of her, her soul welcomed him as a piece of itself forever. A moment, a connection that would always be with her.

And when they moved in slow, then fast, soft then harder, perfect rhythm she looked him in the eye and promised that nothing would ever mar the memory of that moment.

They came together again minutes later, with her on top, sitting on his lap.

And then, in tandem, they reached for their clothes. Handing pieces to each other as they fit and, standing, dressed side by side.

"Do you have to go right away?" she asked him when he zipped his pants and buckled his belt.

He glanced at the pillow and blanket she'd laid on the couch. "The threat from Duran might have dissipated, but while you're still on your mission, I was planning to stay here, as I did last night. Unless you'd rather I go?"

She shook her head. "I'll take the bedroom."

But instead of politely leaving the room, she plopped back

down to the couch. Picked up her glass of wine. Took a slow sip and looked up at him.

The sooner she could find out what she needed to know, the better. She had to get out of San Diego before she did something really stupid. Like fall in love.

But far more pressing, the more quickly she could help Nicole, the better off her sister would be. All day long she'd been driven by the very real fear that her sister might be physically hurt by the man Savannah had seen from the boat. Eduardo Duran? Charlotte's husband? She didn't know.

"I did some research on Charlotte Duran today," she started in right away with the plan she'd made for when she next saw Isaac. Beginning with seemingly casual conversation pertaining to something he'd shared with her about his life. The person he was being paid to protect. "She's a professor." She'd managed to confirm the fact after hours of reading write-ups of charity functions put on to raise money for women's causes. There'd been a mention, not of Charlotte directly but of Eduardo, paying tribute to his "lovely professor daughter."

And the other tidbit that had seemed to jump off her computer screen and down her throat, as she'd been eating dinner, had been Eduardo having been awarded American citizenship through the sponsorship of his daughter, whose mother had been American born.

His adopted daughter...though there'd been no mention of that distinction.

Isaac wasn't talking.

She wouldn't let herself be deterred. Not again. He expected her to continue with her plans, and there was no telling what that would bring.

"I know you probably can't talk about her, and I'm not asking you to," she said, having left the plan to draw Isaac out the night before, after its complete failure. "I just...wanted to get to know you a little better, you know, share a peek at your daily life. And…she sounds…nice."

Nonthreatening. Noninvasive—other than the fact that she'd looked up the woman. He didn't have to know some of the intricate channels she'd taken. The one that mentioned Eduardo's citizenship, in particular.

And…if she'd looked up Charlotte that day, it would mean that she hadn't already done so. That the Durans had been nothing to her until Isaac had come clean about what he really did for a living, who he worked for, and that the gunshot might have come from his employer's staff as a defense measure.

"Anyway," she continued, fear growing that with the huge unknown of the next day looming—having to be out and about to make her story of looking for someone believable— she might not get another chance.

At least not such a clean, accessible one.

He was looking at her. She'd started and stopped. She had his attention. "I…don't really know how to approach this, Isaac, and I hope so much that you take it in the way it's offered…"

Tears pricked the sides of her eyes. She couldn't let them well. No matter how sincere they were. They'd be too much, over the top, for someone she'd never met.

"I just… The other day…when I was on the boat… I didn't know it was Charlotte I was looking at," she continued, her gaze wide open to him, her tone filled with the emotion she couldn't let overpower her.

"And I saw something no one else could have seen."

He sat up then, his gaze sharp. "What?" he asked, all armed protective guard at that point. And, in a way, she fell in love with him a little bit for real, for caring about tending to her little sister so completely. Giving his all to the job.

Nicole was lucky to have him.

"There was a man there…" She was assuming he'd be aware of who was on the premises.

"Yeah."

"Her father?"

"No."

Thank God. Savannah sat a second, letting relief wash over her.

"Savannah," he said, his urgent tone calling her to point.

Embarrassed, she liked that he was so intent on watching over her sister. And had a flash of envy, too. Of wanting to be on the receiving end of his loyalty.

Until it hit her that she was. He was running interference for her so she could take care of something vitally important to her. Which meant…he cared. About her. For her. Personally.

Because she wasn't a job to him.

But Charlotte was. And after the way Isaac had stepped up for Savannah, protecting her, providing her with a safe place to stay…she believed she could trust him.

For her sister, her whole reason for being there, she had to press forward. She'd wanted to make certain that someone was aware that her sister was showing signs of being emotionally abused. Had spent the day looking for an "in," someone in Charlotte's life separate and apart from home where the suspected abuse was taking place, someone her sister would trust to help her through the situation.

Picturing the scene she'd witnessed from that boat, fear engulfed Savannah all over again. The man had been on the premises, which meant he'd obviously been someone Charlotte and her father had trusted. Someone in their circle, perhaps? Someone she'd be loath to press charges against?

Someone who'd been confident enough to continue to touch her even after she'd made it clear she hadn't wanted him to do so.

She shuddered inside. Was swamped with worry. And a quietly building rage.

Who better to tell than the man sworn to keep her sister safe?

As long as she could trust him to go against his employer if that's what it took to keep Nicole out of harm's way.

Which Isaac had proven over the past twenty-four hours. Telling her that Duran's people were on the hunt for her. Helping her stay clear of them. Giving her a place to stay. Even having a friend keep a watch on the place while he was at work.

Promising to continue to do so.

"What did you see?" he asked when she sat there, processing a closing in sense of desperation along with the rest of the overwhelming emotions hitting her one after another.

She still managed to look Isaac in the eye as she said, "The man in the yard kept trying to get close to her, touching her, even after she'd repeatedly brushed him off. He was clearly, and forcefully, refusing to accept the no she was clearly giving him."

"You got all that from a glimpse from a boat more than a quarter of a mile away?"

"I got more than a glimpse," she told him. "When I first saw them, the guy had grabbed her, and she'd jerked away. I couldn't just close my eyes to it." And then added, "And the binoculars are the strongest I could buy. I told you, I don't intend to make contact with…the reason I'm here. I just need to see…to know…" She couldn't say anymore.

Didn't trust herself, in that moment, that night, with all that had happened, not to say too much.

With her father's killer an unknown…and someone— not Duran's people, she felt sure—having taken a shot at her the day before.

"You said you saw something no one else could have,"

he told her. And it dawned on her, he didn't seem surprised by the scene in the yard. She wasn't telling Isaac anything he didn't already know. He'd been on duty that afternoon.

Somewhere in the yard?

Keeping an eye out from the house?

Did he know about the mistreatment? And wasn't doing anything about it?

Maybe he already had.

Maybe Charlotte had told him. Or the mysterious man had.

The way he was looking at her…as though from a distance… For the first time since they'd met, she had the sense that he wasn't all in with the moment. And she stepped up her game, giving him the rest before he started to doubt her. To think that she was crying wolf just to get his attention.

"She was crying, Isaac. She walked to the beach, her back to the house, and stood there and fell apart. Her face crumpled, like she was in agony…" As Savannah relived the moment for him, picturing it all, she felt the blood drain from her face, grew almost light-headed as it dawned on her.

That had been the last sight she'd had of her sister. Nicole's face…crushed in agony…because right then…

The shot.

At the precise moment that she'd seen more than she should have.

She *had* been followed. Someone knew what she'd been watching. What she'd seen. And had tried to make certain she wasn't around to do or say anything about it.

Someone who was aware that she knew who Charlotte Duran really was? And didn't want her to get involved?

Someone privy to her father's murder? At the moment, it was the only thing that made sense.

Was someone trying to control Charlotte, to keep her from finding out the truth?

If Savannah really had been followed, there'd been very real cause for her paranoia. Horrifying reason to fear for her own life.

And now, to fear for Charlotte Duran's life as well.

Eduardo Duran might soon find out that what could be bought, could turn out not to be what one thought one had purchased.

What could be given could be taken away.

A lesson Savannah had learned indisputably when she'd been just seven years old.

One that had driven every minute of her life ever since.

And would drive the next one, too.

With someone from the past truly at her back...she brought them to everyone with whom she came in contact. Her silence wasn't enough to keep others safe, as her mother and the police had told her.

At least not once she'd accessed the Family Finders database.

Had they put Charlotte Duran's DNA in the database on purpose, to lure Savannah out? After Nicole's kidnapping, she and her mother had been given new identities.

Why anyone would purposely seek her out, she had no idea, but she had to cut all ties with everyone until she figured out what was going on. No one was going to die because of her.

Thoughts, possibilities tumbled through the mass of horror enveloping her. All pouring out from a part of her mind that had been frozen by that gunshot. And set free by reliving it. There, with Isaac. Where she'd felt safe.

Turning to him, she let words fall out of her. "I...actually...found what I was looking for today, Isaac. You talking about all the security cameras at the Durans' made me think about others' cameras—and the way people liked to share everything on social media...and I did a social media search and stumbled upon what I..." Weak, too weak. Embarrassingly weak. She was scrambling. Because she couldn't continue to use Isaac. Not with the love they'd made.

Not with the horrifying realization that her worst fears weren't just paranoia. That they were much more likely reality.

In the short time she'd known him, she'd grown to care about him.

She couldn't put his life in any more danger.

Because she couldn't continue to pretend with him.

What if her need to see her little sister got Nicole shot at, too?

What a fool she'd been. Thinking, after nearly a quarter of a century, she could fly into town, get a glimpse of her sister living a normal happy life, and pop back out to a life suddenly made new for herself? One wiped of the past?

"You wouldn't have traveled all this way if you hadn't already done all the social media canvassing you could possibly do."

Statement, not question. With that look that saw right inside her.

And still made her feel safe.

"The bullet hit while you were looking at Charlotte," Isaac's words came softly. "What suddenly scared you about that just now?"

The whole truth almost tumbled out. To serve *her*. Because *she* needed comfort. She'd come to make sure her sister was okay. That niggling worry as to why Nicole had been looking for family...how could she not help her sister find herself?

And then, to witness what had looked clearly like some kind of domestic abuse?

But Savannah had pursued the Family Finders notice for herself, too.

The truth hit hard. She'd been selfish.

And she had to speak the truth that was hitting her hardest.

"What if I put her in danger? Or...*you*? Just by being there?" The question had to be asked. It was lingering in the air between them.

What had she done?

Reaching out a hand, Isaac brushed the hair back from her face, his hand lingering softly at the side of her temple, as though giving her strength to hold up her head. "We've already been over this," he told her. "You've got reason to fear, Savannah—I give you that. Which is why I'm going to do all I can to protect you. But it's a stretch to think that whoever might be after you would go after everyone you look at, don't you think?"

Right. She'd lost sight of his perspective for a moment. He had no idea about the horrible secret she carried. Her connection to the Duran household.

And she was just no good at being two people at once. Or caring for someone she was keeping secrets from.

Which was the whole reason she'd concocted the cruise vacation. So she could go a period without talking to her partners without inciting their worry.

Sitting there, locking looks with Isaac, she almost blurted the truth. Almost.

"Are you ready to call it quits, then?" he asked. "On whatever your mission was here?"

Was she?

She'd told Isaac about the supposed abuse.

But what about the gunshot? Was someone going to go after Nicole next? With Savannah being the only one who could help law enforcement figure out why? The only one who knew that Charlotte Duran was really Nicole Gussman.

Just like she'd once been Sarah Gussman.

The name repeated unfamiliarly in her head. Like it was

something she'd read in a family bible, not like someone she'd ever been.

She needed time to clear her head.

And then to think.

Before she made any more mistakes.

And so, mimicking one of Isaac's moves from the night before, she gave him a noncommittal shrug.

Then leaned in and kissed him. Long but not hard.

The kiss was filled with emotion. With regard for him.

And as she got up and silently left him there, stopping in the bathroom and then grabbing her computer off the table, heading into her room, and quietly locking the door—locking herself in, not him out—she let the tears fall.

She might never know for sure if Nicole was happy and well.

But she was certain of one thing.

She'd just told Isaac Forrester goodbye.

Chapter Thirteen

Isaac slept well for the four hours he allowed himself. And as he quietly let himself out of the house long before dawn, having just taken a look at the closed door of Savannah's bedroom, he had a new question on his mind.

Was it possible that Savannah was being used? That she had no idea what her client really knew or held over Duran?

His gut didn't immediately dismiss the idea.

The way she'd struggled to tell him about seeing Charlotte break down while standing so no one from the house could see—those tears, Wagar's treatment of Charlotte had really hit her hard. There'd been absolutely no reason to tell him about what she'd seen.

Except that her heart had been bothered by Charlotte's distress.

As was he. He'd been standing at the window, had seen Charlotte head to the beach, had seen her standing there, and had had no idea she'd been crying. He'd figured she'd, in no uncertain terms, told Arnold Wagar that she was just not interested and to leave her alone. Had assumed she'd been standing at the beach waiting for the man to take the hint and leave.

Then the shot had been fired, and he'd forgotten all about that little family drama.

In his car, driving to his apartment in the dark, Isaac was looking at the scene with fresh perspective.

Why *had* Charlotte been crying?

And why had Savannah told him about it?

Why was she really in San Diego?

She was a lawyer, not a private investigator. Why hire her unless to make contact with someone? Offer some opportunity or impart legal advice. Maybe a make-believe business offer to the younger Duran—one she'd want to consider, but one of which her father wouldn't approve.

Something that would give someone a hold over Duran. Someone who'd held that last piece of critical information from Savannah?

Did Wagar have something to do with it all?

He'd seen the man at public functions that Duran had attended with Charlotte on and off since he'd been in San Diego. Not part of the inner circle, but definitely part of the crowd.

Isaac had figured Wagar was simply someone with money who took Duran to be exactly who he said he was. An incredibly successful businessman. He was no longer so sure of that.

Just as he couldn't let go of the idea that Savannah was perhaps more of a pawn than a mastermind.

A victim, not a suspect.

Because the woman had noticed his charge's tears? Or because she'd told him about them?

Or was it because he'd just had the most incredible sex of his life with her?

If another agent had told him that he'd had sex with a person of interest and then suddenly was considering the possibility that said person wasn't as guilty as at first thought, he'd think the man's ability to do the job had been compromised.

And maybe his had been. He didn't think so.

Yet he'd somehow failed to get access to her computer, which had been his target when he'd driven out the night before.

But even if he had been somewhat distracted by the sex, he was still too firmly in place to pull out without jeopardizing the case at the critical moment. Wasting more than a year's worth of bureau money and time. And far, far worse, making it possible for Duran to continue doing business as usual.

No way was he doing that. Blurred lines, even sex on rare occasions, were part of undercover work.

He could still get the job done. There was no doubt about that.

To that end, he reminded himself of the case against Savannah.

First and foremost was Duran's knowledge of the woman, warning Isaac to be on the lookout for any attempt the lawyer might make to get to Charlotte. And then, two days later, there she'd been spying on Isaac's charge. Didn't matter that Duran was a dirtbag Isaac didn't trust. He'd known about Savannah, knew her to be a threat, and someone who was acting above board didn't spy from boats.

He'd also verified that Savannah was not working for Sierra's Web. He'd made a quick call to her office, posing as a former client with another job for her.

Next, Savannah had said she was only there to look, not contact. So why be there at all? And she'd also told him she wasn't working for anyone. Again, then why be there?

And how had Duran known about her?

Then there was the computer. The one thing that could have led him to more truth, and before leaving him on the couch for the night, she'd quietly picked it up and taken it to bed with her.

Maybe she'd been planning to use it yet that night.

More likely, she'd been protecting its contents.

Last, she had a secret. Had admitted so during a weak moment. One that would supposedly put his life at risk if she told him about it.

How it all fit together he didn't yet know, but he could tell he was getting closer. And was wide awake, eager to forge on with the day ahead even before he hit his own shower, shaved, and then, dressed in his usual garb, strapped an extra gun to his ankle in addition to the one he'd put in the holster at his waist.

Duran had asked him to spend the day checking out every place Charlotte had gone during Isaac's tenure. Isaac had a log of every stop they'd ever made. Had told Duran so. And fully intended to do as requested. As time and opportunity allowed.

First and foremost, he was making himself available to the team of FBI agents on Savannah Compton. She knew him, so he couldn't follow closely, but he was going to be in her vicinity the second she stepped out of the FBI safe house in case he needed to swoop in with some bogus Duran news if the investigation led them in a direction that needed direct contact with her. Or to stop her from doing something. Like leaving town.

He'd also shared his log of Charlotte Duran's activities with the San Diego office, and a female agent would be posing as a friend of Charlotte's from college to trace their steps. And be able to ask questions without raising suspicions.

And the bodyguards who answered to him, with the exception of Emmajean, still had their regular duties but were fully apprised to be extra vigilant and to report to him, and to house security, the second they noticed anything suspicious.

Emmajean had been fired.

Duran's decision, not Isaac's.

Isaac's teams were in place.

He had no idea what the day was going to bring, but he knew that he was ready for it.

Or thought he was. Right up until eight in the morning when he called Savannah, and she didn't pick up. Neither the burner phone, nor her own personal number.

The one he'd told her to keep off. And had watched her take the card out of. Something she could easily have put back in.

He'd just left Charlotte's favorite coffee shop—a small mom-and-pop place by the university, where they stopped anytime she had an early morning lecture—and had called in to Chuck Knowles, the agent currently on duty at the FBI property, to see if there'd been any activity at the house yet. Then, hearing that they'd seen no sign of movement from the house, he'd called her.

Calling Chuck back, he told the more junior agent to get up to the house. To knock and then enter. And call him back.

His throat dry as he waited, Isaac sat in the vehicle owned by his undercover persona—Isaac Forrester—and felt a far more personal tug inside him. More like a younger Mike Reynolds had felt when he'd first discovered that his little sister's boyfriend was a fairly big-time drug dealer.

Mike Reynolds, the name he went by when he wasn't undercover, had no business showing any part of himself in San Diego. Most particularly not anything as intense as the tension eating away at him during the seconds that turned into minutes while he sat there, thrumming his fingers hard against the leather steering wheel.

Sex or not, he was in no way allowing Mike's personal feelings to enter Isaac's world.

The woman was probably in the shower. Hadn't heard the phone ring.

He'd caught her in the shower the morning before. She'd

answered anyway. Had apologized for the extra couple of rings it had taken her to get to the phone.

For someone living a lie, pretending, Savannah Compton never missed a beat playing the part of a woman grateful to a bodyguard she'd just met, for helping her out.

An expensive silver sedan pulled into the coffee shop parking lot. Scooting down farther in the driver's seat of his own vehicle parked across the street, Isaac watched as Arnold Wagar got out and entered the shop.

If the man came out with two cups of coffee...it proved nothing.

But sure as hell made the man look more suspicious. Already holding Mike Reynolds's phone, waiting for his call back from the San Diego agent, he quickly dialed Juan Billings, one of his own agents in town from Washington, letting him know where Wagar was currently located, asking him to keep a tail on the man and telling him to keep Isaac posted.

Isaac, not Mike.

And had just hung up when his phone rang again.

"She's gone, sir."

What the hell! Sitting up so sharply he cracked his knee on the dash, Isaac swore silently at the pain and barked, "What do you mean *gone*? She drove off the lot, and you missed it?"

"No, sir. The car you loaned her is still here. Keys on the table. Same for the FBI-issued burner phone. The house looks just like it did the day we readied it for her. With the exception of the sheets on the bed. They're gone. Same with the pillow and blanket."

Isaac's gut clenched. "What about her bag?"

"Gone. Whatever she brought in with her, she took back out. Seriously, place looks like she's never been here. Even the trash is gone."

Starting his engine, Isaac pulled out into traffic. "Any sign of a struggle?" He turned, crossed three lanes.

"No. It's weird, sir. The door was locked. Curtains still drawn. Bathroom and kitchen are clean. It's like the woman removed all traces of herself and then evaporated."

Just like Charlotte Duran.

Isaac had a very sick feeling about that.

THE ROOM WAS DANK. It smelled musty. But it had a metal door with a sturdy lock and a window high enough up that she could walk around inside without fear of getting her head blown off.

Savannah had always thought herself the scaredy cat of the bunch. Whatever bunch she was in. Growing up. In school. And most particularly, at Sierra's Web, with every one of her very brave partners seeming to tower over her in the courage department. She had every confidence in her intelligence and her ability to handle any legal problem or court battle that came her way.

Yet she'd moved through life fearing that the boogeyman could be at her back at any minute.

A fear that had turned to more of an obsession when she'd started to feel like he actually was following her. Shortly after Dorian's kidnapping.

Which, she'd confirmed the night before, had been right about the time that Charlotte Duran had first entered her DNA in the Family Finders database. Putting those two things together had only occurred to her after she'd been talking to Isaac about seeing Charlotte cry. The bullet coming when it had...

The way she'd instantly folded in on herself. The intense fear that made her feel helpless. As though she was already a victim.

Dropping her beat-up roller bag on the floor, she leaned over to let her satchel fall off her shoulder onto the one double bed and headed into the windowless bathroom to pee.

She'd suspected in the last couple of days that maybe she really had been followed, that it was possible that someone from the past had somehow known about her before she'd seen the Family Finders notice. But lying in bed the night before, aware that she might have put others in immediate danger, thinking about Dorian the year before, the way she'd felt then, and back to Sierra, too…along with the timing of that bullet…it had all just clicked.

She'd been aware of her need to watch her back since she'd been seven years old. But she hadn't been paranoid.

All the cases the firm had worked on, often putting her partners in immediate danger, hadn't brought on irrational fears.

No, actually being followed was what had made her feel as though she had someone watching her. Because they had been.

And the timing, her sense of being watched coming at the same time as Charlotte's Family Finders entry…

Someone wasn't just watching Savannah. They'd been watching Charlotte, too.

They had to have been to have known about her sister putting an entry in the database. And their knowledge of who Charlotte really was had prompted them to watch Savannah. Before the DNA match. Those results had come much more recently.

Someone had already known that Savannah was Charlotte's biological sister. Someone who also knew about Savannah's identity change.

How, she had no idea.

No one but her mother and the marshal who'd handled their case knew that Savannah Compton had once been Sarah Gussman.

Or so they'd thought.

Current facts were telling a different story.

She'd figured it all out within an hour of going to bed the night before. It was as though sex with Isaac had loosened up the tension holding her prisoner. Or it had given her the strength to believe in herself enough to allow her to see clearly.

Ironically, considering that Isaac had been the catalyst that set her free, as soon as she'd put all the facts together, as soon as she reached her conclusion, she'd known she had to get away from Isaac. From everyone. While she figured out what to do next. She'd put anyone she was with in danger, just by being with them.

Even a rideshare driver.

She'd also leave a trail. Someone they could get to who'd be forced to say what they knew.

Which was why she'd left just an hour behind Isaac the night before. After studying the televised footage from the property cameras for more than a day, she'd not only had a good grasp of the lay of the land, she'd known where all the cameras were located and how to avoid them.

From there, detailed searches on her computer had shown her the best route to move, undetected, the three miles she'd have to walk to get to the old but quaint motel that promised quiet and solitude.

The walk, while arduous, had given her a lot of time to think.

One thing was indisputable as far as she was concerned. Whoever had been watching Nicole knew that she'd had other family for Family Finders to find.

And hadn't wanted her finding them.

Only one person would likely care what Charlotte Duran discovered almost a quarter of a century later. Would care enough to have someone followed, to shoot at them. That was someone who knew that Nicole had been kidnapped.

Whether or not they knew the rest...that her father had

been about to testify against someone really big, that he'd been murdered…she couldn't say.

But it seemed logical to assume so.

Which was why she'd taken the time to disinfect the safe house before she'd left. Removing every trace of her DNA from the place. She'd felt bad about the bedding. Taking it all with her. Had thrown it, with the rest of the trash, into a pond she'd seen on the cameras at the back of the property. Apologizing for having done so to any organisms living within.

Savannah wasn't suffering from paranoia due to Dorian's kidnapping. Her instincts, honed by a lifetime of hiding her true identity, had been letting her know that someone really was at her back.

Yet it turned out that she didn't fear for her life so much when she thought it was a danger to others. She feared more for theirs.

The walk in the dark had been awful—she'd cried a good bit of the way—but she'd had the strength to get it done. And done well.

Reminding herself with every step that she was exceptionally well trained. In several types of self-defense—she'd taken the kitchen knife best suited to throwing—but in ways to evade criminals, too. After more than a decade with Sierra's Web she'd heard enough to arm her well.

One of the big questions remaining was how much Eduardo Duran knew. Had the man just paid top dollar for an adoption, not knowing that Nicole had been kidnapped?

And if he knew more, how much did he know?

Just that she'd been taken?

Or had he known the man who'd killed Sarah and Nicole's father?

And if so, was that all he knew?

Still in the bathroom, she flushed. Washed her hands. Saw

her face in the mirror, the dirt streaks, the brokenness staring back at her but wouldn't let herself cry again.

She'd had her time to mourn, and it was done.

Thankfully, the Sierra's Web investigative team had insisted that every expert carry safe kits with them. Including enough cash to get by for a few days. Savannah had used a little bit at a shady-looking gas station and convenience store with no surveillance cameras to pay way too much for some food and a burner phone that was likely contraband.

All the better for her purposes.

And then to prepay for a couple of nights at the motel—not that she planned to stay that long. Just seemed smart to seem as though she wasn't in any kind of hurry.

Best news, as far as she was concerned, was that she hadn't had the sense of being followed at all during her trek. By the time she'd reached the convenience store, unshowered, hair down to shadow her features, having cleaned the house, cried, and hiked for miles, her disheveled state had fit right in. She'd bet the tired and clearly stoned clerk wouldn't even be able to give an accurate description of her were anyone to stop and ask.

With that thought and one last glance in the mirror, Savannah decided to forgo the shower she'd been about to take. The disguise worked. And it didn't matter how she looked, or felt, if she was dead.

Or if someone else was because of her.

Charlotte.

The woman had been on her mind nonstop.

Worst-case scenario, in her mind, was that whoever had been watching Savannah for most of the past year, whoever was clearly currently after her, and probably Charlotte, too, was someone involved in whatever illegal dealings their father had been about to testify against.

She hadn't broken witness protection protocol by flying

to San Diego or renting a boat. She'd broken it when she'd entered her DNA in family databases. She'd done so privately. Which wouldn't have put her in danger. If not for the fact that her DNA had matched that of someone who didn't know about witness protection guidelines, who'd made their profile discoverable.

Without having any idea of the danger she was putting them in, Charlotte had unknowingly exposed them both to a past that had killed their father.

Was it going to get the two of them killed, too?

If her theory was correct and someone had been watching her for nearly a year without harming her in any way, did that mean she was safe?

Another flash of the gunshot blast on the boat came to mind next.

Shaking her head as she stood on a chair to peek out the rectangular window positioned close to the ceiling, Savannah breathed through the shock of fear that rent through her.

Focused on the one thought that she couldn't let go of. Nicole. Charlotte. The agony she'd seen on her sister's face.

How much did Charlotte know?

And how much danger was she in?

Was she better off if Savannah just faded away? Neither had been in danger over the past year.

And then there was Isaac...

No. *Really.* There was *Isaac.* His car. Parking. Him getting out. Heading for the office.

Looking for her?

He'd said he would protect her. And after the hour they'd shared, naked on the couch...she should have known he wouldn't just accept her leaving without a trace.

Oh, God, what had she done?

But...she *hadn't* done a lot of it. Not if someone had been on her tail for the past year.

But that didn't mean she had to be a victim.

She had to be smart.

Isaac was back in the parking lot. Heading to his car but looking around.

Tension stiffened every muscle, every nerve in her body. He was right there. Charlotte's bodyguard. Did she tell him what she'd figured out?

If her witness protection cover was already blown, if the devil was already upon them, what would it hurt?

But if it wasn't?

He was at his car. Reaching for the door handle. Glancing back.

Was it providence again? Him being there right when she'd been looking out? Was he Charlotte's only chance?

Jumping down from the chair, Savannah turned the dead bolt. Unhooked the chain lock.

And opened the door in time to see Isaac's vehicle driving away.

Chapter Fourteen

Adrenaline pumping, Isaac pulled out into the street in front of the old motel and then pulled back in the drive as it circled the other side of the two-winged building. The desk clerk hadn't recognized the only photo Isaac had had of Savannah Compton—the one from the Sierra's Web site—and he hadn't been all that eager to talk to Isaac, either, most particularly since Isaac couldn't show Mike's badge.

But for enough cash, the man had mentioned that a disheveled-looking woman who probably matched the photo had checked in not long ago. And for another couple of twenties, had even given up the room number.

One way or another, Isaac was going to get Savannah to talk to him. Too many lives were at stake to continue playing nice.

But first, he was doing a perimeter check. And, satisfied that the couple of vehicles in the second drive weren't a threat, he drove around the block twice, too. One last check to make sure he wasn't being followed by whoever Savannah was working with.

And then drove through a somewhat questionable-looking joint for a fast-food breakfast order. Just a guy, hanging out.

The fact that he'd had such great sex with the woman only hours before she'd bolted rankled. More than it should.

He used the feeling to feed his determination to crack her.

To keep his backbone stiff as, a plastic bag in hand, he approached her door. Knocked. If he scared the crap out of her, he did. She hadn't taken her phone. Had left him no way to call ahead and make an appointment.

"Food delivery," he called. He'd bought enough for two. Would decide once he was inside if he was in a sharing mood or not.

The thought was barely complete before he heard locks click and the door flew open only long enough to pull him inside.

Taking him by surprise.

So much for pushing his way in.

How did the woman manage to continue to throw him off course?

"I don't know if it's safe for you to be here or not," she said, standing toe-to-toe with him just inside the door, her gaze wide open, her tone urgent. "I'm not sure if I'm making things worse, putting you in danger, but you're here and..." She broke off.

Glancing away from him to the bag he held.

And then down at herself.

"Talk to me, Savannah." The authoritarian demand he'd intended came out softly.

An urging, at best.

He took in every inch of her, the streaks of dirt on her face, a tear in the sleeve of a shirt he hadn't yet seen. Cotton pants that looked as though she'd slept and then crawled around in them.

No makeup.

Disheveled was an understatement. And after the way she'd run out on him without even giving him the respect of letting him know she no longer needed or wanted his hospitality, the knowledge he had of her subterfuge, how in the hell could he still find her so incredibly...desirable?

More beautiful than any woman he'd ever met.

"I figured out some things, and I'm afraid that Charlotte might be in danger." Concern oozed from her gaze as words poured out fast.

He ignored everything but the fact that hit hardest. "You know where she is?"

"You don't?" Mouth open, brows creased, she stared at him. And then she paled. "Tell me you know where she is, Isaac." The warning in her tone came out of the blue.

Nothing he'd heard from her before.

Her true self coming out?

"She's missing." He didn't couch the words at all and wasn't sorry for the abrupt delivery.

Savannah fell down to the bed, bending over, her head to her knees for a second, and when she came back up rocked front to back. He stared at the trembling in her hands as she asked, "How long?"

If he told her the truth, she'd know he'd lied to her the night before. "Yesterday morning."

She froze then, her eyes narrowed as she stared up at him. "The breach."

He nodded, resisted the urge to sit beside her, to take her hand. "I wasn't at liberty to say anything," he told her instead. Giving her what he could of an explanation for his subterfuge, for no good reason he could think of.

With a nod that felt like a dismissal, Savannah stood. "Tell me what you know." The take-charge tone was back, and for a second, he felt like he was in court. Like he had no choice but to tell the truth, the whole truth, and nothing but the truth. Except that...he couldn't.

"I can't. But you know something. It's obvious that it's eating at you." He let the intimate tone seep into his words.

She glanced up, held his gaze for a second, as she had so many times over the past few days. And then shook her head again. "I need to know what you know first," she said.

And so he gave her something. "She disappeared without a trace. No sign of forced entry. No tire tracks. Her phone, purse, and car are all at home."

She'd stopped pacing, stood right in front of him, the dirt on her face a stark contrast to the sudden whiteness of her skin. He saw the fear in her eyes.

Knew it wasn't faked. And so he fed it.

"Her father is beside himself."

"What do the police say?" she asked then, pacing again. "The FBI?" Her back was to him as she mentioned his agency.

For a second, he considered that she knew. That his cover was blown. But nothing else gave indication of such.

Guilt was nagging at him. A never before occurrence.

"Mr. Duran doesn't want them called." He saw no harm in giving her that much. She'd be able to see for herself, soon enough, that there was nothing in the news. "He's worried that if word gets out that she's missing, unsavory characters will come out, hunting for her, putting her in even more danger. He's hired private investigators, and, of course, the entire security staff is on the case as well."

Looking up at him, she said, "Except for you."

He let her think that. It was the right move for the job. Which was why he was there.

The grateful look in eyes shadowed by worry made him want to take her in his arms. To promise that everything would be okay.

But he didn't believe it ever would be. Not for her, if she was messed up with Duran.

And not for them, either.

"Tell me what you know, Savannah, while there's still time to save her."

Her head reared back at the words, but she held his gaze and nodded, too. "You're right. And you're here. And looking for Charlotte, you're all walking into something and have a better chance if you know what you're likely up against. I'm going to have to trust that I do more good than harm by talking to you." She didn't sound happy about the choice.

He wasn't happy when she took his hand and pulled him to sit on the end of the bed with her. If she thought he was going to fall for any more of her distractions...

"Charlotte Duran is my sister."

All the turmoil raging inside Isaac just...stopped. Like he'd been put in deep freeze. Nothing happened. He just stared at her.

As thoughts tumbled all over.

Was she hallucinating?

Making some kind of sick joke?

Surely she didn't think he was so besotted with her he'd fall for something so ludicrous.

Her gaze was open, locked on his, and swarming with emotion that looked—and felt—real.

How did she do that?

"I told you I was here to look for someone. Not to make contact, but just to see that they were okay. That someone is Charlotte."

She appeared—sounded—so serious.

And was confusing an already upended situation. Wasting time he didn't have to waste. Had he fallen deeper than he'd thought? Had her siren call brought him there when he should've been out busting ground to find Charlotte Duran? As well as the proof he needed to stop her father.

Just the fact that she was making him doubt himself...

Isaac stood. Left his bag of uneaten breakfast on the dresser and headed for the door.

Savannah Compton could stay or go. She could lie and scheme and snag hearts. But not in his world. Not anymore.

He was done.

HE DIDN'T BELIEVE HER.

She didn't blame him. But he couldn't go.

Isaac's hand turned the dead bolt, unhooked the chain lock, and Savannah said, "Her name was Nicole."

She stood as he slowly turned around. Reached for her computer, turned it on. Brought up the proof. Faced him, shoulders straight and head high. Uncaring that she looked so filthy. She had a story to tell.

He didn't come closer. His gaze was clearly assessing. But she had his attention.

"She was kidnapped from her daycare when she was a year old. I was seven." The words slid right out, as though they'd been there waiting for their turn.

As twenty-four years of silence shattered around her, Savannah focused on information pertinent to saving Charlotte. "Almost a year ago, Charlotte entered her DNA into Family Finders. She made her profile public, just her name and an address, so that if there was ever a match, the family member could find her. I'd tried other, much larger databases, but a client referred me to Family Finders, and I entered my information six weeks ago. And just last week was notified of the match."

She held out her laptop.

Isaac watched her as though she might sprout wings and fly away. And then took the computer, studying the screen before looking back at her, his expression stone-like.

Piercing. "I need some time to check this out."

She sat. Held up her hands.

And watched as Isaac's thumbs flew over his phone screen. Stopped as he read. And flew some more. Five minutes passed before he looked over at her again, open mouthed.

Stared was more like it.

As though seeing her for the first time.

As though he couldn't believe what he was seeing.

She waited. Feeling surreal. Her entire world had just flipped into something she didn't recognize. After twenty-four years of silence, she'd said her secret aloud. To a virtual stranger.

She hadn't obliterated.

There'd been no fanfare.

If she'd lost her mind, another calmer one had found her.

Time passed. She lost track of how much. Isaac continued to type on his phone. And then, when the silence was beginning to get to her, suddenly asked, "Why did you disappear like you did in the middle of the night?"

His softer tone reached her more than the actual words. Freeing some of the chains tightening around her chest.

"Last night, some things clicked." She started talking as though she hadn't just dropped a bomb between them, giving him the facts he needed, weeding out the things she needed to say to him. "Telling you about Charlotte crying, reliving the boat blast, feeling that fear. It's not something I've carried with me my whole life. That fear just started a year ago."

"Your partner's kidnapping," Isaac finally spoke. She couldn't tell if he was letting her know he already had that part, urging her to get on with it, or if he was joining in the theory she'd built.

"Right. But what I didn't know until last week, and didn't put together until last night, was that I didn't start to feel as though I was being followed, didn't start noticing random different cars staying a few lengths behind me until after Charlotte put her information in that database."

She'd half feared saying the words aloud would cause them to crumble into ash. More false narrative she told herself. Like being followed at all.

Instead, they grew in stature.

Isaac approached the bed again. Sat on the corner of it, his gaze steady on her. "Wait a minute. You're saying that you think someone who knew Charlotte was kidnapped also knew you were her sister and started watching you when she started looking for you?" His words were clipped.

Hearing her theory aloud, it sounded fantastical. And sat with her in confirmation, too, as she nodded.

Close beside him, she held his gaze, needing him to talk silently with her as he had over the past few days.

Needing some real-life connection.

"I don't think Charlotte was looking for me specifically," she clarified after a long moment. "She was only a toddler. I have no idea if she even knows she was adopted. But she'd obviously been looking for family. And someone knew if I'd put my information in the database, she'd find me."

With a tilt of his head, he continued to watch her as he said, "And it's logical to assume that with all the new DNA technology, someone who'd had a family member kidnapped would definitely enter DNA into those databases."

He spoke to her point, not to the question she'd mentioned but left unasked. Did Charlotte even know she'd been adopted?

Had Isaac known?

His loyalty lay with his employer. She couldn't afford to push.

"Whoever this is who's after me, and now probably has Charlotte...it has to be someone who already knew about me because I just entered my DNA in Family Finders. But

I believe now that I was really being watched all this time. Ever since Charlotte entered hers. Before, when I didn't know about Charlotte's visit to the database, I had only Dorian's kidnapping to explain the sudden change in me. But it didn't really make sense, you know? I didn't have inexplicable anxiety issues after Nicole was kidnapped. Nor when Sierra was murdered. I grieved. I got myself trained in self-defense. I walked a straight line, made conservative choices, and looked over my shoulder, always. But I was never irrationally afraid. Never saw things that weren't there."

He nodded. And more of her words found their freedom. "I'm starting to feel like myself again for the first time in months."

Isaac frowned then. Stood. Putting his hands in his pockets as he took a couple of steps, then turned back to face her.

And the look on his face, the way he was regarding her, as though only just seeing her for the first time made her want to take it all back.

Charlotte Duran was adopted.

On one hand, the news stunned him. On the other, things started to make more sense to him. Eduardo's over-protectiveness of his daughter—spurred, Isaac had long thought, by the billionaire's odd insecurities where his daughter was concerned.

A man's daughter being his weak spot was pretty standard. But Eduardo had seemed to thrive on Charlotte's adoration. And did everything he could to shine a light on it. Mentioning it in conversation every chance he got. Not just praising his daughter but drawing attention to the way she felt about him. To their bond.

A representative from Family Finders had confirmed to the FBI the DNA match between the two samples they'd received.

The birth certificate an agent in the Washington office had just emailed listed Duran as Charlotte's father. And her mother as having died in childbirth. Confirming the story he'd been told.

Birth certificates could be changed.

Falsified.

If one had enough money and knew the right people.

DNA didn't lie.

And the rest, the kidnapping...even without the confirmation upon which he was waiting...he believed Savannah.

And she was holding something back. He was certain of that, too. Didn't like it at all.

But her association with Charlotte Duran...her explanation for her sudden appearance in San Diego...made a hell of a lot more sense than Duran's had.

Which meant that Eduardo Duran knew that Savannah was Charlotte's sister? Was that the big secret? The thing that the fearless man feared?

Charlotte wasn't biologically his.

Isaac would bet his life Charlotte didn't know that.

And the bigger news—she'd been kidnapped before.

Knowing what he did about the Duran empire, Isaac didn't struggle to believe that one at all. Or to assume that Duran had paid a lot of money to buy his daughter.

Some perp kidnapping her again made sense, too. Whoever had taken Charlotte the first time, sold her to Duran, could have taken her a second time to squeeze Duran, remind him of what he'd done, of what he had hanging over him but also to get Charlotte's DNA.

Without proof that Charlotte was Nicole, the perp couldn't blackmail Duran. It would be a scumbag's word against a respected dynasty.

They'd need Savannah's DNA, too, though. But they didn't

need her alive to get it. Or to blackmail Duran. Which put her in immediate danger.

She'd told him the other night that both of her parents were gone. Her father when she'd been little and her mother when she'd been grown.

Something else made a whole lot more sense. Duran not wanting to report his daughter's disappearance to the authorities. The billionaire couldn't risk having someone ask for DNA and possibly discovering that the woman he called his daughter had been reported missing before.

A long time ago.

Agents were searching the national database for the twenty-four-year-old missing person case involving a toddler named Nicole Compton.

As he stood there in the cheap, old motel room, Isaac wasn't any closer to arresting the man he was after. He'd need more. Proof. But he finally had a road to take.

And felt an even stronger urgency to find Charlotte. He didn't believe a kidnapper would kill her. At least not until he got what he wanted from Duran. Charlotte was one person who was most definitely worth more alive than dead.

But not Savannah.

His gut gave a lurch as the thought hit him again.

When he'd thought her complicit, he'd been concerned about her safety but had figured she'd brought danger upon herself. Now that he knew the truth...

The expert lawyer had turned out to be far more fascinating, compelling than he'd thought, even the day before. She was a woman who saw a problem and took it upon herself to solve it.

One who didn't cry into her soup and wait until others helped mop her up.

And one who deserved at least a snippet of a happy ending. If he could at least give her the chance to see Nicole face-to-face. To speak to her...

His senses honed, he looked at the woman he'd been naked with the night before and saw someone entirely different.

A woman who was on his side of the law. Who had been all along.

A woman he'd purposely taken advantage of...not sexually—that had been weakness there—but by frightening her into staying at his house so he could have access to her.

He pushed the image away. Couldn't let himself off the straight and narrow.

And couldn't leave it behind, either.

Duran. The master criminal. "A profile of a highly successful criminal includes the ability to manipulate," he said aloud. "If what you say is true, I'd put money on the fact that whoever knows about you made sure that you suspected you were being followed, without providing enough proof to have you do anything about it. Different cars, behind you long enough, slowing when you slowed, turning when you turned, but then suddenly not there..."

"Yes!" Savannah stood, too. "That's exactly how it happened. Any internet search of me would have shown my vulnerability. A way to get at me. Sierra's Web and Dorian's kidnapping was all over the news at that time. And if he was watching me, he'd have seen me spending so much time in self-defense classes. I gave him the ammunition." She glanced into the food bag.

Watching her, feeling her pain, Isaac took the move as a nervous reaction more than a desire for food. A break from a situation that had to be caging her. She turned to face him, though, after taking that second or two. "That's it, Isaac. I haven't been losing my mind. But he was trying to make me feel like I was." The relief in her tone hit him hard.

He'd been pegging her for conning him when she'd been

busy trying to cope with her life. There was still that "more" she wasn't telling him. His gut got that one loud and clear. The way she held his gaze so completely, until she avoided it altogether. And while he'd have to find a way to get her to confide it all, he didn't blame her for holding back.

He wasn't trustworthy. Not as Isaac Forrester. And Isaac was the only man in the room. The only life he was going to live until Eduardo Duran was behind bars.

And his adopted daughter, too, if need be.

The thought hit, as it always did. But with a force so different, Isaac took a step back. Stared at Savannah. And wondered how on earth he was going to tell her that he suspected her newfound baby sister was not only missing but was also a suspected international criminal?

As he watched her, met her gaze, the answer became clear. He wasn't.

Chapter Fifteen

The way Isaac was looking at her, as though he'd welcome her in his arms again, pulled at Savannah, but she turned away. She couldn't think of herself. Or even him.

"I have no idea who we're searching for, Isaac. There were never any suspects. And if they've already had her for over twenty-four hours…" A brand-new fear took root in her heart. Had she finally found her baby sister only to lose her again? Permanently?

"A stronger question is who was following you? I've heard nothing about any Duran detail at work in Michigan or anywhere else." Not that, in that particular case, he would have.

"Maybe the kidnapper?"

"And how would he have known exactly when Charlotte entered her information into that database?"

She didn't know. Had burst into tears while walking that morning as she'd considered the overwhelming burden her lack of information was putting on any hope of seeing Charlotte happy and then getting on with her own life.

When she shook her head, feeling helpless, Isaac said, "I have to consider that there might be a bad apple in Duran's employ. Someone with an axe to grind who somehow got close enough for Duran to have said something or to have had Charlotte's information or, at the very least, access to her computer. Or was privy to Duran's most private documents. I don't even know where he keeps those. Nor do I think he'd keep record of something like this."

As the challenges before them—the unknowns, maybes, and suppositions—seemed to grow too high to scale, Isaac took her hand. "But what I do know is that whoever has been following you, who shot at you isn't about to stop now. So, the first thing we need to do, for sure, is to keep you hidden."

She heard what he wasn't saying. Whoever they were, they likely had Charlotte. Stood to reason Savannah would be next.

She couldn't go back to Isaac's house. Into hiding. She'd been hiding for most of her life, in one way or another. "Unless we use me to lure them out," she said, knowing she'd just made her plan of action, with or without Isaac's blessing.

The idea might have been forming under the surface, but it had just come to her in concrete thought. She didn't yet know how it would work. She'd need to go to the police. To have someone watching her so that when she lured out the hunters, even if she was hurt or killed, they'd be caught.

"I'm done being a victim, Isaac," she said when he stood there, watching her. Duran thought police involvement would put his daughter at higher risk. But what if one of Duran's own men helped her?

Dare she ask Isaac? Was it fair to do so?

So her plan wasn't fully formed.

She just knew she was the bait. And she had to try. For Nicole. And for herself.

He frowned. "To be clear, you didn't respond to Family Finders in any way?"

His question was succinct, could have been interrogation. It didn't feel that way. And she said, "Not directly. I looked up the address that populated in my private search. Just trying to get a feel for where it was. I did it in a café, just signed in as a guest. And then, when I got to town, I typed it in my phone's global positioning system for driving directions." He'd need to know about anything that could possibly be traced.

Sierra's Web had taught her that much.

"Did you tell anyone?"

She gave him an immediate shake of the head. And then said, "No one in my life—including my partners, who are family to me—knows I ever had a sister." And when she realized the statement would raise more questions, she quickly added a partial truth. "I was a kid when it all happened. My way of coping was to pretend that it hadn't. Mom moved me to another city, and I left it all behind. I felt like it could have been me, you know?"

"Your father was already gone then?" He didn't miss a beat, and so neither did she.

She looked straight at him as she nodded.

His eyes narrowed, his brow furrowed. "Have you, as an adult, ever looked back at the case? With your skills, the access Sierra's Web gives you..."

"No." She still held his gaze, but with some difficulty. He was getting dangerously close to things she couldn't say.

Her mother and the marshals had assured her, over and over, that there'd been no evidence of any link between Nicole's kidnapping and her father's upcoming testimony. Everyone was certain, based on evidence at the scene, that Nicole had been collateral damage.

They could have been wrong. Something she'd considered more than once over the years.

But as far as she was aware, she was the only person left living, other than a retired agent and a marshal someplace, who knew that her father had been about to testify the day he'd been murdered.

Nicole's disappearance, even her last name and exact details of the kidnapping, had been changed on the records as part of Savannah and her mother's entrance into witness protection.

She'd been called Natalie Willoughby in the witness protection report.

And though Savannah had asked her mother many times over the years if the authorities would be able to find them if Nicole was found, she'd always only been told *I don't know.*

As an adult she'd realized that her mother had made the very difficult decision to appear deceased in the event the authorities ever did locate Nicole. Which would have put Nicole into the foster system.

She'd turned her back on any possibility of seeing her youngest child again, of caring for her, and she'd done it for Savannah's sake. To protect her. Keep her from harm.

Which was why Savannah had to do all she could, lose her life if that was what it came to, in order to ensure Nicole's chance at health and happiness.

"Savannah?" Isaac's soft tone called her back to him.

"What?"

"I asked you why you didn't look her up."

She couldn't give him the truth. Reached for the bag of food he'd brought in. Pulled out a couple of foam cartons with lids and plastic-wrapped packets of napkins and disposable utensils. Opened a lid to see rubber-looking scrambled eggs with breakfast potatoes, a piece of questionable sausage, and a biscuit. As she was picking up the dried hard roll, the part of the answer she could give came to her, and she turned, facing him again.

"If the FBI couldn't find her, how could I?" she asked, stating the truth she'd lived with for most of her life. Until Sierra's Web had broken all kinds of records for crimes they'd solved. "And I'd been told, repeatedly, that it wouldn't be fair to her. Whether her life had gone well or not, she didn't need to know what it could have been. Unless she chose to find me." Her mouth still open on that last word, she shoved the biscuit between her teeth and bit down.

Forestalling any other dangerous tidbit that might attempt to spill out.

THE WOMAN HAD no idea she was dealing with an international criminal operation. Whatever deep secret she was keeping about her sister's kidnapping was personal. Isaac read the truth in her body language, the turning away and the straight glance from eyes filled with pain as she'd told him as much as she had.

Every bit of it had rung true with everything he knew about child abductions.

And the things she wasn't telling him. If he had to guess, he'd say that she'd been present during the kidnapping. Had, perhaps, been charged to keep an eye on her sister for a minute while her mother had quickly done something else.

What seemed obvious to Isaac as he sat shoveling in a cold breakfast that would have been only marginally edible when hot was that Savannah Compton blamed herself for her baby sister's kidnapping.

At the small desk in her room, they were sitting side by side on the wooden slatted bench meant to be a luggage rack, eating silently as though the questionable nourishment was actually palatable. She was staring at her food as she ate.

Clearly reliving a part of her life that no one shared.

While he contemplated what came next.

She was going out into the fray—that much was obvious. He wasn't going to be able to change her mind. Short of locking her up, he couldn't stop her.

The thought eased the guilt eating at him somewhat as the plan that had been building since she'd first revealed her connection to Charlotte solidified.

He had to use her. Savannah Compton and her shocking surprise were the world's best chance at bringing Duran to his knees.

Maybe their only chance.

She'd already brought the danger down upon herself.

But his plan would be for her own good as well. Alone, she stood no chance against the Duran empire and whoever the man was warring with. Both sides apparently after her.

With Isaac, she'd at least have a chance to stay alive. She'd have protection. His. Which she'd know about. And also that of the agents he had secretly working with him.

He was risking the case—Duran's bodyguard associating with a woman Duran was after. The fact was there in all its rawness.

If he could get to the arrest warrant with his cover intact, he'd have the win of his career.

Another truth. Not one that motivated him.

His gut was telling him Savannah Compton needed protection that he could provide and, with equal weight, it was letting him know that with Charlotte's disappearance, things were coming to a head. The Sierra's Web lawyer could very well be his last chance to get Duran before the man simply disappeared.

To set up shop elsewhere. Under another new identity. He'd had two that Isaac knew of. A third wouldn't be a stretch.

It was how his type worked. Same money, different name.

And how, international law enforcement had determined, Duran had managed to escape paying for his crimes for decades. He'd perfected the art of becoming someone else.

Isaac waited until Savannah put down the plastic fork she'd been using and pushed her container toward the wall before speaking again.

"My guess is you know more than you realize. Someone

was somehow privy to Charlotte having entered her DNA with Family Finders. Someone who you might have seen in the past. Someone you might recognize, even now. What keeps bothering me is why would they manipulate you, make you doubt yourself from the moment your little sister became part of that database?"

Her gaze wasn't timid, but he could read the concern there. Mingling with shock, he thought, as she said, "I'll know him? That's what this is about? Someone thinks I know something about the kidnapping?"

She frowned then, staring at him, but the look was blank. As though she was seeing something else. And then, shaking her head, she came back to him, her gaze focused on his, and she said, "I can't pull up a picture in my head of anyone I knew twenty-four years ago. And certainly not from around the time of the kidnapping. I vaguely remember what my teacher looked like. I have memories of the neighbors but couldn't describe them to you."

As Savannah focused, showing him her professionalism, the thoroughness with which she approached every task, Isaac's tension settled a bit.

He'd come to Savannah's hotel room thinking she was a criminal. Meaning all bets were off in terms of entrapment or luring her into helping him.

Now that he believed she was innocent… Isaac and Mike weren't getting along as well. To make matters worse, he couldn't separate the two enough at the moment to know which one wanted to protect her more.

"I'd like to talk you out of putting yourself up as bait, most particularly until we have time to try to figure out who we're dealing with…" His pause was deliberate. If she agreed to hold off, he'd have to reassess his current plan to use her to draw out whoever had been following her. Had shot at her.

An agent couldn't ethically engage an innocent civilian in the line of duty without her express consent to assist the FBI.

If Isaac gave her more of what he knew, which he easily could as Charlotte's bodyguard, he could talk her into co-operating.

The line he was skating had become a thread.

Savannah was shaking her head before he'd completed the thought. "My mind's made up, Isaac. No way I hide away while my little sister could be in severe jeopardy, being trau-matized—for a second time in her life."

She left neither Mike nor Isaac any other choice but to get her on the plan. For her own good as much as anyone. "Then, please, let me help you," he told her, falling back into Isaac's life far too easily. "I think you're right in that you represent our best and quickest hope of finding Charlotte. I know that you'll be far safer being exposed to this creep if I've got your back. And there's more chance that we'll be able to rescue Charlotte if my team is there to help." Mike's team. Not Isaac's.

If Isaac did his job right, Duran's people weren't going to know a damned thing.

In the event of a takedown, it would be all FBI agents on deck, with Duran's people in handcuffs. At least until they could be thoroughly checked out and cleared of any wrong-doing.

And those with dirty hands would be offered the oppor-tunity to roll on their top leader.

Savannah's gaze showed a whole lot of doubt. "Your team? Duran's people are on the lookout for me..."

He was ready for that one. "If I do my job right, they aren't going to know I've found you unless we've got Charlotte, too. At that point, your being her sister will be established, and while there will likely be a lot of emotional, and potentially criminal baggage to sort through, with no guarantee how that all plays out, you'll no longer pose a security threat."

Clearly the time to act had come. Duran was feeling heat from a source dangerous enough, bold enough to kidnap Charlotte. If Duran got too skittish, he'd pull one of his suspected disappearing acts, and Isaac would have lost his chance.

The plan was the best he had.

And was relying on a whole lot of *if*s.

Any of which could go wrong.

And get people killed.

SAVANNAH AGREED TO Isaac's offer with only a moment or two of thought. Big picture, she'd be a fool not to. For herself, obviously, but more for Charlotte. What could Savannah, one lone, unarmed woman, do to rescue what could be a drugged or injured body from criminals?

He'd have a couple of buddies, bodyguards that he'd worked with in the past, at their backs.

Isaac was on the payroll of a billionaire, was the head of Duran's protection detail. And was being loyal to his employer, keeping his own counsel about the man and his business, while he did what he could, namely using Savannah, to try to find the man's daughter. Clearly he'd proven to be one of the best at what he did. He thought of things she didn't even know to consider. Field things.

When it came to the law, to making certain that the kidnappers paid for every single crime they'd committed, she'd be the one to get it done.

Isaac had been scrolling on his phone and turned it to her. "I kept a log of every place I've taken Charlotte over the past several months. My guess is no matter who's behind the kidnapping, whoever actually took her knew her patterns, is familiar with those areas. I'm assuming the current kidnapper was hired," he added as she scrolled the electronic list he'd handed to her. "But I could be wrong."

Feeling tears threaten as she read snippets from her sister's everyday life—something she'd never dared let herself hope she'd ever be privy to—Savannah forced herself to stay focused.

"I think we should start with openly, visibly visiting these areas," Isaac continued, his gaze forthright, his tone completely professional. "It's what an investigator would do if they were looking for someone. Visit the places they visit. See if anyone has heard from them. I'll get you a car to drive and be behind you at all times."

She looked up from his list, handed back his phone, her mind reeling with Charlotte's tastes. Coffee. There were a few well-known barista shops. Boutique clothing shops. And women's facilities. From shelters to high-powered charity organizations. "Sounds good," she said. Then stood, reaching into the bag she'd lugged through the woods, pulled out clean clothes and toiletries, and finished with "And please send me a copy of that log." She rattled off the number of her new burner phone as she shut herself in the bathroom just feet away from the remains of their breakfast.

Twenty minutes later, Savannah picked up her phone off the bathroom counter before presenting herself outside the closed door and was relieved to see that Isaac had done as she'd asked. His travel log had been sent to her screen.

If they got separated, she had that much to work with on her own.

She hadn't known Isaac long enough to be putting any lives in his hands. She knew that.

But sometimes, a person just had to trust.

Chapter Sixteen

Mike's people were up to speed and in place by the time Savannah exited the bathroom. Isaac took one look at her and, for that split second, wanted to call the whole thing off.

In a fresh pair of capris with a short-sleeved shirt and tennis shoes and her long dark hair pulled back, the woman looked as though she belonged on an expensive court, racket in hand, sipping lemon water in between serves.

Or in his bed.

While he was decked out for work.

Thankfully the second passed without anything of note coming from it.

As did the entire rest of the morning.

In his car, following behind Savannah in the gray rental sedan, he stayed online with her through the cars' audio systems as they started on the location log he'd sent her. They spoke only about the case and otherwise hung there on a connected line, in contact. Savannah never seemed to lose focus, even for a second, as she scoured everything in sight, anywhere they happened to be. From being aware of the vehicles behind them to the green balloon caught on an electrical wire, the lawyer proved her quick ability to mentally catalogue and recall even the smallest details.

Which made him wonder, again, about her past and the

secret she was keeping from him. Had she seen the kidnapper? Did she know who they were after? Consciously or subconsciously? Had she heard anything that might help them narrow down their suspect?

They were heading toward the university where Charlotte had most recently lectured.

The place where she'd scoped out a hiding place in a women's restroom rather than be face-to-face with Arnold Wagar.

He'd had his people looking into the man Duran wanted his daughter to marry, and so far, nothing he'd learned had pointed to any kind of physical aggression in the man's past. Other than Savannah's testimony regarding the tears the man had caused Charlotte to shed.

What he found interesting, though, was that Wagar owned a portfolio of profitable, tax-paying companies, including a family-run winery that shipped expensive and very exclusive product all over the world.

Someone held in high esteem globally, with international shipping capabilities...

"I'm getting more and more uneasy about the idea of bringing in Duran's people to help when we locate Charlotte." Savannah's voice interrupted his thoughts and captured his full attention, too.

When they found Charlotte. Her goal, of course. But her course of action, making herself prey...she seemed to be gliding right over the fact that she might get found before she found.

He kept the thought to himself as he asked the more pertinent question. "Why?" Was she about to tell him more of what she knew?

A blip of doubt hit as he considered how much he'd risked taking on the woman as completely as he had.

He pushed through the unwanted blow to his confidence. He hadn't been duped. Wasn't being played.

He'd know if his cover had been blown.

Savannah was keeping an eye on him. He saw her glances in her rearview mirror. After a long pause she said, "I've been thinking about everything we've both come up with, trying to fit pieces together in a way that shows us the ones that are missing. And it seems plausible that Charlotte's father knew he'd adopted a kidnapped baby. I'm assuming it's always just been father and daughter, so maybe he wanted a girl with particular characteristics and back then it would have been harder for a single man to adopt. Or maybe he knew the kidnapper and had a reason to buy him out of trouble. Could have been a brother who'd gotten into trouble or something..."

The family-member angle wasn't one he'd considered. Duran wasn't known to have any biological family. At least not in the states. But had Charlotte found out about someone? An aunt or uncle or cousin? Someone from whom her father was estranged? Could that have been why she'd gone to Family Finders?

His mind grabbed the possibilities, finding merit rather than dismissing them outright. An estranged sibling who knew Eduardo's secret, one Charlotte had wanted to find, fit with the facts they had.

Including Charlotte's disappearance. A missing person who'd left no trace. What if Savannah hadn't been the only one who'd been sent a positive match pursuant to Charlotte's database entry? What if someone else had been notified that she'd been looking and had contacted her? A highly intelligent young woman could feasibly have planned her escape to meet up with someone she was related to, in the hopes of bringing him or her home to her father.

It sounded like something Charlotte would do.

The official version, that he'd heard from both Charlotte and her father at separate times, was that Charlotte had been born to Duran and his wife, an American woman who'd died giving birth. What he'd learned that day was that there'd been an American birth certificate and paperwork granting the child dual citizenship.

"What if the kidnapper has been in the picture for a while?" Savannah said, continuing on her own tangent. "Maybe he threatened to tell Charlotte that she was kidnapped unless he was compensated. He could have been getting paid by Mr. Duran for his silence. Charlotte could have told her father that she'd entered her DNA into the Family Finders database. Or—you'd know better than I—maybe her computer is regularly checked to make certain that no one's defrauding her, and they found record of the entry. That's why they were watching me after she'd entered the database.

"As long as I did nothing, I was no threat. But once I flew to San Diego... Maybe the kidnapper and Mr. Duran both know that I'm Charlotte's sister and are trying to get rid of me, so I don't tell Charlotte. Even if Mr. Duran didn't know at first that Charlotte had been kidnapped, when he found out, loving Charlotte as he did... It's believable that he'd buy the kidnapper's silence..."

Savannah's voice trailed off.

Isaac thought about telling her about the family angle her words had just brought to him but knew he couldn't. His assignment was for him and his agents. Savannah could only be privy to what she had to know for the sake of the case.

The fact brought a bad taste to his mouth and tension to his gut as he said, "I think you're onto something..."

Her gasp came crisp and clear over the wireless connection, followed by, "What if Mr. Duran or the kidnapper have taken Charlotte someplace—sent her on vacation out of the country even, just until they're satisfied that I've been dealt with? She might not even know people think she's missing."

He'd considered Duran as the instigator in Charlotte's

absence. Still didn't feel like that one fit. "Which means you're risking your life on a wild-goose chase," he said and added, "I had a text while you were in the bathroom, letting me know that my protection team's mid-morning update from Duran security included the fact that your rental had been returned to the airport but that there'd been no sign of you heading through security to board the flight. So if you want to change your mind and go back into hiding while I sort this out…"

What in the hell was he saying?

And who was saying it? Not Isaac Forrester, that was for sure.

And not Mike Reynolds, either.

Having her exposed was their best shot at ending the case. Including removing the threat from Savannah. She'd been to San Diego once. Had sought out Charlotte. Duran wouldn't be comfortable leaving her out there anymore, a possible threat who could attack at any time.

"No way I'm giving up. If what we think is true, I'm a threat to Duran no matter where I am. I told you, Isaac, with or without you, I'm done being a victim." Savannah's words let him off the hook, with a strong note to get himself in gear, get any softness he might be harboring toward Savannah Compton off the table or get off the case.

Her tone changed, lost its energy as she added, "I'm only guessing here. And not sure I'm anywhere near the truth."

Isaac nodded. Keeping to himself the fact that he believed she was closer to finding their mark than she thought.

And that he admired her ability to get there.

What he allowed himself to celebrate was the fact that with her suspicions on Duran, as his had been all along, they were closer to being on the same page. She'd just negated the need for any lies he'd have had to tell her if they found Charlotte and she pushed him to bring in Duran's men.

Beyond that, she was just a part of the plan to complete the most important job he'd ever had. A part he was sworn to protect.

And he was just Isaac Forrester.

A fake persona.

Period.

AFTER THE CONVERSATION regarding Duran, Isaac seemed to open up to Savannah more. Like maybe he was starting to see her more as her partners did—a necessary cog in the wheel with contributions that no one else could bring to the table.

Or maybe she was just slowly starting to see herself again.

As she passed a popular gas station–convenience store chain, Isaac told her about the time Charlotte had insisted on stopping at that exact location to pump gas. She'd wanted the experience.

Keeping her gaze focused on the traffic, on her surroundings, Savannah felt her heart fill due to the real-life image of her sister that was finally forming in her mind's eye.

And a few minutes later, as she approached the university they'd been heading toward, Isaac told her about an encounter that had taken place just that week—Charlotte planning to cut her lecture to avoid someone in the audience.

He didn't say who—it would've been inappropriate for him to do so—but the way he told her…a man who wouldn't take no for an answer…she knew. The man in the yard with Nicole…making her cry…

Wait. She stiffened, shot a quick glance in the rearview mirror. Locating Isaac two cars behind her in the left lane, she said, "What if Charlotte did leave of her own accord?" Mind clear, inner vision astute, she continued, "She was willing to forgo a lecture to avoid the man. What would she be willing to do to avoid being hounded by him in her own home?"

That was it. The explanation that made sense. Charlotte knew the house, the security systems, the habits of the personnel in place to watch over everything. She'd know how to avoid all of them. How to shut down the system for the time she'd need to escape.

And would have had something in place to get her away once she was off the property undetected. Savannah had hired a boat. Charlotte, with all her wealth, could have swum and then walked before being picked up by a helicopter. Or a yacht. She could be anywhere, with anyone of her choosing. People she'd pay to stay silent.

It was an explanation Savannah could take in without losing a part of herself. Nicole hadn't been kidnapped again—she'd left of her own accord.

A silent Isaac was pulling into the university parking lot behind her. She'd get out. He'd wait in the car until she was far enough away and then carefully follow her. He'd provided them both with earpieces to stay in verbal contact.

Getting out of her car, turning on the earpiece as it connected, she walked toward the building that had housed the lecture hall and asked, "This guy who leaves her no choice but to disappear—who is he?" Her words were soft, but she issued them with definite courtroom interrogation in her tone.

Isaac's silence might have been hard for her to withstand a day or two before.

Not anymore.

She was done being manipulated by the fear her hunters had spent the last year instilling within her. She might've been cautious, but she had a mind that could untangle the most intricately weaved webs.

"Isaac?" Her gaze was moving around her surroundings, just as it had every other time they'd stopped. "Who is he?"

"I'm ten yards behind you. The door we always entered is at the left side of the building. The lecture hall will be the first door on your right once you get inside."

She veered to the left. Looking at everyone in sight. Catching no one looking back. "Who is he?" Her words were staccato.

"That's information I'm not free to divulge." There was no hint of sorrow in his tone.

His words felt like stabs. Until she reminded herself Isaac was skating a thin line, owing his loyalty to his employer—the lack of which could be a career ender for him—and… knowing Savannah.

Knowing. What else could she call the odd connection between the two of them? Virtual strangers who were somehow trusting each other with lives at stake.

Who happened to have had incredible sex less than twenty-four hours before.

"Is he on your radar as a possible suspect?" she asked then.

"Until I have someone in custody, everyone is a possible suspect." The low tone in her ear delivered his message succinctly.

She and Isaac Forrester were working together, reaching for the same goal, but they weren't a team.

And no matter how much he lit her up, he most definitely was not one of her partners.

THE WOMAN HAD as much energy as any good agent with whom he'd ever worked. Isaac listened in on conversations she had with people at the university, most pertinent to him being the one she held with the dean of the women's studies department.

Posing as a journalist doing a story on Charlotte Duran for an online women's publication Isaac had never heard of, Savannah had a heartfelt talk about the different cultures in which women were raised, which she managed to segue into a question about Charlotte's possible motives for being so passionate about her topic.

He didn't blame the lawyer for trying to get to know her sister in any way she could, yet time was pressing at his back. He couldn't be completely absent from Duran property for more than a day or two. Nor did he think that whoever was after Savannah was just going to give up and go home. The longer things drew out, the more desperate everyone was going to become.

The more determined.

And the less likely Duran would be to remain patient. If he didn't feel success coming his way soon regarding the threat that Savannah Compton posed to the life he'd built, the man was going to disappear right behind his daughter.

Dread weighted his gut as he considered that that had been the plan from the moment Charlotte had disappeared. Duran had already started his disappearing act. First Charlotte. And then himself...

"She cares deeply about all aspects of the female psyche, about the unique challenges all women face, regardless of race or nationality or culture, and tries to bring a sense of sisterhood into every group to whom she speaks..." The dean's voice was coming through Isaac's earpiece just as one of Duran's security guards approached the building from a parking area on the other side of the building. A third shifter, they'd never actually worked together. He knew the man by gait.

Sliding his hand to the gun holstered by his pocket underneath his suit jacket, Isaac turned, slid behind some shrubbery, and said, "Get out now. South door. Go behind the shrubs against the building, and don't move."

Without waiting for a response, he rounded the building from the opposite side and, before the guard made it to the door of the building, burst around a corner as though he'd been on the same sidewalk. With surprise all over his face and in his voice, he greeted the man. Told him he was making good progress on his day's responsibilities but had so far turned up very little. Except that Charlotte was passionate about the challenges women faced.

He kept his demeanor serious. Played the guy-to-guy, guard-to-guard card. Showed concern. And then suggested, on the down-low, that he was beginning to wonder if Charlotte Duran had left of her own accord.

When the guard responded in kind, looking Isaac in the eye, expressing his own lack of progress along with a dose of fatigue, Isaac offered to take some of the other man's assignments and was gratified when the man said he'd been specifically charged with speaking with anyone who'd shown up on Charlotte's phone records over the past week, showing them Savannah Compton's photo, and that he would get his job done.

But he thanked Isaac sincerely for the offer as Isaac barreled forward with the conversation to let the man know he'd just interviewed the dean, whom the man had been on his way to see, and had shown the photo to no avail, knowing full well that Savannah could hear the conversation.

If the guard didn't turn around, their jig could be up. Isaac would pull out all stops to prevent the guard from seeing the dean, setting off a sprinkler system or fire alarm if it came to that, but he needed Savannah prepared.

With a grateful nod, along with a comment about Isaac's reputation for thoroughness, the tired security man turned back the way he'd come. And Isaac stood watching him until he was out of sight.

They'd dodged a bullet.

And Isaac took warning, too. Isaac had been charged with looking for Charlotte. At least one member of the security staff was on another mission. Eduardo Duran wasn't going to stop looking for Savannah. He was only going to increase manpower until she was found.

Chapter Seventeen

Following Isaac's instructions completely, zigzagging her way between buildings and trees and then using his vehicle as a cover, Savannah made it back to her rental sedan. Her heart was pounding, and she was breathing heavily.

But she had completed the trek perfectly by focusing on his voice in her ear.

Adrenaline pumped through her as she started her car and pulled off the university lot. Other than her abrupt departure, claiming a sudden stomach ailment, Savannah had enjoyed her conversation with the dean. But more, she was actively engaged in saving her sister.

"We're on the right track," she said to Isaac as soon as she'd segued into traffic. "We know that Duran's men are aggressively looking for me," she said, feeling the shiver of fear the notice brought but also engaging with the sense of power it gave her. "Which means that I mean as much to them as we surmised that I did."

His grunt didn't add to her sense of accomplishment, but she didn't let him diminish her resolve, either. "I'm changing course for our next stop," she told him next, signaling a turn from the directions she'd looked up while hiding in the shrubs. He could follow or not. The fact that she was driving in front of him had been his call.

"This will work better if I have some heads-up." His tone was droll. She didn't miss the warning in the words, though. He'd probably just saved her life.

She needed him far more than he needed her.

While she wanted to be seen, to draw out the kidnapper, she'd fail if Duran's men got to her first.

"Back there, Dean Wilson was talking about Charlotte's passion, and it hit me. There were women's shelters on your log. I'm heading to the one Charlotte most recently visited—just last week. If anyone can give us any insight as to where Charlotte might hide out, I'm thinking it would be someone at the shelter. I've worked with several women's shelters, and one of the things that seems to remain true throughout the entire community of them is that shelters are a safe place for women to talk. About things they might not speak of anywhere else."

She was pulling away from the square mile surrounding the university, entering a roundabout when another vehicle entered at the same time from a perpendicular direction that should have yielded to her.

Except that it wasn't yielding. The vehicle was coming straight at her. Big. Black. Savannah gunned the gas, speeding around, heading for another exit, not slowing—though she should have, and barely escaped another car with the right of way, shooting out in the opposite direction of where she'd been heading. She heard a crunch behind her.

Cringed.

Sent up a small prayer for those involved in the crash that had been clearly meant for her. And with a shaky voice said, "Isaac?"

Fearing the worst when she didn't hear his voice reply in return.

ON THE PHONE with Chuck Knowles, rattling off a license plate number before getting out of his car to observe the wreckage he'd nearly been a part of, Isaac watched Savannah speed off into the distance.

His gut clenched tight—he knew he had to stay at the scene long enough to see who'd just tried to kill her. Someone who'd known she was at the university, who'd seen her turn onto the road leading to the roundabout and had headed her off.

One of Duran's men?

Running toward the wreckage, a three-car pileup, hearing someone say they'd called 911, he was already hearing sounds of sirens when he caught sight of a male—less than six feet tall, shaved head, white T-shirt, jeans, medium-color skin with tats on his arms—running from the scene.

To a car on the side of the road, just off the roundabout. He was in, with the blue sedan taking off before Isaac got sight of the driver. But he managed to snap a photo which, when enlarged, produced another plate number for him to call in to Chuck.

He did so as he climbed back into his own car, backed around, and sped off down the road Savannah had taken. He knew her destination, hoped she was back on the route, and, as soon as he was off with Chuck, called her back.

His jaw was clenched, his gut sick with worry as he waited for the call to connect, to hear the first ring.

He'd had to leave her to fend for herself. Had to stop and get what evidence he could before police had arrived. Car makes and models. Suspect information, if he'd had a chance to retrieve that, too. As a bodyguard he had no legal ground to stand on, but before law enforcement arrived, all bets were off. There was no law against being an overzealous concerned citizen.

Two rings. No answer.

The black SUV entering the roundabout, heading straight for Savannah. A getaway car. Or lookout. Or both.

Had a third vehicle followed her out of the roundabout?

Not immediately—he'd watched long enough to know that, but once he'd turned his attention to the plate number for Chuck...

"Isaac?" Her voice in his ear. Strong. Worried sounding.

Isaac's hand shook on the wheel as adrenaline drained from him, making way for relief. "You okay?"

"Yes."

"In your car?"

"Yes."

"Driving?" He had to know. Direct questions for direct answers. Ones she could give even if someone was listening.

"Yes."

"Alone?"

"Yes." Was that a note of warmth in her last response?

They couldn't afford warmth. Any more than he needed to be weak with relief.

"You on your way to the shelter?"

"Yes."

He knew the route. "On Randolph Road?"

"Yes."

Turning sharply, he took a turn and then another, heading toward a shortcut through an alley. "I'm on my way."

"Oh!" Her surprise was evident. And he was pretty sure he detected relief, too.

"You thought I'd abandon you?" The idea kind of pissed him off. She didn't see him as someone reliable.

And yet leaving her to fend for herself was exactly what he'd done.

"I thought you'd been hurt," she said then. "I knew you were entering the circle behind me. Heard the crash..."

Her voice trembled as her words broke off.

She'd been afraid for him. But had kept going.

As he had.

They were professionals. Focused. The only thing that mattered was the goal.

But that small tremble he'd heard in her voice…it lingered.

SAVANNAH DIDN'T GET much from the shelter. She'd hoped, going in alone, posing as a woman Charlotte had spoken to, asking for clarification on a location Charlotte had mentioned as a place to hide out for a few days, that someone would immediately pop out an answer.

Which was why she was a lawyer, not an investigator. She'd walked into a small, empty room. Had been spoken to through what was obviously bulletproof glass via a metal speaker in the middle of it. She'd been convincing enough to get herself beyond the first locked door and into a private room with a table and two chairs. And then she'd met with a woman who was one of the shelter's volunteers. Someone who only worked two afternoons a week.

And had been told, quite clearly, that no one there would give out any information on anyone else who'd been there or worked there, ever. Most particularly not to someone who didn't have a case on file. Or who hadn't registered with them.

If she wanted to register, they could get that process started, and then she'd be able to speak with a counselor who could help her. Or if she'd rather, she could just sit for a bit, have a beverage and a snack, and when the counselor was free, she could come in to chat. But at no time did anyone give out safe locations to anyone other than someone who'd been deemed to have immediate need of one.

While Savannah was disappointed, she totally understood. Anyone could pay someone to go in and get information that would then be used to allow an abuser to get to his victim.

Which was what she told Isaac. He'd been on the lookout the entire time she'd been inside, and she'd waited for his all-clear before she'd exited the back door of the small, nondescript building and practically held her breath as she'd hurried to her car.

"You think the guy in the crash was the same one who shot at me?" she asked as soon as she was on the road again, driving to their next destination. Another shelter.

He'd said that he'd seen one man and had called in a description of him as well as a license plate number to his team. And that due to the crash, the police were involved as well.

"It's possible." His tone gave away nothing.

"Hired by Duran?" She was trying not to internalize the danger she was in or dwell on it. Doing so would be counterproductive to her possibility of survival. But she needed to understand, as best she could, what she was up against.

"In the year I've been associated with Eduardo Duran I haven't seen a single piece of evidence pointing to him ever putting out a hit on someone. Or proof that he's done anything else illegal."

She'd pretty much expected that to be the case. Isaac wouldn't be working for the man if he thought Duran was involved in criminal activity.

But her heart settled a bit anyway, for Charlotte's sake.

THE GETAWAY CAR had been stolen from a bowling-alley parking lot the day that Savannah had come to town. The black SUV was registered to a ninety-year-old man who'd been dead for six months. Whether it was stolen or being driven by a legal heir was yet to be determined. None of the man's relatives could be reached.

Since witnesses had all stated that the black SUV had come barreling into the circle, causing the crash, the police were designating the incident a hit-and-run crash, sus-

pecting that the driver of the SUV had been driving under
the influence.

The FBI was not involved. Isaac's call. He couldn't afford the risk of blowing his cover. They were getting close.
Perps were running scared. He had to let it play out until he
found proof of more than a vehicular crime.

His agents were following up, quietly, on their own.

And Isaac was finding the case more and more distaste-
ful. And himself lacking the power that generally drove him
to successfully close cases and save lives.

"Do you think someone associated with Nicole's kidnapping and Duran are working together, or do I have two separate entities gunning for me?" Savannah's voice filled the
space of his vehicle so completely, he felt as though he was
being washed with it.

But couldn't get clean.

"I wish I knew," he told her. "My guess would be that
they'd join forces just to get you out of the picture. And then
Duran goes after the kidnapper. But that's before we factor
in Charlotte's disappearance. If we knew who has her, we'd
have a better chance of figuring out who the enemy is and
from there determine how to catch him." He heard his words
too late to take them back.

He'd been talking like an agent. Like himself. Not like
Isaac.

The killers weren't the only ones who were getting pushed
hard enough to act in a way that could get them caught.

Isaac made note. And continued to do his job as he followed the gray sedan a few lengths in front of him. Watch-
ful. Taking in everything he could. Gun on the seat beside
him just in case he had to make a quick shot to save a life.

Worrying about snipers.

Duran's entire empire had been built with unseen, unknown, unprovable tools. Isaac had spent the past year searching for actionable proof of a ghost.

His Duran phone rang, and he glanced at the screen. He didn't recognize the number.

"Hold on," he told Savannah, tense as he cut her off from audio call and lost communication with her.

"Yeah," he barked into the air around him, more vigilant than ever at keeping watch on the woman who was not quite officially, but morally, under his protection.

"Isaac?" His system froze. And went into high-alert mode all at once. There was no mistaking the voice.

"Charlotte?"

"Yeah."

"Where are you?" He glanced behind him. To both sides. Focused on the gray sedan making a left-hand turn and drove on by. He'd take the next street. Approach the shelter from a different angle. Park a block up. Protocol.

It was stifling him.

As was his charge's lack of response.

"Charlotte." His tone carried his tension. "Are you all right?"

"Yes. Are you alone?"

"Yes. What's going on?"

"I just got a call from…someone. There's been a woman asking around about me this morning. Long dark hair, dark eyes, a little taller than me. You know anything about her?"

Breaking all speed limits, Isaac cut up a block, ran a stop sign, and turned onto the street that housed the shelter. Not taking a breath until he saw the gray sedan pulling into the driveway.

And his mind cleared to pinpoint focus as he said, "I need to know about you," he countered. "Are you alone?"

"Yes." The word meant nothing. She'd say anything she was told to say if a gun was pointed at her head. But before he could continue the interrogation long enough to read her, she said, "I'm not going to tell you where I am. I just... I trust you, Isaac. Do you know who this woman is?"

"I need you to give me something first, Charlotte. Tell me what's going on."

Savannah had disappeared into the side door of the shelter. He had to get back to her line. To monitor...

"I shouldn't have called."

"Wait!" He couldn't lose her. She'd said she trusted him. Had reached out to him. "I do know who she is, but I can't tell you more until I know more about your current situation." Did Charlotte know about Savannah, then? Did she know she'd been kidnapped as a child? That she'd been adopted?

Though...his team still had not found verification of the missing-toddler case.

He'd seen the DNA results. Had had them verified. The two women were sisters.

"You work for my father. Your loyalty is to him."

Okay. She was at odds with Eduardo. It was something.

"He pays me to be loyal to you, not him."

"I'm someplace safe," she said then. "Using a burner phone I was given."

He believed her. For the most part.

The woman was a suspect.

He needed her to trust him. To stay in contact until he could figure out where she was and why.

And he had to get to the other line. "Did you leave of your own accord?"

"Yes."

And, a thought repeated...based on what she'd just said, she was at odds with her father?

Had he read Eduardo right? The man had no idea where his daughter was or who'd taken her?

What did Charlotte know? The question burned his gut. Almost as much as his lost contact with Savannah.

"You need to know you can trust me—I need to know I can trust you," he said then. Playing the game he had to play.

"I asked for help from one of the shelters." He'd never heard a defeatist tone come out of Charlotte's mouth. But there it was.

And it made sense. She'd just been contacted.

Right after Savannah had tried to get information from the most recent shelter Charlotte had visited.

Was she trying to tell him that Eduardo had been abusive—no. Truth hit him.

Wagar.

And her father trying to force her to marry the man.

"She's the woman who was shot at in the boat the other day," he said then, taking a huge chance, playing a hunch but needing to get Charlotte to trust him enough to get her back in his fold. "She found out I was your bodyguard and came to me to tell me what she'd seen." He risked much with his skating between truth and lie. His ability to do so well had meant the difference between life and death many times in his career. "She saw Arnold Wagar refuse to take his hands off you when you made it clear you wanted to be left alone. She said that you were in agony, crying on the beach."

He played his strongest hand right up front. Remembering what Savannah had said about the global sisterhood...

In lieu of mentioning the sisterhood about which he would not speak.

"There's something not right about Wagar. He and my dad are thick. My dad trusts him. He's pressuring me to marry him, and I won't. He gives me the creeps. Wagar's the first person to ever come between me and Dad." He heard pain in Charlotte's voice. A break from her normal confident, often pigheaded, way of handling life.

Growing more tense by the second as he watched the shelter with no sign of Savannah and no way to hear what was happening inside, he wondered if the whole Charlotte thing was little more than a spoiled young woman's temper tantrum, until she said, "I know I'm too much of a brainiac to catch all the little nuances in general conversation and I'm often off in my head and miss some of the nonverbal emotional communication that goes on around me, but I'm not wrong about Wagar."

That one sentence, telling him that Charlotte was going through a pretty intense self-evaluation, convinced Isaac, and he sat forward. "Tell me what feels off about him."

"First, he's only been around for about a year, but Dad, who doesn't let anyone but me get really close to him, trusts him enough to want me to marry him?"

About a year. About. A. Year. The words reverberated around the car like thunder. The same time frame in which Savannah had been followed. Didn't prove a damned thing.

But it could.

"And about a month ago he said something that I don't think either of them knew I'd heard. It had to do with my penchant for computer coding. So...several years ago I wrote a proprietary program for my father. Has to do with money management. A way to have it siphon through one global location before dispersing to its various accounts so that he can, at any time, know the current value of anything he owns, but if you put a trace on it, the first stop, the global location, is invisible. We call it Glob. Anyway, I heard Arnold ask my father if he thought, after we were married, I'd do some coding for him. Like, it's not me he wants, but my computer skills. He doesn't want me. He wants to marry me so I can do for him and his businesses what I do for my dad."

All senses on alert, Isaac could feel racing in his veins

as his mind became a calculating machine, and his gut told him he'd found what he'd been looking for.

He had no idea how deep Charlotte's involvement was. But she'd just told him how Duran was able to hide everything he did while still providing clearly traceable money trails. The system, Glob, was part of what had been stopping them. And clearly was much more intricate and complicated than Charlotte had just alluded to. He and his team had serious work to do. Connections to make. Major hurdles to overcome.

But he felt certain that Eduardo Duran's daughter had just told him how to find the proof he needed to take down the entire Duran empire once and for all.

Chapter Eighteen

"Della, can I speak to you for a second?"

Savannah heard the voice come from behind her as she sat on a couch, facing the middle-aged, soft-spoken, yet compellingly trustworthy domestic violence counselor who'd just been addressed.

Looking over Savannah's shoulder, the woman stood immediately and excused herself. Leaving Savannah to suspect that something not good was happening. Either in the shelter, with one of their clients, or...with her.

She hadn't planned to pose as a victim. She'd just...been one. From the second she'd walked in the door, she'd felt as though her story had to be told. Not the real one. No kidnappings, witness protection, or gunfire. No bodyguards or sisters.

But the fear engulfing her whenever she stopped focusing on Charlotte's plight, on finding her sister, had come pouring out. She didn't know who was after her or why, but she knew she was being followed. And had just barely escaped probable death in what had clearly been an intentional car crash. If the black SUV had hit her instead of traveling on to strike two other vehicles, she'd have been crushed.

After that had all fallen out of her, she'd had her plan. Had asked how one went about finding a safe house. She was afraid to go home. Afraid to leave the shelter.

Della had just been about to answer her question—Savannah had hoped for a response that could give her an excuse to bring Charlotte into the conversation, a mention of the professor's name, having been referred by her—and then, she'd been gone.

Isaac wasn't back online yet, either.

Checking her phone, she saw that their lines were still connected.

And it hit her…something had happened outside the safe house. Something to do with Isaac. Someone knew he was working with her.

With fingers trembling so much she had to press three times to get the job done, she disconnected the call. Was sick to her stomach. She'd known bringing Isaac into her sphere would put him in danger…

Savannah jumped as the door opened and then stood, turning to face whatever was to come.

Della was alone, closing the door quickly behind her, her beautiful face creased with concern.

"What happened?" she asked. She wasn't the only victim in the city, maybe not even in the shelter, but…

"We have volunteers who take turns watching footage from our security cameras anytime anyone is in the building," the woman started right in, not reclaiming her seat. As Savannah's heart pounded the woman continued, "There's a man outside—he circled the block behind us twice and then disappeared into the culvert just beyond where you parked your car."

Thank God. Almost lightheaded with relief, Savannah sank back down to the couch. Took a sip of the iced water Della had given her just after she'd arrived. "In a blue suit coat?" she asked, scrambling to find a way to explain Isaac's presence in a nonthreatening way.

If she had a protection detail, why would she need a safe house?

Della was there—sitting beside her on the couch, not across from her as she had previously—before Savannah had finished swallowing.

"No, dear. He's wearing brown pants, a darker brown short-sleeved shirt hanging loosely over the waistband, and tennis shoes. Has hair down to his shoulders and a beard. Sound like anyone you'd recognize?"

Jitters started inside her, making her legs feel as though they might start jerking of their own accord. She was trapped. A sitting duck.

She could die. Without having done a damn thing to help Charlotte.

Unless...she was getting what she wanted. Was drawing out the ghost who'd been haunting her. Was Isaac on to him?

"I don't," she said, trying to think clearly through a wave of fear.

Had they gotten to Isaac?

Did they have his phone? Had they been listening to her conversation? Had she just played into their hands?

The suspicious character had gone into a culvert by her car. Which meant they knew what she was driving. Just like the driver of the black SUV had known.

She'd wanted to be found. But the hope had been to have them apprehended before they actually hurt her, so they'd lead authorities to Charlotte. Where were Isaac's bodyguard friends who were supposed to have his back?

Tears pricked the backs of her eyes, and she straightened. She wasn't going to fall apart. She was still there. Still able to act.

She just had to think.

"Am I the only...one...here?" she asked, not able, most particularly in that moment, to call herself a victim.

Della's nod, while serious, didn't seem to hold fear. More like...determination.

"We can help you get away," she said quietly. "We have a basement with an underground bunker that leads a half mile away. It's rough. I'm guessing from the days of the underground railroad. It's the reason we bought this place. The structure was crumbling, but we've stabilized and supported it all. But it's dark, dank, and only three feet high. You'd have to climb up a ladder through a sewer to get to the street. We'd have a car parked at the sewer, so no one sees you come up. You'd climb in and be driven to a destination of your choice within a five-mile radius. The police station, or someplace else."

The police station sounded heavenly to her at the moment.

But would such a move get Charlotte killed? Duran thought so.

Isaac had seemed to agree.

If the kidnappers had Charlotte and knew that the police had Savannah, would Duran be able to save her?

Would he even try, if his own ass was on the line?

She'd said she was going to be bait. And her plan was working!

The job wasn't done, and she was still able to be out there. Trying to find someone following her before they knew she'd seen them.

And if she did?

Without Isaac how did she get them before they got her?

Or was Isaac already outside, getting them as she sat safely inside sipping water on a comfortable couch with a lovely woman who, in another world, might have been a friend.

Her mind raced as Della sat there next to her, her gaze filled with compassion while she awaited Savannah's answer.

If she was alone and saw someone on her tail, she could call Sierra's Web. Have a meeting with her partners. And let them decide if they wanted to help her or not.

She'd tried to keep harm from coming to anyone else.

But clearly it didn't matter where she went—she was a wanted woman. And eventually that would lead back to her dear friends.

Maybe, the second she was alone, she should call them anyway.

A simple desire to see her sister without poking any bears had turned into something much larger, and more dangerous, than she'd ever imagined.

And Isaac... If she'd gotten him killed...her partners had to find his murderers and make them pay.

The fact that he'd been offline didn't bode well. Even if he was on the trail of someone, he could still have his earpiece on. Would have found a second to whisper a warning to her to stay inside, if nothing else.

"I very gratefully accept your offer," she said. "With one request."

"You need money?"

She had plenty in the bag on her shoulder. Along with her computer. Had been wearing the bag every visit she'd made that day. "No. But... I thought I recognized a vehicle, parked on the next block, as I turned in here. Could you send someone to see if it's still there?"

If Isaac was okay, he'd handle a wellness check from the local police. And if he was sitting behind his steering wheel, bleeding to death...she couldn't just leave him there to die.

"Of course," Della said. "We've already called for a full perimeter check and will add the next block to it. Our volunteer called the police the second she saw the man head to the culvert. It's protocol anytime we see something suspicious in the area. The local officers are definitely our friends here." The woman was close enough to touch Savannah. Had her hands right there, where Savannah could take hold, but didn't make contact.

Staring at those hands, Savannah wanted to reach out, to avail herself of a moment to draw strength but was afraid that if she did, she'd lose her courage and ask to be rescued.

After which, even if no one else blamed her, she'd hate herself for the rest of her life.

Her baby sister had been stolen from home.

Twice.

While Savannah's life, after the loss, had been blessed. Most importantly, she'd grown up with the love of their only living parent. With their mother's love.

Something she carried within her still.

Her mom had had to turn her back on her youngest daughter, and, though she'd never spoken of it, Savannah had known it had not only broken her heart but had eaten at her for the rest of her life. Savannah had a chance to fix that hurt. To ease her mother's eternal heart.

"Do I tell you now where I want to be taken?" she asked and felt as though tension drained out of Della. As though the woman had been personally invested in her choice to accept the chance to forge ahead on her own over going back to what she knew, allowing the mistreatment for a sense of security.

"No," the woman said and then reached over and placed her palm over Savannah's clasped hands. "It's best for you and us if we don't know. You'll tell your driver when you get in the car."

Meeting the woman's dark eyes, seeing the intelligence brimming there, the encouragement, Savannah stood.

Determined to fight, to do all she could to catch the horrible people who'd ruined her family's lives, no matter what it cost.

And to avenge the man she'd known such a short time but suspected that she already loved more than any other she'd ever meet.

He'd put his life on the line for her. Had maybe lost the battle.

She'd never have a life worthy of living unless she fought back.

CHARLOTTE REFUSED TO let Isaac go to her. She'd agreed to have him meet her sometime later in the day, before dark, and would be calling him back with a location. Whether or not he'd end up arresting her at that time remained to be seen.

But he was getting close to successfully closing the case. The familiar sense of heady adrenaline pouring through him was evidence of that.

He hadn't decided whether he was going to take Savannah with him to meet her sister. Didn't have a clear sense of whether or not her presence would be more advantageous to the case.

Charlotte was already doubting her father's judgment where Wagar was concerned. Would meeting a biological sister help catapult the woman further from her father? Or send her closer to him? He'd see how the rest of the day went, what Savannah came up with in her conversations, who they drew out of hiding, and go from there.

Clicking back to his ongoing conversation with Savannah the second Charlotte disconnected, he listened intently. Needing to hear her voice.

Tried to convince himself that his tension at the initial second of silence was case related. That he was only bothered about the conversation he'd missed. But when no sound came on the line for the next second and the next, he looked at the phone's screen. The call had been terminated. And the jolt to his midsection was personal. As was the sudden inner push to exit the vehicle and run to the door of the house-like structure she'd entered.

The agent in him kept him in his seat while he assessed. But barely.

He'd had half of her car in sight, including the driver's-side door, the entire time he'd been on with Charlotte. Hadn't noticed any untoward activity from his view of the front and one side of the house.

And forced himself to sit and wait. Undercover work didn't proceed like clockwork. There were always unforeseen complications. You had to be able to roll with them, to change course on the fly, which he'd proven himself more than able to do.

But when another fifteen minutes passed and there'd been no movement from the house, Isaac's tension had reached breaking point. The call could have just been dropped. Cell service wasn't failproof. And Savannah would have noticed, excused herself to the restroom, and redialed. She was just that kind of detail-oriented person.

Ripping up the carpet at his feet, reaching underneath it, up behind the brake pedal, he pulled out his official creds, took the safety off his gun, re-holstered it, and, with his hand under his jacket, seemingly in his pants pocket but on the butt of his weapon, he approached the side door of the house. Rang the bell he'd seen Savannah ring.

Stood there on the stoop for a full minute with no response.

He rang a second time, turning to see a police car slowing beside his vehicle. And another, coming from the opposite direction, turning into the parking lot directly behind him, moving toward Savannah's gray sedan.

His gut sank.

If someone inside had called the police, that meant there'd been some kind of trouble. With Savannah present. Did he out himself to local law enforcement? Could he trust that they wouldn't blow his cover?

Or did he abandon Savannah? Leave her to find a way to contact him if she could? Abandoning her to likely die at the hands of Duran—or some unknown kidnapper?

Maybe both?

According to a clearly worried Charlotte, Wagar had only been in Duran's life for a year. Isaac could in no way see that as a coincidence.

But while it was just the past year that Charlotte knew about, that didn't mean there hadn't been other business between the two.

Say, twenty-four years before?

What if the men had been acquainted in a previous lifetime? Had had Charlotte in common?

Who'd called whom after all that time? Duran? When he heard about Charlotte's DNA database entry?

Or had Wagar been monitoring databases? And notified Duran?

Wagar appeared to have the upper hand.

Duran was the one who'd be paying the biggest price. To the point of marrying off his beloved daughter to the man just to keep her with him? To keep the secret intact?

Which made Wagar, what, the kidnapper?

If that was the case, why didn't Duran just have the man killed?

Wagar had to have something over Duran, something that would expose Duran's secrets in the event of Wagar's death...

Walking back toward his car, he put the safety on his pistol. Reached into his back pocket for the wallet he carried with him every day and, taking the offensive, approached the officers who'd just looked into the windows on both sides of his vehicle. "Can I help you with something, Officers?" he asked. Getting what intel he could before he even considered something so rash as to blow his cover.

He showed the officer he approached, Jayden, his identification. "I'm personal protection director for Eduardo Duran—is something going on here?"

"This your vehicle?" the second officer, rounding the hood to join Isaac and Officer Jayden, asked.

"My personal vehicle, yes," he said. "I'm here at the behest of Eduardo Duran. His daughter has expressed interest in making a sizable donation to the facility, and I'm making a routine security check as part of Duran protocol." The words poured out of him as though he'd known what he was going to say. As though they were true.

Jayden handed Isaac's ID to Williams, the second uniformed man who'd joined them, who studied it, nodded, and handed it back to Isaac, saying, "We just had a call from inside the facility. Their security cameras caught a suspicious character circling the next block..." Williams nodded toward the street behind the shelter as Jayden took over.

"He then entered the property through some shrubbery and slid down into the culvert," the younger man said, with a gesture toward the second police car, parked at an angle half-behind Savannah's vehicle.

A perp outside. Not in?

Savannah was safe?

Adrenaline spread anew as he headed toward the second police car, a rapid walk, with Jayden and Williams keeping up beside him. The plan was working?

They'd lured out whoever was after her, would have the arrest, and possibly some answers, before his meeting with Charlotte?

Not the proof he needed to take down Duran. He'd need a warrant for Duran's electronics and his best tech agents deep diving on Glob for that. Or...testimony from Charlotte Duran. But if they could expose the man's personal lies... prove that he'd hired someone to kill Savannah Compton... they could lock him up for that much while they built a criminal case that would not only get the man off the street forever but would shut down his businesses, too...

"He's gone." Another cop, thirtyish, was climbing up out of the culvert. "It's wet down there—there are footprints. Looks like he took off, followed the drainage ditch that way." She pointed to the street behind the shelter, the one the man had reportedly come from. "We'll head inside, get copies of the footage, run his likeness through facial recognition, and keep an eye out," she finished, clearly the senior officer on scene.

Isaac needed a copy of that likeness. Would call Chuck. Leave it to the agent to secure it. Run it. Keep him posted.

In the meantime... "And the woman?" he asked, nodding toward Savannah's car. And after Jayden filled his superior in on Isaac's identity, his private security position, registration, and reason for being in the area, the senior officer, Abernathy, turned to him.

She was frowning as she asked, "You know her?"

"No," he lowered his tone, shook his head, showing her his compassion. "I saw her going in as I drove up. Long dark hair, pulled back, capris and short-sleeved shirt. The way she was looking around her... I've been waiting for her to leave before I rang the bell. But after so much time had passed, I figured maybe she was a volunteer and was just ringing the bell when your officers approached."

He was on form. Finding his confidence. Doing what he did best. Pretending to be someone he was not—to save lives.

Right up until Abernathy returned to tell him that no one that fit the brief description he'd given was inside the building. No one other than the shelter's regular volunteers were inside.

He started to push. Saw the way Abernathy's gaze narrowed and immediately backed off. Saying that he'd seen what he'd needed to see to assure Eduardo Duran that his daughter's association with the shelter would be worthwhile.

Thanked her and headed straight to his car.

Either Savannah had enlisted the shelter's help to ditch him.

Or just like Charlotte, she'd disappeared into thin air.

Calling Chuck to get copies—not just of the intruder's image, but of all the shelter's security footage from that morning, and to have someone watching Savannah's gray sedan, too—he pulled away, feeling the eyes of local police at his back.

He had to wonder…were they on Duran's payroll, too?

Was he being followed? Did Duran suspect he knew more about Charlotte's disappearance than he was saying?

Was the man having every member of his current staff watched?

Odd that after just a couple of hours of having Savannah on the road as bait, one of Duran's men had shown up at the university, right where they were at the same exact time.

And yet the security guard had seemed to trust Isaac. Turned around.

Only to have Savannah almost run off the road just a short time later.

Savannah, not him. If his cover had been blown, he'd have been the target. He had no doubts about that. Isaac was a risk to far more than just a family matter.

But that didn't mean that Duran wasn't having him—all of them—followed.

Savannah had disappeared. They had to have known where she was.

Did that mean Duran had her already? Snatching her right from under his nose?

Putting one more call into Chuck, relaying his fears, Isaac drove.

Two women missing who'd been in his care.

And he had nowhere to go.

Chapter Nineteen

Savannah didn't call her partners. Instead, she acted like she was one of them, maybe for the first time since they'd formed the firm. She put her full energy into accomplishing the task in front of her rather than just being legal counsel for those who'd always done so.

Had they all seen her lack of courage over the years? Did they consider her their weak link? No one had ever given her cause to think so. To the contrary, they all came to her for her advice, for her counsel. And always trusted and acted upon the advice she gave.

Was it possible they'd seen something in her she hadn't?

After her half-mile trek, she'd climbed up the ladder, into the back seat of the car, and told the driver to take her to a car rental place.

From there, she used her firm credit card—clearly Duran would already have someone checking anything in her name—and rented yet another sedan. Dark green.

Inside the agency, seeing a pay phone, she used it to dial Isaac's number. Just in case. But fearing that her hunters were in possession of it, that she could be playing right into their hands, she hung up before the first ring.

And didn't pick up when, minutes later, his number

showed up on her screen. What she did do was immediately turn off the location on her phone.

For once, for her mother and Charlotte, for Isaac—and for her scared little self, too—she was going to use the intelligence with which she'd been blessed and the self-defense training with which she'd armed herself and fight back. She didn't need Isaac's physical presence behind her to visit the places where Charlotte was known to have been. She had her copy of his log.

In her new car, she studied the city map she'd pulled up on the internet and memorized the way to the next location. A women's clothing boutique.

Without Isaac behind her, she had to be more vigilant than ever, but after a year of feeling like someone was following her, she'd honed her observation skills.

Which was how she'd been able to avoid the near-fatal collision that could have cost her her life that morning.

A crash that had hurt innocent people.

The thought troubled her greatly as she approached the boutique a good hour after her escape from the shelter. There were sales staff inside. Maybe even the owner. People who'd gone to work that day to earn a living. People with loved ones. Did she put them all at risk by strolling inside?

If she didn't find out everything she could about Charlotte's conversations, how would she be able to put together pieces that might point them to the ghost? If he'd been watching Savannah all those months, chances were Charlotte had been in his sights, too.

And if he was Duran, or hired by the man, chances were good that Savannah would be the only casualty. Car crash aside. Had she not acted so quickly, she would have been taken care of then.

Talking herself out of the fear that paralyzed her, she parked in front of the boutique. Waited long enough to take stock of all other vehicles in the area. Noting people who came and went. She was in a new car. With her phone's location off. Unless the shelter had burned her—and she was willing to bet her life they hadn't—she likely had a little time before anyone caught up with her.

Even if Duran had the police in his pocket.

The thought was fanciful, one based more in the debilitating fear that she'd let consume her life than in reality, but a man with that much money—and a life, a father-daughter relationship to protect—she could see him going to whatever lengths it took.

And, as a partner in Sierra's Web, knew full well how many times money swayed the minds and morals of seemingly good people. Even those sworn to uphold the law.

Particularly those.

Determining that it was safe for her to go inside, Savannah did so. And returned to her car ten minutes later with a new jumpsuit she'd purchased for her good friend, Charlotte, to surprise her for her birthday.

Savannah had learned that her sister didn't present as an uber wealthy woman. Charlotte was polite. Respectful. And, as smart as she was, was sometimes insecure about her knowledge of what was currently in fashion. Which was why she stuck to the few boutiques she trusted for any wardrobe changes.

Charlotte also hated having someone watching her every move and had once snuck out the back door of the shop to avoid her bodyguard and meet up with a woman she'd met at a shelter who'd needed some technical advice.

As Savannah watched her back, driving in zigzags to her next stop, she decided that if she saw imminent danger, she'd call the police. It was the smart thing to do.

And she let her heart talk to her, too. Even if she never

met Nicole as the grown woman, Charlotte, she was getting to know her sister. And loved the person she'd become.

If she died that day, she'd do so feeling as though the last choice she'd made—to find Charlotte—had been the right one. That her life had served in the way she'd most wanted.

She'd go believing that she hadn't let her partners down. She'd proven to be worthy of the best of them.

And she'd go knowing that she'd finally found out what it felt like to fall in love, to make love with the man she'd been meant to find.

But she didn't plan to die.

As she drove and had her own back, the energy pumping through her was too strong to ignore. More powerful than fear.

Because she had one hell of a reason to live.

After twenty-four years, she'd learned how to trust herself. And to trust love to guide her, too.

ISAAC'S BOSS HAD given him an assignment. To visit every location he'd taken Charlotte Duran during the past three months. But that wasn't why he continued down the list he and Savannah had been using that day.

He drove to the next location because in just a matter of days he'd grown to know a woman so intimately that he knew following the list was what she would do. If she were able.

And because the plan was a good one. The tidbits Savannah had learned about Charlotte Duran during her various conversations that day were things he could use to have deeper influence on the young heiress when he met with her later.

Her passion for helping victims—if he could show her some of the reprehensible things her father had done…

Or at least get her to do a deep dive on her own invention, Glob, and let her find out for herself.

He'd promise her the best deal he could give her. Somehow over the past twenty-four hours he'd lost any passion for seeing Charlotte Duran behind bars.

He'd seen her as a suspect. Savannah had opened his mind to the person she was. A helpless toddler who'd been stolen from her family and knew only what Eduardo Duran had taught her.

One who spent her time helping women who'd been victimized.

Good deeds didn't forgive her the crimes she'd likely committed. He'd have to find out the scope of her involvement before he'd know what he could do for her, but he knew, even before he met with Charlotte, that he was committed to doing all he could for her.

Maybe he was going soft.

Maybe after he'd put Duran away, he'd think about taking the promotion that had been offered him and leave undercover work behind him.

The way the case, Savannah Compton in particular, had gotten to him, he had to consider that it was time he got out. Moved up to new challenges.

An hour after he'd left the shelter, he tried her phone again as he rounded a corner to park across from one of Charlotte's favorite restaurants. Just in case someone picked up. If he could keep them talking, he could get Chuck to get a trace on it. He'd been to the boutique which was next on their list as soon as he'd left the shelter. Then on to the exclusive salon where Charlotte got her hair done. Neither location had given him much. The boutique owner and Charlotte's hair designer, knew he was her bodyguard. He used the excuse of her having lost one of her favorite earrings and had learned that neither of the establishments had it.

If Duran was tracking his moves, he'd see that Isaac was following orders. While he waited to hear back from Charlotte.

He prayed that Savannah was alive. That he'd hear something back from Chuck that would tell him where to go, how to find her.

When his phone rang and the agent's number showed up on screen just before he exited his car to head into the dining establishment, he remembered Savannah talking about providence. And hoped to God that some worked in her favor.

Instead of the agent's call giving him any sense of direction or relief, Isaac sat there, stunned, reeling with the urgent information Chuck was giving him.

The secret Savannah had been keeping…he hadn't seen it coming.

Agents in the Washington bureau had finally found record of the disappearance of a one-year-old named Nicole who'd been taken from her daycare by her father, who'd been murdered later that same day. Except that she wasn't Nicole Compton. She'd been born Nicole Gussman.

Had been listed in the missing person database as Natalie Willoughby after her remaining family members, her mother and seven-year-old sister, had entered the witness protection program.

The seven-year-old child had been born as Sarah, but became Savannah—something similar, probably because the chances of her making a critical mistake with the name change would be lessened. Her last name had changed from Gussman to Compton.

Savannah's father, Hugh Gussman, had worked for the IRS and had been about to blow the whistle on a sizable breach he'd found in the system, a hack that had cost the government more than a million dollars.

Information that would never have been disclosed except that Savannah's mother was dead, Savannah was in danger, probably from those the program had sought to protect her from, and because of the ties to an internationally wanted criminal—Eduardo Duran.

Whether Duran had in some way been involved with the IRS hack from El Salvador or had just put in for a black-market baby and had ended up with Charlotte was something Isaac had to try to find out.

Gussman had been going to reveal all, including the source of the hack, to the FBI the day he'd been burned to death and left as a pile of ashes on a sand dune. Investigators had found a piece of skin from the bare heel he'd been digging into the sand, over and over, as he'd died a slow death, from which they'd been able to extract DNA to identify him. His shoes and socks had been found in the woods several yards away. His charred belt buckle had been discovered in the debris.

Sick at heart as he listened, aching for the young girl Savannah had been and for the incredible woman she'd become, Isaac felt his resolve to find her answers harden into a life mission. He couldn't change what Charlotte might have grown into, what she might have done as an adult working with her father, but he could end the ravaging once and for all.

In those seconds, solving the case, the job had ceased to be his motivator. He was out to get justice for Savannah. And for her mother and baby sister, too.

Bringing down Eduardo Duran was no longer a job to him.

It had become personal.

Thoughts of his little sister—who was, based on his social media research, married, an elementary school teacher, and a mother of two—surfaced as he hung up the phone. He'd busted her drug-dealing boyfriend, refusing to look the other way even though it meant she'd had to do a month in juvenile detention for the drops she'd made for him. She'd been on a crash course to hell, on the verge of ruining her life, and he'd done what he'd had to do to save her.

Rather than giving the young couple the second chance they'd begged for, he'd made the bust, turned over the evidence, and cried when he'd watched her being hauled off. Maybe getting caught would have scared them straight. Maybe they'd have made good on a chance to turn their lives around. He hadn't been willing to take that chance.

Because he'd loved her that much.

Something she'd never understood.

She'd blamed him for putting the job above love and family.

And had hated him ever since.

If Savannah was alive—and his gut told him to believe there was still a chance—she'd likely hate him, too, when she found out that he'd been using her all along. That the life he'd presented to her, that of bodyguard Isaac Forrester, had all been a lie.

A job.

Until that morning, he'd taken her eventual loss of trust in him as a given.

But knowing that she'd spent her entire life unable to trust anyone with her deepest secrets…and had still trusted him with one of them—Charlotte being her sister—he could hardly sit with himself knowing that she'd feel he betrayed her.

Telling himself to get it together, to get himself in gear and get back to work, he took another long study of the area around him. Giving a mental run-through of the other details Chuck had given him. Placing them firmly in the puzzle he'd been building in his mind over the past year. They'd found no trace on his phone, so if Duran was having his whereabouts checked, it wasn't through his cell. The grandson of the man who'd owned the black SUV that had caused the crash in the roundabout was wanted by local police for suspected illegal weapons charges, and surveillance footage of the man seen heading into the culvert at the shelter earlier that day had produced no matches in the bureau's facial-recognition software.

He wouldn't have pegged Duran for using low-level criminals with records. He'd pay top dollar for help that was so far off the grid they'd be unidentifiable.

The guy at the shelter could've been one of them. So maybe sent by Duran?

But the driver...were they looking at two groups after Savannah, as she'd first thought? Duran and whoever she'd been running from in the witness protection program for most of her life?

And then there was Wagar. Possibly the kidnapper. A third entity who'd need her permanently silenced.

As his thoughts gelled, terror for her welled for the split second it took him to tamp them down before they prevented him from doing what he did best.

He'd been watching a green sedan as it approached the block where he sat. It was a newer vehicle, the same model that Savannah had rented before. When the car slid into a parking spot in front of the small high-end family-owned restaurant, a place that guaranteed its patrons' privacy and peace while they dined, his senses were suddenly in perfectly tuned gear.

He saw her get out.

And at the same time, a woman who exited the attached establishment next door, an import place that sold fine wine, caught his attention. Held it. The bag she carried bore the label of the store she'd just vacated, but the way she held it, the shape...

Isaac was out of his vehicle and weaving through cars on the road as he gave a holler, pulled his gun, and shot.

The bag flew up into the air, blood splattered, and though he gave chase, the injured woman disappeared around a corner and was lost.

Chapter Twenty

Chest tight, Savannah was shaking as she made her way through the crowd of people forming to what turned out to be a gun on the sidewalk. She continued to shake as she pushed past them to find out where Isaac had gone.

She'd seen him. In that split second after she'd exited her car and stepped onto the sidewalk, he'd hollered, she'd ducked, heard the shot, and when she'd stood, he'd been gone.

She'd have been killed.

That gun on the sidewalk had been meant to send a bullet into her.

She'd seen the woman exit the wine shop. Had wondered if she'd bought a bottle to share with someone she loved...

She hadn't seen a killer.

The mistake had almost ended her life.

So would walking down the street unprotected, in plain view. Turning, Savannah rushed for her car. Climbed inside and drove off in the direction she thought she'd seen Isaac go. Turning into the alley a couple of doors down from the wine shop.

And saw him walking toward her, sideways, as he kept an eye on his back as well.

She stopped next to him. Had never been so glad to see

anyone in her life. Felt the tears prick her eyes. But shifted into Reverse and gunned the gas as soon as he was inside.

He didn't say a word as she backed out of the alley and then took several turns in rapid succession.

Driving like a madwoman until she felt certain that she hadn't been followed. And then it all hit her and she slowed, feeling the weakness in her fingers as she loosened the death grip she'd had on the steering wheel, and glanced at Isaac.

He was studying the side mirror and then ahead of them. And looked...just like Isaac. Strong. There.

"You found me," she said, her voice sounding unfamiliar to her and way too loud in the tension-filled car. She didn't chance another look at him.

Didn't trust herself not to cry.

"Always." The word was clipped. His response...odd. Unless he'd just been referring to every time he'd come after her in the past few days.

Her eyes firmly focused between her mirrors and the road, she asked, "You want me to take you back to your vehicle?"

"No."

"Did you get a good look at her?"

"Not good enough."

He pulled out his phone. Dialed. Said, "Chuck, I've got an update for you." And proceeded, in very succinct terms, to detail everything that had just transpired, including orders for follow-up actions to be taken. Finishing with, "She was clearly a professional. I hit her hand—not sure how bad. There was blood. I've got Savannah with me." And then, without any kind of farewell or indication of his next moves, he hung up.

Chills spread over her. Through her. Isaac, his voice, commanding and professional... Who was he?

Someone hired by the kidnappers? In the employ of whoever her father had been going to testify against?

She couldn't believe it. Was frozen inside as she continued to propel the car forward.

The man had just saved her life.

And pursued the woman who'd clearly been about to shoot her.

She couldn't afford to stop. Didn't want to give anyone a chance to catch up to her. So she drove. Turning randomly, finding a stretch of road with little traffic, she took it, heading nowhere. And when she could, she asked, "Who are you?"

"Take the next right" was his only response.

He'd saved her life.

She had little chance in a battle between them. He had a gun and, from what she'd just witnessed, was an excellent shot. She could wreck the car. Or she could do as he said.

And continued to do so silently over the next ten minutes as he watched their surroundings intently, speaking only to issue instruction.

When fear threatened to take the air out of her lungs, she reminded herself he'd saved her life. And when that quit working, she thought about the night before, when he'd let her pull his clothes off. When he'd touched her with too much gentleness to have been merely body parts seeking satisfaction.

Remembering the look on his face when she'd sat astride him and he'd spasmed inside her for the second time.

Eventually she recognized where they were. And knew where he was taking her.

Back to the house he'd provided to her after she'd been shot at.

Because she felt safer there than out on the streets that seemed to be teeming with people trying to attack her from all sides—and because if he wanted her dead, he'd have let the woman on the street kill her—she drove there of her own accord.

Signaled the next turn before he'd had a chance to instruct her. And pulled into the drive as though she'd been doing so on a regular basis.

Once in front of the house, though, she didn't turn off the car. Or look at him. She sat there with the sedan still in Drive, her hands on the wheel, staring out the windshield, and asked again, "Who are you?"

She heard him move, seemed to feel it, too, and then his gun appeared on the dash right in front of her. Another rustle and a thin leather wallet appeared there next.

"My name is Mike Reynolds. I'm an FBI special agent currently undercover as Isaac Forrester."

Whatever she'd feared he'd say, hoped he'd say—something about Duran and his orders and Isaac choosing at the last minute not to follow them and engaging his bodyguard friends—the FBI had never, for a second, figured in.

She couldn't look at him. Didn't know him.

An FBI special agent.

Who she'd had sex with the night before. Thinking he was her sister's bodyguard.

Believing they were spiritually connected. Meant to meet. That providence had brought them together...

Embarrassed, feeling like a fool, she picked up what she assumed were his credentials. Verified she'd gotten that one right.

"I know that you were born Sarah Gussman. That your father worked for the IRS and was about to testify regarding a hack in the system that had cost the government over a million dollars. I know that you and your mother went into witness protection right after your father was murdered and Nicole was kidnapped. That her missing person report was registered under Natalie Willoughby and that your last name was changed to Compton. I know that your father's body was identified by skin from the heel he'd been digging into the sand…"

She gasped. A spike hitting her heart. She hadn't…

"You didn't know that." The words were different. Softer. Isaac's voice. When he'd been holding her the night before.

No. She shook her head. Couldn't get lost in fantasy. Her whole life had been lived with shades of fake. No more.

She had to be free.

And Charlotte? Where did she fit in?

"Let me guess—you're looking for the man my father was supposed to testify against." She wasn't proud of the sarcastic tone, even as she welcomed it. Sarcasm, any emotion at all, showed him that she'd fallen for his act.

"I am now," he told her. "Along with my original assignment."

Wait. What? "Your original assignment." There, that had been more lawyerlike. And as long as she kept her gaze glued outward, he wouldn't have even a slight chance of reading what she was choking back.

What she couldn't…wouldn't…*ever* let him know. That for a minute or two there, she'd been in love with him.

With *Isaac*.

"To find the elusive proof the United States, along with law enforcement agencies from various other countries, needs in order to arrest Eduardo Duran for theft, espionage, arms dealing, and murder—among other things."

Charlotte's father?

She'd go there. As soon as she got her head on straight.

Had the FBI been following her? Was that how he'd known how to describe to her so exactly how she'd been manipulated by fear over the past year?

Oh, God. Had it been *him*?

Tears blurred her vision. She sat up straight, took a deep

breath, and held them back. And asked, "How long have you known about me? About my past?"

"Less than an hour."

The words he said, the way his voice caught, Savannah's head snapped sideways, and her gaze ran full tilt into his. Getting lost there. Burying her in the warmth she needed to survive the moments.

Finding him.

And rejecting him, too. She'd fallen for Isaac Forrester. A fake persona who'd had a job to do. Not Mike Reynolds.

She turned her attention back to the windshield—the world beyond it.

"Duran called me into his office the day you arrived in town. He told me that his intel had told him that you were in town for a rogue client, someone you'd agreed to help separately from Sierra's Web for a much larger paycheck. Your job was to convince Charlotte that she had biological family in the States, with the ultimate goal of a substantial piece of the Duran pot."

Made sense. A lawyer with supposed proof and paper-work drawn up could easily prove rights to funds, depending on what the funds were, how they'd been designated...

And it hit her...he'd known who she was the day she'd hit town. Before he'd supposedly asked to sit with her. "You... used me."

She told herself not to look at him. But did it anyway.

He didn't even attempt to deny her accusation. Looking her straight in the eye, he nodded.

It was the first thing she found about Mike Reynolds to admire. Now that the secrets were out, he was honest with her.

Even when it showed him for the... FBI agent that he was. Because she could hardly think of him as scum. He'd been doing his job.

And...he'd saved her life.

"What did you hope to gain from our...association?" *Other than sex.*

She'd given him her heart, and he...he'd used sex to get closer to her. To gain her cooperation?

"I didn't know. Multiple governments can trace activities to Duran's doorstep, but no one has ever been able to find proof that would ever stand up in court to convict him of anything. Added to that, he has friends in very high places, both here and abroad. Sending me in was our only chance to find out how he did it. To find something...anything...that we could get a conviction for, that would then give us access to warrants for everything he owns or has ever touched."

He was talking about a man Charlotte adored.

"You told me you had secrets, you were here to see someone. You were shot at. I didn't know what you knew, who you were working for, but the way Duran reacted to your presence, I knew whatever you represented to him was huge."

"So you were using me from the beginning." She had to get that one down pat. Before she could move on.

The lovemaking...the closeness...had all been on her part. Not his.

"I was." He admitted the truth aloud that time.

Her chin trembled. She could feel the tears. Refused to allow them. Didn't look at him. It was time for her to wear her big-girl panties and move forward.

Away from him. From fantasies about love and what was meant to be.

She'd come to town to make certain that her sister was well and happy.

She had not yet completed her mission.

HE'D LOST HER. It was Mollie all over again. Except...in a way, far worse.

Mollie, as a child was to a parent, had been on loan to him, a member of his household, until she'd been old enough to claim her own life.

Savannah had felt like…more than a loan. For a moment in time, she'd made him feel complete. No matter how many times he'd assured himself he knew better than to get personally involved.

"Who knows besides me?"

The way she barely looked at him, as though she couldn't, caught at him. When, since the moment he'd approached her in the bar, they'd seemed to say so much with no words at all. He couldn't let himself get in the way. Had to stay focused on the job, period.

"That I'm undercover?" he asked, though he knew that was what she'd meant.

"Yes." Her chin jutted toward the windshield with the word.

"No one."

"Who's Chuck?"

He'd known the second he'd dialed that he'd made his choice. No more lying to Savannah. He'd found her alive.

Had saved her life.

The honor or prayers answered deserved truth.

"My second-in-command here in San Diego."

She glanced his way. "You have second-in-commands elsewhere?"

"I've been undercover, full time, on different assignments for nearly a decade. I work out of the Washington, DC, bureau."

The windshield got her gaze again. He'd never have thought he'd be jealous of a piece of glass. Or grateful for it, either.

"And this house?"

"An FBI safe house."

Her lower lip jutted some as she nodded. "You've had me under surveillance since I got here."

Not a question. He answered anyway. "No. Just while you were here and I wasn't. I promised you protection."

"Must have made you mad to find out I'd slipped the noose this morning." The bitterness didn't sound natural to her. But it felt horribly real.

Life had handed the woman far more than her share of burdens to handle. But he was the one who'd made her bitter?

"You want the truth?" he shot back at her, every word personal.

She looked over at him. Held his gaze while she nodded.

And with his vow of truth pumping blood through his veins, he said, "I was terrified."

He lost her gaze. Win for the windshield. "Because you'd lost your best chance at solving your case."

"Because I was afraid I'd lost you. That they'd gotten to you."

Her head turned back toward him. "They?"

Leaning in, he gave her every piece of him he had to give in a look, with words he couldn't say. "You know as much as I do, Savannah. Or will in a minute. I know Duran is the worst kind of enemy. I believe my cover is still intact with him, but that doesn't mean he trusts me. A man like that can't fully trust anyone. I fear that Wagar might be the man who kidnapped Nicole. Giving him leverage over Duran. But that's assuming Duran knows Charlotte was kidnapped. And I'm not convinced yet that he does.

"It could be that Wagar was simply the man he used to secure his black-market adoption. Or that he's not involved at all, in the kidnapping or with Charlotte's past. What I'm certain of is that he has some kind of hold over Duran."

He stopped, took a deep breath, and barreled on. "What I also know, and found out after you entered the shelter—"

he quickly stopped himself to clarify before she believed he was really made of stone, before he lost her gaze again "—is that your sister is alive."

Eyes lighting up like fireworks, she burst out with, "Charlotte's alive? You're sure? Is she okay?"

"She called me. That's why I went dark when you were in the shelter." He filled her in on his conversation with Charlotte. Gave her a rundown of his time outside the shelter. Other details that he knew and she hadn't. Pouring it all out because it was the right thing to do.

Because he trusted her with his life.

And, allowing himself to absorb a bit of her essence before he lost her eyes on him, he finished. "Charlotte gave me a major missing piece to the puzzle this afternoon. It was also one that incriminates her." He told her about Glob. And his suspicion that Duran used the coding not only to have one global pool for money that was never seen but to create an entire network of invisible money laundering that landed in accounts that the US and other countries would never have access to and then were dispersed from there.

Eyes wide, filled with alarm, Savannah continued to watch him. "You think she's involved in Duran's criminal activity?"

He had to give her the truth, no matter what it cost him. Because to not do so at that point was going to cost him more. "I'm almost certain she is."

"You're going to arrest her."

Visions of Mollie's hateful look as she'd been taken from the courtroom flashed through his head.

"If she cooperates, and depending on how deeply she's implicated, I'm hoping to offer her immunity. What I can promise you is that I'm going to do everything in my power to make her way as easy as possible. She was taken from her home, her loved ones, her safety and security when a baby needs nothing but those things. She couldn't help but cling to the man who became her entire world. We don't know what he's told her. How he's manipulated her…"

Some depth returned to Savannah's gaze. Not at all like he'd been washed with the night before. But enough of a hint that Mike felt better about himself than he had in a long time. And said, "In private, when we're alone, like now, please call me Mike."

She blinked. Nodded.

Turned away, wrapped her fingers around the steering wheel, and said, "Where to now?"

Chapter Twenty-One

Call me Mike. She didn't know Mike. She'd unknowingly played make-believe with a bodyguard named Isaac.

It might take a minute to wrap her mind around that one. A minute she didn't have to spare.

Charlotte was alive!

"We stay here and wait for Charlotte's call," Mike Reynolds answered her question—"Where to?"—a full minute after she'd asked it. He'd been watching her.

She'd ignored the opportunity to meet his eyes. To see what she read there. The connection that had seemed to give her strength...had any of it been real?

From the very first he'd been playing her.

But Charlotte was alive! Relief was palpable. Smoothing the edges of betrayal.

She'd been falling in love. He'd been doing his job.

Eduardo Duran. Her baby sister's adopted father was an international criminal. Mike Reynolds and the FBI thought Charlotte was involved, too.

She couldn't seem to get a lucid grasp on any of it. Recognized the vestiges of shock. Needed to talk to Kelly, one of her best friends, her partner, Sierra's Web's psychiatry expert, and Savannah's sounding board.

Except that…she'd been pretending with all of them from the moment they'd met.

Charlotte was alive!

"Wait," she turned to the agent, saw Isaac sitting there, doing as she'd just asked, waiting for her to continue.

And so she did.

"You said that Charlotte called you to ask about who'd been asking about her. That she'd received help from one of the shelters."

"Right. I told her that you…"

"Were the woman on the boat. Spun things around, said I sought you out because I was concerned about what I'd seen. Charlotte's tears."

His gaze didn't waver. He sought no mercy. And showed no defensiveness, either. He was who he was. Doing what he did. Same as always. Isaac. Mike. Same guy. Same job.

She saw it all there. Looked away. Wouldn't be taken in again. And heard him say, "I told her the truth I was free to give. That you're a woman who talked to me because you cared about her."

"You played her."

"Maybe." His tone, not Isaac at all and yet as compelling—maybe more so—drew her gaze. And looking her straight in the eye, he said, "It's possible I've been at this too long. Have lost sight of the distinct differences between getting what I need and being honest. I just know that untold numbers of lives are at stake—they're resting largely on my shoulders at the moment. I needed your help. You needed mine."

She swallowed. Nodded again. Then asked, "Was any of it real?"

He glanced away. And she did, too. Couldn't see his eyes as he said, "I don't know."

The nonanswer was a wake-up call to Savannah. Her love

life, any future life at all wasn't of concern at the moment. Glancing back at Mike Reynolds, and Isaac, too—determining that she was going to have to live with both of them in the short go because she couldn't seem to obliterate either one of them—she saw a clear path. Put herself on it.

"I would guess that the shelter Charlotte used was the first one I visited, since they obviously knew how to reach her. I discovered, through my own escape, just how detail oriented and serious these places are about keeping their victims safe." She told him about the thoroughness of her own departure from the shelter. "We need you, the FBI, to go back to that shelter and convince them to transport Charlotte here. Maybe not you. This Chuck, or someone else—probably at least two someones. They'd need to show credentials, to let the shelter director know that Charlotte is in immediate critical danger, far more than she knows, and get her into FBI custody…"

She was talking like a big sister who'd do anything to save her younger sibling's life. But knew, as an expert lawyer, partner in a firm nationally renowned for saving lives in the most extreme of cases, that she was finally, firmly on the right path. "We get her here… Mike…" His eyes darkened as she stumbled over the name, but she pushed on. "We tell her the truth. We give her a chance to help you."

Savannah had no idea whether Charlotte was implicated in her adopted father's crimes, but she knew the truth had to come out to set Charlotte free.

Knew that there was no one better than herself to protect her sister's legal rights.

And…oddly…as she sat there, replaying in her mind what she'd said and studying the undercover FBI agent who'd played them all, she realized that she'd just entrusted her sister's future to him. He'd said he'd do whatever he could to make Charlotte's way easier.

And she believed him.

MIKE CALLED CHUCK IMMEDIATELY. Barked out orders, named two agents from his Washington team that Chuck was to take with him to the shelter, verified that a couple of agents from the San Diego team were already on the safe house, and hung up.

There was nothing left to do but go inside. And wait.

The last time he and Savannah had been in that space together, less than twenty-four hours before, they'd had incredible sex. His best ever. And he'd had probably more than his share in his nearly thirty-eight years.

But because all he'd allowed himself to be since Mollie's disappearance from his life was the best damned cop he could be, he ushered Savannah Compton inside, checked every corner of every one of the spotless rooms, and turned the television on to security camera screens.

She set herself up at the table, computer open.

And then, with a brief glance at him that seemed to be telling him something, except that she glanced away too quickly for him to be sure, she said, "I've just sent a request to my partners for an emergency gathering on our private video-meeting software..." She paused, glancing down at her screen. "Three—no, four—of them have already responded. And there's five..."

"You're asking me to vacate." He'd been planning to walk the perimeter...

"No. I'm apologizing ahead of time for some of what you might have to sit through, but I'd like you to be present to answer any questions they might have." She was all professional, an expert lawyer.

And, God help him, sexy as hell.

She'd also just put him on notice that she was having him checked out by the best of the best. From a private firm that had been fully vetted by the FBI.

As long as her team stuck to business, he'd pass with flying colors.

"You can't take Charlotte back to Duran," Savannah said then, glancing up from her screen when he sat down perpendicular to her at the table. Close enough to touch. Which he was very careful not to do. Not even a knee bump.

Ridiculous, and wholly unlike him to even have the thought. Let alone feel regret for the loss of something he'd never really had.

And the Charlotte thing… "The longer I take to call him and let him know I have her and will be bringing her back, the more we risk someone tipping him off. He'll bolt. We could lose him forever. We have no idea how high up his power extends, who's in his pocket, which is why my team and I, along with a couple of agents in the San Diego office, are all who know about this case."

He could almost see her mind spinning and then watched as reality dawned. "You think someone at the shelter's going to tell him."

"I think it's possible. The Durans donate to all the local shelters."

"I'm assuming, then, that you have agents on him already."

"We do. But without proof, which we still do not currently have, we can't touch him. You're a lawyer. You know…"

She was nodding. Frowning. "You think it's possible that Charlotte might have to go back to get the proof?"

He shrugged. He hoped not. Saw the plausibility. Knew anything was possible. And knew, too, as Savannah would, that depending on how deeply Charlotte Duran was involved, she could risk her life to take on her father, to get them the proof she needed to buy her freedom.

And was saved from any further conversation on the matter when Savannah glanced at her computer and said, "We're on."

She didn't immediately involve him. Didn't have him on screen or include him in conversations. Instead, he sat there and watched expressions chase themselves across her face as she greeted each of her six partners, calling them out by name—for his benefit, he was sure—letting them know that FBI agent Mike Reynolds was in the room.

He found it difficult to swallow over the next several minutes as he heard her telling her partners that she'd been lying to them the entire time they'd known her. In very lawyerly terms, interspersed with her own difficult swallows, she told them she had a sibling and, without pause, gave them the rest of the details of her past. The secrets she'd been forced to keep. Talking about the danger she'd recently brought upon herself. Admitting that she'd never been intending to go on a cruise but rather to see that Nicole was well and thriving. Ending with an apology for her subterfuge, along with an offer to resign from the firm if they thought it was necessary.

He heard voices then, male and female, talking over each other, and then Savannah again. "Stop." Her tone seemed to shock her partners into silence. "You guys need to talk about this among yourselves. You know I love you. You're my family. And that doesn't change either way. But we're who we are because we trust each other implicitly. If even one of you feels as though you don't really know me and can't fully trust me, then I'm stepping away. We can reconvene on the matter later. Right now, many lives are at stake and the FBI—and I—need the firm's help."

She didn't expect all her partners to forgive her. Which said to him that she wasn't going to forgive him. He'd lied for good reason. Because he'd had to. And so had she, to her partners. Witness protection as well as undercover work were only successful as long as necessary lies were told. But the lies still had consequences when it came to trust and relationship building.

She didn't believe they'd all still be able to trust her because she didn't trust him. Her message couldn't have been clearer.

And, note taken, he went to work as she turned the screen and moved over so that both of them were within camera range. The respect with which her partners treated him was noted as well. And appreciated. While they were still in the meeting, Mike got on the phone and had his people send over everything they had in the Duran file to Sierra's Web. He told them what he knew about Glob's capabilities. And tech expert Hudson Warner and financial expert Winchester Holmes were both going to work immediately, together and with their teams, to work their magic and see what they could discover without Charlotte's help.

Mike was impressed, if a bit intimidated, and more taken with Savannah Compton, too, as the meeting drew to an end. But when he'd thought they were all about to sign off, Glen Thomas, the science expert and quietest of the bunch, said, "Savannah?"

They were all staring straight into their cameras. Sitting next to the lawyer, Mike felt their pinned look strongly, though it wasn't aimed at him.

She looked right back at them. He felt her stiffen, though. "Yeah?"

"We've taken a vote, by text, and we need you to know. All these years, you've been here serving us, and we didn't look deeper. We're sorry that we didn't know. That we took you for granted and at face value. We trust you with our lives. You are one of us. Now. And forever."

Mike saw her face on the screen. Saw the love brimming from those eyes he'd somehow thought only talked to him. Saw the tears forming.

And got up and left the room. Left Savannah to her real life.

Only just starting to realize what he might have had.
And had lost.

HER TEAM HAD her back. Savannah felt their support as an hour later, just after dark, she paced the living room of the small house, listening for the sound of the online-store delivery van that was being used to bring Charlotte Duran to them.

Mike had made grilled-cheese sandwiches paired with applesauce.

It had taken a while, but she'd gotten it all down. And then washed the dishes. Would have liked to shower again, to change clothes, put on fresh makeup, look her best for her and her sister's first meeting, but her things were still at the old motel.

And as much as she wanted to care about something easy, a topic as superficial as looks just didn't matter.

Hard to believe it had only been that morning that she'd unlocked the door of her clandestinely rented room. A mere twelve hours since she'd broken a twenty-four-year silence, showered, and set out to save lives. Only to find herself back where she'd been before her backbreaking trek through the woods.

Sometimes when life came full circle, it didn't look at all as you'd imagined it would.

She was about to meet her little sister face-to-face.

Was knowingly letting Charlotte walk into an FBI trap.

Because if she didn't, her little sister's life would never be safe and secure. She'd spend the rest of it dealing with the Arnold Wagars her adopted father shoved on her.

And in danger of arrest, too.

The idea was to reveal Savannah's identity to Charlotte first, to establish a place for Charlotte to belong, separate and apart from her father, before pressuring her to turn on him.

While Savannah hated that they were knowingly making choices in order to manipulate Charlotte, she completely understood the necessity.

And fully believed that it could be the only way to save Charlotte's life.

But her heart was pumping hard with dread as much as anticipation when she heard the van drive up.

She saw Mike pause, glancing her way, as though waiting for her to join him at the door. She stepped back to the far end of the living room—as far from the front door as she could get without losing sight of it.

Standing there shivering, she heard Nicole's voice first. "Wow, Isaac, you sure know how to make a girl uneasy." The tone, while flippant, had an undercurrent of fear that struck Savannah's heart.

And reminded her of her mother, too.

She tried to draw a deep breath, but the battle against tears won out, and as she fought and blinked, her chest tightened.

Her heart pounded.

And then, with just one blink to the next—an occurrence that happened with regularity every day of her life—she saw Nicole standing there in jeans, an expensive-looking button-down shirt, and ankle boots, looking at her.

And frowning. "What's she doing here?" She shot the question over her shoulder to Mike. Isaac.

The agent glanced at Savannah, and she knew he was leaving the call up to her.

"We've got some things to tell you, Charlotte," she said, finding the name rolling off her lips with ease. Charlotte, not Nicole. Just like neither of them had been Gussman in decades. "Have a seat." She motioned to the couch and chairs across from her, waited for her little sister to take a corner of the couch before choosing the opposite corner for herself.

Leaving a chair for Mike.

The outsider.

"Stop staring at me," the younger woman said then, her tone somewhat autocratic. But Savannah was certain she heard insecurity nestled inside it. "Not only is it rude, but you're giving me the creeps."

Speaking her mind. Savannah held back a smile. And then, as the moment had fallen upon her, her lips trembled. She glanced at Mike. Needing Isaac.

Saw the look in his eye, a glint that somehow reminded her of her own strength, told her she didn't need him, and turned back to the woman with her same long dark hair, also pulled back, the same dark eyes. And Charlotte's own more uniquely oval rather than round cheeks that Savannah looked at in the mirror every morning.

And the words were there. "A year ago, you entered your DNA in the Family Finders database," she said, her tone filling with confidence as it always did in court when she knew she had an open-and-shut case.

She paused, waiting for Charlotte's nod. Just as she would have had her baby sister been on the witness stand. Only difference between court and the couch in that moment was the love brimming her heart and the overwhelming need to wrap her arms around the witness and never let go.

"I entered mine as well," she said then, slowly. Giving Charlotte time to hear, to comprehend every word. "Except that, due to something that happened in my past, I didn't make my profile discoverable."

Charlotte crossed her arms. And her legs, too. "Yeah, what's that got to do with me?"

"A week ago, I was notified of a match," she said. "Between you and me."

Charlotte's arms dropped to her sides, her legs were flat on the couch, her mouth open. When her eyes lit up, Savannah smiled, teared up, ready to open her arms and finally have them filled again with the tender body of her baby sister.

Waited for Charlotte to catch up with the bombshell she'd just had dropped on her. For her little sister to come to her. "You're, what, my aunt?" the woman asked. "My mother's sister? You look awfully young for that. Or wait, you're a cousin! I knew there had to be someone out there. Wow!" She looked at Isaac. "You knew! That's how you got the shelter to bring me here. Though, really, Isaac, all you had to do was tell me when I called." She looked back at Savannah. "Wow, this is so great."

Charlotte was babbling. Savannah had a feeling it wasn't a normal occurrence. Glancing at Mike, she read confirmation in his raised brow and head tilt.

A move that Charlotte caught. "What?" She looked between the two of them. "Isaac? Tell me what's going on."

Mike pointed to Savannah. And when Charlotte looked over, Savannah said, "I'm not your cousin. I'm your sister."

"My...*what*?" Charlotte's raised tone, the shake of her head, indicated shock. But no pleasure.

Feeling her sister's distress, and with a nod from Mike, Savannah quickly filled her sister in on the tragic details of their past. Including their father's murder. Keeping her courtroom tone and sticking to provable details, she laid it all out.

Waiting for the moment when Charlotte, who'd been looking for family, finally realized that she'd found the mother lode. The younger woman's mouth dropped open one more time. Closed. Opened again as she kept glancing from Mike to Savannah and back to Mike again.

"You're telling me I'm adopted?" The question was clearly aimed at Mike. And lacking even a hint of joy.

Savannah's heart felt the crush, but she remained, back straight, ready to give Charlotte whatever she needed. The load of information she'd just dumped onto her couldn't be helped, given the circumstances, but Charlotte didn't know that.

And deserved time to comprehend. To digest.

"She's your sister, Charlotte. I had the DNA results verified," Mike homed in on the point that he could prove right then, right there. She understood what he was doing. Was grateful he was there.

Because they all knew that if Charlotte was Savannah's biological sister, Eduardo Duran couldn't possibly be her biological father.

The younger woman shot up from the couch. Wrapping her arms around herself, she paced back and forth between Mike and Savannah and then stopped in front of Mike, stood over him, and said, "She's lying, Isaac. I don't how she's managed to convince you of this horrible falsehood. Or why she'd even want to. But her story—it's just not true. Family Finders screwed up, or she provided you with wrong DNA, but my father was not murdered. Nor was I kidnapped." She dropped to her knees in front of him, her tone as confident but softening as she said, "I know for certain that Eduardo Duran is my father. I went through a time after we came to the US, rebellious teens, whatever..." The passion with which the woman spoke—only to Mike, her back to Savannah— had Savannah holding her breath. "...I was tired of hearing any time I asked about any relatives, maternal or paternal, that they were dead. The one thing I'd wanted to do most when we came to America was see my mother's grave. To leave flowers there."

Savannah gasped. Mike looked at her. Held her gaze. But when Charlotte kept talking, without turning around, his attention returned to the younger woman. "My last straw was when he told me that the graveyard had been vandalized. That several graves were robbed. My mother's being one of them. Which meant there was no grave to visit. It was too much. I demanded right then and there that he submit to a paternity test. I needed proof he was really my father."

Savannah couldn't fight the tears that were streaming down her face. She'd quit trying. Charlotte stiffened when Savannah sniffled but still didn't turn around.

"It was the biggest fight we ever had, Isaac. But I wasn't backing down, and he submitted to the test. Which came back positive. But I wasn't going to stop there. I took hair from his bathroom sink and had it tested. I *know* he's my father."

Savannah couldn't breathe. Couldn't think. What Charlotte was saying…it couldn't possibly be right. Wide-eyed, Savannah looked at Mike, saw him staring at her, let herself sink into his gaze.

And stay there.

Chapter Twenty-Two

The blood had drained from Savannah's face. He could feel her sinking. Willed her to stay with him. They'd sort it out. Figure it out.

"How sure are you two of the validity of the samples you sent to Family Finders?" The FBI had done their own testing of the samples. He was certain of the accuracy of the results.

He was grasping. He knew that. But Savannah needed a lifeboat.

"I work with one of the nation's leading forensic scientists." He hardly recognized the deadpan tone in Savannah's voice. Kept hold of her gaze.

Charlotte wasn't going anywhere. The job would get done.

"He wore gloves as he extracted hair from my skull and then carefully packaged it. And did a buccal swab as well."

"I went to a lab at the university. Did both as well. And had them sealed before I personally sent them off. I was present, with eyes on the samples, the entire time."

So unless Family Finders or the mail service had switched samples and one of the sisters had a different sister—which was unbelievable at best—the two were sisters.

Savannah wasn't fully with him yet. He wasn't sure she ever would be. She needed support from loved ones. Her partners.

If what Charlotte had said about the paternity testing…

His adrenaline started to flow and, knowing what he had to do, that he had to work quickly, get the sting over with so that he could be a friend to Savannah, he broke eye contact with her to look at Charlotte.

"I'm not Isaac Forrester," he said, succinctly. "My name is Mike Reynolds, I'm with the FBI, and this house is surrounded." As Charlotte's face paled and she sank to her butt on the floor, staring at him open mouthed yet again, he proceeded to tell her why he was in San Diego, working at her home, guarding her. And was ready, every second, to grab her if she tried to run.

Whether she didn't try because she knew she wouldn't make it far, didn't want to be shot at, or because she simply couldn't, he didn't know.

He didn't hold back describing her father's crimes, stretching back twenty-five years—that they knew of. The timing hit him. He stopped. Quietly finished with, "But we're certain that he was busy building his empire long before that. No one has been able to determine what country he was born in, where he started out, but we will…"

Unless they just had.

On his phone, he dialed his Washington office. Had them do a deep dive on Hugh Gussman, his gaze shooting between both sisters as he did so.

And then, taking it upon himself, he dialed Sierra's Web. Had had the number programmed into his phone from the moment he'd been told about Savannah Compton.

Hudson Warner answered, and while Mike sat with two statue-like women, both looking as though they might be sick, both avoiding looking at the other, he made his request for the Gussman deep dive a second time.

And then listened as Hudson Warner told him a thing or

two. Hung up. And looked at Charlotte. The time had come. "I don't know how much you know about Eduardo Duran's money laundering," he said, all business. "And until I have the full scope, I can't offer you anything concrete, but considering the egregious circumstances, I'm prepared to try for full immunity. But only if you cooperate right now. We need to get a warrant to arrest the man before he's certain that we're onto him."

"I'll call him," Charlotte said, her voice cracking. "I'll tell him what I did, how I got away. Tell him that Arnold makes my skin crawl and that I'll come home only if he promises me that I won't have to marry the man. He'll wait for me. Which will buy you some time."

Mike didn't even glance in Savannah's direction. He couldn't. Not then. Keeping his eyes fully on Charlotte, he nodded. And waited while she made the call. She hadn't said she'd cooperate with the rest. But she'd given him a show of faith.

When the call was done, he looked at Savannah, who was staring at the back of Charlotte's head as she nearly whispered, "I can show you your mother's grave..."

Charlotte turned slowly. Mike couldn't see her expression. But he saw the trembling in her shoulders as, on her knees, with her arms reaching out in front of her, she moved over to meet Savannah, who'd fallen to the floor to catch her.

No words were spoken. The two women clung tighter than anything Mike had ever seen. Both were crying what were clearly a lifetime of unshed tears.

Moisture pricked his eyes, too. But the emotion was vicarious only.

Wasn't personal.

He couldn't possibly be jealous of two women who'd been robbed of the chance to grow up together.

MIKE REYNOLDS HAD closed his case. Within an hour of Charlotte working together online with Hudson Warner's team, giving them full access to Glob's coding, the original programming she'd written to provide her father with a single location to store all his money intake, they'd been able to have enough proof to get an arrest warrant for Eduardo Duran.

Savannah had been given a chance to see the man face-to-face. She'd seen photos, had heard the facts about his multiple surgeries for a supposed deviated septum that had resulted in a new nose and occipital bones, and had no desire to look at the man eye to eye.

She'd heard that he'd begged to see her.

But he'd lost that right the day he'd faked his own death, just as he'd fabricated his intention to blow the whistle on whoever had been stealing from the government. He'd been the one pilfering money, double the amount the government had known about. He'd known he'd been about to be caught and had gone to his boss, pretending that he'd just discovered an intricate hack in the system and had offered to testify in exchange for protection for himself and his family.

He claimed that the government moved up his date to testify and that was why he'd only had the chance to take Charlotte.

Savannah believed differently. He hadn't taken her or her mother because he hadn't been certain of their cooperation. Her mother, at the very least, would have figured out that something had been grossly wrong when they'd have had to leave the country. Witness protection didn't stretch that far. And Charlotte…sweet little baby Charlotte…she hadn't known any better.

But in the end, she'd known enough.

To stop the man.

Put him behind bars.

And to be able to prove that she hadn't had any part in their father's illegal empire. She'd written Glob when she'd been a bored, off-the-charts intelligent teenager with no friends. Hugh, who'd started out a regular guy, also with an above-average intelligence quotient, had been so bored with his IRS cubicle and daily grind that he'd found ways to make enough money on the side to quit his job. At first, he'd just dabbled for fun. For something to do. But when he'd seen how he could manipulate the tax system databases, he'd been hooked. Addicted.

And the addiction had been driving him ever since. As Kelly had said on numerous occasions, as they'd worked on various cases over the years, it was a sad truth that sometimes it was more of a challenge to be bad than to be good. Which was why prisons oftentimes had inmates who measured with above-average intelligence.

Arnold Wagar had been a kid then. Barely an adult. Nobody Hugh had known. But he was wealthy. More so even than Duran. Came from a well-respected family. His father had been a Salvadoran dignitary in the US at one point. And when Charlotte had told her father that she'd entered her DNA into that database, Duran had known that he could be exposed at any time. He'd simply wanted Charlotte married, with a prenup that gave her half of her husband's wealth were he to divorce her, to secure her future in the event that the worst happened. In exchange, Wagar not only got a beautiful young wife with excellent skills he could use, but he got a sizable chunk of Duran's legitimate business dealings as well.

Charlotte had relayed a lot of the personal facts to Savannah. She'd gone home the night she'd met Savannah at the FBI safe house, as promised, had insisted on doing so, and had been present when, at two that morning, their father had been arrested.

She'd said she needed the closure.

Savannah wasn't sure they were ever going to have that. Not completely. But they had each other, which was more than either of them had ever dreamed possible.

Most of Eduardo's assets had been frozen. The property was up for sale. Charlotte had had a sizable savings of her own, earned from her lectures and a couple of the computer programs she'd written and sold.

But she didn't seem to care all that much about money. Most certainly wasn't driven by it as their father had been.

She'd moved to Phoenix, into Savannah's sizable home in a gated community, and was helping out at Sierra's Web as a private contractor until she figured out what she wanted to do with the rest of her life.

Kelly had cautioned Savannah that it would take time, a lot of it, for Charlotte to be anywhere near healed. Her entire life, every memory she'd had, had been built on lies.

But a month after Duran's arrest, Charlotte was already singing when she made coffee in the morning. And talking about applying for a professorship in women's studies at Arizona State University. She'd been offered a job at Harvard but wanted to stay close to Savannah.

A choice that Savannah wholly embraced.

Other than necessary separations during working hours— Savannah had chosen not to travel for a while—she was with Charlotte. They'd even slept in the same bed a night or two, when Charlotte's demons had been getting the better of her in the dark and she'd come to Savannah's door asking if she could stay, just for a few hours.

Savannah had her own internal struggles to get through and was working on them with Kelly, unofficially, and with one of the experts on Kelly's team, officially, too. But she was coming from a much easier starting point. She was the lucky one, having had the honor of being raised and loved by their mother. Only a small portion of her life had been a lie.

The lies she'd told all her life...that was one of the things she was working through.

Along with the whole Isaac thing. She'd left San Diego without telling him goodbye. How did you offer a farewell to someone who hadn't been real? But her heart continued to ache.

She'd wake up in the middle of the night with a vision of his eyes sharp in her brain. She couldn't make herself believe that the connection between two souls hadn't been real.

And so, though she barely acknowledged the fact to herself, she waited for him to contact her. He knew her name and where she worked. If he ever wanted to find her, he could.

For all she knew, he was already off on another undercover case somewhere. Living a new pretend life, among other criminals. Having sex with another suspect.

At least, that was all she knew until one Sunday afternoon, while she and Charlotte were lying on rafts in their backyard pool and her little sister said, "Mike gave up undercover work and took a promotion they'd been offering him for years." Just dropped the words into the middle of their peace. Casually. As though she'd mentioned the dove in a nearby tree.

Mike. Charlotte didn't seem to have a problem seeing Isaac Forrester and Mike Reynolds as the same man. But then, her sister hadn't slept with him.

Mike. Isaac. Whatever.

He'd given up undercover work. Because he'd lost his professional perspective with Savannah? The possibility sat there in her mind. Taunting her.

"He has a sister, you know." Charlotte dropped another bomb into the air just as Savannah had started to relax again.

"No, I didn't know," she said, trying to sound as though she was half asleep. Hoping Charlotte would take the hint and let her wallow her way out of the frame of mind she'd sunk into. Her little sister seemed truly fond of the man who'd guarded her for several months. It was one of the few good memories Charlotte had carried with her to Phoenix. At least that she talked about.

Savannah's job was to welcome the conversation.

"Her name's Mollie," Charlotte said. Whether her sister of such high intelligence had missed the hint or, more likely, had simply chosen to ignore it, Savannah didn't know. But the wondering gave her a place to focus her thoughts.

"Their parents were killed when Mike was barely out of high school. She was still a kid. He raised her."

He'd raised his little sister on his own? Right out of high school? She didn't want to care.

"Yeah, but then she fell for this bad boy. Truly bad. He was dealing drugs at their high school. Mike was a cop then, and he busted them. Sent the guy to prison, and his sister ended up in juvie for a month."

"He told you all this?"

"Some of it."

"When?"

"The night that dragged on to the next day when Eduardo was arrested."

Charlotte and Mike had spent hours at the San Diego bureau. While Savannah had been helping a Duran housekeeper pack up the list of things her sister had said she wanted immediately and then checking Savannah and Charlotte into a hotel by the airport.

"Anyway, Mike figured he was saving his sister's life.

Tough love. All of that. She hated him for not loving her enough, trusting her enough to give her a second chance before busting her."

"I'm guessing he'd already warned her to stay away from the guy. And the stuff," Savannah said, eyes wide open as she drifted over to the deep end of the pool.

"Yeah, knowing him, I think that's probably a given. Anyway, they haven't spoken in years. She's married now. Has a couple of kids."

"He told you that, too?"

"Nah, I looked her up. And... I wrote to her."

Sitting straight up, Savannah upended herself, falling back first into the water, and came up sputtering. Holding on to her raft, she looked at her sister. "You what?"

"I wrote to her. Told her who I was. Told her about us. And how Mike had risked his career to bring us together. And how even though he'd have had to turn me in if I'd been involved in Eduardo's dealings, you were both there for me."

Savannah stared. "And?"

"She wrote back. We're kind of pen pals now."

Whoa. What in the hell was going on. Pen pals? With Mike's sister?

"Does he know?"

"He does." The voice...male...came from behind her. Swinging away from her raft to verify that her eyes weren't playing tricks on her, Savannah went under again.

Considered staying there. For all of a second.

She wasn't a quitter. Never had been.

Shooting up, she looked to the cool decking around the pool. And saw Mike Reynolds, in swim trunks, drop a towel next to hers, just as Charlotte, still on her raft, leaned over and grabbed her arm, dragging Savannah out of the deep water. When Savannah's feet were on the bottom of the pool,

Charlotte rolled off her raft, leaning in to whisper, "You love him."

She shook her head. "I only knew him for a few days," she whispered back, imploring her sister to tell her she'd just imagined what she'd seen. To tell her that she hadn't set her up.

And praying that she had.

"I knew I loved you an hour after I met you," Charlotte whispered then. "Love is funny that way. It doesn't care about our rules, our understandings, our logic. It just lives. And spreads. And is ready, whenever we are, to bloom inside us and gift us with its bounty."

With that, Charlotte made a small, graceful dive that took her into a glide to the side of the pool. She passed Mike, grabbed her towel, and was gone before Savannah had the wherewithal to go with her.

"You coming out, or should I come in?" His tone was teasing. The look in his eyes as his gaze connected with hers was anything but. She read pain. Sorrow.

Need.

When her body flared in response, she figured she was better to stay covered by water rather than stepping up to him in her very brief bikini.

"You can come in."

That was it. He was allowed in her pool. Nothing more.

She watched as he walked down the steps, the journey so excruciatingly slow she couldn't help but notice every muscle, every cluster of dark hair...and the enlargement in his groin area. All of which she'd seen before.

She stood firm, waiting for him to make his move so she could reject him.

She'd been home a month. He could have called.

Or texted and asked her out for a drink rather than sabotaging her at home.

He came into the water slowly, walking in deeper.

God, he looked good.

So good.

Too good.

The water was up to his belly button. She was glad for the respite. Honestly glad. She had to think.

To exist in reality all the way.

She didn't quite meet his gaze as she said, "Charlotte told me you took a promotion."

"Did she also tell you it's in the Phoenix bureau?"

Ahhh. So her little sister had been...the thought stopped. She wanted so badly to yell at the man standing before her, absorbing her with his gaze. Telling her things she'd needed to hear.

For maybe her whole life.

Everything had always been so complicated. The secrets she'd had to keep. The lies she'd had to tell. Or risk lives.

Kind of like him. His duplicity had had one motivation. To save lives. Like Mollie's.

"I take it she didn't tell you," Mike said, taking a step closer to her. She could step back. Thought about it. Didn't move.

And then he was right there, a couple of inches of water between them, still looking at her. Compelling her to look back.

"You asked me if any of it was real," he said to her, his gaze glistening and pointed.

And she waited. She needed truth. Not pretense.

He nodded. Then said, "The things that mattered—the fact that you showed me a part of life I'd never seen before, a part I wanted, the fact that I couldn't do my job if it meant not protecting you, the fact that I've never, ever had such mind-blowing sex before...those were all real.

As is how excruciating these last four weeks have been without you."

"You could have called." She'd tried for levity laced with sarcasm. Her words came out as a needy whisper.

"I needed to get my life in order, to figure out who, and what, I had to offer first."

Tears filled her eyes as she asked, "So who and what do you have to offer?" She was crying—and smiling, too.

"I'm offering dinner," he said. "A real date. Tonight. And then, another one. And another."

"And if I said that, after only those few days together, I think I'm in love with you?"

His eyes glistened as he slid his arms around her and murmured against her neck, "I'd say, thank God."

He kissed her then. Desperately. Without air. And then gasping, more softly. With stomachs pressing together, skin to skin, he lifted his head. Met her gaze and said, without words, everything she'd ever need to hear.

"I love you," the words were like icing on the cake. She saw his lips move. Put her fingers over them.

"Just don't ever quit looking at me like that," she whispered. "It's all the *I love you* I'll ever need."

He kept his eyes trained on her as he lowered his head, breaking the connection only when their lips joined again.

And she let herself fly. Really fly. For the first time since she'd been seven years old. She was young again. Older than the sky. She was a daughter. A sister.

She was a woman.

And had finally found the security that had set her free.

The love that had been with her from the beginning. A love that didn't care about rules or understandings. That didn't answer to logic. It just lived. And spread. And was always ready to be accepted.

To live through anyone who would let it. Anyone.

Instead of living in fear, Savannah was going to spend the rest of her days spreading the greatest truth in the world. Love, not logic, conquers all.

* * * * *

COMING SOON!

We really hope you enjoyed reading this book.
If you're looking for more romance
be sure to head to the shops when
new books are available on

Thursday 27th February

To see which titles are coming soon, please visit

millsandboon.co.uk/nextmonth

MILLS & BOON

LET'S TALK
Romance

For exclusive extracts, competitions and special offers, find us online:

- **f** MillsandBoon
- **X** @MillsandBoon
- **◉** @MillsandBoonUK
- **♪** @MillsandBoonUK

Get in touch on 01413 063 232

FOUR BRAND NEW BOOKS FROM
MILLS & BOON MODERN

The same great stories you love, a stylish new look!

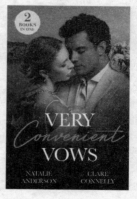

OUT NOW

Eight Modern stories published every month, find them all at:

millsandboon.co.uk

Afterglow Books is a trend-led, trope-filled list of books with diverse, authentic and relatable characters, a wide array of voices and representations, plus real world trials and tribulations. Featuring all the tropes you could possibly want (think small-town settings, fake relationships, grumpy vs sunshine, enemies to lovers) and all with a generous dose of spice in every story.

♪ @millsandboonuk

◉ @millsandboonuk

afterglowbooks.co.uk

#AfterglowBooks

For all the latest book news, exclusive content and giveaways scan the QR code below to sign up to the Afterglow newsletter:

SCAN ME